James Nelson has served as a seaman, rigger, boatswain and officer on a number of sailing vessels. He is the author of the five books comprising *The Revolution at Sea Saga* and *The Brethren of the Coast* trilogy. He lives with his wife and children in Maine.

His web site can be found at www.jameslnelson.com.

ALL THE BRAVE FELLOWS

The Revolution at Sea Saga
Book Five

James Nelson

CORGI BOOKS

ALL THE BRAVE FELLOWS
A CORGI BOOK: 0 552 14964 0

First publication in Great Britain

PRINTING HISTORY
Corgi edition published 2005

1 3 5 7 9 10 8 6 4 2

Copyright © James L. Nelson 2000

Ship diagrams and map by James L. Nelson

The right of James L. Nelson to be identified as the author
of this work has been asserted in accordance with sections 77
and 78 of the Copyright Designs and Patents Act 1988.

Set in 10½/12pt Galliard by
Kestrel Data, Exeter, Devon.

Corgi Books are published by Transworld Publishers,
61–63 Uxbridge Road, London W5 5SA,
a division of The Random House Group Ltd,
in Australia by Random House Australia (Pty) Ltd,
20 Alfred Street, Milsons Point, Sydney, NSW 2061, Australia,
in New Zealand by Random House New Zealand Ltd,
18 Poland Road, Glenfield, Auckland 10, New Zealand
and in South Africa by Random House (Pty) Ltd,
Endulini, 5a Jubilee Road, Parktown 2193, South Africa.

Printed and bound in Great Britain by
Cox & Wyman Ltd, Reading, Berkshire.

Papers used by Transworld Publishers are natural, recyclable
products made from wood grown in sustainable forests.
The manufacturing processes conform to the environmental
regulations of the country of origin.

To Nathaniel James Nelson,

who was kind enough to wait until
Daddy was done writing this book
before being born.

And as always,
to Lisa,
whom I love

The several Commanders . . . will have . . . a chance of immortalizing their own names besides enriching all the brave fellows under their command.

—RESOLUTION OF THE MARINE COMMITTEE
APRIL 29, 1777

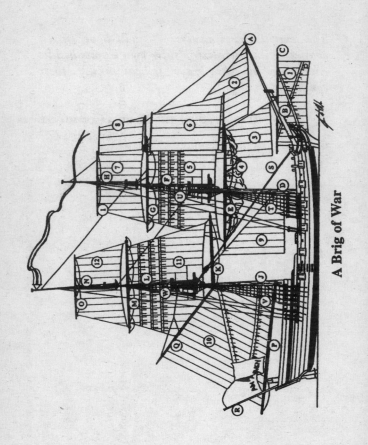

A Brig of War

Sails
1. Spritsail
2. Jib
3. Fore Topmast Staysail
4. Foresail (clewed up)
5. Fore Topsail
6. Fore Topmast Studdingsail (removable)
7. Fore Topgallant Sail
8. Fore Topgallant Studdingsail (removable)
9. Main Staysail
10. Mainsail
11. Main Topsail
12. Main Topgallant Sail

Spars and Rigging
A. Jibboom
B. Bowsprit
C. Spritsail Yard
D. Foremast
E. Foreyard
F. Fore Topmast
G. Fore Topsail Yard
H. Fore Topgallant Mast
I. Fore Topgallant Yard
J. Mainmast
K. Mainyard
L. Main Topmast
M. Main Topsail Yard
N. Main Topgallant Mast
O. Main Topgallant Yard
P. Boom
Q. Gaff
R. Ensign Staff (removable)
S. Mainstay
T. Fore Shrouds and Ratlines
U. Fore Topmast Shrouds and Ratlines
V. Main Shrouds and Ratlines
W. Main Topmast Shrouds and Ratlines

*For other terminology and usage see Glossary at the end of the book

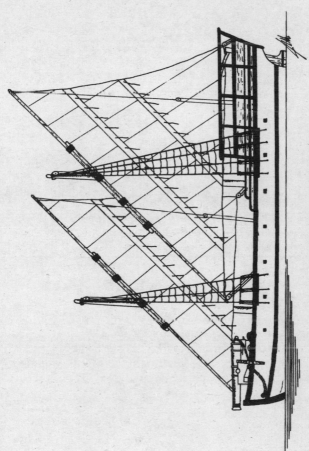

The Continental Navy Xebec Expedient

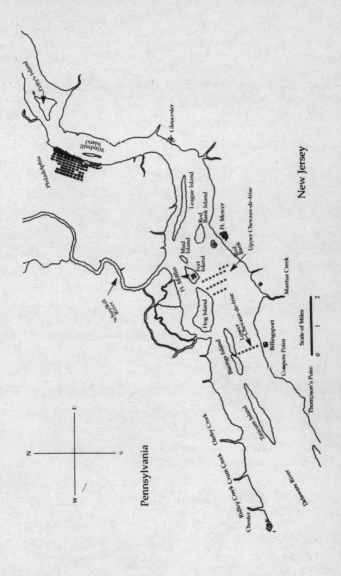

Pennsylvania

New Jersey

Philadelphia

Petty's Island

Windmill Island

Gloucester

League Island

Red Bank Island

Ft. Mercer

Mud Island

Schuylkill River

Ft. Mifflin

Fort Island

Red Bank

Upper Chevaux-de-frise

Hog Island

Lower Chevaux-de-frise

Billingsport

Mantua Creek

Crispers Point

Thompson's Point

Billings Island

Tinicum Island

Darby Creek

Crum Creek

Ridley Creek

Chester

Delaware River

N

S

E

W

Scale of Miles

0   1   2

ALL THE BRAVE
FELLOWS

CHAPTER 1

I am now Applying myself with all diligence to the Business of the Navy Board . . . but I think it peculiarly Unhappy that we Enter on this Business when the Circumstances of the Fleet are far from being such as promises any Hopes that we can gratify the Expectations of the people . . .

—JAMES WARREN
WRITING TO JOHN ADAMS
SEPTEMBER 7, 1777

The wind blew cold, steady and strong, striking the New Jersey coast at an oblique angle and sending up a line of breakers miles long. The Continental brig-of-war *Charlemagne* was half a league off the coast, far enough to be beyond the immediate threat of the breaking surf, but close enough for her people to be wary and concerned.

The sky was ugly, gray, the color of boiled meat. The sea was gray as well, taking its mood from the muffled daylight, and covered over its surface with whitecaps that flashed in long rows extending seaward to the horizon.

The hair was white, pure white.

Capt. Isaac Biddlecomb leaned closer to the mirror, one hand on the washbasin to steady himself against the roll of the ship, bits of shaving soap still clinging to his chin.

There it was, nestled among the long, black hairs that swept back along his head and were bound up in a queue. A white hair. A ghostly harbinger of creeping age. He was only thirty-one. It seemed altogether too early for that sort of thing.

'Have you only now noticed that?' Virginia Biddlecomb, his wife of just over a year, sat on the locker aft, her back against the weather side of the great cabin, her feet against the big table, which was in turn lashed to the deck. In that position she held herself motionless against the roll and plunge of the brig, as casual as if she were sitting on her porch. Virginia was entirely at home on shipboard.

Biddlecomb turned and met her eyes. Her look was mischievous, teasing. In her lap, a great bundle of cloth and lace, and in the center of that, two-month-old Jack Biddlecomb. All that Isaac could see of his only child was a tuft of dark hair, a pink cheek, and a tiny ear as the baby took his breakfast at Virginia's breast. The sight no longer made Isaac uncomfortable, and he congratulated himself on that.

'Yes, it is the first I have seen of it,' Isaac replied, 'though the great wonder is that I am not entirely gray, with all I carry on my shoulders. Ship captain, husband, father . . .'

Virginia gave him a pouty expression. 'Surely your family is not a burden to you? I should think we would be a great comfort to you in your time of trouble.'

'You are, my dearest. You are always a comfort to me.'

'And you, sir, I pray, are a better sailor than you are a liar, or we shall never see Philadelphia.'

Biddlecomb smiled and wiped the remaining soap from his face. He stepped aft and kissed Virginia and kissed his son on the head, though the boy took no notice of the gesture.

'In any event, my love,' said Virginia, 'did Shakespeare not say that "infirmity, which decays the wise, doth oft make the better captain"?'

'Something to that effect. But I had thought that misquoting Shakespeare was my province.' He leaned low and peered out of the salt-stained windows at the portion of sea that lay astern of them.

Two vessels were in view, one about two cables astern of the *Charlemagne*, the second two cables astern of the first. They were plunging along in the brig's wake, their sails shortened to avoid overtaking the battered naval vessel.

They were both privateers, newly built and fitted out in Boston. The nearer of the two was a brig, the farther ship-rigged, what they would call a sloop of war in the naval service. They were sailing in company with the *Charlemagne*, in hopes of aiding the American cause and, more importantly sharing in any prize that might come the way of the often fortunate Capt. Isaac Biddlecomb.

'We've a regular little squadron here,' Isaac observed, 'at least until we fetch Cape Ann. Still, I think we will have no opportunity to make use of them.'

But Virginia's mind was no longer focused on the fight for independence, and the passion she had once had for politics had now mostly yielded to motherhood. 'Isaac, do you think the sleeping cabin aboard the *Falmouth* will have room enough for our bed as well as a hanging cot for Jack? If the fitting out should require some months, then it would be well to have it thus arranged.'

'We should be able to figure that easily enough.' Isaac crossed the cabin and from a shelf crammed with charts withdrew a roll of paper nearly a yard long, thick and heavy. He unrolled it on the table, carefully setting various objects down to keep it from rolling up again. 'Let us just see what the dimensions are of the sleeping cabin.'

'Isaac, do not for one moment pretend that you have got that draft out just to answer me. In truth, you are using my question as an excuse to leer at the thing again. I swear, if you looked at a woman the way you look at that paper, I would have her eyes out. And yours.'

Biddlecomb looked up at his wife. He smiled. She was right. As usual. 'You know me too well, dear, too well by half. But if it is of any comfort, I confine my longings to you and the frigate.'

The frigate, the *Falmouth*, lay stretched out across the table in two dimensions, a black-and-white rendering of what was to be the next command of Isaac Biddlecomb, Captain, Navy of the United States.

She was not one of the original thirteen frigates, ordered in those heady days of December 1775, when John Adams and Stephen Hopkins were leading the charge in the naval line. Of those thirteen, only four had got to sea. Of those four, the *Hancock* had already been captured and the *Randolph* was languishing in Charleston, dismasted and crippled. As

20

for the other nine, the *Congress* and the *Montgomery* had been burned to avoid capture on the Hudson, and the balance remained in various states short of completion.

But despite that, and seemingly despite the ugly face of reality, Congress had ordered more ships late in the year '76: a brig of eighteen guns, five frigates of thirty-six guns, and most unbelievable of all, three seventy-four gun ships of the line.

And along with that, and almost as an afterthought, the *Falmouth* of twenty-eight guns. William Stanton, Biddlecomb's father-in-law, and now chair of the Navy Board of the Eastern Department, told him that the contract was a payoff, a plum thrown out to a political crony of one of the committee members.

That was fine. Biddlecomb did not care about the ship's parentage, did not care about the circumstances that caused her to be raised up on the stocks. He ran his eyes over her lines as they had been drawn, the beautiful, fine entry, the gentle deadrise, the elegant sweep of her stem and cutwater, the suggestion of tumblehome at her gunwales. Stanton had got him the drafts from the designer, Joshua Humphreys, and now Biddlecomb was in love, like falling in love with a woman's portrait. He was seaman enough to know how sweet a vessel the drafts represented, if properly built.

He had received his orders a month before: proceed to Philadelphia where the ship was building in the yard of Wharton and Humphreys; assume command; see to her rigging, armaments, and final fitting out. Then get her to sea, quickly, before the British were able to seal her up in the confines of the Delaware River.

No sooner had he set his eyes on the drafts than he was anxious to be rid of the cramped and tired brig that he had been commanding for two years. Every time he unrolled the plans, the *Charlemagne* seemed to grow smaller and more inadequate.

Biddlecomb picked up his dividers, adjusted them against the scale of the draft, held the points against the drawing of the sleeping place. 'Yes, I think there shall be ample space for all the Biddlecombs to bunk,' he said, thinking of the restless nights in his future. Every time little Jack called out, it jerked Isaac out of his sleep; every time he bawled for his mother, which was often, Isaac was up as well.

'I fear we will have to share the cabin with the great guns, though,' Isaac continued, caressing various features of the draft with the brass dividers. 'Though I will be much surprised if there are guns aboard her now.' He stared at the black ink squares that represented the *Falmouth*'s gunports. Twenty-eight twelve-pound guns. Just one of the frigate's broadsides would throw a greater weight of iron than the entire pathetic armament aboard the *Charlemagne*. What he would do with that.

'I do so hope that the British have not taken Philadelphia,' Virginia said. 'I long to see that city again, and to show off little Jack to Sophia and Mrs Clark and the rest.' It was as if they were having two different conversations.

'I do not know, my dear,' Biddlecomb said. He laid one of the divider's points against the *Falmouth*'s gun deck, measured the distance to the overhead. He would have standing headroom. He would be able to stand upright unimpeded anywhere in the great cabin. Such luxury.

He scowled at the *Charlemagne*'s deckhead, under which he stooped. 'Before we sailed I had heard no more than those rumors of a fight along the Brandywine Creek, and the word was that things had not gone well. As they generally do not.' Twenty-eight big guns, he thought.

'If the British have taken Philadelphia, then surely they have taken your silly frigate as well,' Virginia observed. Isaac looked over at her, guessed that the words had come out more bitter than she had intended.

'I think not.' Isaac carefully rolled the drafts up again. He was learning the limits of Virginia's patience. 'I have it on good authority that the British fleet is still in the Chesapeake, and if they do not control the Delaware Bay and the river, then it is unlikely they were able to capture the frigate. I have no doubt but she was moved to some place of safety.'

'That is if she was launched, which you do not know.'

'That is true.' Isaac had not thought of that. The last he had heard, she was still on the ways, all but ready for her launch. It was quite possible that the British had taken the city and found the *Falmouth* high and dry, vulnerable as a beached whale. They might have burned her or taken her for themselves. The thought frightened him, and he was annoyed with Virginia for having brought it up.

'I'm sorry, my beloved,' Virginia said sincerely. 'I have no doubt that your ship is in a safe place, waiting for you to sail her away.' Her contrition was genuine, but the truth of her earlier observation could not be denied, and so Isaac was not much

23

comforted as he crossed the cabin and they kissed in mutual apology.

Jack was at last finished and Virginia handed him to his father, who took him up in his arms, stealing a glance at his wife's lovely breasts as he did. 'Good morning, my little man,' he said, tickling the baby under the chin, marveling at the tiny features, only now losing their newborn wrinkles.

Jack blinked wide, stared up at his father. He was not yet quite in control of his facial muscles, and his eyes opened and closed, and his mouth twisted in the oddest expressions, which made Isaac laugh, delighted. The baby seemed entirely at ease with his surroundings, though his world swooped and rolled and yawed, creaked and slammed around him.

'I had thought . . .' Virginia began when she was cut off by a voice, faint through the skylight, singing out from the mainmast head those words that superseded all others on board a man-of-war: 'Sail, ho!'

Virginia kept silent, listened as intently as Isaac. 'Where away?' came the booming voice of Ezra Rumstick, the *Charlemagne*'s first officer, a great bear of a man, Biddlecomb's oldest friend.

A pause, and then the first note of the lookout's reply, and then Jack let out a yell, tiny in its volume but quite enough to drown out what the man aloft had reported. Isaac sighed in exasperation and handed the baby off to Virginia, who put him over her shoulder and patted his back, coaxing a surprisingly loud belch from his tummy.

Biddlecomb heard footsteps through the gunroom outside his cabin, a knock, and then the door was partially open. 'Midshipman Gerrish,' the marine sentry announced, and Biddlecomb said, 'Come.'

The *Charlemagne* had been a regular naval vessel, complete with a marine contingent, for over a year and a half – indeed, for as long as there had been a navy of the United States – and Biddlecomb was at last becoming accustomed to the formalities of the service.

Not quite so was Mr Midshipman Samuel Gerrish, who, in his midthirties, was on the old side for a midshipman. He stepped into the cabin, looked around, squinting through round spectacles. At last he looked up at Biddlecomb, as if surprised to find him there, and said, 'Mr Rumstick's compliments, sir, but a sail has been sighted, ship-rigged, bearing due south on a starboard tack with single-reefed topsails.'

'Indeed.' Biddlecomb considered the information. The ship would be sailing roughly parallel with the coast, making toward his little ad hoc squadron, would most likely tack soon and claw off the coast, before his leeway set him down on the beach. Biddlecomb had been considering just that thing himself.

'No colors that the man could see?' he asked, and Gerrish said, 'No, sir.'

'Very well, then. Pray tell Mr Rumstick that I shall be up directly, and please take a glass aloft and see what you can see.'

'Aye, sir,' Gerrish said, making a poor job of disguising his feelings about going aloft on that cold, wet morning. He saluted and disappeared and Isaac turned to his wife.

'Duty, and all that,' he said as he pulled on his coat and his greatcoat over that.

'Of course, my love. Your scarf is on the sideboard. Please put it on before you go on deck.'

Isaac smiled, wrapped the scarf around his neck. He had been all of thirteen when his mother had died. He was not accustomed to such feminine concern, and was not sure if he liked it.

The difference between the great cabin and the quarterdeck was startling, a sudden shift from the comforts of domestic life to cold and ugly war, as if the cabin that housed his wife and child and the deck that supported the officers, men, and guns of the brig were two entirely different places, and he had somehow gone instantly from one to the other. It took genuine effort for Biddlecomb to shift his concerns from Jack's need to be burped to his ship's need to be driven into battle.

The *Charlemagne*'s officers – Rumstick, Second Lieutenant David Weatherspoon, Marine Lieutenant Elisha Faircloth – gave their 'Good mornings' to the captain and retreated to the leeward side, save for Rumstick, who saluted and said, 'Strange sail's just visible now, sir, on the rise.' He nodded in the direction of the *Charlemagne*'s larboard bow and Isaac followed the gesture.

The gray sea was rising up before them, a moderate swell that came even with the brig's rail as the vessel twisted and sank into the trough. Then she shuddered as her bluff bow hit the bottom and began to rise, coming up and up as the roller passed under them.

And on the crest of the wave Biddlecomb was able to catch a glimpse of the distant vessel; spindly topgallant masts and yards, dark against the gray sky, like bare trees in winter, topsails full and hard, shortened by the length of a single reef, their weather leeches distorted by the pull of bowlines, the better part of a jibboom with fore-topmast staysail set and

26

drawing. The distant rig dipped, as if nodding a greeting, as the vessel went down in some unseen valley of water. And then the *Charlemagne* went down herself and the stranger was gone.

'Indeed,' Biddlecomb said quite involuntarily. He stared blankly at the horizon, examined the image that was fixed in his mind. Such a brief glimpse did not tell him much, so he had to assume the strange sail was not friendly.

'Ferguson,' Biddlecomb called out to the foretopman who, among other things, assisted Gerrish with the signal flags, 'signal the privateers "strange sail in sight," and once they have acknowledged that, do "tack in succession" and "clear for action."'

'Aye, sir.' Ferguson began to bend the bright flags to the halyard.

The *Charlemagne* began her rise again, the fast swooping motion of a ship coming up on a wave, the motion that causes so much distress to the stomachs of those unaccustomed to it. And on the top of the rise Biddlecomb could see the sails of the distant vessel begin to flog in disarray, and from aloft Gerrish called out, 'On deck! Stranger's coming about!'

'Sir, I beg your pardon.' Lieutenant Faircloth, commanding officer of the Second Battalion, Fourth Company, of American Marines, the *Charlemagne*'s marine division, stepped up on the slanting deck and saluted. 'I had thought to have my men see to mending their uniforms. Would this not be a good time?'

Biddlecomb turned, considered the marine officer. He was dressed, as was his custom, in his immaculate bottle-green uniform, his small cocked hat pushed down on his head. He was a wealthy man, and he

27

and his men were always tricked out in high style. Faircloth took seriously the equipment, training, and welfare of the marines under his command. And that, as far as Biddlecomb could tell, was the only thing he took seriously.

'Pray, Lieutenant,' Biddlecomb asked, 'how long have you been formulating that question?' Faircloth was not concerned with uniforms, he was probing to see if Biddlecomb thought there might be a battle.

'About ten minutes, sir.'

'Very subtly done. In reply, let me say that, no, I do not think this is a good time to mend uniforms. This fellow has come about, and if he does not then run off to the south'ard, I think we can presume him to be of the Royal Navy.'

'Very good, sir. Or, I should say, "Aye, aye," keeping in the nautical vernacular, and such.'

'Privateers have acknowledged "tack in succession," sir,' Ferguson reported.

'Very good. Mr Rumstick, hands to station for stays.'

The order was shouted forward, and Mr Sprout, the boatswain, made his pipe squeal as he called men to their places for putting the brig about. Biddlecomb pulled his eyes from the horizon. Virginia was making her way aft, her arms uncharacteristically unencumbered.

'Jack is asleep in our cot,' she reported, and Isaac felt his one life overlapping the other. 'What of this strange sail?'

'We know nothing yet, my dear,' Isaac said. The *Charlemagne*'s officers were all making a great pretense of not listening to their captain's conversation. 'But to

28

be cautious we are going to come about, gain some more sea room, and then clear for action.'

'And then?'

'And then we shall do the one thing that this service has best prepared us to do. We shall wait. And wait and wait and wait.'

CHAPTER 2

Our main difficulty will be to procure hands – as
we are daily robb'd of our men by both privatiers,
& merchant men & the Extravagent wages given
by the Latter, & the great Encouragements given
by the former.

—CAPTAIN HECTOR MCNEILL
TO THE CONTINENTAL MARINE COMMITTEE
OCTOBER 9, 1777

For the next five hours they waited, tense at first, and
then bored, and then with a real and growing sense
of anticipation.

With the American squadron and the strange sail
on opposite tacks, they found themselves sailing
almost directly away from one another, both clawing
their way off the New Jersey coast. The *Charlemagne*
making north by east, the stranger almost due south,
until at last she was lost to sight, her skeletal topgallant masts dipping below the horizon.

Not wishing to lose contact with the distant ship,
and judging his ships to be far enough offshore
to have a reasonable margin of safety, Biddlecomb

tacked the squadron again, and in less than an hour they had the stranger in sight once more.

The stranger had tacked as well – she was not trying to escape – and now the four vessels were once again closing, four ships plunging toward that place on the sea where they would come together and do battle for supremacy of that patch of gray water.

Biddlecomb did not know what was going on aboard the privateers – he had not talked with the captains of those ships since leaving Boston – but he had to imagine that they were as excited as he was by what must be a pending fight. In times of war, merchant ships did not go out of their way to close with other ships of unknown nationality. The stranger had to be a man-of-war, and the sheer number of vessels that the Royal Navy had in North American waters made it likely that she was British.

'On deck!'

Biddlecomb craned his neck to see the lookout aloft, as did all the officers on the quarterdeck and all the men forward. 'Deck, aye!'

'She's just hull up now, sir! Looks to be a sloop of war, no bigger!' A pause, then: 'She's broke out colors, sir! She's British!'

The officers exchanged smiles, nods of congratulations, as if they had already taken her as a prize.

'Gentlemen,' Biddlecomb said, 'you are all of you veterans of a number of bloody campaigns. I would think that your past experience would be enough to inform you of the folly of celebrating victory even before the iron has begun to fly.' And then, because he wanted to calm the officers' ardor but not quash it, he added, 'Still, I'll warrant we have every reason to be optimistic.'

31

Nor was he lying in that assessment. This ship with which they were closing was a sloop of war, probably eighteen to twenty guns, probably six- or nine-pounders. She was more powerful than any one of the three American vessels, but she was no match for the three of them together, and the privateers were nimble and heavily manned. They could all lay off the bows and quarters of the enemy, pound away at her, and then, if the seas permitted, board with their overwhelming numbers. As a prize, the sloop of war would not be as valuable as a fat merchantman loaded with military stores, but the action would be worth ten times that in glory.

'Mr Gerrish, let us have our ensign aloft. This will be our first opportunity to carry it into battle.'

Gerrish removed the flag, wrapped tight for hoisting, from the canvas-covered locker and bent it with great care to the halyard running to the truck of the mainmast. It was a new ensign, just that summer designated by Congress, and sewn by Virginia as her present to the ship. The *Charlemagne* had only flown it on a few occasions.

Gerrish hauled away until the bundle bumped to a stop at the masthead. Then the midshipman jerked the halyard and the bundle broke open. Thirteen red and white stripes with a blue canton and thirteen white stars in a circle spilled out, caught the breeze, and fluttered to leeward.

'Lovely, lovely,' Biddlecomb said with enthusiasm.

'Thank you, Captain,' said Virginia. 'Now I think I shall take Jack and retreat to the breadroom.'

The last time Virginia had been on board during a fight, Biddlecomb had not been able to drive her below, had had to endure the sight of her standing fully exposed to the enemy's broadside, firing at a British frigate with a pistol. Now the mother bear would defend her child with the same callous disregard for her own desires, her own life.

'I think that would be best.'

He had not wanted to expose her and Jack to this kind of danger. Indeed, he would not have allowed them to accompany him if he had thought that they might run into a fight. But Howe was in the Chesapeake and Biddlecomb had reckoned it unlikely they would meet a man-of-war, the Charlemagnes' hopes notwithstanding.

But here it was, and Virginia knew better than to ask him to avoid the coming battle for her and Jack's sake, or to say something foolish about his promising there would be no trouble. Instead she kissed him, full on the lips, despite the gawking cadre of officers, wished him Godspeed, and hurried below.

Biddlecomb turned and looked at the two privateers astern, his anxiety and guilt concerning his family swept away with the tide of tactical considerations. The privateers had their ensigns streaming at their mastheads, plain fields of red and white stripes. Like the *Charlemagne* they had put their boats over the side and were towing them astern to avoid the horrible splinters that would result from their being hit with round shot. They had set more sail and were gaining rapidly on the *Charlemagne*, plunging through the quartering sea and sending up great sheets of spray as they drove into battle. They would attack in force, not line ahead, just as they had discussed over many a glass in the *Charlemagne*'s great cabin, swinging at the hook in Boston harbor.

Biddlecomb could see the crowds of men on their

decks. With their short enlistments, easy discipline, and promise of great monetary rewards, privateers had no trouble attracting the best seamen, all to the detriment of the United States Navy. And just as attractive to potential recruits, privateers did not generally go after the enemy's naval vessels. They confined their interests to merchantmen, a strategy that carried considerably less chance of bodily injury.

The Continental Congress's 'Instructions to Commanders of Privateers' specified that at least one-third of their crews had to consist of landsmen, in order that some seamen be left for the navy, but Biddlecomb doubted that that regulation was strictly followed. It was irritating, but if those men would not join the United States Navy, at least today they would assist.

He turned and looked down on to the waist of his own command. With sixty men aboard, the *Charlemagne* was undermanned, but not by much. He had lost a number of hands after their late return from France, some lubbers whose backsides he was glad to see, some able-bodied seamen whom he missed dearly.

Nor was it only foremast hands who were eagerly joining the private men-of-war. He had lost his purser, which was a great annoyance, and his surgeon, Grim, which generally did not matter, except in those few instances when he was needed, and then it mattered very much.

Still, Biddlecomb's good fortune in the matter of prizes, and the fame he had achieved through no plan of his own, had made recruitment easier for him than for most captains in the navy. They did not flock to him as to a privateer, but when he sent his men around Boston to paste up the recruitment posters offering 'Great Encouragement for Seamen' who would rendezvous at the sign of the Green Dragon, they came in sufficient numbers. There were some captains who could not leave port for lack of men.

The Charlemagnes stood at quarters, checking over equipment, craning necks to see the enemy, stamping the deck and blowing on hands to keep warm.

We'll be warm enough directly, Biddlecomb thought, then turning to the helmsmen said, 'Let us fall off a few points,' and to the officers, 'We shall come up on the leeward side of this fellow, let the privateers attack from the weather gauge.'

He was yielding the most advantageous position to the privateers, not from any sense of consideration, but because he was not certain of how steady they would be in a fight. The captains of the two ships were all fearsome bluster over brandy, but that did not convince Biddlecomb of how they would perform when the cannonballs began to fly.

Not that the coming fight would be any great test of courage. The odds were so lopsided that Isaac did not think there would be much of a fight at all. His greatest fear now was that the commander of the British sloop would smoke that fact, turn on his heel, and run. It would be the most reasonable thing for him to do.

Lieutenant Faircloth crossed the deck, steadied himself on the binnacle box. 'Do you reckon, sir, that there is too big a sea running to board?'

'Too big by half, I should think,' said Biddlecomb. 'I believe your marines would be put to best use in the tops.'

'Aye, sir.' Faircloth turned to the sergeant in the

waist. 'Sergent Dawes, let us get the men aloft, if you will, and those fellows aft that are designated for the quarterdeck.'

Biddlecomb watched the marines as they formed queues on the deck and climbed one after the other into the shrouds. Their regimental coats were all new, all a uniform shade of green. Faircloth had replaced them after the *Charlemagne*'s return from France. Though Washington's army was clothed in rags there were always merchants ready to sell scarce supplies to men with Faircloth's cash.

They climbed slowly, muskets slung over their backs, round black hats pushed down on their heads, their shoes polished and gleaming dull in the gray light. Their breeches and cuffs and lapels were bright white.

Biddlecomb thought of his white hair again. He was not just Jack's father, he thought. He felt like a father to all of these men. And when he had command of the *Falmouth*, it would be much worse, all of the same problems increased in proportion to the size of the vessel.

But despite that undeniable fact, the thought of the frigate brought on the tingling in the soles of his feet, gave him a thrill akin to the anticipation of his wedding night.

'Fall off another point!' Biddlecomb called to the helmsmen. 'Sail trimmers, a little sharper up! That's well! Belay!'

The first of the privateers, the brig, was abeam of them now, half a cable off, and quickly overtaking. Even if she was not carrying more sail, she would have been faster than the *Charlemagne*, with her clean bottom and new sails and rigging.

The captain of the privateer stood alone at the weather rail, man-of-war fashion. He turned, gave Biddlecomb a half-hearted wave, and then shifted his attention back to his ship and the approaching enemy.

Biddlecomb did likewise. The British sloop of war was half a mile distant, her canvas reduced to topsails and jibs. Fighting sail. Her big guns were already run out.

'Look at this son of a bitch, bold as brass,' Rumstick offered, nodding toward the enemy. 'Oh, God, but we will do for him! Oh, yes, we will!'

Biddlecomb looked over at his first officer. The big man was rubbing his hands, literally rubbing his hands in anticipation. Isaac looked to see if a line of drool was hanging from Rumstick's lips. Biddlecomb would not have been surprised.

Rumstick seemed to sense he was being watched. He paused, met Biddlecomb's eyes, dropped his hands to his side. 'We'll . . . we'll take the bastard's lee bow, is it, sir?' he asked sheepishly.

'Yes, Mr Rumstick. Pray go see to the great guns.'

Rumstick hurried forward. Biddlecomb swung himself up into the main shrouds, ran his eyes over the tactical situation. The first privateer was past them, the second coming up fast. The *Charlemagne* was moving away from them both at an oblique angle. The three ships were crocodile jaws, opening up and welcoming in the British sloop of war. And still the enemy came on, a quarter of a mile now. Whatever the captain of that ship lacked in discretion, he made up for in courage. And that had been enough to win the day on more than one occasion.

'Run out, Mr Rumstick!' Biddlecomb called. His

hand moved automatically to the hilt of his sword, the beautiful weapon he had taken off of a British lieutenant. The brass wire binding the grip was cold and damp. It felt good under hand.

The deck trembled as the Charlemagnes hove the big guns out, straining to pull them up the slanting deck. The privateers were running their guns out as well. Fifteen minutes, perhaps less, before they would be locked in it, pounding away at each other. A whole day's maneuvering leading up to this moment, then half an hour of thundering terror, and then the weird quiet after the fight. Biddlecomb had seen it before. But this time Virginia was aboard, and their son.

'This time it is three ships on one,' Biddlecomb said.

'Yes, indeed, sir,' Lieutenant Weatherspoon agreed.

'Yes.' Biddlecomb had not meant to speak out loud and he tried to cover the fact. 'Please see the sail trimmers at stations, Mr Weatherspoon. I think we shall heave to under this fellow's lee bow, let the privateers lie to on his weather side.'

'Aye, sir.' Weatherspoon hurried forward, leaving Biddlecomb alone with his thoughts, his plans.

A cable length away now. Soon the first privateer would be broadside to broadside with the enemy. Then the *Charlemagne* would round up and rake him fore and aft. Then the second privateer, every inch as big as the enemy, would be alongside as well. Biddlecomb did not think this would take as much as half an hour.

'Enemy's falling off!' Weatherspoon shouted, bounding back up onto the quarterdeck with the energy of his eighteen years.

The sloop of war was turning, turning her bow toward the *Charlemagne*, bringing her broadside to bear on the privateer. The British commander would not let the Americans call the tune.

'Fall off!' Biddlecomb shouted, and the *Charlemagne* turned as well, keeping her same position relative to the sloop.

Then the British ship fired her starboard broadside straight into the big privateer one hundred yards away. Her jibboom was shot away, the fore topgallant mast hung broken, but Biddlecomb could see no more damage beyond that.

'Mr Rumstick, fire as we cross her bow!' Biddlecomb shouted down into the waist, and almost immediately the first of the *Charlemagne*'s guns went off, flinging round shot the length of the sloop's deck. One after another the six-pounders fired, flying inboard to be loaded again by the well-drilled men.

The privateer, the brig, was firing as well, a dismal effort, one gun at a time in ragged order. Jets of water shot up around the sloop of war, holes appeared in her sails as the round shot whistled uselessly by.

No matter, no matter, Biddlecomb thought. He noticed that his sword was in his hand. He could not recall drawing it. Soon we shall all be alongside one another, where we cannot miss. Only the number of guns will matter then, and that is all in our favor.

The first of the *Charlemagne*'s guns were firing again, their second round, even as the aftermost were firing their first.

The privateer brig was not faring well, her gunfire having dropped off even from the previous sorry rate. She was taking a beating from the British man-of-war, whose rate of fire was a wonder to behold. There seemed no break in the fire, just a continuous series of cannon blasts, more like the firing of ranks of troops then the broadside of a ship. Great clouds of gray smoke, the same color as the sky, erupted from her weather side and rolled in banks and clouds and long streamers away downwind.

'They are well drilled,' Biddlecomb observed to Weatherspoon, shouting over the gunfire.

'They are, sir. Look, here goes that fellow's main yard.'

The privateer's main yard was hanging at an odd angle, flopping fore and aft with the plunge of the vessel, and looking as if the jagged butts of the damaged wood were the only thing holding it together. A swarm of men raced aloft to save the spar, for without it they would lose the use of their main topsail and half of their driving power.

The *Charlemagne* was all but past the man-of-war's bow, running downwind of the enemy. It was not a good position, with the coast of New Jersey two miles away and under their lee, but it was where they had to be to trap the British man-of-war in a cross fire between themselves and the privateers.

'Sail trimmers! Stand by to heave to, mainsails aback!' Biddlecomb shouted forward. The sloop of war was charging down on them, and the first of her big guns were finding the *Charlemagne* in their arc of fire.

'Come up, come up, you bastard,' Biddlecomb muttered, 'come up under all of our guns.'

Now, now, now. He turned to give orders to the helmsmen, swept the horizon to weather as he turned. Saw the two privateers just as they completed their tacks, spinning around, showing their fine painted transoms to the British man-of-war as they raced to get away.

'No! You blackballing sons of bitch cowards! Come back here!' Biddlecomb screamed. He could do no less, despite the uselessness of the gesture. The glass in the one privateer's great-cabin windows was blown away by another of the man-of-war's broadsides, but she did not falter at all in her flight. The other privateer, the big one, was already at extreme cannon range.

And then the two privateers in their headlong retreat were lost to Biddlecomb's sight, blotted out by the bulk of the British man-of-war ranging up alongside.

CHAPTER 3

Several Privateers have been chased by different Cruizers: But from the better Sailing-State in which the former can with facility be kept, and other local Advantages, without Effect.
—VICE ADMIRAL RICHARD LORD HOWE
TO PHILIP STEVENS,
SECRETARY OF THE ADMIRALTY

Even as the *Charlemagne* shuddered under the man-of-war's broadside, even as great splinters whistled through the air around him and shattered rigging plunged down from aloft, Biddlecomb had to marvel at how fast a situation could change, and how stupid he could be.

On further reflection he had to admit that the privateers had behaved exactly as he would have expected, if he had been honest with himself.

The man-of-war and the *Charlemagne* passed by each other on opposite tacks, swapping their dispro-portionate broadsides, and Biddlecomb was afforded one last bitter look at the two fleeing ships – now a good quarter mile away – before he had to turn such thoughts out and concentrate on what he would do next.

As it stood, they were pinned between the sloop of war to weather and the coast of New Jersey, now a mile and a half away to leeward. Wriggling out of that box would be the first priority, but his enemy was not going to let that happen with any ease.

The sloop of war swung up into the wind, coming about, tacking on a lee shore with shortened canvas and a big sea running. It was a bold move, and well executed, and it prevented any easy escape the *Charlemagne* might have found.

'Damn, damn, damn.'

Soon they would be broadside to broadside on the same tack, lying alongside one another, and it would be gun against gun. He could not let that happen. He could not win in that event.

He thought of Virginia, down below, staring wide-eyed around the breadroom, little Jack howling in fear, his mother trying to console him, trying to console herself. It was so much worse when you did not know what was happening.

He could not let that distract him. He looked over the larboard quarter. The man-of-war had settled on her new tack. If he tried to tack the *Charlemagne* now, he would run aboard the bigger ship.

'Stations for wearing ship!' he shouted. Perhaps they could duck under the enemy's stern, get to weather of them, and sail off in the privateers' wake. 'Brace in the afteryards! Up helm!'

The *Charlemagne* turned, her bow swinging away from the man-of-war, presenting her vulnerable stern, taking the raking fire of the enemy as she tried to duck behind her. The shoreline was noticeably closer now; even as they tried to work their way off, the wind and sea were setting them down on the beach.

Isaac had hoped, had gambled and prayed, that the captain of the sloop of war would wear as well, would follow the *Charlemagne* around. Once he had the sloop of war in his wake, he could get to windward of her, and thus out of the trap.

But his enemy understood that as well. The sloop of war's helm was put down again, her bow swung up into the wind, tacking rather than wearing, blocking off the *Charlemagne*'s escape.

Rumstick prowled the waist, keeping the men at it, seeing that as much iron as possible was fired into the enemy's momentarily exposed stern. If they could take out the helm, or the captain, there might be a chance. But the sloop settled down on the new tack, yards braced up sharp, great guns firing as the ship's oversize crew worked them, fast and accurate.

Biddlecomb felt the rush of air as a ball passed close by, like a minor hurricane that grabbed him and sucked him in, and then he was covered with splinters, a hundred little pinpricks on his face. The passing shot had torn through the main boom, cut it clean in two, and as it collapsed, it tore the gaff-headed mainsail from foot to head.

Isaac grabbed the rail, shook his head, looked forward. One of the great guns had upended, flung halfway across the deck, the stunned gun crew staring stupidly at the impotent weapon. But there was Rumstick, grabbing men by the jackets, shoving them to other guns to augment their crews, to fill in the holes left by the wounded and the dead.

Overhead in the tops the marines were performing

wonderfully, pouring a steady stream of small-arms fire onto the enemy's deck. The Americans had been raised with guns in their hands, unlike the British marines, who more often than not had never held a gun until their enlistment, and the Americans' fire was notably more accurate. But they were too far away to do any real harm that day.

The two ships were again sailing on the same tack, broadside to broadside. The *Charlemagne* could not take that kind of punishment. Nor could they tack without running into the enemy. There was no choice but to wear again, but every time they did that they were driven closer to the beach. From the quarterdeck Biddlecomb could see the shoreline clearly, the long white lines of breaking surf, row upon row of shark's teeth, ready to devour them if they ventured near.

'Stations for wearing ship!' he shouted. He had no choice. He had no good choices left.

And then, quiet. Biddlecomb paused, mouth open, stared at the man-of-war. The expected question, odd-sounding through a speaking trumpet. 'Do you strike?'

'Brace in the afteryards! Up helm!' he shouted. It was all the reply this enemy needed. He had surrendered a ship once before, and it had been a mistake and he knew he would never do it again.

They were granted a reprieve, at least, from the devastating cannonade, for the *Charlemagne*'s wearing around forced the enemy to tack to prevent the Americans from slipping around her stern and heading for open water. The two combatants turned, transom to transom, coming around with larboard tacks aboard.

'He is tacking again?' Gerrish said, loud and incredulous. 'Dear God, does he not see the beach? This fellow's testicles must be made of much the same stuff as his round shot!'

The comment elicited a smile, if not an outright laugh, from Biddlecomb, as Gerrish's words often did. But then there was reality again, like a cold boarding sea.

They were just over half a mile off the beach. With the mainsail gone and the *Charlemagne*'s generally poor condition, Biddlecomb did not know if he could keep the brig out of the surf even if he did not have this enemy hovering near.

And in that instant he decided that he no longer wanted to. There was no escaping the man-of-war. It was surrender, sink, or run the brig aground. It had devolved to those choices, no more.

'Mr Gerrish, we are going to run her up on the beach, make our escape that way.'

'Aye, sir.' There was nothing flip in Gerrish's tone. He understood what this meant. The ship would be lost. Not all of them would make it through the surf.

'Go and tell Mr Rumstick and Mr Weatherspoon. I'll have the boats alongside, and all them that can't swim go into the boats. Put a good quantity of small arms, powder, and shot in each boat. Put Ferguson and Woodberry in charge of the boats and the oars double-banked. The rest of us will see the brig ashore. Mr Faircloth, your marines down from aloft, if you please.'

'Aye, aye, sir.' In chorus. Faircloth passed the order to Sergeant Dawes. Gerish hurried toward the quarterdeck ladder.

Something was gnawing, something forgotten.

'Oh, dear God . . . Gerrish!' Biddlecomb shouted. 'My wife, get my wife out of the breadroom. Do it yourself, I want her on deck in two minutes!'

'Aye, sir, wife out of the breadroom.'

Gerrish hurried off to inform Rumstick of the plan and then disappeared below, and Biddlecomb put the helm up and ordered the yards braced square.

The *Charlemagne* fell off, with the wind between two sheets, and her motion changed as the rollers came perpendicular to her keel. She went stern high, and then her stern dipped and her bow came up and obscured Isaac's view of the not-so-distant beach.

The gunfire stopped, the jarring underfoot ceased, leaving only a dull echo in Biddlecomb's ears. The captain of the sloop would have guessed what the Yankees were about. There was no need to waste further powder and shot.

The boats were hauled alongside and the Charlemagnes began the tricky business of getting aboard and getting away while the brig raced toward her death in the surf.

Virginia appeared on deck, Mr Gerrish leading her by the arm. She had taken a bit of duck and fashioned a sling for Jack, as the African women did, allowing her to carry the boy and still have use of both arms.

She had apparently understood, even from the confines of the breadroom, that things were not well with the *Charlemagne*. Isaac could tell, intimate as he was with every aspect of her body, that she had removed her stays and a number of petticoats so that she would be more free to move. She had torn a good foot of cloth off the hem of her dress to prevent her feet from tangling in it and had wrapped herself and Jack up as warm as could be. Two pistols were clipped to her belt.

No look of fear or panic was about her, just determination and resolve that she and her baby would live. Isaac could not recall having loved her more than he did at that moment.

He raced down the quarterdeck ladder, ran up to her, put his hands on her waist, pressed her and Jack to him. 'We are going to run the ship ashore, my love. You go in the boat with Ferguson, he'll see you safe through the surf. I shall follow directly.'

'Be careful, Isaac.'

'I will. No cause for concern.' He looked down at Jack, wrapped up in Virginia's caraco jacket and his own oilskin coat, staring out from the bundle, that look of perpetual surprise on his little pink face. His mother was holding him and his father was there and he seemed to think all was right with the world.

'Brave little man.' Isaac kissed him. 'I'll get a bit wet, no more than that,' Isaac to Virginia. He kissed her, kissed Jack again. There was every likelihood that one or all of them would be dead within the hour, they both understood that, but they said nothing more.

Biddlecomb returned to the quarterdeck and climbed into the main shrouds to see the launch get away from the doomed brig. A dozen of the Charlemagnes, of whom all were passionately in love with Virginia, helped her and little Jack down into the boat. The rest sat on the thwarts, oars held up, Ferguson standing like a tree in the stern sheets, despite the wild bucking of the boat, the pounding she was taking against the *Charlemagne*'s side.

Isaac longed to shout out orders, to control every

aspect of getting the boat under way, the boat that held his life, for if that boat foundered, then there would be nothing left for him. His mother and father had died when he was a boy, and he had not even realized the chasm that was left in their passing until Virginia and Jack had come along and filled it once again. He knew he could not endure that emptiness again.

But he said nothing, because he knew that Ferguson was seaman enough to get the boat off safe, and he was captain enough to know when his interference would be a hindrance. Instead he muttered a soft prayer as Ferguson flexed his knees, felt the motion of the boat relative to the ship, took a quick look at the seas astern, and shouted in a clear voice, 'Shove off! Give way all!'

The bow of the boat spun away from the brig's side, and one by one the oars found the water and pulled, and a second later it was clear of the *Charlemagne*'s side and as safe as it could be with that sea running. Biddlecomb breathed again, wondered how long he had been holding his breath. The boat was safe until they tried to get it through the surf, but for that he could do no more than trust in Ferguson and God.

With an odd mix of concern and relief Isaac pulled his eyes from the great bundle of cloth that shielded his wife and child in the center of the boat, swung inboard, and dropped to the deck, to be greeted there by Weatherspoon's anxious 'Sir! Sir! The man-of-war's launching boats!'

'Indeed?' Biddlecomb stepped up to the taffrail, took the proffered telescope. The sloop of war was three cable lengths astern now, hove to with her mainsails aback. Her boats were stacked amidships on the booms, and the topmost was just going over the side. Through the glass Biddlecomb could see the red coats of the marines waiting for the order to clamber down the side and take their places in the landing party.

The Royal Navy was not going to be satisfied with seeing the *Charlemagne* break up in the surf. This captain was going to hound them onshore, chase them through the dune grass, make them fight it out on dry land, that foreign element.

'Persistent son of a whore, ain't he, sir?' Weatherspoon voiced Biddlecomb's thoughts.

'Indeed he is. Well, he may see the *Charlemagne* wrecked this day, but we'll yield him no more.' The *Charlemagne* wrecked. The words, ash in his mouth. 'We'll need to stream cables, see the hatch boards up, whatever we can do to help those left aboard through the surf. Let us get to it.' He forced his mind to fix on the problem of getting the remainder of his men safe ashore, ignoring the fact that he was destroying the *Charlemagne*, his beloved *Charlemagne*.

They were a half mile from the beach. Isaac did not know how steeply the land fell off. They might be aground any minute, if the shallows ran far out to sea. It would behoove them to lighten the vessel.

'Mr Rumstick!' Biddlecomb shouted forward. 'We shall cut away the mainmast! Get some hands aft, quickly now!' It was the most expedient way of ridding the *Charlemagne* of several tons of weight and would at the same time provide the men with great quantities of debris on which they might float to safety.

Rumstick grabbed up an ax, shouting orders even

as he ran to the base of the mainmast and took a swing. The blade struck just above the fife rail, bit deep, cut a great gouge in the wood. He twisted the handle, jerked the blade free, and Sprout, standing opposite him, swung with an ax of his own. Like two woodsmen they hacked at the mast while others took their places on the channels, ready to cut shrouds and backstays free.

Biddlecomb squeezed the hilt of his sword, stared past the bow to the oncoming beach. Not long now, fifteen minutes perhaps. He looked astern. The *Charlemagne*'s boats were well behind them, the brig under full sail moving much faster then they ever could. They looked like water beetles crawling toward shore. He could make out no more detail than that. If he lived, he would make it to the beach before Virginia and his son would be there to greet them.

'That's well!' Rumstick's voice boomed. He and Sprout had cut away enough wood to assure that the mast would break off in that spot. 'Cut them shrouds and backstays away! Starboard side only!'

Cutlasses, axes, and knives fell on the lanyards, and one by one the standing rigging went slack until at last the entire weight of the leaning mast was born by one shroud.

The men cleared out of the way as Sprout brought his ax down on the bar-hard lanyard. The cordage parted with a sound like a gunshot, and the great towering mainmast leaned farther and farther to larboard, falling with a cracking, tearing sound, ripping up the running gear, pulling at the foreyards as it went. It paused, as if gathering strength for its last fatal effort, and then crashed down into the sea, sending spray as high as the foretop and dragging the *Charlemagne*'s stern section around in a drunken lurch.

Biddlecomb staggered, grabbed on to the quarter-deck rail for support. Turned to the helmsmen. 'You may as well lash that and get ready to go in the water.' The helm had no effect now; the pull of the foresails, the drag of the mainmast, and the relentless surf were in control, and they were all conspiring to drive the brig up onto the sand.

'Cut that debris away! Cut it all away!' Rumstick shouted, but Biddlecomb yelled, 'No! No! Belay that! We shall use it as a raft, once we're aground.'

And then it was quiet again, with nothing for the Charlemagnes to do but marvel at the strange emptiness in the place where the mainmast had stood and wait for the keel to grind up on the sand.

Isaac thought about the *Falmouth*, about his passion for her, how he had cursed the inadequate brig. The *Charlemagne*. The ship with which he had brought gunpowder to George Washington's munitions-starved army. The vessel that had played her part in the first United States naval action on the island of New Providence. The battering of the frigate *Glasgow*. Twice. The ship that had brought Benjamin Franklin to France and had wreaked havoc on English shipping in the Irish Sea, flirting with a crisis of international proportions.

His command.

He felt like a man returning from an illicit affair only to find that his faithful wife has been mortally injured.

Well, he thought bitterly, I shall not be looking at those drafts in the great cabin again.

And that thought sent his mind down another avenue. He took a step toward the main shrouds, intending to climb up a few feet, a reflex action, before he recalled that the main shrouds were no more. But even from the deck he could see all that he needed to see.

The beach was six or seven hundred yards away. The *Charlemagne* bucked and hawed and pitched as the rollers passed under her and broke in long lines along the shore, pushing her closer and closer.

A long, dark swath of wet sand bordered the water and ran as far up and down the beach as he could see. The tide was out. If he ran her aground now, the tide might lift her off again before the sea pounded her to bits. And then she would become the property of the Royal Navy, those familiar guns turned on his own countrymen.

He recalled with a flush of guilt that he had not thrown overboard the signal book and orders and such, and all of that would be in British hands as well. That could not happen, it could not be allowed.

Isaac let go of the rail, staggered forward. The quarterdeck rose up under his feet as a wave passed under, and then the *Charlemagne* came down in the trough, slamming down, shuddering through her whole fabric, seeming to stop for a beat before the next wave lifted her again. The keel had struck bottom. No good. The beach was still too far away.

Biddlecomb lurched to the quarterdeck ladder, moving from one handhold to the next, and nearly tumbling down into the waist as the *Charlemagne*'s keel struck again.

'Mr Rumstick!' he shouted, and Rumstick was there, hand on the mainmast fife rail. It looked like the Medusa's head with torn rope trailing off in every direction. 'Ezra, we must cut the foremast away. We are striking now and we are still too far out.'

'Aye!' Rumstick agreed.

Biddlecomb paused, thought again, decided. 'You see to that. I am going to fire the ship.'

Rumstick hesitated this time, glanced at the beach, tried to gauge the rate of spreading flames against the speed with which they were being driven ashore. 'Aye, aye, sir!' he said at last, then leaned forward and jerked his ax from the stump of the mainmast and shouted, 'Hands to cut away the foremast!'

Biddlecomb snatched up a cartridge case, a long black leather cylinder, used by the powder monkeys to carry the powder from the magazine to the great guns. The case had been abandoned in the frenzy. He could tell from the weight that it contained at least two of the tight-packed flannel cartridges of gunpowder. That was enough.

'Mr Gerrish, fetch a pistol from someone and come with me!' he shouted, and dove down the main scuttle to the lower deck and raced forward. He could hear Gerrish's shoes on the deck behind him, the midshipman's breath as he panted. They raced past the big brick galley oven, cold now, as the coals had been thrown overboard when the brig was cleared for action, and forward, into the gloom of the bow section of the tween decks.

Biddlecomb found himself groping along, feeling from one storage-room door to the next. The dull sunlight on deck had rendered them blind in the dark space, and like the oven, all the lanterns had been extinguished.

But that was no matter. There was no part of the

Charlemagne that Biddlecomb did not know, not an inch of wood he had not personally seen. He had participated in every moment of this ship's life, from the laying of her keel to her launch and fitting out, to the design and setting up of her spars and rigging. She had never moved an inch but under his command.

He felt the deck drop under his feet, the keel slam into the bottom. The shudder was transmitted through the brig's fabric, through Biddlecomb's legs. Now he was seeing to her death.

He came at last to the bosun's stores, the farthest forward of the several cabins arranged in the bow. His eyes were adjusting to the dark. He could make out the white bulkheads, the handle on the door.

'Gerrish, are you there?'

'Aye, sir, right here.'

'Find the sailmaker's stores, pull out whatever cloth you can lay your hands on. Pile it up there, by the breast hook.'

Isaac pulled open the door to the bosun's stores and was greeted with a great mixture of smells: tar and turpentine and paint and linseed oil. It smelled of volatility.

He pulled out his pocketknife and cut away the lashings that held the butt of turpentine in place, rolled it out of the cabin. Suddenly the brig lurched, rolled, her whole motion changing, and Biddlecomb was flung to the deck, just able to grab the heavy butt before it rolled over him. He heard Gerrish crashing down somewhere in the dark.

'Are you all right, sir?' Gerrish called.

'Fine. Are you hurt?'

'No, sir. I fell on the pile of sails.'

'I suspect the foremast has just gone by the board. Let us hurry.' Isaac pulled himself to his feet. The motion of the brig was wild now, with the dampening effect of the mast gone, a violent roll and snap back, twisting and corkscrewing. He rolled the butt forward, and Gerrish helped him push it onto the pile of sailcloth right against the stem. They broke the spigot off and the powerful smell of turpentine filled the space.

Biddlecomb fumbled with the cartridge case, pulled one of the flannel cylinders out, cut it open with his knife, and sprinkled the mealy powder over the cloth. 'Here, set that off with the pistol's flintlock.'

Gerrish pulled the lock back, held the gun sideways over the cloth, a dim gray pile to their now accustomed eyes. He pulled the trigger. The flint snapped against the frizzen and a trail of sparks fell from the steel and onto the scattered grains, which puffed and smoked as they burned, spreading the flames one to another and grabbing onto the cloth.

'That's well, step away,' Biddlecomb said, and they had not taken three steps back when the sparks found the turpentine and the canvas flared into a genuine conflagration, flames spreading fast in all directions.

'Good. Let us get some more combustibles about and then get topside.'

It was hard just to stand on that rolling deck; wrestling stores from the bosun's locker was nearly impossible. Biddlecomb and Gerrish were soon sweating with abandon from the effort and from the great heat thrown off by the burning canvas. They poured paint around, and linseed oil, balls of marline and more cloth from the sailmaker's locker.

The flames were roaring and snapping and eating away at the paint on the bulkheads, threatening to overwhelm them with heat and the toxic gas of the many burning materials, when Biddlecomb decided that the ship was on fire and would remain that way until the fire had consumed all that there was to consume.

He slapped Gerrish on the back, pointed to the deck overhead. Gerrish nodded, followed, and the two men staggered aft, coughing, stumbling, gasping for fresh air. They found the ladder up to the waist, clung tight as the rolling ship tried to fling them to the deck, and climbed up into the watery sunlight.

The whole world had changed in the time that they had been below. The foremast was gone, draped over the starboard side as the main was draped over the larboard. The beach was perhaps two hundred yards away, the *Charlemagne* careening toward it, turned sideways and taking the seas on the beam, rolling wildly with only the wreckage alongside to keep her from rolling over completely.

'Sir, are you all right?' Rumstick was there, looking concerned.

'I am fine, Ezra. The ship's afire, she won't go out now.'

'I'm sorry, Isaac.'

'As am I. But better she should burn than become a part of the British navy. I surrendered her once, you will recall. I shan't do it again.'

Then the *Charlemagne*'s keel hit again, a great crash and shudder that flung all the men to the deck as if they were swept away by grapeshot. Biddlecomb felt the ship roll, saw the gray sky overhead spin past as the ship slewed around and the waves picked her

57

up again and drove her on, then dropped her again on the sand.

He pulled himself to his feet, staggered forward, holding on where he could. Smoke was pouring up from the forward hatch, thick and black and stinking of all the things that were ablaze below.

Again the *Charlemagne* was lifted high, flung toward the beach, dropped with a crash. He wondered how many of those she would survive before breaking up. Which would kill her quicker, the fire or the surf?

'Listen here, you men!' he shouted. 'Listen here!' And when they were listening, the thirty or so still aboard, he said, 'We have to get off her, now! You men climb down onto the wreckage of the mainmast. Plenty to hold on to, just take a care you don't get tangled up. I'll cut it away and you'll float ashore!'

No one argued, no one could think of a better idea, and it was unlikely that there was one. The Charlemagnes struggled aft, and one after another they climbed onto the main shrouds, now leading down into the sea rather than up into the top-hamper. They moved fast and sure – most of those still aboard were topmen – and grabbed onto whatever solid thing they could find.

'That's the lot of 'em,' Rumstick said.

Biddlecomb turned, surprised to find the lieutenant still aboard, more surprised to find Weatherspoon, Gerrish, and Faircloth behind him. He opened his mouth to order them off, realized that he would meet with argument if he did, and there was no time for argument, so he said, 'Cut it away.'

The officers fell on the shrouds and backstays with their axes and cutlasses. Biddlecomb drew his sword, slashed at the main royal backstay, severed it

58

in three strokes. The last of the standing rigging, that umbilical cord binding mast to ship, was cut through. A roller passed under, lifted the brig high above the wreckage. Biddlecomb held his breath – it looked as if the *Charlemagne* would roll right over the men in the water – but then the wave dropped the ship with another smashing blow and the mainmast was lifted high and whirled away toward the beach.

The next wave came and the brig did not lift so high, and Biddlecomb guessed that her back was broken, her bottom stove in. Smoke was pouring out of the main hatch now, half the tween decks consumed. Rats were skittering across the weather decks, too terrified to bother keeping to the shadows.

'We best think of a way off, I reckon,' Rumstick offered.

'Gratings make famous rafts,' Biddlecomb said. 'Quick, let us get some off of the hatch before they burn through.'

The small clutch of officers hurried to the main hatch, staggering like sailors coming out of a public house. Flames were licking up through the small squares in the grating, but the wood had not yet taken. Eager hands grabbed the aftermost grating, pulled it free, then dropped it again as the *Charlemagne*'s keel struck and sent them scattering like ninepins. Isaac fetched up against the larboard bulwark, lay still, groaned. He felt a kinship with his beloved *Charlemagne*. Like the brig, he could not take much more of this battering.

Then water was swirling around him, over his arms, over the back of his head. He gasped at the cold, shuddered, leapt to his knees and his feet. The brig was lodged in the sand, no longer rising to the sea, the waves pushing her over, water pouring in through the gunports. Rumstick and Weatherspoon were still clutching the grate. Gerrish was on his back, half underwater.

'Here! Get that grate down here!' Biddlecomb shouted, grabbing Gerrish by the coat and dragging him to his knees. The midshipman muttered something, Biddlecomb could not hear what, and his head lolled about as if the muscles of his neck were gone.

Rumstick and Weatherspoon and Faircloth half walked and half crawled to the low side of the deck, pulling the grate behind them. They could feel the sea welling up again, lifting the broken ship, swirling up through the gunports. They grabbed onto the grate, locked their fingers through the square holes, and grabbed onto various parts of Gerrish's clothing as the sea rose up under them, lifted them off the deck like the hand of God, and swirled them away over the bulwark.

One second they were on hands and knees on the *Charlemagne*'s deck and the next they were in the water, clinging to a hatch grating, looking up at the bulk of the brig. And then the next wave had them, lifted them, and they were looking down on the deck of the stricken ship, which they were quickly leaving behind.

They held on, gasped at air, spit mouthfuls of salt water back into the sea, spun around like a leaf in a stream. The breaking waves might well have flipped them end for end, but the bulk of the *Charlemagne* served as a breakwater, holding back the worst of the surf, until at last they felt the gritty sand under their shoes. They stood and dragged themselves out of the water, Rumstick and Faircloth supporting Gerrish, their clothes heavy and dripping.

Biddlecomb moved with some difficulty over the sand, tried to focus his thoughts and ignore the many aching points on his body. Not all of his men had made it. He saw a few bodies in the surf, flopping back and forth as the water came in and out, as if making one last halfhearted effort to get ashore.

The rest of the Charlemagnes were drawn up in a group, Mr Sprout getting them organized by mess. There did not seem to be many men standing there, given the size of the brig's company.

'Here's the boats coming, sir,' someone said.

The boats. Of course. Virginia and Jack. How could he have forgotten? It seemed wrong. This was not a backdrop against which he would think to see his wife and baby.

He turned, looked in the direction the man was pointing. The two boats, the launch and the pinnace, were driving hard for the beach with double-banked oars. Ferguson and Woodberry had realized the advantage of ducking in under the lee of the *Charlemagne*'s broken hull. The boats swooped past the stern section, turned hard, and settled in for the pull ashore in the relatively smooth water beyond the ship. They pitched in the remaining waves and took some water over their transoms and then ran up onto the sand with a grinding sound.

Biddlecomb ran back down the beach, splashed out to the launch, resting in a foot of water. 'Virginia, Virginia, are you all right?'

'Yes, very well, thank you,' said Virginia. 'I'm fine, Jack is fine.'

Biddlecomb stepped back, made room for the men

61

piling out of the boat and dragging it farther up on the beach. Then yards away the wreckage of the mainmast was pushed up on the sand. The United States ensign was still there, wrapped around the royal pole, clinging tenaciously to its rightful spot. They had never struck it.

'Ferguson, cut that ensign free and bring it along,' Isaac ordered. At least they had not lost the colors. It was not much, but it was something.

The *Charlemagne* was hard aground, fifty yards away, half-rolled on her side, the seas breaking around her. Black smoke was pouring out of her main hatch and the great cabin windows. She was completely involved, would burn right down to the waterline. Biddlecomb felt the tears well up, blinked them back. What had he done, what had he done?

He looked past the wrecked and burning brig, farther out to sea. The sloop of war was hove to still, her boats all in the water, making their way toward the beach. There was no time now to reminisce, to mourn the loss of the *Charlemagne* or to wallow in his feeling of guilt and defeat. There was no time for that. The redcoats were coming.

CHAPTER 4

We proceeded up the river to cover the landing of the troops, which they did without opposition to the number of 22,000 in one day. They had intelligence, that George Washington was about five miles off, but he thought proper to march into the back country, there to make a stand. General Howe is gone off in pursuit of him. We expect to hear in about a month's time of Philadelphia being taken.

— A LETTER FROM A YOUNG GENTLEMAN
ON BOARD HIS MAJESTY'S SHIP *SPHYNX*

Malachi Foote shifted uncomfortably, ground the tobacco in his mouth between stained teeth, spit a long stream on the ground. This was not at all how he had pictured it.

Not the ship, of course. She was exactly right. The *Falmouth*, sitting proud on the stocks, her hull embraced by the launch cradle, ready to go down the ways and into the Delaware River.

She was just as he had pictured her, from the first moment he and Humphreys had laid blank paper on

63

the table and taken the first tentative stabs with their pencils, creating elegant hull shapes; top timber sweep, reconciling sweep, floor sweep, dead rise; out of experience and thin air. He could see that perfection made manifest now, sitting patiently, like a bride being made ready.

She was one hundred and twenty-six feet, three and one half inches long between perpendiculars, one hundred and five foot, seven and a quarter on the keel. Her extreme beam was thirty-four feet, ten inches. She was six hundred and eighty-one and fifty-three ninety-fourth's tons burthen.

Her topsides were oiled, the lovely, darkened wood glowing dull in the weak sunlight. Her upper and lower wales, those heavy planks that ran her full length from stem to stern, were painted black, accentuating the lovely run of her hull. Her upper rails were painted red, a thin, understated line, and below that a strip of deep sky blue. Her bottom was coated with a great smear of white stuff, consisting of tallow, sulfur, resin, and broken glass, Malachi Foote's own concoction, guaranteed to stave off shipworm and seaweed for months to come.

Those parts of the *Falmouth* that Foote could not see he could picture, for he had supervised the fitting of every piece of the twenty-eight-gun frigate. He could see the huge hanging knees, the gentle bend of her clamps, the cant frames, the massive timbers throughout. No, there was not a thing wrong with her.

It was the launching.

He had pictured it many times over the past months: bright sunshine warming the masses of spectators, flags waving, bands playing, members of the

Continental Congress turned out to give long-winded speeches to which no one would listen. Barrels of wine, beer, and West Indian rum broached and emptied. Firkins of ham and tongue and corned beef. Some bit of mutton to smash a bottle over her cutwater. It had been that way for the *Randolph*, built on those same stocks, a ship of middling qualities, and even for the *Washington*, that ill-crafted, misbegotten tub built at the Eyre shipyard, upriver.

But not for the *Falmouth*. There were none of those things that day. Not even the sunshine.

And for that, at least, Foote was glad. A sunny, cheery day would have served only to further darken his mood, if that was possible.

Instead, the clouds hung low in an unbroken gray and black blanket, casting the shipyard, the river, the city of Philadelphia, in somber, funereal tones. A cold wind clawed its way around the buildings, picking up the fallen leaves and sundry shipyard debris and hurling them malevolently at the river. It snatched at the tail of Foote's long coat and slapped it against his legs, and the stronger gusts forced him to clam his hand down on his hat. It was as if God Himself was proclaiming this was a dark day for the profession of shipbuilding, that such a ship as the *Falmouth* could go in the water unheralded.

Those few workers that they could scrape up for the launch were applying soap and tallow to the ways, and showing no great enthusiasm for their task. Foote stepped forward, opened his mouth to shout at them, then checked his anger.

He cleared his throat and formulated a calmer entreaty. 'Come along, you bastards, God ain't gonna hold the bloody tide for us all day!' Then, satisfied that his words had had their intended effect, he folded his arms again and continued to glare at the gray river.

'We are just shy of high water now, I should think,' observed Joshua Humphreys.

They were standing side by side, and the two men could not have looked more different. Humphreys was in his mid-twenties, tall, thin, and pale of skin, dressed in Quaker black, round glasses perched on his nose, magnifying pale blue eyes. He had the nervous quality of a deer, seemed perpetually afraid. It had taken Foote some time to realize that in fact he was not.

Foote, by contrast, was not above five feet five inches in height, dark skinned with dark salt-and-pepper hair tied back in a queue, more gray than one might expect for a man of forty-three. He was powerfully built, with a strength born of swinging adz and maul and mallet over a lifetime of ship-building. He had done such hard labor all his life, from apprentice to master shipwright, and even when he was in charge he did not shy away from hefting a tool. He shaved infrequently and that made him look as if he were always growing a beard.

He squinted down at the water's edge. The river was creeping up over the ways, far beyond the normal tide line. The current was slowing. It was nearly slack water, the day of the spring tide. Time to launch.

'Give it half an hour, I reckon.'

'I'm certain Adams would have been here,' Humphreys observed, 'and Stephen Hopkins too had the spring tide been even a few days earlier.'

Foote glared at the young Quaker, turned, and spit another brown stream on the ground.

'Hmm, you seem to be conjuring great quantities of spittle today, sir,' Humphreys said.

'There's some days, my dear Humphreys, that it's the only way to properly express what I feel.'

It was September 25, 1777, and Philadelphia was a very different place than it had been a year before.

Back then, all of the capital city was enraptured with thoughts of liberty and the noble fight against the ministerial army of England. The first ad hoc navy of the United States had successfully captured the island of New Providence. Ben Franklin was in France, coaxing from Louis XVI enough military stores to keep the army in the field. Washington had crossed the Delaware and served out retribution to the German butchers in winter quarters at Trenton.

And all along the waterfront in Philadelphia, noble frigates rose on the stocks and were launched into the Delaware River with all the fanfare of an optimistic and patriotic people. It seemed a hundred years ago.

Foote and Humphreys had played their part, working together on the frigate *Randolph*, Humphreys doing the lion's share of the design work, Foote as master shipwright.

They had known each other for years, each being something of a fixture on the Philadelphia waterfront, had harbored a vague dislike for one another. But thrust together on that project, they had fallen into long discussions of what made the perfect man-of-war and had found in one another fellow zealots in the art and science of ship building.

The *Randolph* was the first time either of them had

built a vessel of war, and it proved to be a fascinating exercise in design and construction.

Then, in November of 1776, the Continental Congress, in yet another flight of enthusiasm, had ordered up more ships: packet boats, brigs, frigates, even seventy-four-gun ships of the line. And among them, the twenty-eight-gun *Falmouth*, a gift of a job given to John Wharton from a friend in Congress who owed him a favor.

Wharton in turn gave the job to his young partner, Humphreys, and Humphreys had seen in it the chance for him and Foote to put into practice all of those things they had discussed over coffee and tea and, in Foote's case, rum at the City Tavern. And so their odd partnership was born.

And from that partnership came what both men believed to be the finest frigate of her size ever built, the perfect combination of strength of hull and quickness of form. A stable gun platform and a fast bottom. A symphony in white oak and long-leaf yellow pine. A ship that could work to windward in light air and stand up to the worst pounding the sea could give.

But even as the great ship had come together on the stocks, the situation in America had fallen apart.

First came the news of Burgoyne's push south through Canada, his taking the mighty Fort Ticonderoga with no resistance. And then Howe had embarked his troops and disappeared out to sea. A month of terrified speculation, and then the British appeared at Head of Elk, the northernmost point of the Chesapeake Bay, forty-five miles from Phila-delphia.

That had happened exactly a month earlier, and

since then Washington had met Howe at the Brandy-wine Creek and had been defeated. Again. Congress had been told that Philadelphia could not be held, and so they had abandoned the place, moved the capital to Baltimore. There were no congressmen there at the *Falmouth*'s launch because there were no congressmen left in the city.

Four days earlier, over three hundred Continental soldiers had been bayoneted in their sleep on a nearby killing ground called Paoli. Howe was only a few miles outside the city, having lured Washington's army north and then slipped around them to the south. Philadelphia was about to be overrun. Her people showed little interest in celebrating the launch of an already doomed frigate.

'Never a word from the captain?' Humphreys asked.

'Should have been here by now. Biddle. No, not Biddle, Biddle's the other one. Biddle-something. Biddlecomb. No, never a word.'

'One would think he would want to be here for the launch.'

'One would think.' Foote wanted to spit again and vent disgust, but he resisted. Instead he picked up the canvas bag at his feet and turned to Humphreys. 'Come along, then, we're going to do this thing proper as we can.'

Foote led the way across the muddy yard and up the ladder still propped against the frigate's side. He stepped out onto her gangway, the light section of deck that ran along the top of her bulwarks from forecastle to the quarterdeck.

Below him was the waist, the two main hatches amidships, the row of empty gunports staring blankly

69

at the gray city. Under the overhanging quarterdeck he could see the bulkhead that sectioned off the captain's day cabin and great cabin aft. Forward, just under the break of the forecastle, the big brick galley oven. Directly above it, on the edge of the deck, stood the belfry with its polished brass bell, the raised letters facing aft: FALMOUTH. Named for that poor town in Maine that had been so violated by the British.

Humphreys struggled up the ladder, stepped carefully onto the gangplank. With the ship up on the hard it was a long fall to the ground below.

'Damn me to hell, she is a beauty, ain't she?' Foote said.

'She is that. I marvel just to look on her.'

'Here, let's see her done up proper.' Foote dug into the canvas bag, pulled out a red-and-white-striped bundle, handed it to Humphreys. 'Jack for'rd, pennant amidships, ensign aft, eh? Go run that up the jack staff.'

The day before, Foote had stepped the jack staff on the bowsprit, the ensign staff on the quarterdeck, and the temporary pole amidships where the mainmast would go. He knew the launch would receive little in the way of fanfare, but he would be damned if she went down the ways with no bunting aloft.

Humphreys made his shaky way forward as Malachi dropped down the quarterdeck ladder and into the waist. He pulled the pennant from the bag and bent it to the halyard, then hauled away. The flag was thirty feet long and forked at the end like a snake's tongue, with three stripes, red, white, and blue, running its length. It flickered and lashed out as it unfolded from the bag and ran up the pole, until at

70

last the bitter end came free and flew away, and the whole pennant waved and twisted in the wind.

He watched it for a moment. Smiled. He climbed back up to the quarterdeck. Forward, Humphreys was just tying off the jack, a series of red and white stripes, across which spread an uncoiled snake and the words DON'T TREAD ON ME.

Foote made his way aft, past the capstan and the binnacle box and the big double wheel, to the ensign staff, lashed to the taffrail. He dropped the bag on the deck. Peered over the rail to the ways below that emerged from under the transom and ran straight into the river thirty feet away. The men had finished the greasing. Now they were pounding away the chocks. In a minute only the shores would be left to prevent the frigate from sliding unbidden into the water.

Foote turned, looked over the bows. More dockyard hands, arranging the cables that would prevent the *Falmouth* from floating away downriver after she was launched. Humphreys was making his way aft. Just run up the ensign and let her go. No more to do than that. But he was having a hard time doing it. It seemed there should be more.

Then from somewhere away to the west, carried on the wind, came just the faintest hint of artillery fire. Washington's Continental Line fighting it out with Howe over some sorry piece of Pennsylvania countryside.

Foote pulled the ensign from the bag, bent it onto the halyard. It was huge, fifteen feet on the fly. He had paid for it himself, from his own purse, and it had cost him a huge sum. Specie, not that Continental paper trash. He had had to go to a sailmaker, and they had

71

enough business from the privateers that it took serious money for an ensign to be worth their while. But in the end he got it, and he was glad for it.

He hoisted away. The flag spilled from the bag, blossoming out as the wind caught the folds and spread them out, and then it was free. Thirteen red and white stripes, a blue canton, thirteen white stars representing a new constellation.

'Lovely, lovely!' Humphreys clasped his hands together, looked up at the big flag with delight.

'Like a fucking dream,' Foote said. He had already displayed more sentiment than he cared to, and he did not want Humphreys to get carried away either. Afraid the poor bastard might weep, or some such. 'I reckon we best see if this bucket'll swim.'

Foote leaned over the taffrail again, then looked forward, saw that all was in readiness. There was an odd feeling in his stomach, a tightening of his muscles. He was nervous, he realized with some surprise. About what, he could not imagine. He squirted a stream of tobacco juice out, watched it fall the long way to the ground.

'Very well, then,' he shouted, 'cut them away!'

On the ground below the men fell to cutting away the shores, great lengths of timber running at an angle from the ground up to the *Falmouth*'s stern and now bearing the entire weight of the ship. They worked with a will, saws biting deep as the two-man teams heaved them back and forth.

The starboard shore was cut through first. The heavy timber fell to the ground and the *Falmouth* gave a lurch that made Foote and Humphreys stagger.

Foote frowned. For five months now he had been waiting for this day, this moment.

72

From the yard below a voice shouted, 'Stand clear!' followed by the heavy thud of the last shore hitting the packed earth, and then the *Falmouth* was moving, for the first time in her life, sliding down the ways toward the element for which she was created.

It was a frightening sensation, for the turn of her bilge blocked their view of the launch cradle and it seemed impossible that she would not topple over. The ship that had seemed as solid as an outcropping of granite was now a moving, precarious platform. Foote took a breath, placed a hand casually on the ensign staff, hoped he did not look half as frightened as Humphreys. He had done this many times, but his mind could never convince his gut that there was no reason to worry. For pride and exhilaration and delicious fear, there was nothing to match riding a big ship down the ways.

The hull gathered speed as she slipped closer and closer to the river. She seemed to be careening beyond control, though she was going no faster than a fit man could walk. The town appeared to recede, and the foremost stocks came into view under the bow as the ship shot down the ways. Foote could now see the men tending the lines, the bow-fasts, running from her hawscholes.

And then the river was there, on the edge of his vision, and he knew the rudder and sternpost were wet, and then more and more of the hull. The after end seemed to rise up as the water lifted it, the *Falmouth* now part in the river, part on the ways, a baby halfway born into its element.

The bow plunged down and then up, and she was free of the land. The steady, linear motion of a ship confined on the ways gave way to the fluid bob and roll of an unballasted ship, fully afloat. Foote closed his eyes, enjoyed the sensation of the ship moving under him, the organic feel of the hull in the water, acted upon by those many influences of wind and tide and current.

He opened his eyes, met Humphreys's, smiled. 'She swims, Humphreys.'

'She does, my dear Foote, she does.'

The men ashore were already hooking up the tow ropes to teams of big-shoulder oxen so they could pull the frigate around to the wharf and tie her up in a place where she could be safely abandoned. They moved quicker and with more enthusiasm for the job at hand than Foote was used to seeing from dock workers, and it annoyed him greatly.

The *Falmouth*'s stern swung around to the pull of the stern-fast, and the bow-fasts were eased away, and in that manner the ship was moved one hundred feet downriver. She bumped gently against the wharf that had been cleared away for her arrival. Eager hands made the lines off. The top of a ladder appreared over the edge of the gunwale and two of the men clambered aboard, and ten minutes later the lines were doubled up and re-enforced with springs and breast-fasts.

With no further comment, Foote and Humphreys made their way to the ladder and down onto the wharf. They walked along the edge, shipwright and naval architect, ran their eyes along the frigate's waterline, observed how she floated, how she seemed to take to the water.

With no masts or rigging, guns, stores, or even ballast, she rode unnaturally high, so that six strakes that would normally be below the water were now above. Despite that, Foote and Humphreys could see that she was on an even keel, that she sat perfectly in the water, like royalty on a throne. They walked her length twice, their eyes never leaving her side. Perfect.

When at last they paused and looked up, the shipyard was deserted, the dockworkers had taken their leave.

'Well done, Mr Foote, well done,' Humphreys said.

'And you too, Mr Humphreys.'

The young man took a long, last look at the *Falmouth*, then turned back to Foote. 'I suppose there is nothing more for us to do here,' he said, half sighing as he spoke. 'And given the circumstances, I really must be off, see to affairs at my home.'

'Of course, sir, of course.' Foote could hardly blame him for wanting to leave. If Foote had any family himself, or anyone about whom he gave a damn, he would probably leave as well.

He held out his hand and Humphreys took it, and they shook. Foote wanted to say something more, but such moments were not his long suit. 'Of course,' he said.

And then he was alone, he and the *Falmouth*. The wind built, backed and veered and whipped in gusts, struck the new vessel broadside and made her strain and pull at the dock lines. And Malachi Foote had no idea what he would do next.

September 25, 1777. The year of the hangman.

And the redcoats were coming.

CHAPTER 5

July 1777
Tuesday 22nd Cape May No Cape Henlopen WbS
at 6 a.m. made the Merlins Signal to weigh at ½
Pt 6 Tack'd Ship Cape May WSW 5 Leags In 2nd
Reef Topsails ½ pt 7 saw a Sail & gave Chace out
2nd Reef T. Sls Sent the Barge & Cutter to cut off
the Chace from the Land Fired several Guns at the
Chace

—MASTER'S LOG
HMS *ROEBUCK*

From the vantage of the beach, the *Charlemagne*
looked even more pathetic, convulsing in her death
throes, rolling farther over with each breaking wave
and then rolling back again, as if she were trying to
work her way off the sand and back out to sea, as if
she were trying to get to some secret place where
brave ships go to die.

But she could not break free from the grip of the
sand or shake off the tentacles of fire. She was
doomed to die in that place, and a month later there
would be no evidence at all of her tragic passing.

Winter storms for years after would heave up on the beach charred bits of her skeleton, until there was nothing left of her, no more blackened wood for beachcombers to find and cause them to stare out at the water and wonder what unfortunate wreck lay hidden there. The great guns that had lashed out at the most powerful navy on earth would bury themselves in the sand, and at some point, in a future that Biddlecomb could not even envision, they would become an indistinguishable part of the ocean bottom. Ashes to ashes, dust to dust.

The marines were formed up in column, their regimentals soaked through, looking more black than green. The powder and shot and small arms had been distributed to the others. The British boats were two cables offshore, no farther. It was time to go.

Isaac pulled his eyes from the *Charlemagne*, determined that he would not look on her again. 'Rumstick, Faircloth, Weatherspoon, to me,' he called, and the officers hurried over. 'I think we will have to fight these fellows, what do you reckon?'

Faircloth glanced out at the approaching boats. 'If we just try to run for it, they'll be right on our arses, and us with no kind of organization. Hard to say how determined they are, but if they are set on a fight, I don't reckon we can avoid it.'

'Mr Rumstick?'

'I got to agree with Faircloth. If there's a chance we must fight, better to be ready for it.'

'Mr Weatherspoon?' The former midshipman was only eighteen, but he looked much older than that. They all did, those who had been waging this war at sea for nearly three years.

'I think we best stand and fight, sir.'

77

'I concur,' Biddlecomb said. 'Mr Faircloth, this is more your purview, how should we mount our defense?'

'Wellll . . .' The marine drew out the word, looked over the beach and the grassy dunes. The soft sand stretched for one hundred feet from the water's edge to the first hump of dirt, which was all but lost under a thick mat of dune grass.

'Not much to anchor a line . . .' Faircloth equivocated some more and then said with finality, 'I think we should spread out on the dune down there.' He indicated a spot a quarter mile down the beach. 'If we just run for it, these bastards will think we're retreating. Once we're out of their sight, we'll form up, keep hidden. With any luck they'll chase after, pell-mell, and run right into us.'

'Good. Let us do it.' Biddlecomb turned back to the men on the beach. 'We will hurry to yonder dune, and once we are out of sight of these whore's sons, we'll form up to give them a proper greeting. Come along, hurry, all of you.'

He pulled his sword and waved it forward and the men moved off in a half run. He heard Faircloth yelling to his marines, 'No, no, don't march, just run! You are supposed to be fleeing, not parading for General bloody Washington!'

They jogged across the beach at an oblique angle, making for the far dune. The sailors were all powerful men, but life in the confines of a ship had robbed them of their wind. Their wet clothing weighed them down and their feet sank in the soft sand and soon all of them were breathing hard, their pace slowing. All, save for Virginia, who, as an avid equestrian, was more conditioned for such exercise.

'Are you' – Biddlecomb gasped, swallowed, gasped again – 'are you well, my love?'

'I am, but you and your men look as if you will faint here on the sand,' Virginia said, adjusting little Jack in his sling.

'Quite, quite.' Biddlecomb gasped again, and then in a louder voice called, 'Let us slow up a bit, we are nearly there.'

The grateful men slowed to a walk. By the time they filed through a gap between the dunes and disappeared from the sight of anyone on the beach, their breathing had returned nearly to normal.

'Mr Faircloth, I leave these arrangements to you,' Biddlecomb said, and the marine lieutenant immediately began issuing orders, pushing sailors in one direction, marines in another, giving orders concerning volley fire, flanking attacks, use of edged weapons and bayonets.

Faircloth had gained a tolerable amount of practical experience aboard the *Charlemagne*, and he possessed an extraordinary amount of theoretical knowledge, being as he was a dedicated student of warfare, so Biddlecomb turned his thoughts elsewhere, confident that the marine had things under control.

The sun was dropping toward the horizon, which meant it would be at their backs and in their enemy's eyes. Biddlecomb reckoned it to be around five o'clock, with no more than two hours of daylight remaining. The captain of the sloop of war would not care to lurk that close to shore once it was dark, no matter what his balls were made of. That meant the shore party could not dedicate more than an hour or so to their capture.

Gerrish was sitting on the sand, half slumped over.

By some miracle his round glasses, which he kept lashed to his head with spun yarn, were still intact. 'Mr Gerrish,' Biddlecomb said, 'are you quite all right?'

'No, sir, but I think I shall recover,' the midshipman offered.

'Good, good.' The signal telescope was still slung around his shoulder. 'Now, if you do not mind, I shall relieve you of the glass.'

Gerrish made a pathetic attempt to unsling it himself, but Biddlecomb said, 'No, no, let me get it,' and eased it over Gerrish's head. The midshipman flopped onto his back as if passing out.

Biddlecomb examined the telescope. He expected to find just the shattered remnants of the lens, the tube half-filled with water, but by some miracle it had survived unscathed. He took a step up the sand dune, then lay on his belly and wriggled snakelike to the crest until he could just see the beach through the grass. He rested the telescope on the sand and peered through.

The sloop of war's longboat, the first of the boats, was just reaching the outer edge of the surf. They were landing close to where the Charlemagnes were hiding, which told Biddlecomb that they had indeed taken note of the spot where the Charlemagnes, in their disorderly retreat, had disappeared behind the dunes, and they intended to follow.

Because they were landing farther down the beach, the British did not have the *Charlemagne*'s hull to serve as a breakwater. The longboat rose on an incoming wave, then disappeared from Biddlecomb's view, then reappeared in the midst of the breaking surf. It sloughed around, nearly broaching before the expert crew pulled it straight again for the last ride onto the beach. The sailors with their wide trousers and blue jackets tumbled over the gunwales and hauled the boat farther up the sand, and then the red-coated marines got stiffly out.

The second boat, the barge, did not fare so well. Biddlecomb watched it rise on a swell, just like the first, and like the first it sloughed around, turning broadside to the waves. Through the glass he could see men straining at the sweeps, backing water, pulling for all they were worth, the seaward side of the barge rising higher and higher until Biddlecomb was looking right at the floorboards. And then the entire boat was over, rolling like a log in the surf, spilling half of the men out and rolling on top of the others.

Then it was gone, in the trough of the waves, and then it was up again, closer to the beach, and surrounded by thrashing figures, blue coats and red. Another swell and then men and the boat were pushed closer ashore and the men's feet found bottom. Some walked from the surf, some crawled, and some lay still in the water. The sea surged again, rolling the barge once more, leaving it on the hard-packed sand, sitting upright on an even keel, as if the rolling over and over had been some acrobatic trick, followed by a perfect landing.

Biddlecomb watched from his hiding place, did some figures in his head. About thirty men in the boat. Each would be carrying around thirty-five cartridges, now soaked and useless. One thousand and fifty bullets that would not be fired at his people.

Faircloth shuffled up beside Biddlecomb, and Biddlecomb handed him the glass, though all of the

81

landing party was now so close as to make it unnecessary. Two more boats landed in succession, the pinnace and the cutter, coming through the surf with some difficulty but managing to stay upright and reasonably dry. The four boats were pulled up to the edge of the dry sand, and the officers, naval and marine, began pushing the men into loose ranks.

There looked to be around forty marines, which seemed to Biddlecomb quite a lot for a sloop of war, and twenty sailors. The marines went through their ritual of loading their weapons and fixing bayonets, each movement precise, mechanical, and done exactly like his neighbor's. It was almost inhuman, the way they moved. Perhaps a sergeant was calling the manual of arms, but Isaac could hear nothing over the roar of the surf.

The sailors were loading weapons as well, more casually and at their own pace, though at least two of them were loading to the marine's instructions, with great exaggerated movements, mocking the bullocks. Everyone seemed to be taking quite a bit of time, which made Biddlecomb wonder at the initiative of the officer in charge, who was presumably trying to chase down a fleeing enemy.

'Taking their time about it all, what?' Faircloth said, echoing Biddlecomb's thoughts.

'Indeed. Here, now they are moving. Are you quite ready?'

'Quite, sir. Particularly if they are going to be as informal as all that. I've sent away a small detachment with Mrs Biddlecomb and your son, about a hundred paces back.'

'Good. Thank you.'

The landing party was marching now, marching

directly at the American's position, stepping out at a casual pace, weapons held over their shoulders. The sun in the west illuminated them beautifully, glinting off buckles and bayonets, making the scarlet coats blaze, bleaching the white waistcoats and breeches until they seemed as pure as new snow.

But of greater importance to Biddlecomb, and more fine to behold, was that they were all squinting and half turning their heads away from the glare, or looking down at the sand to avoid the painful on-slaught of light.

Biddlecomb could see the officer in charge, wear-ing the white lapels and waistcoat of a navy lieutenant, walking ahead and to one side of the column. The man had to believe there was no hope of catching the enemy he was ostensibly chasing, or he would certainly not be so lackadaisical in his pursuit. He certainly could not think that the enemy was hunkered down less than a hundred feet away.

Isaac twisted around, looked down at his men arrayed behind the dune. They were grim, clasping and unclasping weapons, letting their eyes wander across the sand since they could not see their enemy, the thing they most wanted to see.

'A minute more, lads, and then it will be like a turkey shoot,' Isaac said in a loud whisper, and was greeted by thin smiles.

He thought, If they could only see how un-prepared these bastards truly are . . .

The king's forces so often underestimated the ability of the Continentals. It bought them their slaughter at Bunker Hill and Washington's escape from Long Island and his successful raid across the Delaware River.

Sometimes the lack of respect was justified, but sometimes not, and the enemy had no way of knowing when the Continentals would run and when they would fight like bears. It was one of the few advantages that the forces of the United States enjoyed. And it was a mistake that was never reciprocated.

The first of the marines was less than fifty feet away. Biddlecomb put his hand on the hilt of his sword and gripped it tight. He wanted desperately to draw the weapon, but he did not for fear the sun would glint off the blade. He imagined that this was how it had been on Bunker Hill. But in fact the Charlemagnes had a great advantage over those men of Boston. This time, the enemy did not know that they were there.

Twenty-five feet away, and Biddlecomb wanted to ask Faircloth what in all hell he was waiting for, but he did not dare speak. And then he had the awful thought that Faircloth was waiting for him to give the order. If there was some confusion of command, the whole thing could turn into a debacle.

He inched closer to the marine lieutenant, was going to breathe the question into his ear, when to his surprise Faircloth leapt to his feet, sword in hand, and waved to the men below.

'Forward! Forward!' he shouted, and the men, sailors and marines, surged up that dune and the one beyond and formed ranks, half of them standing, half kneeling.

Biddlecomb struggled to his feet in the soft, sloping sand, drew his sword, did not know what to say. Ferguson pushed up beside him, grinning like an idiot. He held a long, stout stick, bleached gray by the sun and salt water, and tied to the stick was the ensign, flogging nobly in the breeze.

'Front rank! Make ready!' Thirty or so flintlocks clicked back against taut springs.

The landing party's reaction would have been comical in a less deadly situation. The front of the column stopped short, their weapons coming half off their shoulders, hands flung up to shield their eyes. But they were marines and would do no more than that without orders.

The back of the column did not stop and careened into those in front, making them all stagger. And behind them, the sailors, who lacked the training and discipline of the marines, began to fall back the instant they sensed the danger.

All of that took place in the two seconds before Faircloth yelled, 'Take aim! Fire!' and half of the Charlemagnes' muskets went off. The front of the column was cut down before they could even see who was firing at them. More would have died if they had been in ranks and not column, but arranged as they were in a narrow line, the men in front were struck multiple times while those behind were un harmed.

'Rear rank! Make ready!' Those men who had discharged their muskets stepped back; those with loaded weapons stepped forward. The marines on the beach were stepping back as well. Panic was starting to take hold, Biddlecomb could see it in their shuffling backward movements, in their faces as they looked around for orders. But the naval lieutenant was nowhere to be seen, and the marine officer was occupied with clamping a hand over his rapidly bleeding shoulder.

'Take aim! Fire!' The Charlemagnes fired again, and more of the British fell and one or two even threw their weapons down as the spirit of defeat swept over them.

That was the second that they would have broken and run, fleeing heedlessly before this enemy in the sun, if the marine officer had not at that moment decided to ignore his wound and take command.

In a voice that was clear and loud, cutting like a sword through the screams of the wounded and the thunder of the surf, he shouted, 'Form ranks! Take care to fire by company! Company, make ready! Take aim! Fire!'

The words came fast, but each one was enunciated, and suddenly the near panicked mob was calmed and steadied by the voice of command, the superhuman effects of discipline and training. They moved as fast as the orders came. From chaos they formed into ranks, cocked firelocks, leveled muskets, and a volley of fire cut through the Americans, knocking several back down into the sand.

'March! March! Charge, bayonets!' the officer shouted, and the whole scarlet mass rolled forward again, pushing before it a long row of glinting, stiletto-sharp blades. Through the steadying effect of a single officer the rout had been transformed into a bayonet charge.

'Front rank! Take aim! Fire!' Faircloth shouted again, and the Charlemagnes fired and more of the redcoats dropped, but the officer was not one of them, to Biddlecomb's regret.

The naval officer was there as well, running up behind the marine, sword in one hand, pistol in the other, and Isaac was struck with the odd sensation

86

that he recognized the man, as impossible as that might be, but before he could look closer, Faircloth was shouting, 'Charge bayonets! March, march!'

They screamed like lunatics as they poured over the dune and down onto the sand, and Biddlecomb, in the lead, with Faircloth on one side and Weatherspoon on the other, was afraid that the men would run right over them and crush them underfoot. He stumbled on the soft sand, heard a bullet whiz by, recovered, took another step. King's men and Continentals were nearly on top of one another, but now the British marines had the advantage, for they were all armed with bayonets, while on the Americans' side only Faircloth's marines were so equipped.

Biddlecomb did not see what happened when the two lines smashed into each other. His eyes were fixed on the marine officer. He was determined to drop that fellow, who had turned his easy victory into something quite uncertain. He ran at the man, sword and pistol out, his feet finding little traction in the soft sand, like in a restless dream.

The officer was shouting, waving his sword, urging his men on. Like Biddlecomb, he had a blade in his right hand, a pistol in his left. The shoulder of his regimental coat was torn open, the cloth dark from spreading blood.

Biddlecomb pulled up, breathing hard, hand shaking from exertion. He leveled the pistol, pulled back the lock. The marine seemed to sense the threat, wheeled around, brought his own pistol up. Both men fired, fifteen feet from one another, like duelists.

Isaac was stunned by the scream of the ball, the rush of air, the sharp pain as a piece of his left ear was cut away. He dropped his pistol, clapped a hand over the wound. The blood was hot against his palm.

The marine officer was down, flat on his back, and behind him was the navy lieutenant, a stunned look on his face. He looked down at the marine, up at Biddlecomb. Isaac saw the man's eyes go wide, felt his own do the same.

'Smeaton?'

The only thing that would come to Biddlecomb's lips. John Smeaton, first of the *Icarus*, the man who had pressed Biddlecomb into the Royal Navy, who had killed his shipmate Haliburton, who had given him his first foretaste of hell.

He watched Smeaton's face go from horror to recognition to fury in the space of a second, saw the lieutenant raise his still-loaded pistol, level it, pull back the hammer. And then Weatherspoon was there, in front of Biddlecomb, pushing him back, aiming his own pistol when Smeaton fired.

Weatherspoon spun around as he fell and his eyes met Biddlecomb's, and Biddlecomb saw the great rent in Weatherspoon's throat where the bullet had ripped him open. He collapsed in the sand, kicking, flailing his arms.

Biddlecomb looked down at the young man, sick, horrified. He looked up at Smeaton. The lieutenant was coming at him, sword raised.

'You bastard! You bastard!' Biddlecomb shrieked with all the despair of the ages. He raised his sword, met Smeaton's blade as it came down, turned it aside. The stream of memory came flooding, jumped its banks; the duel with Smeaton on the *Icarus*'s deck after the mutiny, how Smeaton had nearly killed him, how the return of the wind on that becalmed day had saved Smeaton's life. But nothing would save his life now. Biddlecomb fell on him like a madman, slashing right and left, with a fury that drove Smeaton back, frightened him, judging from his eyes. Smeaton was a good swordsman, an excellent swordsman, but Biddlecomb was as well, and he had the anger driving him.

Step by step he drove Smeaton toward the water, and though his anger did not subside, he felt his strength of arm giving way. He cut right and Smeaton met his blade, but this time the lieutenant did not step back, but rather held his ground and made an offensive move of his own, forcing Biddlecomb to go back half a step, to defend himself.

There was a shouting, a row, a surge of noise to Biddlecomb's left. From the corner of his eye he saw green regimentals charging in on the pack, saw bayonets on musket barrels. A volley fire, a wild cry, and then red-coated marines were running for the surf, throwing guns aside, with the sloop of war's sailors leading the way.

Smeaton looked quickly over his shoulder. He was being left behind by his retreating men, but he did not dare turn his back on Biddlecomb.

Then he made his choice. He took two steps away and looked Biddlecomb in the eyes, a malevolent glare. 'Damn you, you bastard, damn you to hell.' He pointed with the tip of his sword. 'This is not over, do you hear me? Bastard!' he shouted, his words mixing with Biddlecomb's 'I'll kill you yet, you son of a whore!' drowning each other out, but it did not matter, for each was shouting for his own benefit.

Smeaton turned and ran, stumbling after the

fleeing redcoats and sailors. Biddlecomb dropped his sword on the beach, turned, and knelt beside Weatherspoon. His head was lolling back, his eyes open, but lifeless, like marble. The sand was black beneath his rent neck.

'Oh, Davey, oh, Davey. No, dear God, no, he was just a boy . . .'

'Sir?' The voice was gentle, respectful. Biddlecomb looked up, blinked, saw Faircloth standing over him. 'Sir, shall we go after them?'

Biddlecomb thought on that a moment. Turned, looked toward the surf. The panicked men there were pushing the boats off, falling over the gunwales, waiting for the Continentals' deadly thrust while they were so vulnerable.

'No, no, it's pointless.' Consideration began to vie with the grief. 'No, we must find some shelter for the night, set up some defense.'

He looked down at the earthly remains of Lt David Weatherspoon, Navy of the United States. Reached over and shut his eyes. 'We must see to our wounded and then find some place to rest.'

CHAPTER 6

As I am well apprized of the importance of Philadelphia you may rest assured that I shall take every measure in my power to defend it ... I am at this moment favored with yours of this date and thank you for your compliance to my request for removing the continental Troops who may be loitering in the City.

—GEORGE WASHINGTON
TO THOMAS WHARTON JR.
PRESIDENT, PENNSYLVANIA SUPREME
EXECUTIVE COUNCIL

Malachi Foote woke the next morning, after what could only euphemistically have been called sleep, the first man ever to spend the night aboard the frigate *Falmouth*. He wondered if he would be the last, and the only.

He had slept in the first officer's cabin, which was somewhat smaller than the room that he rented in town, but had the advantage of being considerably cleaner and filled with the perfume of fresh paint and oil and new-cut wood. Nor did he have to endure the grating voice of the shrew who rented him his miserable cell, shore-side.

He could have slept anywhere on the ship, of course, including the captain's cabin, but he could not bring himself to do that. Not that he had any fear of this Biddlecomb showing up and finding him there. The goddamned navy and their goddamned captains. If the brothers Howe and their sons of whores were coming this way, then you could bet the navy would be the first to get the hell out of their way.

Still, he could not sleep in the captain's cabin. It was just not right.

Foote threw the blanket off, half rolled out of the bunk, allowed himself the luxury of groaning as loud as he pleased at the creaking and protesting of his muscles. He sat on the edge of the bed for some moments, staring into the gloom.

The first officer's cabin was situated in the gunroom, one deck below the captain's great cabin. The only natural light was provided by two small ports in the transom, which could only be opened at anchor or in extraordinarily calm weather. They were open now, and Foote could see the dull gray dawn casting its indifferent illumination around the after end of the deck. It would be another cold, overcast, miserable goddamned day. Son of a bitch.

Dressing was not a protracted affair, as he had slept in most of his clothing. He reached over and grabbed his boots and pulled them on, then pulled on his waistcoat. He stood and scratched himself thoroughly, then buttoned the waistcoat and pulled on his coat over that.

He slung a cartridge box over his shoulder and

clipped a navy-issue pistol to his belt and slung his musket over his shoulder. He jammed his hat down on his head, picked up a jug of small beer, a loaf of bread, and a ham.

He stepped out of the cabin, made his way forward, past the long row of identical wood-frame doors that enclosed the officers' cabins. Climbed the ladder that brought him to the after end of the main deck, over which the quarterdeck spanned like a roof. Aft of him was the bright white bulkhead that separated the captain's great cabin from the open deck. Forward, beyond the overhanging quarterdeck, the waist, a great, open space without the guns. The next ladder brought him through a midships hatch onto the quarterdeck.

He stepped out into the morning he had envisioned. The sun was still below the horizon, but high enough to reveal the gray, featureless sky. The wind had dropped off at least, and only an occasional weak gust disturbed the leaves and wood chips in the shipyard.

The city beyond seemed deserted, lifeless. Usually at that hour, sunrise, it was bustling with carts heading for market, laborers off to work, ships along the waterfront rousing out hands for scrubbing down and swaying aboard. Usually the blacksmiths' hammers were ringing out already, the fishmongers' voices singing, and the apprentices and journeymen and masters at Wharton and Humphreys at their tools. Sunrise was not the time for waking in a city such as Philadelphia, the biggest and the busiest city along all of the United States. Sunrise was the time for the work to begin.

But not that morning. That morning the city lay

paralyzed with uncertainty, holding its breath, not knowing what even the next hour would bring.

Malachi Foote understood. He felt the same way.

He stood for some time, watching, listening. At length he was satisfied that nothing was happening, not yet. He checked the priming of his weapons. What he might accomplish with two guns he had no idea, nor did he wish to think about it, but still he did not feel that he could go about unarmed. He represented the *Falmouth*'s entire line of defense.

That done, he pulled his sheath knife from his belt and cut a thick slice of ham, tore off a chunk of bread, and made his breakfast. He wanted coffee, more than anything else, but his unwillingness to trouble with building a fire outweighed even that desire. He took a long pull of the small beer, cut another slice of ham.

He did not know, had no way of knowing, what was really going on. That was the most damnable thing about it. He had heard nothing but rumors for a month; the British army was pursuing Washington north, they were flanking him and marching for the city, they were making winter quarters to the west, they had been beaten by Washington at Brandy-wine.

The truth? Who the hell knew? The closest one could get to the truth was to believe the rumor that gained credence by being repeated the most. And the latest rumor to gain that status was the one that had General Howe and his redcoats and German butchers marching into the city that day. That morning, perhaps.

He stopped in midchew, cocked his head toward the city, certain he had finally heard something that was not a rooster crowing. He frowned, squinted, as if that would help his hearing.

Horses. He was hearing horses. And not just one, but several, perhaps a dozen. They were coming toward the waterfront.

'Aw, first thing in the goddamned morning,' he said out loud, spraying bits of bread on the quarter-deck rail, which he wiped up with his sleeve. More likely than not they were an advance guard of the British army, cavalry scouts sent on ahead.

He swallowed, sighed, pulled a plug of tobacco from his coat pocket and bit off a wad. There were decisions to be made, big decisions, and he did not have the information he needed to make them.

If the British army overran the city, then he could kill two of them at best before they shot him and took the *Falmouth*, and that would not do much good. He didn't care to die, though if he had to, he could live with it. But the *Falmouth* could never be allowed to become part of the Royal Navy. That would not happen.

He could burn her, set her ablaze that moment. But then if the British did not take the city, he would feel pretty stupid. Wouldn't care to explain that one to Humphreys.

He turned and ran his eyes along the river. It was the last of the ebb. If he cast off the dock lines, the *Falmouth* would float away downriver, perhaps even as far as the American defenses below the city. The *Delaware* was down there, but of course she was rigged, armed, and manned, not a floating shell like the *Falmouth*. If he could get the *Falmouth* there, she might be safe, at least until the British took that part of the river as well. But he did not think he could.

The frigates *Effingham* and *Washington*, both launched months before, had already been towed upriver to places of relative safety. That was the best plan, but it would be impossible. They had been lucky to find men enough just to launch the *Falmouth*. Even though she was light and high in the water and would be easy enough to tow, he could never hope to find the men to pull her upstream.

The sound of the horses' hooves on the cobblestone streets grew louder. Foote picked up the musket.

'Damn it, damn it all to hell.' He climbed down the ladder to the wharf.

They came into view at last, clattering down Chestnut Street. Mounted troops, to be sure. But not British. British troops would have been flogged for looking as disreputable as these.

He leaned on the musket, spit a long stream onto the wharf, and waited. They made right for him. He knew they would. They looked as if they were anxious to harass someone, and he was the only one abroad at that hour.

There were eight of them. They reined in hard and came to a stop with a flourish, forming a loose semicircle in front of him. On closer inspection they did not look so bad; the officer in charge was dressed out in a blue coat with buff facings, a red waistcoat, and buckskin breeches, which disappeared into tall black boots. The others were similarly attired, to varying degrees.

The officer took a long and dramatic moment to run his eyes over the *Falmouth* before looking down from his tall horse and saying, 'Good morning, sir. I would ask you, who are you and what is your business?'

Foote stared at him, made him wait just as long as he had been made to wait, then spit a stream of tobacco juice and said, 'M. A. Foote. Master shipwright. You?'

The officer seemed to consider whether he should answer, finally said, 'Lieutenant Jackson, Third Regiment of Light Dragoons. We are attached to the Life Guard, on provost duty.' He had a soft voice, lilting. A southerner. Virginia, no doubt. Wealthy.

'We've lost some of these rascals in this last fight. Run off,' Lieutenant Jackson continued, 'and we are trying to round them up before the city is taken. Have you seen anyone this morning? Anyone who looked to be a deserter, at all?'

Provosts. Marvelous. Hunting down some poor bastard who had run from the British guns just so they could bring him back and hang him. Foote wanted to ask the lieutenant if he was riding the same horse he used for hunting down foxes and runaway slaves back on the plantation.

'You gentlemen are the only living things I've seen come by this way since sundown last night,' Foote answered.

'You are quite certain?'

'Quite.'

'Very well. I fear you will not be so lonely for long. General Howe is not three miles to the west, and I reckon he will be entirely ensconced in the city by this evening. Are you the keeper of this ship?'

'I am.'

'It has no masts? No guns, or such?'

'No.' Well spotted, dumb arse, Foote thought.

'I fear she is in some jeopardy. You might think of towing her off, or in the last instant sinking or burning her. Better that the British do not take her. Good morning, sir.' Lieutenant Jackson touched his gauntlet to his hat in salute, then, with a wave to his troops, he and the detail of the Third Dragoons pounded off across the hard-packed dirt of the ship-yard and north along the river. Soon Foote was alone again, with only the fading sound of their hoofbeats to remind him that he was not the last man on earth.

'"You might think of towing her off." There's a grand fucking idea.' Foote spit on the wharf again. Ran his eyes over his beloved frigate. Thought about putting her to the torch. Wondered if this was how Abraham felt, looking down at his son Isaac on the altar.

Jackson had said that the enemy was coming, and Jackson was in a position to know. It was nearly slack water. If he cast off the dock lines now, the *Falmouth* would drift a half a mile downstream, and then the tide would turn and she would drift right back again.

'Damn it! Goddamn it! Damn it!' Malachi swore, cursed, stomped his foot. It was too cruel, that he should get to this place, that the *Falmouth* should be swimming at last and he had to burn her. Better that she had never been built at all.

He pulled himself back up the ladder and climbed down to the berthing deck. A fire there, around the mainmast partners, would have the best chance at spreading and consuming the entire ship. Malachi swallowed hard, tried not to be sick. Just thinking in those terms was making him nauseous. He could always light himself on fire, roll around the deck, set her ablaze that way. Didn't seem such a bad idea.

He considered the combustibles aboard. A good part of the *Falmouth*'s sail inventory had already been

98

made, and much of her rigging cut and readied to go over the mastheads. The masts themselves were floating in the mast pond not one hundred feet away, but since there was no chance of stepping them now, Foote had ordered all the material – sails, rigging, cordage, blocks, deadeyes, and small stuff – loaded aboard and stowed down so that it at least could be saved along with the frigate. Now it appeared that it would best serve as fuel for the funeral pyre.

Foote shuffled aft. There was the straw mattress on which he had slept, that would make a good start to things. He pulled it off the bunk and dragged it forward into the gray light filtering through the gratings on the main hatch above.

And then he stopped, froze, listened to the new sounds overhead. He heard a thump, the dull reverberation of a footfall on the deck above. Then another. Tentative, hesitant. He heard the squeaking of leather shoes, the soft, barely audible sound of bare feet on wood decking.

'Anyone aboard, then?' a voice called out, loud and bold, and Foote jumped in surprise. It was the accent of a native Continental. Now, far from being afraid to burn his beloved ship, Malachi was afraid he had not burned her soon enough.

He laid the mattress down softly and pulled the pistol from his belt. He pulled the lock back while finessing the trigger so that it cocked without a sound. He placed a foot on the ladder, eased his weight down on it, and climbed silently up.

Malachi peeked over the hatch coaming into the waist, but whoever was aboard was on the quarterdeck, or the gangway above. He stepped up onto the main deck and back into the shadows. From there he could see up through the quarterdeck hatch, while those above would not be able to see him.

He did not wait long, for those men on the deck above were apparently convinced that the ship was deserted, and they were spreading out around the quarterdeck.

To his great relief he did not see red regimental coats. Rather, he saw blue, dark blue, bleached and faded in the sun, dirty white lapels, pewter buttons in those cases where there were buttons at all. There were various sorts of breeches, mostly buckskin, and sundry shirts and waistcoats, cocked hats, flat, wide-brimmed hats, forage caps, but still their dress was more uniform than was generally seen on the eclectic Continental Line. There were perhaps a dozen men. Malachi could well imagine who they were, what they were about.

He stepped forward, into the waist and up the ladder to the quarterdeck. The soldiers were eating the last of his ham and bread. They were gathered around the binnacle box, exploring its contents, hoping, no doubt, that it was the ham storage locker.

They did not see or hear him approach. Pathetic. They were dead men, all of them. He eased the lock back to half cock.

'Morning. Can I help you gentlemen?' he asked, loud and sharp, and half of the soldiers jumped. Muskets came around, thumbs rested on flintlocks, but their expressions were the guilty smiles of boys caught stealing apples.

'Well, good morning to you, sir!' One of the band stepped forward.

It was the voice that had called out earlier, and it belonged to a man nearly six feet in height with a ruddy face, red hair bursting from under a cocked hat and tied behind in a queue. He wore a blue, faded regimental coat with buckskin breeches. Stockingless feet were pushed into battered shoes.

'I am Sgt Angus McGinty, Third Company, Fifth Pennsylvania Regiment, Continental Line. These men are with me.' He doffed his hat, a big, ingratiating smile across his meaty face.

A Teague. There's a famous fucking turn of luck, Foote thought. 'That so? A ways from the front, ain't you?'

'Yes, well, we've become a wee bit separated from our regiment, in the late fighting,' Angus explained. Smooth as butter.

Foote pulled his plug of tobacco from his pocket, tore a piece off, and worked it between his teeth. Noted the hungry look on the faces of the men watching him, their eyes on the brown weed.

'They ain't here,' Foote said.

'And who might that be?'

'Your regiment. They ain't here.'

McGinty smiled, less sincere this time. 'We'd not thought they were. Just looking for a bite, you see, and a drop, before we get on with our looking.'

'I can bloody well reckon how hard you're looking. As to food, you just ate all there was to eat on board.'

'I pray, sir, you forgive us, eating your breakfast,' McGinty said, pure contrition. 'But as to victuals, I suppose we'll have a wee look around first. There could be something you overlooked, d'ya see?'

Malachi Foote genuinely did not care if a man deserted the army. It seemed to him a perfectly reasonable thing to do, and he certainly had no love for provosts. But this McGinty was an oily fellow, a toothy-smile-and-slap-on-the-back kind of fellow, who made his way in the world with his false bonhomie. Foote had seen his type before and liked it less than anything.

He worked the plug in his mouth, held McGinty in his gaze, watched the big man's confidence falter under the eye of someone who was not taken in by his airs. 'No, Teague, I don't reckon you'll look about the ship.'

'Now see here . . . your name, sir?'

'Foote. M. A. Foote.'

'Oh, Ma Foote is it? Well, see here, me good Mother Foote, I don't reckon your—'

'Hold a minute.' Foote held up a hand, cut him off. Cocked an ear toward the city. 'Ah, you gentlemen are delivered. I wish you joy.'

'Oh, now, Ma, what are you on about?' McGinty asked, and then he too heard the sounds of the hoofbeats, not so far off.

'Oh, damn me, it's the bloody provosts!' one of the others said, the first besides McGinty to speak. All heads turned shoreward. The provosts were in sight already, riding back the way they had gone.

'I should think they'll be happy to show you gentlemen back to your regiment,' Foote offered, but no one was paying attention to him.

'All right, everyone, down below!' McGinty ordered.

They were already moving when Foote stopped them short. 'Hold up there, you stupid bastards! They've already seen you, hiding won't do you any good now.'

'Stow it, Mother Foote, we've no time for you

now,' McGinty snarled, even his pretense of good humor gone.

He made to push past Malachi, but the shipwright grabbed his sleeve, jerked him back, said, 'Hold up. There's another way.' An idea was forming.

'Aye, turn us into the provosts, is your way—' McGinty began but another of the band cut him off.

'Shut yer gob, McGinty. Damned provosts are here now.'

Foote shot a look at the man who had spoken. An ill-tempered-looking sod in torn canvas breeches, a slouch hat pulled low over his eyes. Foote liked him immediately.

'You wait here, and keep your goddamned mouths shut,' Foote said in a harsh whisper. He walked over to the quarterdeck rail, looked down at the provost below.

'Lieutenant Jackson, have you found your deserters yet?'

'Yes, I believe I have, and an abettor as well. Now, all of you, lay down your arms and come down here—'

'Hold up! Hold up! What are you on about?'

'Sir, do not pretend that these men are not deserters. They—'

'Deserters!' Foote was pleased with the genuine tone of outrage he managed. 'These men are from the Fifth Pennsylvania. They are assigned to me to guard the ship.'

'Oh, indeed? And you have written orders to that effect?'

'Orders? Yes, I got orders. I stuck 'em up my arse, so General Howe wouldn't find them, but you're welcome to come up here and have a look.'

He let Jackson have his moment of shock and disgust at the vulgarity of the lower classes before he went on, 'See here, Lieutenant, there was no time for orders and such. I sent a note to . . . ah . . .'

'Colonel Johnson,' McGinty supplied in a whisper.

'—Colonel Johnson, and he dispatched this platoon. All he could spare, and not much help it'll be. There was no time for orders, all written out pretty and the like.'

Jackson frowned. His horse shifted nervously under him. Foote could see he was wavering, not sure if he should believe the crude shipwright or his own instincts.

'Now see here, Lieutenant,' Foote continued, 'General bloody Howe and his whole motherless army will be marching down that street any minute, like you said, and before then I got to get this frigate outta here. So if I might beg your leave, I would like to set the few men I got to it.'

Jackson continued to frown. He turned his horse, looked down the length of Chestnut Street, looked back again. Foote could well imagine what Jackson was considering: the possibility that Foote was telling the truth weighed against the probability that he was not. The difficulty of extracting a superior number of armed deserters from the deck of the ship, high overhead. The chance that they would be trapped by Howe's army while they fought an internecine battle.

'Very well,' Jackson said at length, opting for discretion. 'Get these men to work immediately, there is not a minute to lose. The Fifth Pennsylvania is camped north of Germantown. See that these troops get back there, once your ship is safe.'

'Yes, sir. Never doubt it.'

'Very well, then,' Jackson said, and with a final frown, and a look that said he would be pleased to wash his hands of all of it, he turned and rode off, his men following behind.

A big hand fell across Foote's shoulder. 'Now that was bloody well done, mate,' McGinty said, the smile back in its place.

'Shut your gob, Teague, and get your goddamned hand off me.' McGinty removed his hand fast, as if he had suddenly realized he were hugging the wrong person. 'All right, I saved your bacon, for now, but I reckon I can find more provosts if need be. And if it ain't the provosts, then it'll be Howe and his bloody butchers.'

'We best not tarry then. Let's move.' It was the ill-tempered one who spoke.

'To be sure,' said McGinty, 'but which is the safe way out of the city?'

'I'll show you,' Foote said. 'It's that way.' He pointed upriver. 'The best way out is up the river, and it just so happens I have a boat for the convenience of you gentlemen.'

'Well, isn't that right Christian of ya!' McGinty exclaimed.

'You are goddamned right it is,' said Foote. 'And while you're rowing yourselves to safety, you can damn well pull my frigate along behind.'

CHAPTER 7

July 1777
Tuesday 22nd Cape May No Cape Henlopen WbS
The Boats found the surf on the Beach too High to
Board the Chace, the Tenders Join'd & Kept
Firing on the People that was throwing some things
over Board out of the Chace till she filled when the
Signal was made to call them off at 6 the Merlin
Join'd and Anchor'd

—MASTER'S LOG
HMS *ROEBUCK*

Philistine. Bloody Philistine. Bloody, bloody cretin.
Bloody, damned Philistine.

Second Lieutenant John Smeaton ran the words
over and over in his head, a silent chant. They
comforted him, helped shield him from the lam-
basting.

Bloody cretin.

He stood before the desk, hands clasped behind his
back, face impassive, like a convict long past the reach
of hope listening to his final sentence.

Behind the desk sat Comdr Samuel Reeve, captain

106

of the *Merlin*, His Majesty's sloop of war, mounting eighteen nine-pounders, currently patrolling the Delaware Bay and the Capes. He was Smeaton's senior in age by only a few years, but in terms of the hierarchy of the *Merlin* he may as well have been the First Lord of the Admiralty.

Socially, of course, he was nowhere near to the Smeaton family, and it gave the lieutenant some satisfaction to remind himself of that.

Damned Philistine.

'So, you bloody sauntered right into it? Walked right into their guns?'

'Yes, sir,' Smeaton spoke for the first time in some moments. 'I had mentioned to Lieutenant Page that perhaps we had best send a patrol ahead of the main body, fearing such a thing, but the lieutenant thought that unnecessary. Said the rebels would never stand and fight his marines. I felt it best to yield to his judgment. I am no soldier, sir, I am a naval officer.'

'Humph,' said Reeve in a tone that left his opinion of that in some doubt. 'I take it no one overheard this discussion between you and Lieutenant Page?'

'No, sir. Our words were not for the ears of subordinates.'

'Corporal Wilkenson is of the opinion that it was you who ordered the marines and sailors up the beach in no particular order, against Page's wishes. That Lieutenant Page nearly rallied them after you led them into a trap.'

'Corporal Wilkenson is a marine, sir. It is only to be expected that he would try and defend his own, and besmirch the navy.'

Commander Reeve sighed, threw his pen down on .

the desk, letting the ink splatter over Smeaton's written report.

The cabin was silent.

Smeaton stared just over the captain's shoulder at his own reflection in the great cabin's aft windows. It was well past midnight, and the glass might just as well have been painted black for all he could see through it. He noted that his uniform was fitting a bit loose.

Rotten, stinking food on this bucket. Must have some new uniforms made up.

'I suppose there is nothing more to be said on this,' Reeve said at length.

I suppose not, Smeaton thought. Bloody luckiest thing that ever happened, that bullock Page being shot down. Might have been a bit awkward had there been an officer of equal rank to Smeaton left to give a report. Thank you, Isaac bloody Biddlecomb. *Morituri te salutamus!*

'Let me say, sir,' said Smeaton, contrite yet flattering, 'that I am very sorry for the events of this afternoon, though still I must congratulate you on bringing about the destruction of the rebel brig.'

Reeve sank his head in his hands and remained in that position for an awkward moment. 'Smeaton, the Dear knows if I had a penny for every time . . . never mind. Pray, get out of here.'

'Aye, aye, sir.' Smeaton saluted, turned on his heel, and left. He stomped forward to the edge of the waist and stopped, considering where to go.

It was Colcot's watch, First Officer Lieutenant Richard Colcot, which meant that Smeaton would find no peace aft on the quarterdeck. Colcot would talk to him, and he would have to answer, because the Billingsgate swine was his superior in rank.

The only other place for him was the gunroom, on the deck below. He was loath to go there, to thrust himself into the foul and unwelcome company of his shipmates, but he had no choice. If he were a captain, as reasonably he should have been, then he could have found some privacy in his great cabin. But he was not, for reasons he knew all too well, and so he was doomed to the company of his inferiors.

He stepped at last through the scuttle and down to the gunroom, that fetid and hellish place. It was lit by four pathetic lanterns that strained to pierce the thick cloud of tobacco smoke that hung eternally from the overhead and gave the gunroom all the charm of a mean boiling house, shut up tight on a winter evening.

The midshipmen were chattering and screeching like a cage of monkeys. Thomas Oldfield, the master, and the pilot, Matthew Croell, were playing at all fours, a game that, to Smeaton's certain knowledge, was created solely for the pleasure of idiots and enjoyed by them alone.

Corporal Wilkenson was drunk.

'Here, Smeaton, I reckon you got what for from the old man, eh?' the marine called out. 'Bloody drummed out of the service, should be.'

Smeaton stopped, glared at him. The noise in the gunroom fell off, eyes turned toward them. 'Shut your gob, you stupid, filthy bullock. Or perhaps you would cross swords with me? Or pistols? Would you play the man?'

Wilkenson just glared back. There was nothing more that he could do. Not only did the second officer outrank him, but Smeaton was far better with sword and pistol than the marine. Smeaton was better with those weapons than anyone else aboard the *Merlin*. That knowledge formed the only bit of wreckage to which Smeaton's drowning pride could cling.

After a few seconds of this, Smeaton said, 'Right, then, that's all I care to hear from you,' and he ducked into his tiny cabin and shut the door.

The babble in the gunroom returned slowly to its former level, but Smeaton ignored it. He sat in the tight chair in his tiny, single room, feet splayed out in front of him, hand moving unbidden to the bottle of the finest West Indian dark that he kept on his bunk. He stared into the half-light filtering in through the screens.

Biddlecomb, Biddlecomb, Biddlecomb.

In the eight hours or so since it had taken place, he had not really thought of the meeting on the beach, not in any profound way. It was too much, too overwhelming, too unreal for him to grasp, with everything else that was going on, the retreat, the explanations. But now, alone in his cell, he thought.

He saw the moment, over and over again, like a dream so disturbing it haunts you all the next day. Lieutenant Page falling, the sick feeling of being suddenly alone and in command of those stupid bullocks. They had walked right into a trap – why hadn't Page been more insistent, the stupid bastard?

And then . . . *him*.

How many times had he dreamed of killing Isaac Biddlecomb? How many hours had he whiled away on watch, running a mental sword through that rebel bastard's guts? Biddlecomb, who had allowed him to live after besting him in a duel, the ultimate humiliation.

They had fought with cutlasses, a barbaric weapon to be sure, and not the choice of a gentleman, but still he, Smeaton, should not have lost. One stupid mistake, one second of leaving himself open to Biddlecomb's boot, and his victory was gone. Worse, his defeat was followed up with the public humiliation of Biddlecomb magnanimously sparing his life, and the private humiliation of remembering the terrific relief he had felt.

The son of a bitch had ruined, literally ruined, the life of his best friend, James Pendexter. James, finally given the command that he deserved, with his best friend, John Smeaton, as first officer, had tried to turn the *Icarus* brig into a decent fighting ship. But Biddlecomb and that big ox Rumstick had infected the crew with their rebel treachery, had led a mutiny and taken the ship from them.

Pendexter had been acquitted by a court-martial, but he had quit the service nonetheless. That incident had left a black mark on his reputation. Everyone in the navy knew he had been acquitted more for the good name of the service, and through the influence of his uncle, Admiral Graves, than out of any conviction that he had done no wrong.

Now he was a pathetic drunk, flopping around his family's home in Kent, or embarrassing himself and all of decent society with his unwanted presence during the season in London. He was treated as if he had suffered some horrible disfigurement or contracted an incurable and contagious disease.

Smeaton shook his head at the bitter thought. He had not fared any better. Worse, one might argue. He had been acquitted as well, but his miserable father had got it in his head that Smeaton had somehow shamed the family. Now, due to certain gambling debts that the tight old bastard had refused to pay, Smeaton was not in a position to be seen around London at all.

Instead he had to remain in the service, with little money and no patronage, taking whatever scraps the navy threw at him. He had gone from first officer of the *Icarus* to second on the miserable, cretinous floating Billingsgate of a sloop, the *Merlin*.

Biddlecomb.

Biddlecomb.

It was all starting to coalesce now. It was all because of Biddlecomb.

They had been living like admirals on that fine brig. Indeed, they would have become admirals one day, the elevation was inevitable, had their names not been sullied. He remembered the party they had had aboard, while anchored in Boston Harbor. It was like their own yacht on the government's chit. What a night! Oh, the joy, the joy they had known, for that brief time, before Biddlecomb had come aboard! And then that smirking, base rebel whore's son had taken it all away.

Smeaton drank the rum, right from the bottle, let the hot liquor run down his throat, felt it spread around his belly. He had always hated the bastard, but until that moment he had not understood how fully responsible Biddlecomb was for Pendexter's ruin, for his own misery.

Biddlecomb.

And now the whore's son was back, and responsible for this latest nightmare on the beach.

Smeaton began to feel a warmth spreading through his body, a warmth that was more than just

112

the rum. Was it a coincidence that he and Biddle-comb had come face-to-face on the sand? It could not be. The chances against that happening were too great.

It had to be something else, a gift from God, a chance to redeem himself. It could not be a mere coincidence. The entire British fleet under Admiral Lord Howe was at that very moment making its way around from the Chesapeake to the Delaware Bay, and of all of them, *Merlin* was one of the few vessels sent on ahead to patrol the Capes.

Coincidence or no, it was still an extraordinary opportunity, a last chance to regain his honor, to finish the duel that should have ended in Biddle-comb's death. Such things did not come about very often, it could not be suffered to slip away.

Vengeance is mine.

He took another drink of rum, felt good, satisfied and optimistic.

Once again there was purpose to his life.

CHAPTER 8

Gun-shot Wounds, of all others, are more complicate, and much more difficult to cure, than an incised Wound . . . They are more or less dangerous, according to their extent, and the part in which they are seated.
—EXTRACTS FROM *THE MARINE PRACTICE OF PHYSIC AND SURGERY*
WILLIAM NORTHCOTE, SURGEON

The Charlemagnes were not on New Jersey proper, but rather on one of the many long barrier islands that guard nearly the whole length of her shoreline like a palisade, though they did not realize that right away.

Nor did it matter much at the moment. The fighting had ended with the rout of the British marines and sailors. The Charlemagnes had not pursued them, but rather had left the enemy to their headlong rush for the boats. The Americans were looking for no more than escape, and they had enough to concern themselves with the wounded and the dead.

It was nearly dark by the time those men who were wounded and still alive, British and American, were tended to and arranged as comfortably as they could be on the sand. Rumstick ordered the boats dragged up and tilted on their side to form windbreaks. He told off a party to gather the copious wood scattered around and stoke it into a huge fire.

Beyond the blinding light of the flames, Faircloth threw out lines of pickets to guard against surprise. By the time night was full on, the living were as comfortable as they were likely to be in that barren place.

The dead were moved behind the dune. Their faces were covered with their coats; the blue jackets of the sailors, the green or red regimentals of marines.

A quarter of a mile away the *Charlemagne* continued to burn, the flames growing brighter and more distinct as evening came on. Around six o'clock her magazine exploded, shaking the beach like an earthquake and blasting two decks' worth of planking, beams, and carlins a hundred feet aloft. The wreckage seemed to hang in the air, suspended as if in liquid, and then it all rained down again around the flaming mass of her hull.

The *Charlemagne* was a great fire on the water no more. She looked as much like a ship as did the bonfire they had built on the beach.

For most of the evening hours Virginia sat on a driftwood log, nursing Jack and shielding him from the wind and reading a book as best she could in the failing light. Beside her stood a marine sentry, set there by the solicitous Faircloth, and though Isaac could see that such attention annoyed her, she did not object or even comment on it.

115

When at last it was full dark, and Isaac had attended to all the things that needed his attention, Virginia appeared at his side, Jack snug in his sling, a haversack in her hand.

'Oh, Virginia, forgive me, I have had not a moment,' he said.

'Of course, never think on it.'

The night was quiet now, save for the crackling of the fire and the moans of the wounded. 'I saved a few things from the great cabin, before we abandoned,' Virginia said, holding up the haversack.

'Bless you, I thought all was lost.'

'Among them, I saved this. I think we will need it. Tonight.' She held up the book that she had been reading, so that Biddlecomb could see the cover in the light of the fire. *Extracts from the Marine Practice of Physic and Surgery*, he read, *With Some Brief Directions to Be Observed by Sea-Surgeons in Engagements, &c, Including the Nature and Treatment of Gun-Shot Wounds*. It had been in his library for years. He had always intended to study it.

Biddlecomb sighed, looked at the fire, looked back at Virginia. She was right, of course. The wounded had to be treated with more than just bandages, and if no volunteers were forthcoming, then it was up to him. This was when he missed the generally useless surgeon Grim. As a ship's captain he had plenty of experience in setting bones and bandaging wicked gashes, but gunshot wounds and bayonet thrusts were an altogether different matter.

'Listen up, you men,' he said in a loud voice. Faces turned toward him. 'We must do something about these wounded. Is there any here who has experience at all in such things?'

116

Silence. Crackling flames, moaning wounded. More silence. 'Very well,' Isaac said. The Charlemagnes' relief was almost audible. The men thought little of doling out vicious wounds, but they did not care to try their hands at patching them. Isaac turned to Virginia. 'I shall see to them myself.'

Virginia held his eyes, and her mouth was set in that way that meant she was about to say something that would meet with objection. 'Isaac, I have been reading on this all afternoon, and I dare say I have the smallest and most nimble fingers here, unless there is one among your men who has done more needlework than me, which I doubt. I think it would be best if I saw to the wounded.'

Biddlecomb felt at once relief at having that cup taken from his lips, as well as disgust with himself for thinking such a thing and shock that Virginia could suggest what she had. It was impossible, a woman acting the part of surgeon. 'Really, Virginia, you cannot—'

'I most certainly can, Isaac Biddlecomb, do not for a minute tell me what I can and cannot do.'

They held each other's eyes, tight lipped, silent. Isaac had known her nearly all of her life, had been her husband for just over a year. That was long enough to know the folly of arguing with her when she had that look on her face.

'Very well then, Doctor. I will assist in any way I can.'

Isaac had the small satisfaction of seeing his wife thrown off-balance by his easy acquiescence, but she recovered quickly and said in a commanding voice, 'Rumstick, pray come over here.'

Rumstick ambled up, his feet making no sound

in the soft sand, his bulk half-lit by the big fire. 'Ma'am?'

'I shall need you to tend to little Jack.' She pulled the child from the sling and handed the bundle to the huge seaman.

Biddlecomb smiled, anticipating the fun of Rumstick's discomfort, for though he was Jack's godfather, Rumstick did not seem the nanny type. But to Isaac's surprise Rumstick took up the infant with a gentle ease, placing a finger like a can-hook under the boat cloak and drawing the cloth away from his tiny face. 'How's my little man, how's my little man? Sleeping, are we?' he cooed.

On the edge of the fire Biddlecomb could see men stumbling out of earshot, hands clapped over mouths, not daring to be heard laughing at the first officer.

'Good,' said Virginia, and leaving Rumstick to further embarrass himself, she took Isaac by the arm and led him toward the wounded. 'We shall need two loblolly boys, I think.'

'Woodberry, Burke, over here, please,' Biddlecomb called and the two men shuffled reluctantly over. 'Do as the lady instructs.'

Virginia was already kneeling by the first of the wounded, a British marine private with a bandage around his arm. The man, more a boy really, was asleep, or passed out. The blood that had saturated the bandage looked black in the firelight, and the cloth was stiff as cardboard as Virginia peeled the dressing back.

'One of you, pray fetch a light of some kind. I cannot see a damned thing,' Virginia called without looking up. Woodberry fetched a lantern that had been among the things in the longboat and brought it over, shining the light down on the marine.

The young man stirred, let out a little groan, as Virginia examined the wound, then came wide awake as she poked at it with her finger.

'Ah, bloody hell!' the marine cried, hurt and terrified all at once. He tried to sit up but Virginia pushed him down and said, 'Be still, I am looking at your wound.'

The combination of pain, surprise, and confusion, as well as the sudden presence of a beautiful woman, was enough to render the man cooperative. He lay back and clenched his fists as Virginia probed further.

'Bullet passed through,' she said. 'Quite a deal of bleeding, but beyond that he is doing tolerably well. Burke, pray fetch some clean seawater and wash this wound out, then tear this into bandages and dress his arm again.'

She handed Burke a bundle of white cloth, a thin, fine material, edged with lace. It was the bottom half of her shift, which she had evidently torn off at the waist. Burke flushed with embarrassment. Isaac wondered when she had managed to do that.

'Aye, aye, ma'am.' Burke fled down the beach.

Virginia stood, moved on to the next man, also a British marine. His head rocked side to side, eyes closed, and he moaned in a steady rhythm. Virginia pulled back his regimental coat and waistcoat. She gently spearated the thick wool cloth from the thinner shirt below, the two being pasted together with dried blood, then she peeled the shirt back as well.

'Ahhhhh!' the marine gasped. His eyes flew open,

119

he half sat up, but Virginia put a hand on his chest and said, 'Lie back, pray, and let me look at your wound,' and the marine did as he was told.

'Isaac, get that light right down here, please.'

Biddlecomb knelt beside her, held the lantern just over the wound. 'Do you have your pocketknife?' she asked.

'Yes, here.' He fished the knife out of his pocket and handed it to her. Watched her as she unfolded it, slit the shirt, and peeled it back. Thought, *Over thy wounds, now do I prophesies, which like dumb mouths to ope' and gape at which to pray.* He had never looked so close at a gunshot wound, not at those he had dealt out, not at those he had received. How very apt was the old man's simile.

Virginia leaned close, peering into the wound, as if looking through a keyhole. She reached into the haversack and pulled out the little bottle of laudanum that had been in the medicine chest in the great cabin. She uncorked it, dropped three drops into the marine's mouth, and told him in a soft voice to swallow the medication and try to relax.

Biddlecomb shook his head. He had considered rescuing the signal book from the great cabin, and his orders, and the drafts of the *Falmouth*, but in the end he had let the fire have them all. It would never have occurred to him to grab the contents of the medicine chest. He doubted if any man aboard would have thought of it.

'This ball is not very deep, and I do not think it borders any considerable artery,' Virginia said. She looked at the young soldier's face. He was lying still, seemed comfortable. She fished around in the haversack and pulled out a pair of small forceps.

Looked up at Isaac, gave him a half smile. 'Let us get on with it, then.'

Biddlecomb went down on both knees, held the lantern as close as he dared. Virginia leaned over the wound and ever so gently reached through the gaping flesh with the little tongs.

The marine gave a jerk, a sharp intake of breath, and Virginia paused until he was still. The light from the lantern gleamed on the thin veneer of sweat on her brow, but her fingers were steady. She slowly, slowly, closed the forceps, felt their grip on the lead transmitted through the instrument, and then gently, gently, extracted the ball.

It came free from the wound, a mangled bit of metal, but seemingly whole. Virginia smiled, relief, triumph, in her face. Held the ball up for Isaac to see.

'Well done, Virginia, well done.'

They looked down at the wound. A little fresh blood was leaking out, but not so much as to cause worry. 'Shall we bandage him up?' Isaac asked.

'No, no. The book warns to be most careful of wadding, clothes, and splinters and such carried into the wound. Here, get the light in close again, if you please.'

Once more Isaac leaned the light close, and once more Virginia reached into the wound with the forceps, but now the marine was deep in the arms of the laudanum and did not stir. Virginia probed, grabbed at something with the forceps, and withdrew them again. In the lantern light they could see, gripped in the instrument, a shredded patch of thick regimental jacket, waistcoat, and shirt, all dyed the same deep red color.

'Now, I believe, we can dress him. Burke, pray

wash the wound as best you can and bind him with dry lint against the opening.'

They moved on to the next man, who had a bullet lodged in his shoulder and a hole in his left calf where a bullet had passed clean through. He was less cooperative, requiring the services of Burke, Woodberry, and another to hold him still, despite the administration of six drops of laudanum. But in the end the bullet was plucked from his wound, and a bit of cloth as well, and he was dressed and left to rest.

And so the work went on, consuming four hours, with some bullets coming out whole, some in two or three pieces, some men lying still and some fighting their would-be saviors.

Virginia grew more confident and more sure with her forceps and her treatments. In only one case – where the wound was right in the gut, and the man, a British marine, writhed and screamed in agony as she probed with her finger, and even then she could not feel the bullet – did she decide that anything she might do would cause more harm than good.

It was one of Faircloth's men, and with her face set in a mask of disinterest she ordered the marine given ten drops of laudanum in addition to the five she had ordered for all of the wounded men. The opium, they all understood, would do no more then ease his pain as he waited on his pending and inevitable death.

The last of them she had thought was not so bad: a British sailor with an arm broken above the wrist by a bullet and another bullet wound in the thigh. The laudanum had worked its magic and the man seemed comfortable. The ball that had broken his arm was still visible, a dull gray hump like a wet stone in the sand where the wound had been washed free of blood. Virginia plucked it out, along with whatever else had been carried with it.

'You are the master with the forceps, dear,' Isaac said, 'but I believe I can claim some expertise at setting sailors' bones. If you would care to look to his thigh, I should be glad to attend to this.'

'Thank you, Isaac.' Virginia looked tired, but pleased, pleased with herself, satisfied at having been able to help in that manner.

Biddlecomb had actually become accustomed to seeing her performing the surgeon's duties, seeing her fine, delicate hands coated with the blood of seven different men, the skirts of her dress smeared where she had wiped her hands clean before performing her next task. He hardly flushed at all as she sliced open the sailor's wide trousers from the cuff to halfway up his thigh, exposing a shapely, well-formed leg, a thing not generally considered proper for a lady to see.

Virginia seemed to take no notice of the impropriety as she peered at the wound in the thigh. She certainly took less notice than Woodberry, who held the lantern for her while Isaac attended to the arm. The seaman was flushing red and coughing in low and protracted tones, as if trying to warn someone that something improper was taking place.

Isaac never ceased to marvel at how prudish sailors could be, particularly in light of his having personally seen Woodberry, on several occasions, stumbling drunk down the steps of a Barbados whorehouse. It was very annoying.

123

'Woodberry,' Biddlecomb said, testy, 'is there something the matter with your throat?'

'Well, no, sir . . . I mean to say . . .'

'Good, then please stop your infernal noise.'

Before Woodberry could explain further, Virginia said, 'Please get that light a bit closer, I cannot see a goddamned thing.'

Biddlecomb looked up, startled by the tone, and the words. Virginia was frowning, looking down at the wound, but she still had the air of the confident. 'Deeper than I had thought,' she said, as if speaking to herself.

Carefully she probed through the flesh, down the gap cut by the passing lead. The sailor gave a guttural sound, rolled his head. Virginia paused, probed again, and the sailor groaned loud.

'No . . . Dear God, I do not know . . .' She looked up at Isaac. 'Is there not an artery, close by—'

Then the wound exploded in a gush of bright red blood. It shot up like a spout, splattering Virginia in the face, shooting across her dress in long red streaks.

'Damn it! Damn it! Damn it all!' Virginia exclaimed, turning her face from the spurting blood, clamping her hands down on the wound. She looked at Isaac, their eyes met, and he saw uncertainty, panic. 'The artery! The artery must have ruptured! Whatever can we do?'

'I . . . I don't know . . . I . . .'

'It must be sewn up, what the book said, stop it immediately. Quickly, the needle and thread, it is in the haversack!' she said this as she plunged her fingers into the wound, disregarding all niceties, the blood spurting up around her hands, soaking her dress, the sailor now moving his head, groaning, flapping his arms.

'Hold him, goddamn your eyes!' Virginia cried, and four men stepped forward and grabbed the man's arms and legs as Virginia probed.

Isaac tore through the haversack, tossing aside lint and bottles and small boxes of medicine, holding up the lantern, searching out the surgical needle and thread.

He saw them, a glint of silver at the bottom of the bag, grabbed them up. Looked up at Virginia. 'I . . . can't . . . reach,' she said, frustration flowing like the blood. She snatched up the pocketknife, cut at the wound, widening it, trying to get to the ruptured artery.

The sailor gasped, twisted, gave a rattling, gurgling sound in his throat, and then fell limp. The blood stopped shooting out from the wound. Everyone was silent. The fire crackled, filling the empty space.

'He's gone,' said Ferguson, who was holding the sailor's right arm. He reached over, closed the man's eyes.

Virginia looked at the body, at the blood on her hands and her dress. The tears rolled down her cheeks. She threw the pocketknife down in the sand.

'Damn it, damn it!' she said. 'Trying to play at doctor, trying to bloody . . . thinking I was just so fine a thing . . .'

She stood, turned her back to the men. Isaac went over to her and put his hands on her shoulder and pulled her against him. 'Virginia, Virginia, you have saved the others. You could not save them all. He was dead already. Would have died the moment we tried to move him.'

125

Virginia had her face in her hands and was sobbing. He held her closer. He understood her tears, had felt them himself. They came with the bloody resolution of action, the mind and body coming down from that heightened state brought on by a fight, in this case a fight for a man's life. No words would help the situation, so he remained silent.

At length she turned to him, her face streaked with tears and blood, her eyes red, her hair falling in all directions. 'Thank you, Isaac, but I shall have to live with that doubt for all my life. The consequences of my hubris.'

'You did save the others. There is no doubt on that point. I . . . we . . . the rest of us would have left them to die. Told ourselves we were no surgeons. We would not even have tried.'

'Thank you.' She gave him a flicker of a smile, turned, and walked off toward the beach. He let her go, understood that she needed to be alone in the dark, to wash the blood from her hands and face in the cold, pure water of the Atlantic Ocean.

He did not know what more to say, in any event. The death of the *Charlemagne*. His wife's despair. His men. His son. The *Falmouth*. It all seemed too much at times, too much for one man, alone.

Ezra Rumstick sat on the dune, his legs drawn up as near to his chest as they would go, staring out at the glowing embers of the *Charlemagne*, remembering, remembering. He thought of the batterings that brig had taken and doled out, the times bowling along with studding sails aloft and alow, how she loved twenty or more knots of wind off her quarter.

He had been with her when her keel was laid. His ax and adze had bitten into every part of her frame. Her spars and sails were built to the specifications that he and Isaac had discussed and together decided upon. The *Charlemagne* was something that was uniquely theirs.

Like their friendship.

Indeed, since the fight with Britain had begun, they had been together: him, Isaac, the *Charlemagne*. People had moved in and out of their lives like flotsam on the tide, but the constant had always been him, Isaac, the *Charlemagne*. There was not one inch of the vessel he did not know and love, and her passing grieved him as much as any death he had yet witnessed in their more than two and a half years of war.

He stared at the bright orange spots on the black ocean, his mind blank.

'Sir?' The voice was quiet, respectful of his somber mood.

Rumstick pulled his eyes away, saw Gerrish standing there, illuminated by dull reflections of the fire.

'Yes?' he said, but Gerrish seemed to understand that he had interrupted something more than a simple quiet moment and said, 'Oh, forgive me, it is not important . . .'

'No, no, what is it?' Ezra had already sated his limited need for silent introspection and was ready for whatever was next.

'Well, sir . . . do you mind?' Gerrish gestured toward the dune on which Rumstick sat.

'No, please, sit.'

Gerrish sat down heavily, stared out at the *Charlemagne*. 'I hope I am not out of line sir, but I am

127

quite consumed with curiosity. This afternoon, when we were fighting those marines, I was a few paces away from the captain. Indeed, I was going to his aid when Lieutenant Weatherspoon pushed me aside, more's the pity. But in that brief instant, it seemed to me that the captain and the British naval officer knew one another. I thought I heard them call each other by name. But mind you I took a good knock on the head, so I could well be wrong.'

Smeaton. Of course. Rumstick had seen him too, the bastard. Couldn't believe his eyes. In all the madness he had put it clean out of his mind.

'No, you were right, Mr Gerrish. That bastard was Lt John Smeaton, and a more vicious son of a bitch you are not likely to find.'

'What . . . how, if I might ask . . . do you happen to know this Smeaton? I don't see a lot of the king's officers in your social circle.'

'I reckon not. No, Smeaton was the first officer aboard the *Icarus*, the brig that the captain and me was pressed into. You heard that story?'

'Not many in the States have not, sir. You are famous for it, you know.'

'Humph. Well, I reckon like most famous actions there's only a little of it that's true, as the story is told. But that Smeaton, he was everything a man could hate in a British officer – cruel, stupid, no seaman at all. As arrogant as they come. Fellow by the name of John Haliburton was pressed with us. He jumped overboard in Barbados, tried to swim to shore. Would have been no effort at all to get him back, but rather than try that, Smeaton put a bullet in his head. Just shot him and let him sink away.'

'Dear God . . .'

'Oh, Smeaton was some hand with a pistol. I've never seen the like. He used to stand there on the quarterdeck making some poor sod throw bottles into the water, and he would shoot them as they went by. Didn't miss too often. Quite a hand with a sword as well. Almost bested the captain.'

'He and the captain fought?'

'That's right. It was after Isaac took the ship. We were becalmed, you see. All hands were damned anxious. Like when we were running from that two-decker just out the Delaware Bay? You recall that?'

'Oh, yes.'

'Well, it was like that, except the men didn't have anything to do, which makes it much, much worse. Smeaton and the brig's old captain, Pendexter, they were on the quarterdeck, and there's Smeaton, just baiting Isaac and baiting him, like a bear staked out, and Isaac getting madder and madder.'

'It's hard to imagine the captain being drawn into that. It is usually him that plays others like a flute.'

'You're right, and I don't know what it was, but Smeaton knew just what to say. I think he kept treating Isaac like he was some kind of peasant, and that's something the captain don't suffer gladly. In any event, they fought, with cutlasses, and Smeaton proved to be a hand with a blade as well. Nearly bested him. Lucky for Isaac, just before Smeaton split his head open, he got a chance to kick the whore's son right in the balls.'

Gerrish smiled, his teeth dull white in the light of the dying fire. 'So why are they both alive?'

'The wind came up, just as Isaac was ready to run that Smeaton through. His life was spared by a breeze. It was an affair of honor, and they never did finish. And then, off Long Island, when we were being run to ground by a British frigate, the captain set Smeaton and Pendexter adrift on a grating. We got clean away while the frigate stopped to pick them up.'

'They must have been utterly humiliated.'

'I hope.' After a moment Rumstick added, 'I never heard what happened to them. Always imagined they left the service after that. But here comes Smeaton, just a lieutenant on a sloop of war, after all this time. I reckon his name was ruined by what Isaac did to him.'

Rumstick stared out into the dark night, wondered if the sloop was still out there. He shook his head slowly.

'What, sir? You look concerned.'

'Yes. It's nothing. I am a mother hen, I swear. But that Smeaton has got to hate Isaac with all that's in him, and Isaac must feel the same. God knows I do, especially after that bastard killing poor David Weatherspoon. Smeaton's the only one I ever seen can lead Isaac into a fight.'

'You are afraid of their meeting again?'

'Afraid? I don't know about that. I got faith in the captain's arm. I just . . . well, I suppose I'd rather that little Smeaton sail away and never cross our wake again.'

CHAPTER 9

*I confess myself unable to give any Advice as to the
disposition of the navy . . . and shall therefore be
glad to have the opinion of yourself and Officers
upon the subject.*

— GEORGE WASHINGTON
WRITING TO COMMO. JOHN HAZELWOOD
NOVEMBER 1777

The marine with the gut wound died in the night and
his body was moved without ceremony behind the
dune. That left two gaps in the line of wounded in
the shelter of the boats. The big dark stains of blood
in the sand were covered over, and no mark of their
passing was left on the spots where they had died.

Isaac left Virginia to herself, off in the dark, but
soon Jack's tiny cries called her irresistibly back. He
was hungry, and all of Rumstick's and Biddlecomb's
cooing and chucking could not distract him from
thoughts of his mother's breast. And so she reappeared in the circle of light from the fire and took
up the baby and gave him sustenance from her own
body, and that did more to ease her guilt and

uncertainty over the death of the sailor than all the words Biddlecomb could have uttered in a lifetime.

At last she and Isaac found their own spot of sand and lay down with Isaac's cloak spread over them like a blanket and slept. And despite the wild tempest of thoughts in his head, Isaac slept soundly, being quite overcome with exhaustion.

The sun was already up when he awoke.

He pushed himself up on an elbow and looked around. The day was gray, cold, somber, as all the days had been for a week at least. Some of Faircloth's marines were milling about, munching on the biscuits that had been in the longboat. The rest of the Charlemagnes were still asleep.

He stood up, gritting his teeth against the ache in his joints, the stiffness, as if he had not moved in days. His eyes moved immediately to the sea, scanning the gray line where ocean met sky, from the northern horizon to the south. It was empty. The sloop – Smeaton's sloop – was gone.

Smeaton. He had not really considered their meeting. How very odd it was. He had occasionally wondered what had become of them, James Pendexter and John Smeaton. Losing the *Icarus* to a pair of rebellious colonials and a mutinous crew could not have done much for their professional reputations. But Smeaton, at least, was still in the navy.

Biddlecomb thought of the pompous, arrogant bastard John Smeaton, felt his mood turn black. He pictured the smirking son of a bitch standing at the *Icarus*'s rail, smoking pistol in his hand, as Haliburton's body slid below the surface of the harbor in Barbados. He recalled Smeaton's condescension –

132

why had it infuriated him so? – even after he had relieved the two officers of their vessel.

He should have killed Smeaton in that instance when he had had the chance, while the bastard was lying fetal on the deck, grasping his aching testicles. Smeaton had been a second away from killing him, right before Biddlecomb's boot had connected. Smeaton would not have hesitated.

If he had killed Smeaton, then Weatherspoon would still be alive. As he thought on it, he realized how very much he wanted to run his sword through Smeaton's guts, if for no other reason than to avenge David Weatherspoon. And John Haliburton. And Bloody Wilson and all the other men who had died aboard the *Icarus*.

Well, perhaps I shall get the chance yet, he thought, staring off at the empty horizon.

'Captain?' Rumstick loomed up beside him, handed him a canteen. 'Ain't coffee, but I reckon it's the best we'll get.'

Biddlecomb put it to his lips, took a long drink. The water carried no more than a hint of the familiar taste of wooden cask. It had not been above a week in the barrel.

'We'll need a cart of some sort,' Biddlecomb began, turning from thoughts of vengeance to more immediate concerns, 'for the wounded.' He ran his eyes along the dunes, scanning the western horizon, the shore side. 'I've no tolerable notion of where we are, beyond New Jersey. How are the people of New Jersey disposed towards the current war?'

'Like everywhere, I'd reckon. Some for it, some against, a power of 'em don't care. Loyal to whatever army happens to be marching through. Faircloth's pickets found a road half a cable west.'

'That should be as good a place as any to start. Let us tell off a shore party . . . well, I suppose we are all a shore party now . . . let us tell off some men to go with us. We will leave Faircloth and his marines here with the wounded; I reckon they are more to be trusted than the seamen. Cutlasses, pistols, whatever we can round up to arm the men. Ready to move in fifteen minutes?'

'Fifteen minutes, aye, aye, sir.' Rumstick saluted, turned, was bellowing orders before he was halfway back to the fire.

Eight minutes later the men were told off, armed, and standing in two loose files, ready to move.

'Very well, let us go,' Biddlecomb said, and off they marched, over soft sand, coarse dune grass, and at last down a well-packed dirt road leading generally south and west.

They marched for the better part of an hour and encountered nothing beyond low-lying marsh and sand dunes, and fast, plump little birds that skimmed the ground in their rapid flight.

When they did at last stumble into the local militia, it was on one of the few curves in the road, one of the few places where they could not see at least a mile in any direction. The Charlemagnes came around the bend, turning to the right, and in doing so nearly collided with two dozen armed men coming from the other direction.

The surprise was complete on both sides, with many a startled shout and leveled musket and even a few men on either side plunging into the dune grass for cover. But fortunately for all, Biddlecombe,

Rumstick, and the officer in command of the militia realized at nearly the same instant that they were all on the same side; and guns were put up before anyone was hurt.

'Somers, Col. Richard Somers,' said the officer of militia, extending a hand to Biddlecomb and running an eye over his uniform. 'Gloucester County Militia.' Somers himself was dressed in wool stockings, canvas breeches, wool shirt, a coat of plain-woven broad-cloth. 'And what might you be, artillery, or some such?'

'Capt. Isaac Biddlecomb, United States Navy.' Biddlecomb shook the calloused hand.

'So you would be one of Hazelwood's boys?'

'Beg pardon?'

'Commo. John Hazelwood. You would be one of his.'

'Ah, no. If I am not very much mistaken, Commodore Hazelwood is attached to the Pennsylvania Navy. I, we, are of the Navy of the United States.'

'I see,' said Somers, though he did not appear to. 'We heard a report that a ship had gone aground on the beach here, heard there was some fighting, that's why we're turned out.'

'Yes, that was us. Continental brig-of-war *Charlemagne*. Total loss. We skirmished with a British landing party. We have wounded,' said Biddlecomb.

'Well, we best get them to some place where they can be looked after. Billy' – Somers turned to a man behind him and to his right – 'run back to the Quigleys' farm. Patrick has a dray, should serve to move these fellows to the boat.' Somers turned back to Biddlecomb. 'Where are your wounded at?'

'About a league down the road, on the beach.'

'Hear that, Billy, about a league down the road here. Get that dray and catch us up. Rest of you, follow me.' Somers headed off down the road again, Biddlecomb and Rumstick falling in beside him, the Charlemagnes mixing in with the militia behind. Isaac could hear muted talking, his men inquiring after flasks or bottles.

'Oh, say.' Biddlecomb recalled the question he most wanted to ask. 'Where are we?'

They were not, as it turned out, at the end of the earth, though Somers assured them they could see it from where they stood. They were on Absecon Beach, a long, desolate, nearly deserted stretch of barrier island that had its northern terminus at Absecon Inlet and its southern at the entrance to Great Egg Harbor. Some fishing and small-time shipping went on there, and a few families such as the Quigleys tried to scratch a living out of the ground, but that was about it. Like much of New Jersey, that part of the coast was largely unpopulated.

Billy and the dray, driven by Patrick Quigley, who was apparently unwilling to let the vehicle out of his sight, arrived not half an hour after the Charlemagnes and the militia had reached the others on the beach. The dead were loaded first, then the wounded were eased with greater care into the back. Virginia and Jack were helped up into the seat, and then the rest fell in and marched off behind the groaning, creaking wagon.

It took all the daylight they had to cross the island, ferry them all out to the sloop aboard which the militia had come, and sail the five miles or so across Great Egg Harbor to the small cluster of buildings that constituted the town of the same name. There

136

was a public house, of course, and a scattering of homes, a blacksmith, a chandler of sorts. A few schooners and a brigantine in various states of repair swung on mooring or were tied to wharves. A small fort, mounting four guns, stood watch over the sheltered harbor. It was not much, but the Charlemagnes did not require much at the moment.

Biddlecomb saw Virginia and Jack and the wounded made comfortable in the public house and secured housing for the rest of his men as well, all with the able assistance of Colonel Somers, who wielded some authority in that little community. It was approaching midnight when Biddlecomb and Rumstick, Faircloth and Somers, found a table by the fire in the tavern room and ordered up rum and beer and slings, made strong, or 'well to the northward,' as the sailors put it, and evaluated their situation.

'We were bound away for Philadelphia,' Biddlecomb explained to the militiaman, 'where I was to assume command of a new frigate building there, and my men were to form the nucleus of the crew. It is generally believed that Howe will move on the city, so I think it crucial that we get there and get the *Falmouth*, the frigate, out before they arrive. And out of the Delaware Bay. I should think Black Dick will soon see the need to bring the fleet around and take control of the water approaches to the city.'

Somers nodded thoughtfully, took a long drink, then nodded some more. 'We don't hear much, away down here, save for rumors. Word is that the British are already in Philadelphia, but that don't mean your boat's been taken, no, sir. *Effingham* and *Washington* was towed upriver, I understand, and it could be this *Falmouth* was too.

137

'As to Black Dick and the fleet, we hear all sorts of things, none sure enough to call the truth. By some reports they're still in the Chesapeake, some says they're up to Philadelphia, which I don't reckon is so. That much we would have heard. Besides, there's a power of defenses on the Bay, and obstructions, what they call *chevaux-de-frise*.' He pronounced it *shevoo de freeze*. 'You familiar with them?'

'I believe so,' said Faircloth. 'Are they not these great wooden poles tipped with iron points and anchored in cribs filled with rocks? The idea being that a ship running into one would impale itself?'

'That's them, described most eloquent.'

'But is it not necessary to support such things with land fortifications?' Faircloth continued. 'Otherwise the enemy should just remove them at their leisure.'

'You've been studying again, I perceive,' observed Rumstick.

'Oh, they got fortifications, never doubt it,' said Somers. 'On Red Bank, just below Eagle Point. Do you know it?'

'We were unfortunate enough to be frozen in the river for many weeks in just that area,' Biddlecomb said, 'in the winter of '76. We know it better than we care to.'

'Well then,' Somers continued, 'there's Fort Mercer on Red Bank, and just across that is Fort Island, where they got Fort Mifflin. They also have a power of galleys and row galleys and floating batteries in addition, and the Pennsylvania Navy, and between 'em all they well command the river. If Black Dick reckons on pushing his way up, them Pennsylvania boys got a lot to push back with.'

'That is good news, at least, and there's been a

bloody dearth of it thus far,' said Isaac. 'Now the question remains, how do we get to Philadelphia?'

'I would think either by land or by sea,' Faircloth supplied.

'Astutely observed, sir,' said Isaac. 'What think you, Colonel Somers, of the travel overland?'

'Overland? Oh, bless you, sir, but I can't recommend it. There's no town of note between here and Gloucester Town, just below the city. New Jersey, sir, is a thin populated place, with scarcely a road worthy of the name. That's why we few that live here stick close to the water.'

'Very well, by sea it is, which I prefer in any event. Tomorrow we shall see which worthy in this town will sell us a vessel.'

'We have funds to buy a vessel?' Rumstick asked.

'Yes, as it happens, the money I had from Congress, and from William Stanton, more to the point, did not perish with the *Charlemagne*.'

If the other officers wished to think that he had had the foresight to rescue it, Biddlecomb would not disabuse them of that thought. In truth, however, it had been Virginia's quick and daring action that had saved the money – script and specie – from the great cabin, along with the medicine and Surgeon Northcote's *Extracts*.

'It's too bad you couldn't have saved the journals and logs as well, before the brig was lost,' Rumstick observed.

'Yes, well, one can't think of everything.' The words sounded more peevish than Biddlecomb had intended, so he moved on quickly. 'Mr Somers, do you know of any vessels locally that might be purchased?'

'Wellll,' Somers drew out the word. 'Not much to be had, tell the truth. We do a fair amount of privateering out of here, I sponsor a few of the ships myself, and most vessels has been taken up with that. There is but one that I know of, available. A fellow, Hoffman, has a schooner. The one with the round tuck stern tied to the wharf, you may have seen her. I understand he's had a mind to sell her.'

'Good, then we shall see this Mr Hoffman in the morning.'

'Yes, I reckon you could.'

'Is there a problem?'

'Oh, no, sir. No problem. It's just that, well, Hoffman has a reputation; he's a bit . . . well, let us just say he can be a difficult man, at times.'

Difficult he was, or so Biddlecomb found out the next morning. An hour after dawn he sent the publican's son around to Hoffman's house to wake him and request he join them on the wharf, Biddlecomb being anxious to keep ahead of Howe and get on his way.

It still took Hoffman the better part of an hour to make his way down to the waterfront. He wore no hat or wig, and his close-cropped hair stuck out in every direction, making his skull look like a sea urchin. His clothes were a good quality, though well past their prime. A scowl was carved into his face.

'You Biddlecomb?' he asked.

'Capt. Isaac Biddlecomb, Navy of the United States, at your service, sir.' Biddlecomb gave a shallow bow.

'My service? You reckon this is for my service, rousing me out before my breakfast? What is it you want? Want to buy my schooner, that what I hear?'

140

'Yes, sir. My men and I were on our way to Philadelphia, there to take command of a frigate building at Wharton and—'

'I don't give a tinker's cuss what you were doing, or why. Don't care about this asinine war, so don't tell me how bleeding important you are. Here, what are they about?'

Rumstick, Faircloth, and Gerrish had already gone aboard the schooner and were probing around her cabins, shaking shrouds and stays, and pulling folds of sailcloth off the booms to gauge the general condition of the vessel. From where he stood dockside, Biddlecomb did not gauge the condition to be very impressive, and judging from Rumstick's and Gerrish's expressions, a closer inspection did not alter that assessment.

'They are inspecting the vessel, sir. It is customary when a purchase is being considered.'

'Well, damned bold, I say, going aboard without my permission.'

'Forgive me, sir, but we are in a great hurry.'

'Well, I ain't, and it's my schooner.'

'Indeed.' Biddlecomb drew a deep breath, held it, exhaled softly, let his irritation settle. 'Perhaps we should discuss the terms of a sale, the price you would ask?'

'Price? Why, sir, with the dearth of shipping to be had on this coast, I do not see how I could let this fine vessel go for less than one thousand dollars.'

Biddlecomb frowned. The expression was genuine, but also the proper lead-in to a counteroffer. Such negotiations were his forte, he having learned many hard and valuable lessons as a merchant captain before the gathering fight with England had driven him into a naval career. But this Hoffman would be a tough one. 'A thousand dollars, sir? I think not. I think—'

'I do not care what you think, sir, the price is a thousand dollars and the point is not open to debate.'

At that moment Rumstick's head appeared above the mainhatch coaming as he climbed up from below, a scowl on his face, and Biddlecomb thought, We shall see, sir, about that.

'You there,' said Rumstick in a tone that even Biddlecomb found frightening. 'Are you the black-guard who is trying to sell us this schooner?' The first officer stepped from the low bulwark across to the wharf. He stood five inches taller than Biddlecomb and nearly ten above Hoffman. His bulk alone would have made him a threatening presence, even without the black expression on his face.

'Do y'see this here, sir?' Rumstick held a handful of dark brown fibrous material under Hoffman's nose. It looked like wet tobacco, or last autumn's leaves revealed by melting snow. 'That, sir, is from your keelson, pulled it up with my bare hand, and the rest of the bottom is no better!' Rumstick flung the fistful of rotten wood at Hoffman's feet. It hit the wharf with a liquid sound and splattered over his threadbare silk stockings.

Biddlecomb tried not to smile. It was all great theater, a game he and Rumstick had played many times.

'Now see here, you have damaged my vessel and you will pay for that, sir, depend upon it,' Hoffman sputtered.

Biddlecomb was impressed. Rumstick had failed to

142

intimidate the greed and unpleasantness out of the man. For the moment.

'Still, I think under the circumstances one thousand dollars is a bit high,' Biddlecomb said, acting the conciliator.

'Very well, then, eight hundred dollars, not a penny less.'

'Eight hundred dollars?' Rumstick spluttered. 'The bottom is compost, for the love of God.'

'So say you. I say the bottom is sound, and more to the point, there is no other vessel for purchase within fifty miles.'

'Damn this little Tory rat, Captain,' said Rumstick. 'We represent the Navy of the United States. Just take the damned schooner, I say, and let this villain claim his money from the Continental Congress.'

Biddlecomb genuinely did not know if Rumstick was bluffing, for he had thought of the same thing himself. But such arrogance was counterproductive, in the grander scheme of things. General Washington had been strict with his foraging parties that they were to pay fair price for anything they commandeered. It was a good policy, and one Biddlecomb wished to follow. It would not help the cause if the people feared and resented the army. But Mr Hoffman was trying Biddlecomb's sphinxlike patience.

'Perhaps that is the best solution to this impasse,' Biddlecomb ventured.

'Now wait here, wait just a moment. I can be reasonable.' Mr Hoffman's mood changed quickly when faced with the possibility of these armed men simply taking the vessel and leaving him with only the fantasy of ever getting money from Congress. 'Four hundred dollars would be fair, would it not?'

143

Biddlecomb smiled. 'Four hundred dollars would be fair indeed.' He dug into the haversack, pulled out a pile of script, began to count it out.

'Now see here!' Hoffman exploded anew at the sight of the paper money. 'I mean four hundred dollars in real money! That there, that is not worth even the paper—'

'Mr Hoffman,' Rumstick spoke softly, deliberately, leaning over the shorter man, 'that there is Continental currency, issued by our very own Congress. Are you impugning the worth of that, sir? I would take that to mean you are impugning the worth of our government, perhaps even the worth of these several states. How do you stand, Mr Hoffman, on this question of independency? Closet loyalist, are we? Perhaps it was thirty pieces of silver you were hoping for?'

By that point Rumstick had backed Hoffman to the edge of the wharf, and Hoffman, sensing the real danger the naval officer represented, shook his head in dumb protest. At last he was able to stutter, 'No, sir, no, sir, I have nothing but loyalty to the Congress and General Washington! I much admire the script they are issuing!'

In the end Biddlecomb gave Hoffman half of the purchase price in paper and the other half in hard currency, milled Spanish dollars, given Isaac by his father-in-law, William Stanton. For all of Rumstick's insinuations, Hoffman was right about the general worthlessness of Continental paper money, and Biddlecomb felt the man should at least get something of value for his vessel.

They left the schooner's unhappy former owner on the wharf and made their way up to the small cemetery on the hill outside of town. The Charlemagnes had been set to work at first light digging the graves that would receive the earthly remains of those men who had fallen in their nameless and soon-to-be-forgotten little battle on the beach. Eight rectangular holes, all in a line, six feet deep. Eight pine boxes run up by a local boatbuilder, eight wooden boards painted with crosses and the names of the dead, in those instances where the names were known.

Biddlecomb stopped and let the others go ahead, ran his eyes over the boxes and the holes ready to receive them. There had been a time when this sight would have filled him with anguish, these men dead on account of decisions that he had made. But that was a long time ago. Two years. It seemed like a hundred. Now he just looked and felt nothing.

Lt David Weatherspoon. He read the wooden board. He, Biddlecomb, was as responsible as anyone for the young man's death, but he could not blame anyone but Smeaton for it, and for that he hoped very much to one day find Smeaton again and kill him, though he could not imagine how that might happen.

In any event, blaming himself would be a disservice to the man's memory. Weatherspoon would not have tolerated it, nor would he have suffered any patronizing talk about keeping the young officer from harm's way. Weatherspoon had been a patriot and a naval officer and he himself would have said that his death was as good a one as such a man could hope for. Better, to be sure, then dying in his cot of bloody flux or yellow jack.

Isaac pulled his eyes from the fresh-cut wood, the bright paint, looked around the cemetery. A number of new-looking headstones, granite, were neatly carved. He beckoned the caretaker over.

'Who carved these granite headstones, these new-looking ones?'

'Fellow up the road does it, and he's quite a hand, as you can see.'

'We must be away this morning, but would you have him carve one for me?' He fished some coins out of his pocket. 'Here is five dollars, will that suffice?'

'Bless you, sir, yes, and then some, I should think.'

'Good. Mr Gerrish, paper and a pencil, please.'

The midshipman – acting lieutenant – who was rarely without those things, hurried over and handed them to Biddlecomb. Biddlecomb put the paper down on a nearby headstone, stared at it, stared up at Weatherspoon's coffin, then began to write.

Lieutenant David Weatherspoon
Second Lieutenant of the United States Brig
Charlemagne
Officer, Gentleman, and Patriot
Died fighting for his Country's Independence
In the Battle of Absecon Beach
September 25, 1777
They that go down to the Sea in Ships
And do their work on Great Waters
These see the works of the Lord
And his Wonders in the Deep.

There. Now at least Weatherspoon's name would not be worn away in the passing of a few seasons, nor would his death be a part of some obscure skirmish. Let future generations figure out what the Battle of

146

Absecon Beach was. For all the good that it would do Weatherspoon. But a headstone, Biddlecomb understood, was not for the benefit of the dead.

He looked at the words of the psalm, thought, as he had often times before, about the ancient seagoing worthy who had penned those words. Whoever he was, he was a man who had understood, genuinely understood, what it meant to be a sailor.

CHAPTER 10

I have another Reason for scuttling them [the frigates Effingham *and* Washington], *which is, that I fear the Enemy will possess themselves of them, and with the Assistance of them and the* Delaware *Frigate very much annoy your Rear – I am –*

—GEORGE WASHINGTON
WRITING TO CAPT. ISAIAH ROBINSON

It had been a close thing with the *Falmouth*, a very close thing indeed, pulling her away from the city and the vanguard of the British army.

The provosts had raced away, clattering off down the cobblestone streets, afraid, like Foote, that they had overextended their stay, pushed their luck beyond its natural limits.

McGinty was the first to speak, to no one's surprise.

'Tow the frigate away, just the thirteen of us? The bloody thing weighs six hundred ton if she weighs a pound. You're mad, Mother Foote.'

Foote turned and ran his eyes along the river, along the pilings supporting the wharf, gauged the

148

run of the tide by the amount of water piling up around the obstructions. Said, 'No towing involved, Teague. We're at the first of the flood now, and the wind's just about right. We cast off the fasts and away she goes upstream. Just need you boys to keep her head straight and I'll man the helm to keep her in the middle of the river.'

'Yer daft if ya think that's all there is to it,' McGinty began again, but the short, surly one cut him off.

'Stow it, McGinty. This bastard saved us from the provosts, reckon we can do this thing for him.'

McGinty glared at him, glared at the others clustered around, judged the prevailing mood with the fine-honed insight of a politician or a snake-oil salesman. 'Very well, then, Freeman. You lot. It's your bloody backs. And necks.'

Foote pulled his plug of tobacco from his pocket, tore off a piece, handed it to Freeman. Freeman accepted it with a nod, tore off another piece, and put the remainder in his haversack.

McGinty was literally licking his lips. 'Now, why don't you hand some of that all round, Mother Foote?'

Foote looked at him, long and hard. 'You be a good Teague, perhaps I will.'

A distant smattering of small-arms fire recalled to the deserters their sense of urgency and the need for haste. They stacked their weapons and packs on the deck and climbed down to the wharf, surrounded the big longboat, and lifted all together, carrying it down to the ways and slipping it into the river.

Foote made his way forward, through the forecastle and out onto the beakhead, and from that high

149

perch he was able to watch the soldiers climbing awkwardly into the boat.

He was not surprised to see McGinty forgo the oars, but rather step aft and man the tiller.

What was surprising was the ease with which the big infantryman took his place in the stern sheets, the authority with which he doled out instructions to the men on the thwarts.

'Very well, then, listen here,' he said. His accent sounded musical to Foote's ear. 'When I says "ship oars," I mean put yer oars down between them two pins, and when I says "give way," it means to pull the oars, and I bloody hope you know how to do that. I might say "give way, starboard" or "give way, larboard" or "give way, all." Are you with me then, laddies?'

One of the young soldiers piped up. 'Are we starboard?'

From the other side of the boat, another offered, 'You'd be starboard if you was facing forward, but looking aft, you're larboard, you great ignorant calf.'

'Oh, for the love of God!' McGinty shouted. 'See here, I'll call it Freeman's side and William's side. Can you keep that straight, then?'

By this means, and with much cursing and yelling and strained patience, the former soldiers of the Fifth Pennsylvania worked the boat off the shore and under the *Falmouth*'s beakhead.

'Well done, Teague,' Foote shouted down. 'Now I'll need some of you boys to help get the light hawser rove out through the hawse pipe.'

'Damn the bloody hawser, Ma Foote, we haven't the time,' McGinty called back. 'That forward breast-

150

fast is plenty long enough and as strong as you could want. Just take it up on board and reeve it through the gammoning hole and pass both ends down to us. That way we won't be towing the bloody tub sideways up the river.'

Malachi spit a stream of tobacco and watched it hit the water a foot astern of the longboat, watched it swirl away upstream. 'For a foot soldier you seem to know a lot about seamanship, there, Teague.'

McGinty grinned, sheepishly, the most genuine expression Foote had yet seen from the man. 'Well, I may have spent a wee bit of time in the British navy, do ya see, before taking up arms in defense of me new homeland.'

'For the love of God, Teague, is there any military organization from which you ain't a deserter?'

'The breast-fast, there, Mother Foote? Or shall I just run the Union Jack up the staff right now?'

'Shut your bloody mouth,' Foote muttered, not loud enough to be heard. He didn't care to have McGinty giving orders or even expressing thoughts, particularly when the Irishman was right.

He scrambled down the ladder to the wharf and cast off the breast-fast.

It took ten minutes to rig the tow rope, and by the time they were done the quiet of the early morning had given way to chaos, the kind that only natural disaster and war can bring. They could hear sounds, not so distant, confused and threatening. A low rumbling. Marching men, perhaps. The occasional bugle or drum or small-arms fire.

There were people in the streets now, people near panic. Wagons rolled past, laden with the furniture and families of those who had refused to believe

151

the rumors and were now trying to flee before the advancing enemy. A band playing martial airs sounded from far away and then was gone.

They could hear the clatter of horses' hooves on the cobblestones, running, growing louder. They would not be Continentals this time.

'Come along, Ma, cut the bloody fasts!' McGinty shouted up from below.

'Take up the strain, Teague, or we'll be hard on the far shore directly!'

'We've taken it up, now will you . . .'

It was pointless. They had known each other for an hour and were already arguing out of habit. Foote tossed off the head-fast and the bow began to swing away from the wharf. From beyond the beakhead he heard McGinty calling, 'Give way, all! Pull, ya bastards, pull like them German butchers was coming for yer sweet mothers!'

Foote ran aft along the gangway. The bow was swinging off, caught by the wind and the tide, and it had drawn the after breast-fast bar taut. He pulled his sheath knife from his belt – the blade was like a razor, Foote having spent a lifetime sharpening tools – and he slashed at the rope. It parted with just the lightest resistance and fell from sight and the *Falmouth* swung farther out into the stream.

There was only the stern-fast left, and that too fell to Foote's knife.

From somewhere forward came McGinty's voice, shouting, 'Starboard yer bloody helm, Mother Foote, starboard your helm and meet her!'

Foote backed away from the quarterdeck rail, hand reaching out for the wheel, eyes locked on the shipyard and the town and the end of Chestnut

152

Street falling quickly away. Horsemen were coming their way, riding hard, riding with purpose.

Foote felt his palm hit an oiled spoke and he spun the wheel to port, heard underfoot the groan of the new tiller ropes hauling the helm to starboard. The *Falmouth*'s bow responded, twisting around and aiming upriver, reacting to the rudder and the pull of the men in the longboat.

The horsemen burst from the confines of the street and spread out across the shipyard, racing for the waterfront. Green regimentals, red facings, shining black boots, curved cavalry sabers slapping at their thighs. Two dozen of them, trim and uniform.

'Bloody Hessians,' Foote muttered. Dragoons. A German jaeger corps. If they had arrived a minute sooner, there would have been real trouble, but now a good hundred feet of water separated the *Falmouth* and the wharf.

'I hope you can swim, ya bloody German bastards!' Foote roared at them. 'Or fly!' He brought the helm amidships, felt the great relief that comes with a narrow escape.

The jaegers had apparently been sent to the waterfront for the express purpose of preventing the escape of any shipping there, judging by their unwavering approach. And judging by their continued determination, they did not consider the *Falmouth*'s escape to be a fait accompli.

They raced north along the waterfront, past the frigate's bow, past the place on the river where McGinty and his crew were pulling for midstream. They charged to the foot of the Morris and Company wharf that thrust itself one hundred feet out into the river, flung themselves off their mounts, and raced out over the water, carbines in hand.

'Oh, bloody hell!' Foote shouted, his elation gone like the wisp of a dream. It took no art to guess what the Germans were up to. If they killed even a third of McGinty's men, then the *Falmouth* would be adrift, would fetch up on the bank somewhere and be easy pickings for the jaegers.

Or, more likely, the deserters would cut the frigate free, save their own hides.

Foote abandoned the helm. He grabbed three of the men's cartridge boxes, each with a big *5th* painted in white on the black leather, and slung them over his shoulders, snatched up as many muskets as he could carry, and raced forward along the gangway.

He reached the forecastle head at full run, the muskets slipping from his hands, just as two of the jaegers' carbines cracked off.

'Ma Foote, we've a bit of trouble here, and you with all the guns!' came McGinty's voice, floating up from beyond the bow.

'Don't you cast off that fucking line, Teague!' Foote shouted. He deposited all but one of the muskets on the deck, brought the one in his hand up to his shoulder, pulled back the lock, hoped the gun was loaded.

He peered over the smooth barrel, found the jaeger officer, placed his head just below the end of the muzzle, and pulled the trigger. The powder in the pan flashed and the gun went off, kicking hard against Foote's shoulder. He discarded the weapon, picked up another.

The smoke had blown past as he took aim again, and he saw that the officer was still standing, so he aimed at him again, and again he fired. On his best day he was a mediocre marksman, and he was two hundred feet from the Germans, so he held out little hope of killing anyone, save by accident. He wanted only to break their concentration, to give them something to think about besides McGinty and the boat crew.

He dropped that gun, grabbed another. They were closer to the Germans now, with the current sweeping them along and the boat pulling the frigate upstream. The jaegers were firing at the boat, loading and firing with the speed and precision of the well trained. It was lucky for the men in the boats that the troops carried only carbines; if they were armed with rifles or even long muskets, they might have easily picked them all off in the first volley.

McGinty, for his part, had put the boat's tiller over and was heading for the middle of the river, pulling the *Falmouth* out into the stream and as directly away from the gunfire as he could.

Foote spared the longboat a glance. One oar was gone, the man who had pulled it slumped over, bright red blood covering the hand he had clapped over a wound. But the rest were still pulling, and McGinty still stood in the stern sheets, giving no indication that he might cast off the tow and run for it.

Malachi looked back at the jaegers over the barrel of the next musket he snatched up. One of them was lying on the wharf, and though it was not the officer, Foote was glad to have had some effect. He fired, tossed the musket aside, grabbed another.

He saw the jaeger officer pointing directly at him, redirecting some of his men's fire. Half a dozen men swiveled around, leveled carbines.

'Bite my arse, you bloody German bastards,' Foote muttered, and then the jaegers were lost behind the smoke of his gun. He stepped away from the gunwale in a half crouch, pulled the spent muskets with him as a few balls whistled overhead and more smacked into the *Falmouth*'s side.

He flipped open a cartridge box, surprised to find only two cartridges left, wondered if perhaps those boys had seen some fighting before they ran. He pulled a cartridge from its hole, bit off the end, and loaded the gun, as fast as his inexperienced hands would move.

More shots from the jaegers, some hitting the frigate, others aimed at the boat. Foote rammed the charge home, returned the rammer, and wondered whether he should fire or load another. He decided to fire, so he approached the edge of the fore-castle head again, crouched low, gun held across his chest.

The Morris and Company wharf, and the jaegers grouped there, were already abeam of the frigate and drawing astern as the current and the men in the longboat pushed and pulled the big ship upstream. Foote aimed, after a fashion, and fired. The *Falmouth* was blocking the German's line of fire on the boat, and they could do nothing to the ship itself with carbines, so they raced back down the wharf to their horses, in hope, no doubt, of finding another place upriver from which to fire.

But there was no place, because McGinty was pulling the frigate to midstream, and even halfway across the wide Delaware River was farther than they could hope to reach with their short-barreled weapons. Foote's ship was safe, for the moment, and

156

he felt the relief blossom and well up until he could not help but shout, 'There, you bloody German butchers! You sons of bitches! Try and lay your filthy sausage-eating hands on my ship, will you?'

And then from beyond the bow came McGinty's voice. 'Here, Mother Foote, we're doing all the work and yer doing all the celebrating! Would ya mind steering the bloody tub, or need I ask you a third time as well?'

But even the Irishman could not quash Foote's mood, and he yelled, 'Ah, Teague! You're the right man for the job when it comes to running away!' Foote left the muskets on the forecastle head, jogged aft, took up the helm, and spun it to larboard and brought the *Falmouth* in line with the tow rope and the wake of the longboat.

They pulled for an hour, the crowded waterfront of Philadelphia passing slowly down the larboard side, the many spires of the city seeming to cross one in front of the other as the perspective changed. Malachi watched the buildings grow less dense, watched them yield at last to brown, open fields.

The flooding tide helped them on their way, as did the wind, which was a steady ten knots over the larboard quarter. Still, towing the frigate was not nearly as easy as Foote had implied that it would be. Nor had he really believed his own representation of the job, but he did not want the men of the Fifth to be discouraged, at least not until they had pulled the *Falmouth* out of harm's way.

They were moving noticeably slower by the time they closed with the southwestern tip of Petty's Island, that triangular-shaped island a mile or so north of the city that split the river like a fork in the

157

road. Foote frowned, abandoned the helm, walked forward along the gangway.

The *Washington* and *Effingham* were all the way up in White Hill, over twenty miles upriver, which was still far from safe though vastly safer than the place where the *Falmouth* was. But there was no hope of getting the *Falmouth* that far upriver. The boat crew was spent, and Foote had his doubts as to whether they would ever be coaxed into towing the frigate again.

He stepped out onto the forecastle head. 'Teague! Hoay!' he called.

'Holloa, Mother Foote!' McGinty twisted around so he could see the shipwright. 'Up from our nap, are we? Hope our creaking old bones didn't wake you!'

'Fagged yourself out, have ya, Teague, pushing that tiller side to side?'

Foote pulled his twist of tobacco from his pocket, bit off a chunk, and worked it between his teeth, in part to calm himself and in part to irritate McGinty. When he finally felt he could speak civilly, he said, 'Listen here. Reckon we've gone about as far as we're going to go. Make her head for the left fork, and once we're well in behind Petty's Island, we'll put her hard by the Jersey shore, make her fast to whatever is there.'

It took another hour of laborious pulling to tow the *Falmouth* past Petty's Island, despite the relief provided by the backwater behind the land. Foote could see the weariness of the boat crew, the crabbed oars, the slow rhythm of the strokes.

Another man might have felt sorry for them, but it never occurred to Malachi Foote.

158

At last they pulled around the far side of the island, and Philadelphia was entirely lost from view. There was only the low, wooded Petty's Island to larboard and to starboard the sparsely populated New Jersey countryside.

'We can put her alongside anyplace here!' Foote called to McGinty, indicating with a wave of his hand the Jersey shore. 'I see a famous tree for the head-fast, just over there!'

With no prompting from Malachi, McGinty untied one end of the doubled-up towline and tied it with a bowline around the other part, then let it slip up to the gammoning hole, thus allowing the line to pay out to its full length. He steered the boat into the shore, clambered out, and slogged through the mud to the reedy bank, where he made the new head-fast off to the tree that Foote had selected.

Having done that, he climbed back into the boat and brought it alongside the *Falmouth*. A minute later all of the men of the Fifth Pennsylvania were back aboard the frigate, sprawled out on the quarter-deck, save for the one man who had taken a Hessian bullet and died of his wound.

The *Falmouth* tugged at its head-fast, swung in the current, and eased against the bank. Foote could tell that the keel was pressed into the mud. As the tide went down, she would settle in the ooze. That was fine. She would be safe like that.

Malachi went below to the first officer's cabin and retrieved the pouch that held, among other things, the four twists of tobacco he had left. The boys might as well have what little reward he could give them, he figured, though by his reckoning they still owed him for saving them from the provosts.

He did not imagine McGinty would see it that way, however.

And Foote had to admit, to himself at least, that they had pulled like slaves on a Roman galley. He could do this one little thing for them, supply them with what tobacco he had, before the men, late of the Fifth Pennsylvania, were on their way to wherever the hell they had been going when they arrived in the yard of Wharton and Humphreys.

By the time he regained the quarterdeck, his small contingent of infantry was asleep, all of them, snoring with abandon. He looked at their lean, dirty forms sprawled out, unmoving. Imagined that was how they would have looked after the provosts were done with them. It occurred to him that it might have been days since they had last slept. Certainly it had been more than that, weeks at least, since they had slept so safe and undisturbed.

Foote let them sleep, ambled forward, sat down on the break of the quarterdeck with his feet on the ladder leading down to the waist. Someday the *Falmouth* might have a captain, and he would never allow anyone to do what Foote was doing, to sit in that place, which was why Foote took pleasure in doing it while he could.

Goddamned navy, he thought, goddamned tarrying, lazy son of a bitch Biddlecomb, whoever he was. The navy did not deserve that fine ship.

He sat for two hours, watching intently the various approaches to the frigate, the river heading off northeast past the bow, and astern making nearly a right angle to the west, the barren fields of New Jersey stretching away on the starboard side, Petty's Island to larboard. He saw no activity of any kind. The jaegers had apparently found something else with which to amuse themselves. No one else seemed to care.

The sun was in the west, inches above the horizon, a dull glow behind the thick cover of clouds, when the others began to stir. He gave them a minute, then stepped aft, found the men – boys, really, save for McGinty and Freeman – stretching, groaning, rubbing aching muscles and half-shut eyes.

Foote fished around in his haversack, pulled out a twist of tobacco. 'Here, Teague. I said if you was a good boy, you could have one of your very own.' He held it out and McGinty took it and bit off an end.

'Rest of you boys can share this out.' Foote handed the other twists around, wondered how he would ever replace them. 'Any of you spits on the deck, I will personally wipe it up with your face.'

'Ah, that's the stuff, sets a man up proper,' said McGinty through a mouthful of half-masticated leaf, 'and the company so congenial.' The others were silent, enjoying the reviving effects of their rare indulgence.

At last McGinty said, 'That was fine, Ma Foote, fine indeed, but I should think me boys are famished and a bit of food would do well for us.'

Foote continued to chew and stare at McGinty, then he ambled over to the side and spit a stream into the river. 'I've got no food aboard, Teague, did you think I was lying to you this morning? You ate my ham and bread already. You're welcome to any of that beer that's left, but that's it. Don't reckon there's even any rats on board.'

McGinty and the others exchanged glances, but it

161

was clear that no one, save he or Freeman, was going to make a decision.

'You didn't think this out in any grand fashion, did you, Ma Foote,' McGinty observed.

'Stow it, McGinty,' Freeman said, his voice like a growl. 'Looks like a farm yonder, reckon they must have some food. Collect yer gear, you lot, and let's move out.'

The boys had gathered muskets and cartridge boxes and stood by the gangway, the equipment slung over their shoulders. Foote looked them over, tried to think of the right words. At last he settled on, 'Teague, you thieving feather merchant, you run a line from that longboat to the frigate so I can haul it back once you're gone.'

McGinty took a bite of his twist, taking care to imitate Foote's every mannerism, and said, 'Never worry about the boat, Mother Foote, we'll bring her back in two hours, or three at the most.'

'Bring . . . bring her back? What, yer coming back here?'

That prompted more glances among the young men of the Fifth.

'Reckon if you don't mind,' said Freeman, 'we had a thought to spend the night here.'

'Humph,' was all Foote could manage. It hadn't occurred to him they would want to stay. He wasn't sure how he felt on that point. But again, they would bring back food, and he was as hungry as any of them. 'All right, you can stay the night.'

'That's most agreeable of you,' said McGinty, bowing low at the waist, 'to offer us lodging aboard . . .' He straightened, looked around. 'What is the name of this fine craft, anyway?'

162

'*Falmouth.*'

'What? The *Foul-Mouth*? Named after you, was she?'

'Shut yer gob, Teague, I've stood for—'

'Stand easy, gentlemen,' said Freeman. 'Thank you, sir, for your offer. We'll find us all some food. Be back directly.'

'Hold a minute.' Foote dug in his haversack, pulled out some coins, an eclectic collection, pennies, halfpennies, some Spanish silver and French sous, an Irish token, typical of the heterogeneous currency circulating in the colonies. 'Here, Freeman, pay for whatever you take. And don't let Teague get his grabbbing hands near that.'

Freeman took the money, nodded, deposited it in his own haversack. McGinty led the men down to the boat and they took their seats and pulled for the shore.

Foote stood and watched them for a while, watched them pull the boat up into the tall grass, watched them assemble and tramp out across the fields with McGinty and Freeman at their head.

At last the men were no more than small, dark spots set against the bleak New Jersey landscape, and Foote pulled his eyes away. He fished a lantern and flint and steel from the binnacle box and with a practiced hand had a light burning in half a minute. He climbed down into the waist and down to the berthing deck, which was all but black.

In the carpenter's stores forward he found his tools and a bosun's chair and collected them up and went topside again and through the forecastle to the beakhead. He made the bosun's chair fast to the headrails, stepped into it, and swung himself outboard so that he was facing aft, his feet planted on either side of the figurehead, his face level with hers.

'Oh, my prettiest, my prettiest.' He ran a loving finger along her smooth wooden cheek, adjusted the lantern until he was satisfied with the way the light fell across her, sighed deep, and stared at her face, her eyes.

No specific image came to mind, no obvious subject, for a figurehead that might represent Falmouth, Maine, and no one, during the frigate's construction, had seemed in the least concerned with what carving might adorn her stem. But Malachi Foote had been concerned, most emphatically. He would not tolerate some ponderous heap of rubbish nailed under the bowsprit, so he had found a big block of cured apple heartwood and set to work.

She was Columbia, that patron saint of America, liberty in female form. Her robes, rendered in wood, clung to her breasts and flowed back over the waist and hips and twisted behind, as if the *Falmouth* were plunging ahead under a towering press of canvas rather than slowly burying her keep in the mud. In her right hand, held half against her chest, a heraldic shield; in her left, a staff that rose up above her head, on which was hung a red liberty cap.

Her neck was long, suggesting grace and strength, not effete delicacy. Her hair seemed to be held against her head by an intricately carved laurel wreath. The curling locks tumbled down and over her shoulders and, like her dress, swept back in elegant twists and curls.

But it was her face that Malachi stared at, her face that was so near perfection. Every night for four months he had worked on her, starting with the wide

164

swirls of her dress, roughing out her arms and hair. He worked slowly, building his skill, until at last he felt ready to release that beautiful face from the apple wood.

Only then had he been ready to call Susan in, to let her see his work, to sit there for hours while he caressed her face with his eyes, and with his sharp-edged tools coaxed it out of the wood.

Anyone looking at her would have judged her complete, but she was not finished in the eyes of Malachi Foote, and he doubted that she ever would be.

'My prettiest,' he said again, and drew a half-inch chisel from the haversack. He laid it against her cheek, like a lover laying a rose on his beloved's pillow, pushed it with just the slightest pressure, watched the tiny curl of wood coming off the blade.

He leaned back in the bosun's chair, observed the effects of his stroke. Not perfect, not yet, but closer, closer by the width of a single wood shaving.

They would never take her, not while there was breath in his body. Not while there was strength in his arm.

CHAPTER 11

October 1777 Wednesday 1st At Anchor off Chester a.m. at 9 made the Signal for the Troops to embark in boats and afterwards the boats were employed landing Troops on the Jerseys.
Dº.
Light Airs at 6 Calm at 8 Light airs and Hazey ½ past weigh'd and dropt up, at 10 Anchored at Chester in 5 Fathom ¼ mile off the Town at 11 Swept the small Bow[er] Anchor and got it up.
—MASTER'S JOURNAL OF HMS *ROEBUCK*
CAPT. ANDREW S. HAMOND

Wherever in that semibarbaric land Isaac Biddlecomb was, it was not here. Wherever in that savage, uncivilized backwoods wasteland that His Royal Majesty and assorted minions were trying so bloody hard to preserve, for reasons unfathomable, wherever Biddlecomb was in that vast landscape, it could not be here.

Smeaton stood on the *Merlin*'s quarterdeck, tapped his fingers rhythmically on the rail, directed his contempt west at the town of Chester. Tried to

166

imagine the place to where Biddlecomb had been bound.

When the *Merlin* had come up with his 'squadron' – the word made Smeaton smile – they had been on a southerly heading, and not so far offshore, which would suggest the Delaware Bay. But no rebel, particularly one as slippery as Biddlecomb would make for the Delaware Bay if he knew that nearly the entire British North American fleet was bound there as well, and Smeaton did not see how they could not know. Philadelphia was in British hands, and a fleet was a hard thing to hide.

But now Biddlecomb was on foot, and there was no telling where he would go. It was absolutely maddening; the bastard had been right there, right at the end of Smeaton's sword, and he had let him slip away. Again.

If only he had killed him, God, if only he had stuck his sword right through him or shot him instead of that other rebel, the boy dressed up like an officer.

If he had killed Biddlecomb the first time he had had the chance, his entire life would be different. How many times had he relived that moment in his mind, the sheer stupidity of it, standing there, exposed, virtually begging for Biddlecomb's boot? His seamanship might not be of the first order, but John Smeaton did not expect to lose in swordplay.

Even if he had killed him this second time on the beach, it would have gone far to improving his lot, restoring his honor, his sacred honor.

A coarser man would have pounded the rail in frustration, but Smeaton just continued to tap, continued to stare.

Now that Smeaton had come to understand how

Biddlecomb alone had been the instrument of his downfall, he could think of nothing but how he might run him to ground. There was nothing he would not do to achieve that, to regain his name, including deserting the *Merlin*. But if he had no tolerable idea of where the bastard was, then it was futile even to think on it.

'Here, then, a signal from *Roebuck*,' growled Matthew Croell, the pilot, from the other side of the quarterdeck. 'Anchor.'

Croell was in a foul mood because he was forced, by his office, to be on deck at that moment and not in the great cabin breakfasting with the captain, the first officer, and one of the midshipmen, who rotated turns for that honor.

Smeaton felt no such anger. He did not care to dine with those villains and whatever midshipman they had selected as their pet for the day.

And that was fortunate, because there seemed to be a concerted effort on their part not to invite him. He noticed how often it happened that the meal at which Captain Reeve entertained was the meal during which Smeaton was on watch.

Smeaton turned to the midshipman beside him. 'Pass the word for the bosun.'

'Pass the word for the bosun!' the midshipman called out, and the word ran forward until the bosun, blue-jacketed, a tall hat on his head, the heavy, intricate lanyard holding his bosun's call draped over his neck, came aft and saluted and growled, 'Sir?'

'Is everything in readiness for anchoring by the best bower?'

'Beg pardon, sir, but Mr Colcot give orders to lay out for the small bower, sir, and that's what I done.'

'Oh, very well, is everything in readiness for anchoring with the small bower?'

'Yes, sir.'

'Good, then, we shall be coming to anchor directly.'

'Sir,' said the midshipman, 'shall I inform the captain?'

God, Smeaton thought, am I never to have a moment's peace?

'Oh, very well.'

Captain Reeve appeared just as Smeaton was rounding the *Merlin* up in her berth. With a curt nod and a 'Thank you, Mr Smeaton,' he took over the quarterdeck and saw the sloop of war brought to an anchor, sails furled and the barge alongside, with the town of Chester in the Colony of Pennsylvania bearing west northwest, one-half west, and a quarter mile off.

This was not the main body of the fleet, this squadron to which *Merlin* was attached, not even a small portion of it. Those ships, over thirty in all, were gathered around Admiral Lord Richard 'Black Dick' Howe in the sixty-four-gun *Eagle*. They were well to the south, having not yet even passed through the Capes of the Delaware Bay. The fleet was making its way around from Head of Elk, at the very northern extremity of the Chesapeake Bay, where on August 25, Lord Howe had deposited his brother, General Sir William Howe, and his army, en route for Philadelphia.

General Howe had fought his way overland, meeting Washington at the Battle of Brandywine and a number of smaller skirmishes, before marching unopposed into Philadelphia.

Now that the British had the city, the problem

was holding it. No one, including Howe and Washington, doubted that the Americans could prevent supplies coming into the city overland. That meant that the army's supplies had to come up the Delaware Bay and the Delaware River. And that meant that the Royal Navy had to be masters of the river and bay, which at the moment they were not.

'There's the signal from *Roebuck* for all captains,' Reeve said to Smeaton tentatively.

Lieutenant Colcot appeared through the scuttle, and Reeve brightened, said, 'Ah, here you are, Lieutenant.'

Reeve turned his back on Smeaton, left him standing where he was, and stepped forward to join Colcot. 'I'm off to *Roebuck*. I should think you would not go far wrong to get the marines in readiness and the boats in the water with their crews. I shall be back directly.' With that, Reeve hurried forward and down into his barge. He seemed to have entirely forgotten Smeaton's presence.

Smeaton noticed, as he always did, and as always he did not care.

Silly ass, he thought, and stepped over to the starboard side of the quarterdeck and stared out over the water. They were Lilliputians to his Gulliver.

The *Merlin* was part of an advance squadron, pushing its way up the Delaware River ahead of the main body. The squadron was under the command of Capt. Andrew Hamond of the forty-four-gun, fifty-rate *Roebuck*. In company with *Roebuck* was the frigate *Pearl* of thirty-two guns, the *Liverpool* and *Solebay*, both twenty-eights, *Camilla*, *Merlin*, and two victuallers. Spread among those vessels were elements of the Tenth Regiment of Foot as well as the Forty-second Royal Highland Regiment, the famous Black Watch.

Chester was as far upriver as the squadron could go. Six miles farther, at a place called Billingsport, the rebels had built underwater obstructions, *chevaux-de-frise*, across the only part of the river deep enough for the big ships to pass. The sunken defenses were protected by fortifications on the shore. The advance squadron was there to clear it all away, like sweeping the streets clean in readiness for the king's passing.

Captain Reeve returned an hour later and summoned all of the officers to the great cabin. 'No surprises, gentlemen, I'll warrant. We shall begin landing these troops directly, at Paul's Point, mouth of Raccoon Creek. Most of the squadron's marines as well. It'll be up to the army fellows to see about clearing out the fortifications, and then we shall begin to clear the channel.

'Hamond has ordered a party from *Merlin* to help in that, support for the carpenters, whatnot. Mr Smeaton, I think perhaps I shall give you command of that, see to getting the channel clear?' Reeve tried to make it sound like an honor, a great responsibility bestowed on the second officer, but his tone was embarrassed, and the effect was a failure.

'Aye, sir,' said Smeaton. It was humiliating, a job for a midshipman. Reeve was just trying to shunt him off, at the very least to be free of him for a while, perhaps even to get him to resign his commission, and everyone in the cabin knew it.

It was humiliating enough for a man with his connections to be second officer aboard a sloop, which he was, thanks to Biddlecomb. But even then he might have worked his way back up to a position

171

of respect and authority, had it not been for the debacle on the beach, thanks again to Biddlecomb.

So he would accept with equanimity Reeve's degrading assignment. It did not matter. He had a greater quest in life.

It took them the rest of the day to ferry the troops upriver and deposit them on the low, marshy shore of Paul's Point. It was dull work, and for Smeaton the tedium was relieved only by staring through his telescope at the swarms of boats pulling to and from the fortifications at Billingsport as the rebels removed everything they could – ammunition, powder, food – before it became once again property of the Crown.

It was funny, really. Smeaton did not expect an epic battle.

The British army made camp that night, right where they had come ashore, and Smeaton, on what Reeve would call detached duty but what Smeaton understood to be temporary exile from the *Merlin*, had his first opportunity to sleep in a tent.

It was actually a pleasant experience, the greatest privacy he had enjoyed since stepping aboard the sloop, with its crowded, unbearable gunroom. Rather than the inane, cretinous ravings of his fellow officers, Smeaton enjoyed the trill of birds, the rustle of leaves, and the soft, barely audible voices of men around campfires. Rather than the choking smells of tobacco and unwashed bodies and bilge, he enjoyed the clean air that came off the water, the hint of wood smoke from the campfires, which was familiar and comforting and bore no relation to the output of the *Merlin*'s officers' pipes.

He sat outside his tent on a folding camp stool, pulling at his own pipe, relishing the evening. He

172

knew no one in the camp, really. There were the *Merlin*'s boat crew and marines, of course, who were off somewhere, but they were just sailors and bullocks and would have no business speaking with an officer. There were also the marine officers from the sloop, but they would certainly not be interested in keeping his company.

It was just the way he wanted it. He let his mind wander, unfettered by trivial concerns and conversations beneath his contempt. He had to figure out where Biddlecomb would go, and how he would find him, how he would issue a challenge. Everything depended upon that.

He had understood from the first the need to kill Biddlecomb, from the moment the *Cerberus* had picked up Pendexter and himself after Biddlecomb had set them adrift on a hatch cover. He had understood, but he had forgotten, until, like the ghost of Hamlet's father, Biddlecomb had appeared on the beach to remind him of his all but blunted purpose.

He would not forget again. He tried to concentrate, tried to reason it out, but his mind kept coming up with the image of Biddlecomb lying on the *Icarus*'s deck, kept reworking the scene so that this time he, Smeaton, ran him through, pinned him to the deck like a specimen of a bug to a card.

At last he gave up, dumped the embers from his pipe, and retired to his blessedly clean and sweet-smelling cot.

He woke before dawn to the sound of some idiot blowing a bugle, but he supposed that that was how they did things in the army, so he rolled out of his cot and pulled his clothes on.

There was not much for him to do at that stage of

the operation. He imagined that his proper place was with the *Merlin*'s marines, but he was *persona non grata* with that crowd, so he just lurked around various parts of the camp, looking as if he belonged, a subterfuge at which he was well practiced and capable. He breakfasted with the officers of the *Roebuck*, a more tolerable set than those of the *Merlin*, and stuck by them when the time came to move out.

It was a thrilling sight, really, the marines, in their red coats and white cross belts, formed up, the Black Watch in their rigid columns, dressed in short red jackets and blue bonnets trimmed out with fur, a swath of the tartan across the front. Their kilts had been replaced by trousers and gaiters, but the officers still wore their basket-hilted broadswords at their side.

Smeaton hung back with the other naval officers. This was not their affair, this fighting overland.

Loud orders were passed down the line, and a certain tenseness came over the men, as if they were ready to bolt, and then the bagpipes shrieked and found their melody and the scarlet mass surged forward at an even, deliberate pace.

If there was one thing that Smeaton could not stand, it was the bagpipes, the howling voice of an inferior race, but even he had to admit that the sound was fitting for this enterprise, good music for bloody work. He thrilled to the sound now, understood why it put men in a fighting spirit.

As keyed up for a fight as the men might have been, they found little release for their ardor that morning. They marched along the hard-packed dirt road to the sound of the pipes and drums, from

Paul's Point to the fortifications at Billingsport, about five miles away.

It was still early morning when they arrived, the fallow fields and cornfields still wet with the dew. The officers rode up and down the lines, arranging the men for the assault, pointing there and there to the subordinate officers to indicate where on the earthworks they were to hit.

When at last the order came to move, the marines and the Forty-second and Tenth Regiments of Foot surged forward, shouting, bayonets down, trampling down a field of corn between themselves and the fort, pouring up and over the redoubts, smashing down heavy gates, spreading out across the inner yard.

They almost caught the last of the rebels, who were busy spiking up the last of the guns, but at the sight of the red-clad troops the Continentals dropped their hammers and spikes and fled for the river and into a waiting boat, and away to the safety of Fort Mifflin, three miles farther up the river. The advance troops of the British army had captured a virtually empty fort.

Nor was there much disappointment, for the more sober heads of His Majesty's forces, those who were not swept away with martial passion just by the sounds of the pipes, understood that it was much more difficult for the British to replace casualties so far from home than it was for the rebels, who lived here. The British could not afford to throw men's lives away. Nor had they forgotten Bunker Hill, and how easily that could happen. No, if every fort fell as easily as that at Billingsport, there would be no complaints.

Smeaton stood on the dirt parade ground in the

middle of the small fortification. He watched the officers going competently about their work, acting from experience. They posted sentries at the well, the spirit room, set armorers to unspiking the guns. There was still nothing for a naval officer to do.

Prisoners.

The thought came to him, even as he tried to think of some business he could undertake to make himself look occupied. There must have been some prisoners taken; in fact, he knew for certain that there were, he had seen them himself, caught by the first wave of Highlanders over the wall. They might know something. They might know Biddlecomb's whereabouts. It was long odds, but Biddlecomb was apparently something of a hero to the Yankee-Doodles, and as such his movements might be known. It was worth a try.

Smeaton felt absolutely buoyant as he went to search out the officer in charge of prisoners, or whatever his official title might be. This was a possibility, a step that might lead him at least to the path that might lead him to absolution.

Lt John Smeaton would be avenged.

CHAPTER 12

This morning 36 Sail of the Enemies' Ships went past this Town up the [Delaware] Bay, and this Evening 41 more were seen from the light House Standing in for the Cape, and while Writing being Nine oClock, find by the lights in the Bay and firing Signal Guns, they have Anchor'd in our Road, I hope they also will pass by without Visiting us.

—WILLIAM PEERY
WRITING TO MAJ. GEN. CAESAR RODNEY
OCTOBER 5, 1777

As anxious, as desperately anxious, as Biddlecomb was to be under way, to get to sea, to fetch Cape May and work his way up the Delaware Bay to his beloved *Falmouth*, there were certain things that he could not control, such as wind and tide, and others he could only barely control, such as procurement of stores for the schooner.

The latter held them at Great Egg harbor for two full days. They really did not need much; food and water for a couple of weeks at the outside, assuming

177

the worst luck in trying to reach Philadelphia, more medical supplies, on Virginia's insistence, some clothing and blankets. But Great Egg Harbor did not have much to offer, and what they did have was not always parted with willingly, not for Continental script and sometimes not even for ready money.

For two days Biddlecomb and Rumstick and Gerrish wrangled and threatened and bribed, while Mr Sprout readied the schooner as best as he could and Mr Faircloth drilled his already perfectly drilled marines, to the delight of the women and boys of the little town.

The former Charlemagnes continued to lodge in the public house, eschewing the damp and cramped schooner for as long as they could. After supper on their third day in that place, Sprout, along with the carpenter and a small contingent of the crew, appeared in the front room, where Isaac and Ezra were enjoying a smoke.

'Beg pardon, sir, but might we trouble you to come down to the schooner?' Sprout requested. 'There's something that the fellows wanted for you to see.'

Biddlecomb shot a questioning glance at Rumstick, but Rumstick only frowned and shook his head.

'Of course, Mr Sprout,' Biddlecomb said, standing, not inquiring further.

'Oh, and, uh,' Sprout continued, getting to the more ticklish part of his request, 'might it be possible, sir, for Mrs Biddlecomb to come as well? And, of course, Mr Rumstick.'

'Humph,' said Biddlecomb. It was an odd request, but Isaac knew that Virginia had not yet retired, and that she would certainly be game for whatever it was

178

that the men had cooked up, so he fetched her from their room and the entire party left the public house to make their way down the slight hill to the wharf where the schooner was tied.

There was no moon yet, and Biddlecomb found his eyes needed to adjust to the dark, even after the dim light of the public house. The dirt road was a black band leading between the few buildings in the town and down to the waterfront. One of the men unshuttered a lantern and led the way, the light on the road swaying to the rhythm of his steps.

They came at last to the wharf against which the schooner lay, bow toward the town, her jibboom reaching out over the quay. The man with the lantern continued on down the wharf until he came to the vessel's quarter and stopped, and Sprout gestured for Isaac and Virginia and Ezra to follow.

'So mysterious, Captain Biddlecomb,' said Virginia. 'I do hope your men do not intend to throw us in the water and make off with the schooner.'

'It would not be the first time my crew has wished to do so, dear, but you are a strong swimmer, I know.'

'Oh, ma'am, nothing of the sort! Never, please never think on it!' Sprout protested, clearly embarrassed.

'I am only teasing you, Mr Sprout,' she assured him. 'Your loyalty could never be in question.'

They made their way to the end of the wharf, and the man with the lantern shuttered it again, leaving them blind in the dark. And then Sprout said, 'Very well, lads!' and three men, standing unseen at the schooner's taffrail, unshuttered lanterns.

The light spilled over the schooner's transom and onto the dark water lapping around the rudder. The small windows in the great cabin were black squares, only the upper edges of their frames catching the light. And below them, the vessel's name, carved into a great sweeping arc of wood, graceful, flowing letters, gilded against a dark blue background, the words *Lady Biddlecomb*.

Virginia gasped, put her hands to her mouth, said, 'Oh my goodness.'

Isaac smiled, shook his head.

'I beg your pardon, sir, we took great liberties,' Sprout was explaining, 'naming the schooner ourselves, and bringing you down here, but the lads wanted to . . .'

Taking it upon themselves to name the schooner, and naming her after the captain's wife, and carving and fixing a name board, all without an officer's permission, was far more presumption and initiative than Mr Sprout was comfortable with, as was indicated by his spluttering, halting explanation. But Isaac cut him off in midprotest and said, 'Mr Sprout, I am delighted and honored that you people have seen fit to do this. I do not know what to say, beyond thank you.'

The 'thank you' was appreciated, to be sure, but his next words, about sending to the public house for whiskey and food for an impromptu christening celebration for all hands, were appreciated much more than that. The party commenced not ten minutes later, and Isaac let it continue on until the early hours of the morning, because it was clearly doing much to lift the men's spirits and because the Lady Biddlecombs née Charlemagnes were well

180

behaved, even polite, in the presence of the captain's wife, this despite their draining the breaker of whiskey with inhuman speed.

Biddlecomb rose the next morning at dawn, his head pounding, his legs unsteady, having gone to bed just three hours before. He reckoned the Lady Biddlecombs would be a sorry bunch indeed, getting the schooner under way.

And he was right, at least as far as the men being a sorry bunch, when Mr Sprout woke them an hour later, shouting in his substantial voice and going around to the places on the deck where they had collapsed and giving them what he considered to be a gentle nudge with his shoe.

Biddlecomb was wrong, however, about getting under way, because the morning was as still as the air in a dungeon cell, not a breath of wind, not even the hoped-for puffs from offshore that morning often brings. Not until midafternoon did they feel anything that could be described as a breeze, and that was from the south and right on their nose, offering no hope of clearing the tricky sandbars and barrier islands and getting to sea

It was another two infuriating, unproductive, frustrating days before they got the blessed wind off the land as the sun came up, enough to blow them across Great Egg Harbor and out through the gap in the islands and into the Atlantic. At the first puff of air Biddlecomb ordered gaskets cast off and halyards laid along and all but the head- and stern-fasts taken aboard.

Richard Somers came hurrying up just as they were stowing the fenders down. 'Say, Biddlecomb,' he called from the wharf, and Biddlecomb stepped over

181

to the rail, which was no more than two feet from where Somers stood.

'Meant to give this to you earlier,' Somers said, handing a canvas bag across the narrow gap between wharf and schooner. Biddleomb looked inside, saw bright-colored cloth.

'Had that lying around since before the troubles,' the colonel explained. 'I know you navy fellows are forever playing with the bunting, false colors, that sort of thing.' Biddlecomb pulled a corner of the cloth out of the bag. It was a Union Jack.

'I don't know where the bloody English fleet is,' Somers continued. 'Could be anywhere. If you run into 'em, that might do some good.'

Biddlecomb smiled, met Somers's eye. 'I thank you. You are in every way correct.' If they did run into a British vessel, any British vessel, that flag would be more help in saving their bacon than all of the few guns they could muster. He reached over the rail, took Somers's hand, and shook farewell.

'Well, good luck to you, I say,' Somers said, then turned and walked away. Biddlecomb thought, here again, two lives have met for this one moment, come together for this instant and then moved apart again. Touch and go.

He pulled himself from his pointless reverie, handed the flag to Gerrish, said, 'Mr Rumstick, let us cast off, fore and aft.'

The head- and stern-fasts were let go and hauled aboard, and the *Lady Biddlecomb* drifted slowly away from the dock, the strip of still water between her and the old pilings growing wider as the ebbing tide gently coaxed her away from the shore.

'Let us have the fore topsail and jib,' Biddlecomb

called next, and with the patter of bare feet across the deck and the squeaking of halyards, those sails were set and trimmed. They slapped in a gust, then filled, and the *Lady Biddlecomb* was no longer a passive vehicle, but rather under the command of those men on her decks, moving to their whim, not that of the thoughtless tide.

They sailed across Great Egg Harbor, their heading due east, straight into the rising sun, adding foresail, mainsail, and main topsail to the canvas aloft. Biddlecomb took bearings off the various landmarks, working his way out of the harbor in accordance to the various bits of local knowledge he had gleaned from the masters and pilots along the waterfront. Aloft, Woodberry stood on the foremast crosstrees, scanning the water, looking for the deadly bars of sand, singing out, 'Sandbar, three points off the larboard bow and a quarter mile off!' Or 'Shoaling to starboard, broad on the bow, half a cable distant!'

Virginia, the schooner's namesake, stood to leeward and aft, holding what looked to be a great bundle of cloth but was, at its center, little Jack Biddlecomb, and enjoyed the morning. The sky was bright blue, cloudless, and the air not so very cold given the lateness of the season. It was a fine day for a sail, and Virginia clearly relished it. But she said nothing, did not intrude on her husband's concentration, and Isaac was once again thankful for a wife who knew her way around a vessel, who knew when conversation was appropriate, and when it was not.

It took them nearly two hours to make their way across the harbor and out into the open ocean, leaving the sandy island called Absecon Beach to the north and Peck Beach to the south. Biddlecomb tried, and failed, to resist the temptation to look for the wreckage of the *Charlemagne*. He ran his telescope north along the shoreline, but he could see nothing of her, and he guessed that that was all there was to see.

Soon the short, gentle motion of the schooner in sheltered waters gave way to the long, familiar swoop of the ocean swells. The *Lady Biddlecomb* was free from the shore and the dangers lurking there. Sandbars and submerged obstacles were no longer their concern, and Woodberry turned his eyes from the waters just beyond the bow to the far horizon, looking now for foul weather and the enemy's ships.

But neither were to be seen on that perfect morning, and the mood aboard the schooner was jovial, relaxed. With visibility as fine as it was, they would be able to see any danger while it was still many miles away, and that was as much as any sailor could hope for, in the early-autumn North Atlantic, on a coast controlled by a vastly superior enemy.

The land breeze deserted them an hour after they'd left the harbor, and the schooner wallowed and rolled on the oily sea before the ocean breeze filled in from the south. They made their course south by east, close-hauled on the starboard tack. The schooner could lie much closer to the wind than a square-rigged vessel, which meant they could make more southing than they might have with the *Charlemagne*, and for that Biddlecomb was glad. More southing meant less time to Cape May, to the Delaware River and the *Falmouth*.

On that point of sail the *Lady Biddlecomb* rolled

little, but rather she pitched, fore and aft, like a teeter-totter, and even Rumstick looked a bit like a drunk as he made his way aft, now walking slowly as the stern rose on the swell, now nearly tumbling as the bow came up. He climbed up the short quarter-deck ladder, approached Biddlecomb.

'I wouldn't worry about carrying the topsail in this breeze if I had a tolerable idea of them topmast shrouds,' Rumstick reported.

'If it builds another five knots, then we will have the topsail in, I think,' Biddlecomb replied. 'By the way, Lieutenant, there is something that I have wanted to ask you, but it forever slips my mind. You recall when we were talking with that villain Hoffman, from whom we purchased this vessel?'

'I do, the ill-natured brute.'

'You came up from below with that handful of rotten wood and told him it was from the keelson, and well done, I say. But wherever did you get it? The wood, I mean?'

Rumstick looked surprised. 'Why, from the keelson, like I said.'

'From the keelson? Truly, it was from the keelson?'

'Well, yes. Odds my life, I thought you knew that. I was not exaggerating the fitness of the bottom.'

'Oh.' Isaac could think of nothing more to say.

'I should think it will serve, mind you,' Rumstick said by way of assurance. 'I wouldn't care to make for the East Indies in this bottom, but I reckon she'll hold together 'till Philadelphia.'

'Well, let us hope. Of course, if she does take on water so the pumps can't keep up, there is every likelihood of a British frigate being nearby, which will no doubt be an instrument for our rescue.'

185

'You have a famous way of giving a man hope, Captain, I have always thought as much.'

They stood on to the southeast through the forenoon watch and the afternoon watch, the men working the pumps more often than not. With that effort they were able to keep ahead of the inflow, despite the fact that sailing close-hauled and nearly into a head sea worked the vessel as hard as she could be worked in tolerable weather.

At the change of the first dogwatch they laid her on the larboard tack. An hour later Cape May came up over the horizon, and soon after that Cape Henlopen. Behind the headlands the sun blazed orange, coloring the whole horizon so that it looked as if all of Delaware and the Jerseys were in flames, and then it was gone.

'I had intended to stand in past Cape May,' Biddlecomb said to Rumstick as they watched the last of the daylight fade in the west, 'but now that we shall not fetch the Capes before dark, I think not. Let us play it safe, stick to the main channel. We'll slip in past Cape Henlopen and anchor in Whorekill Road for the night.'

'Best course of action, I think, sir. Damned tricky shoals, just south of Cape May.'

Virginia came up from below, having put Jack to sleep in the tiny hanging cot that the carpenter and the sailmaker had run up for him, and joined the men at the rail.

'This is lovely, just lovely,' Virginia said. 'But still, I shall be glad to reach Philadelphia.'

'The British may have reached it first,' Isaac reminded her.

'I shall still be glad to get there, see old friends.'

186

'But, if the British . . .' Isaac had assumed that if the city was occupied, then Virginia would not be able to go there, but he realized that that was not necessarily true.

'I shouldn't think the British would molest an innocent young woman such as myself, a baby in my arms.' She smiled at Isaac. 'Besides, who knows what useful things I might overhear while dancing with the handsome officers at General Howe's balls?'

'Indeed.' He did not know if she was kidding and did not want to ask, so he just smiled and turned his attention back to the distant headlands.

It was nearly full dark now. From the quarterdeck they could see the lighthouses on Cape May and Cape Henlopen winking their warnings to approaching ships such as theirs. But beyond that there was no sign of life. The sea was deserted, as if it had been left to them for their private enjoyment, and the passing of the daylight meant one more day that they had not fallen victim to their powerful enemy.

They stood on for Cape Henlopen, and the beacon of the lighthouse seemed to rise higher and shine brighter as they closed with the land, like an intermittent comet, while overhead the stars grew more distinct and numerous. The watch changed, and Mr Gerrish came aft to relieve Rumstick, but Rumstick remained on deck after his men had gone below, enjoying the night along with Isaac and Virginia.

It was nearing midnight by the time they were close enough to see the loom of Cape Henlopen against the dark horizon, a low and irregular shape against the backdrop of stars. They were a mile at least from the closest headland, a nice wide berth. The flashing light moved from its place fine on the bow to broad on the bow and then slipped down the larboard side as the *Lady Biddlecomb* doubled the Cape and stood into the dark Delaware Bay. They could feel the motion of the schooner change again, the long rise and fall of the open ocean once more yielding to the slight, choppy motion of the inland water.

It was too dark to see much of anything. Rather, they felt the presence of the land, the shoreline enveloping them on three sides, the confines of the Delaware Bay, the smells from off the land, the tangy odor of marsh and mudflat.

A light appeared off the larboard bow, until that moment hidden by the headland. It was down low, not far above the water. From the bow the forward lookout sang out.

'House, I should reckon, sir,' said Rumstick. 'There was that fellow lived there, outside the town of Lewes, right near the mouth of the Whorekill.'

'Yes. What was his name? In any event, I imagine we can use that light as a mark for the anchorage.' Biddlecomb turned to the helmsman, mouth open, ready to instruct him to steer on the light, then another light appeared, and then another and another. 'What the devil?'

They watched in silence as Cape Henlopen fell away and more and more lights appeared behind it, a dozen, two dozen, like a new constellation, but brighter than those in the heavens.

'Anchor lights,' Rumstick said with finality.

Biddlecomb nodded. He had reached that same conclusion, not a second before Rumstick voiced it. 'I can think of but one organization that can boast that many vessels.'

'Pray, gentlemen, must you be so cryptic?' Virginia said. 'What do you mean by . . . oh . . .' She paused. 'You mean it is the Royal Navy?'

'What else could it be? No convoy of Continental vessels, not that big. Certainly not the United States Navy.'

'Just like the bloody British,' Gerrish observed, 'they have taken the best anchorage all for themselves.'

'Perhaps a strongly worded letter to the First Lord is in order,' Biddlecomb said.

'I agree, sir, and I shall write it directly.'

'I don't wish to interrupt your fun, sir,' Rumstick said, 'but hadn't we ought to do something?'

'Yes, well . . .' Biddlecomb said, silently examining options. He could come up with only three. The first was to anchor where he had intended, which was a famously bad idea. Beyond that, there was coming about and heading back into open water, or pressing on.

'I believe we shall press on, Mr Rumstick. In the turn of a glass we shall have left the fleet astern, and I see no difficulty in keeping ahead of them all the way to Philadelphia.'

There was silence on the quarterdeck, and Biddlecomb could all but hear the questions in his officers' heads: And then what? We shall be trapped upriver. And then what?

'Aye, sir,' said Rumstick. Gerrish echoed his words.

And Biddlecomb was glad that the questions remained unasked, because he did not know the answers. He knew only that he had orders to go up the river, to take command of the *Falmouth*. His frigate. And that was what he was going to do.

CHAPTER 13

Sir   *Fort Mifflin October 6. 1777.*
From the best Intelligence the Enemy have
withdrawn all their men from Billingsport (the
night of the fourth Instant) except two hundred
who seem much discourag'd . . . One of their Ships
has just now come in close to the Chevaux-de-frize
with intent I suppose to weigh it, the Gundolas are
down to annoy her. Our men are very sickly.
              —LT COL SAMUEL SMITH
                TO GEORGE WASHINGTON

The Lady Biddlecomb stood on, up-bay, until
Biddlecomb was certain that they were in among
the various flats and ledges and bars that naturally
defined the channels for shipping on the Delaware
Bay. At that point the danger of taking the ground
became greater than that of being found out by the
British. They anchored in five fathoms with the best
and only bower and the single, dubious cable that
Hoffman had left aboard, and that only after further
haggling and veiled threats.

Biddlecomb was woken an hour before dawn by

Mr Gerrish, who crept into the great cabin and gently rapped on the door. With a groan Isaac untangled himself from Virginia and extracted himself from the cot.

He was perfectly adapted to the height of the *Charlemagne*'s cabin; it was second nature for him to avoid striking his head. But of course he was not aboard the *Charlemagne*, which in the dark and in his semi-awake state he forgot, until he came up hard against the even lower deckhead of the schooner. He cursed softly, not wanting to wake Jack, not wanting Virginia to hear him using foul language in front of the baby, because it made her angry when he did, as irrational as that seemed to him. He feared that the tone for the day was set.

He dressed and made his way to the quarterdeck, where Mr Gerrish, who was learning to be a perfect subordinate, was waiting with a pot of coffee. Rumstick was awake as well, and Lieutenant Faircloth and Sergeant Dawes were mustering the marines. Biddlecomb had not ordered dawn quarters – there really were no quarters to go to on the merchant schooner – but Faircloth turned out his men nonetheless.

The sky overhead showed just the suggestion of dawn, a vague easing of the blackness, a slightly gray quality to the light. Biddlecomb breathed deeply, relished the smell of brine and foliage, the clear air of autumn. Took a long drink of coffee, let the smell of that mingle with the rest. Felt he could speak civilly.

'Mr Gerrish, let us loosen off all sail and get the anchor to short peak. I wish to be under way the moment we can see even half a cable.'

'Aye, sir!'

'Oh, Lieutenant?' Biddlecomb caught Gerrish half-turned around.

'Sir?'

'Pray, help yourself to some coffee, when you have a moment.'

Gerrish hurried off, giving instructions to Mr Sprout, who rigged the windlass, and to the topmen, who ungasketed the sails. Ten minutes later, Biddle-comb saw a cormorant lift off the water, a half a cable length away, by his best reckoning. He thought he recalled something about the army's benchmark for dawn being the ability to see a gray goose at one hundred yards, figured that the cormorant would do for them, that in the naval service they had to be flexible.

In a matter of minutes the anchor was broken out, caked with mud, and the schooner ghosted away from the anchorage, northeast, and Mr Gerrish laid aft for his coffee. The gathering light stripped the shadows from the far banks. Biddlecomb took bearings on the familiar landmarks, gauged where on the Bay they were.

The *Lady Biddlecomb* had left the British fleet ten miles behind, and as the sun approached the edge of the low land to the east, Isaac could see the ships huddled together in Whorekill Road. His telescope revealed a great tangle of masts, like Boston Harbor in the old days. He could not begin to count how many vessels there were; forty at least, and no doubt more. Men-of-war, transports, victuallers, the awesome firepower and logistical might of the British navy.

· The upper rim of the sun flared above the eastern shore, and in that instant there was a great cannonade, a distant and muted gunfire, like hearing a battle a long way off. The fleet had fired their morning guns. They would up anchor soon and be under way, not even aware of the little rebel schooner racing to keep ahead of them.

A steady breeze carried the *Lady Biddlecomb* up the Bay, past the markers that delineated the many shoals: Brandywine, Outer Fork, Upper Middle, Cross Ledge. A low, thin haze drifted in, reducing visibility to a couple of miles and obliterating the view of the great British fleet astern, or more to the point, obliterating the British fleet's view of them.

In that happy isolation they tended northwest, past Little Duck Creek, Great Duck Creek, Bombay Hook, where the Delaware Bay began to narrow into the Delaware River. It was in the middle of the afternoon watch that Reedy Island came into sight, fine on the larboard bow.

'Here, Mr Rumstick, is this neighborhood familiar to you?'

Rumstick grinned, shook his head. In the winter of 1776 they had spent long weeks frozen in the Delaware River, right next to Reedy Island. 'Never cared to look on this place again, Captain. Thank the Lord we are able to just sail on by this time.'

'Amen to that.' Biddlecomb looked at the low island, the shore where he had once chased down a bunch of deserters across the frozen river. He could see the old barn where he had found them, holding Mr Weatherspoon hostage, recalled the relief he had felt on Weatherspoon's release. Never thought the boy had only another year and a half to live.

Soon they would pass Marcus Hook, where he had taken aboard Dr Benjamin Franklin and his party, bound for France, and Mud Island, where they had also been frozen in. Where he had ordered his first flogging. So many ghosts haunting that stretch of water.

The haze had persisted throughout the day, despite Biddlecomb's belief that it would dissipate with the rising sun. They could still see several miles at least, more than enough to navigate the river, but navigation was not their only concern, and the schooner's company could not be at their ease as long as they did not know what lay beyond the limits of their vision – how close astern the fleet behind them had come, what lay ahead.

They rounded the dogleg at Fisher's Point, turning from northwest to northeast, and Biddlecomb called his officers down to the tiny cabin, where he had spread out on the table a chart of the upper reaches of the Delaware Bay.

'Gentlemen,' he said, once the others had gathered around the table. Virginia sat on the lockers aft with little Jack, ignoring them. 'I should like your thoughts regarding what we might find yonder. I know this stretch of water prodigiously well, but I know no more than you about the military situation. I had hoped that if we piece together every rumor and half-truth we have collectively heard, we might come up with some tolerable notion of what lies ahead.'

'Well, sir,' said Faircloth, a native son of Philadelphia, 'I have always heard it said that the chief of the defense is here,' he put a finger down on the chart, 'on what used to be Mud Island, now called Fort Island. The fortifications are called Fort Mifflin.'

'Fort Island? When last we were through this way,

they were calling Mud Island "Liberty Island." I wish they would settle on something. So here, you say, at Fort Mifflin?'

'I believe that is the primary point of defense, and at Red Bank across the river, at Fort Mercer. The two anchor down a line of *chevaux-de-frise* across the river.'

'Then we shall approach with caution, indeed. I think we shall just make Mud . . . Fort Island by nightfall. If we can anchor there, we should be able to gain some intelligence of the circumstances in Philadelphia, perhaps even of the *Falmouth*.'

'There is also some fortifications here, sir, I believe,' Rumstick added, 'here at Billingsport. River narrows, and there's no going around the north side of Billings Island, as you know, not for anything that draws more than a sloop, so the guns there can play well on the shipping.'

'It is in American hands, to your knowledge?'

'Aye, sir, it is an American fort, but with that fleet chewing on our arse, I don't reckon it will be for long.'

'And no underwater obstructions? No *chevaux-de-frise*?'

'No, sir. Not to my knowledge.'

'How good is your knowledge?'

'Not very.'

'Well, then we shall—' Biddlecomb began, but the cry of 'On deck!' cut him off, and the tone of the lookout's voice suggested their luck might not prove so famous after all. They heard Mr Sprout, who was running the deck, reply, ' Deck, aye!' and the rest was lost as the officers shuffled deferentially aside to allow their captain to exit first, though it was clear they would gladly have trampled him and each other in a race to the deck, if discipline had not held them back.

They emerged in a gaggle on the tiny quarterdeck and saw without asking what the lookout had reported. A few miles ahead, near the edge of their visibility, they could see the hazy, vague silhouette of a ship, more the suggestion of a ship than an object clearly seen. Indeed, an eye not accustomed to the sight of a ship as seen through a haze would never have guessed what it was, but to the men of the *Lady Biddlecomb* there was no doubt.

Biddlecomb stared at the vessel, considered sending Gerrish aloft with a glass, but decided against it. In the hazy weather Gerrish would be able to see no more from the masthead than they could see from the deck. Instead he put his glass to his eye and stared.

It was a big ship, a two-decker of fifty guns or more, which meant, of course, that it was one of the battleships of the British navy. He frowned, squinted, and as he watched, the dull outline of another ship became apparent, ahead of the one he was watching, smaller, but still big enough.

He put the glass down, turned, and stared astern, but there was still nothing to be seen there. He looked forward again. A third ship was visible now. They were all standing northeast up the river under topsails and topgallants, their courses hanging in bunts.

'It's a squadron of the Royal Navy,' Biddlecomb said at last. 'It could be nothing but.'

'But we left them in our wake,' said Rumstick, not sounding so sure, 'did we not? Sure, they could not have passed us by in this haze?'

'I cannot imagine it. Is it possible that what we saw at Whorekill yesterday was but a part of the fleet? That this is the vanguard of the attacking force?'

The four men – Biddlecomb, Rumstick, Gerrish, and Faircloth – stared at one another and then back at the fleet. Details revealed themselves as the schooner closed with the slow-moving ships, Hannibal's war elephants making their ponderous way along.

The implications of this were frightening in the extreme. The fleet they had seen anchored off Whorekill Road was an overwhelming sight, a force that could roll over anything in its path, that could crush any pathetic resistance that the rebels might throw up. And now it appeared that that was but half of it.

And of course the *Lady Biddlecomb* was now caught between the two. Not in the Delaware Bay, where there were creeks aplenty into which they might duck, but on the narrow river, where there was no place for secreting the schooner. Whether they stood on or turned and fled back down to the Bay, they would have to pass under the eyes of the British fleet.

'I reckon we had best look as British as we can,' Biddlecomb said at length, realizing that the moment for gawking was long past. 'Mr Gerrish, let us run up that ensign that Somers was so kind to provide. And pray go to the cabin and inform Mrs Biddlecomb of the situation and request that she remain below. Mr Faircloth, none of your marine uniforms on deck, please.'

Biddlecomb looked down at his own naval uniform: blue coat with red lapels and cuffs, red waistcoat, and blue breeches. 'It dawns on me that this was bloody shortsighted. We should have made our uniforms to look as much like those of the British as we could, for just this sort of thing. Gentlemen, I guess it shall be boat cloaks all around, and hope these villains don't wonder why we look like a parcel of undertakers.'

A seaman was dispatched below to fetch up boat cloaks, and the marines were ordered to remove their beloved green regimentals, which led to much low and disgruntled muttering. Mr Gerrish had the Stars and Stripes down on the deck, was bending the Union Jack to the halyard rove through a jewel block at the peak of the gaff.

'Hold up there, Mr Gerrish!' said Rumstick, and Gerrish froze, the bunting in his hand. 'That's a jack, it ain't an ensign. It goes on the jack staff . . . which we ain't got,' he added after further reflection.

Biddlecomb turned from watching the vessels ahead of them to join the discussion. 'It can never go to the peak of the gaff, only an ensign should fly there. Any British midshipman would know as much.'

'But it's the only flag we have, sir,' Gerrish pointed out.

'The mainmast truck, perhaps?' Rumstick offered.

'I suppose . . .' Biddlecomb really was not certain what a schooner of the Royal Navy would fly, by way of flags. 'We have no paint or anything with which we might make up an ensign?'

'Not a damned thing. That villain Hoffman picked her clean, a roach would starve for want of a crumb.'

'Well, then, run it up to the mainmast truck, please, Mr Gerrish. We shall see who we fool, and for how long.'

More and more ships revealed themselves as the *Lady Biddlecomb* ran upriver in their wake – more men-of-war of all sizes, more transports, more victuallers. It was almost too much to be believed, that one nation could summon up such force and unleash it at will. And that this was only a portion of the Royal Navy, and the biggest men-of-war in this squadron were only third-rates, paltry in comparison to the first-rate ships of the line, seemed beyond comprehension.

And it was just those things, by Biddlecomb's reckoning – the size of the ships, the size of the fleet, the admixture of merchantmen and hired vessels – that was at that moment saving their bacon, for no one seemed to take the slightest notice of the schooner slowly passing up the line. He imagined that the captains, the lieutenants, the masters, of those big ships had their hands quite full navigating between the various mud banks and avoiding running aboard the ships in front of them.

What was more, he supposed that none of them could imagine a rebel schooner having the audacity to do what he was doing. He did not believe it himself.

'Here's the flag,' said Rumstick, nodding toward the two-decker they were now overtaking, the name *Eagle* in gold letters under the wall of glass and ornate carvings that made up her stern section. It rose like a cliff over the schooner, like the looming presence of a cathedral.

From the staff on the flagship's poop flew the white ensign, the cross of St George, the Union flag in the upper left quarter. It rippled and swelled in the breeze, draping itself over the unseen poop deck. At the foremast head flew a similar flag, lacking only the Union Jack.

'Viscount bloody Howe, Vice Admiral of the White . . .' Rumstick muttered, staring at the huge ship as they passed slowly up her starboard side.

'Sir,' asked Gerrish, 'should we salute the flag? I mean, as part of this charade, would that be the thing?'

'I am not certain . . . I don't believe so . . .'

'I think the regulations call for a salute only if the ships have not seen one another for six months or more. We're pretending to be part of this fleet, ain't we, Captain?' Rumstick offered.

'Just so. No, no salute.'

They had drawn ahead of the break of the *Eagle*'s quarterdeck when at last someone noticed them. 'Hoa! The schooner, ahoy!'

The officers looked up together. It was a lieutenant on the *Eagle*'s quarterdeck, peering over the hammock netting and calling through a speaking trumpet.

'Holloa!' Biddlecomb replied.

'Where is your ensign?'

'Blown out, sir! I've sent over for a new one!'

There was a pause, not a comfortable one. The lieutenant turned and spoke with someone on the deck, someone whom they could not see. He turned back to them.

'What schooner is that?'

'*Dispatch*!' Biddlecomb replied, naming the only British schooner he could recall on the North American station, hoped fervently that this fellow had no personal knowledge of that vessel. Of course, in another minute they would draw ahead of the *Eagle*'s quarterdeck, and the bright new name board on the

Lady Biddlecomb's transom would put the lie to that story.

The lieutenant brought the speaking trumpet to his lips again, paused before speaking. Looked back down to the *Eagle*'s deck, a frustrated look on his face, pulled between one thing and another. He looked back at the *Lady Biddlecomb*, then stepped down behind the bulwark.

'Curious bastard. Let us hope he is gone,' Rumstick said.

'Let us, indeed.' Biddlecomb looked up at the canvas aloft. Foresail and mainsail and the headsails. He wished very much to crack on; the wind was right for the square sails on the foremast, but he did not want to draw attention to what he hoped was an innocuous little vessel. He looked along the shoreline. The tide had turned, it was the first of the flood, but of course the nonpartisan current would carry all the ships faster, not limit its help to the Americans alone.

He looked back at the flagship. They were past her quarterdeck, up with her bows now, and the curious lieutenant was still nowhere to be seen. A minute more and they might be too far along for the man to read the name board.

'Chester is but a few miles away,' Biddlecomb observed, 'and Billingsport, just beyond that, is in American hands, we are given to understand. I should think these fellows' – he indicated the British fleet with a nod of his head – 'must anchor up in Chester. We shall stand on as we are and hope we are not challenged, then once we have Chester abeam, we shall crack on like the devil is on our heels and away upriver. Mr Rumstick, pray have all things in

201

readiness for the square foresail and fore topsail and the driver as well. But softly now, let us not give our purpose away.'

Rumstick went forward to see the things laid along in an unhurried manner, quite in conflict with his natural inclinations. The *Eagle* was astern of them, and nothing more had been heard from her. The vessel they were now passing was a victualler, a hired merchantman who would not give a tinker's cuss about the protocol of the schooner's bunting.

Biddlecomb could catch glimpses of Marcus Hook in the narrow gaps between the leading vessels, and beyond it a few of the outlying buildings of the town of Chester. An hour of daylight left, a few miles to go. This was the worst moment, when they were this close, when there was actual reason for hope.

On up the river, past the victualler, past two transports, past the mighty *Somerset*, which had once chased them clean across Boston Harbor. What would her captain think if he knew that that impudent little bastard Biddlecomb was under his guns again, Isaac thought. Let us hope he does not discover it.

And then they were past, with the *Somerset*, the first in the line of ships, turning away and making for the anchorage at Chester. How would the *Lady Biddlecomb* appear from her decks? A dispatch boat, bound for . . . where? It did not matter. They were clear of the fleet, and no questions had been asked, save for the query regarding their ensign.

'Mr Rumstick, let us have the squares and the driver, if you please,' Biddlecomb called out, and in a flash the men aloft laid out and let fall. The schooner heeled a few strakes more, her pace grew noticeably faster, as the canvas was sheeted home.

Six miles upriver, on the southern bank, lay Billingsport. Biddlecomb knew it well, just as he knew every foot of the river. Six miles to the American fortifications, and once past those, they were safe from the fleet.

The breeze, which had held steady all day, began to build with the setting sun, pushing the *Lady Biddlecomb* farther over, increasing the note of the water gurgling down her side. With the lift provided by the flooding tide they were moving along briskly now, probably eight or nine knots over the bottom.

They were no more than four miles off Billingsport when Biddlecomb saw the smoke, a great black column rising up and leaning to the northwest, where it was pulled apart and carried away on the wind. Something was burning, something more than a cookstove or an oven for heating shot.

'Sir, shall I strike the Union Jack?' Gerrish asked.

'No, hold a moment.' Perhaps Chester was not as far as the British fleet had gone. Was there perhaps a third advance squadron, one that had taken Billingsport?

He put his glass to his eye. There were ships at anchor in the river. One, two, three, and a sloop, all within a mile of Billingsport, and since they were not Continental ships, it meant that the fort could not still be in Continental hands.

'We've one more gauntlet yet, I fear,' Isaac said, snapping his glass closed. He looked aloft. The sails were drawing well, trimmed to perfection, the schooner was moving at a fine clip. The ships and the fort would not fire on her until they were certain that she was a rebel, and they would not be certain of that until she had sailed right past them and into the arms of the American forces, and then it would be too late. Tiny Billingsport might have been taken, but he could not imagine that Forts Mifflin and Mercer had fallen as well.

A mile from the fort they drew abeam of the first of the British men-of-war, a sloop of eighteen guns, which showed no interest in them. It was lucky that the flagship and the vanguard of the fleet had arrived at that moment; a strange schooner might have raised suspicion, but with so many vessels arriving at once, it went unnoticed.

Biddlecomb's attention moved to the next vessel, and then with a start he looked back at the sloop, muttered, 'Damn me all to hell . . .'

It was Smeaton's sloop, he was sure of it. There was that unmistakable figurehead – what it was supposed to be he did not know – but he would not forget it. The dull yellow paint on her sides, the black wales, the red below her gunwales, the queer arch of her taffrail – they were burned into his memory from when he had watched her drive his beloved *Charlemagne* to her death.

'Son of a bitch . . .' he muttered, pivoting as the *Lady Biddlecomb* sailed on, keeping his eyes on the hated sloop. So Smeaton was here, was probably aboard the sloop, not two cable lengths' away. But what chance was there of bringing him to a fight, one-on-one, of sticking a sword through him in appreciation for what he had done for Weatherspoon, releasing the boys' immortal soul from its frail human bonds? None he could think of.

'Captain, see here,' Rumstick was saying, and Biddlecomb pulled himself away from his vengeful reveries. He followed Rumstick's finger. The British flag was flying over Billingsport, and behind it rose the column of smoke.

'They take it and then burn it?' Biddlecomb asked.

'Looks that way, unless the defenders set her ablaze when they run. But I see no capital ships upriver, so I reckon this is as far as the damned British got.'

'For now.'

Billingsport was broad on the starboard bow and half a mile off; the sun was nearly to the horizon, right in the eyes of those watching from the fort. The *Lady Biddlecomb* was tearing along, racing upriver. Rumstick studied the fort through his glass. 'I see no sign they're alarmed. Don't seem to be much of anything going on.'

'Good. Another five minutes and we are past and safe.'

The fort was now all but abeam of them and still no alarm, no guns firing, none of the British ships slipping their cables in pursuit. It was too late for the British, the *Lady Biddlecomb* was safe, beyond their reach.

Isaac felt two days' worth of extraordinary tension sloughing off, felt himself relax, like the moment of lying down in bed and stretching out.

And then the *Lady Biddlecomb* shuddered underfoot, came to a crashing stop, going from eight knots to nothing in an instant. Isaac was flung forward, his feet going out from under him. He had a notion of the quarterdeck coming up at his face.

He hit with hands down and tumbled forward, his boat cloak wrapping around him as he rolled along the quarterdeck, Rumstick next to him. A glimpse of Gerrish going headfirst over the binnacle box. The sound of smashing, tearing wood, like a round shot striking home, but much, much worse.

He sat up, thrashed out of his cloak, looked up. The sails were set but the mainmast was leaning over, seconds away from going by the board. The *Lady Biddlecomb* was immobile, straining to make headway, moving not an inch.

Biddlecomb got to his feet, staggered forward. They had hit something, but he could not think what. There was not one submerged hazard in that part of the river, he knew it as sure as he knew his name.

He leapt down into the waist and down the ladder to the lower deck. He could hear water rushing in, could feel the schooner settling. He pushed his way forward, ducking low in the narrow space. Stopped short by the bow, gasped, said, 'Oh, dear God . . .'

Jutting out of a ragged hole in the deck was a great wooden shaft, its pointed, serrated, iron-tipped end dripping, gleaming in the dull light. The ship-killer barb of the *chevaux-de-frise*.

CHAPTER 14

Octob^r 1777
Monday 6th
Billings Port Fort E^t 2 miles
Fresh Breezes and Hazy Weather, at 2 p.m.
Anchored Here the Eagles Tender, at 4 d^o saw
Billings Port all in flames, Same time a Signal on
Board the Solebay *for Seeing 5 Sail in the SE Q^r*
. . . Saw His Majesty's Ship the Egle *anchor off*
Chester with Lord Howe's flag on Board.
               —JOURNAL OF HMS *CAMILLA*
                CAPT. CHARLES PHIPPS

Lieutenant Smeaton moved to the southwest corner of the redoubt that made up the outer defenses at Billingsport and pushed himself into the narrow corner overlooking the river. From there, the chief of the smoke from the burning barracks passed to the north of him and over the river, obscuring his view of Billings Island and the far Pennsylvania shore. The sun was settling behind the smoke, lighting it up orange and red from within, and that, mixed with the swirling tendrils of black and gray, made a rare and awesome sight.

Smeaton glanced at it, glad he was no longer choking to death on the acrid fumes, and turned his attention back downriver. He put his glass to his eye.

The *Merlin* was still at anchor a half a mile away, though he had no delusions about Reeve summoning him back on board. Billingsport had been taken, then largely evacuated, and now the barracks and other wood structures were being burned for whatever idiot reasons the army had decided upon. Only a small contingent was to be left in the fort, and he, of course, would be one of them. If only one man was to be left, Reeve would see to it that it was him.

Not that it mattered, the villain. Reeve would get his turn, after Biddlecomb.

Smeaton turned his glass downstream. The vanguard of the fleet was up with Chester; in fact the first of them, the *Somerset*, it looked like, was already on her hook.

His view of the big two-decker was cut off by the foresails of a schooner, heading upriver, already past Chester and the rest of the fleet. It looked for all the world like a Yankee boat, the Union Jack at the mainmast head notwithstanding.

Probably one of the many, many small vessels captured from the rebels. Bugger-all chance of making any prize money in this war, Smeaton thought. The rebels had so few ships that were worth anything.

The schooner was driving hard for Billingsport under all she could set. Carrying dispatches, no doubt, or orders of some sort.

There is the boat for me, he mused. If I am not to

208

be made master and commander at any time soon, a schooner such as that would answer well.

He watched the vessel draw closer, considered the advantages of such a command. Detached duty, carrying dispatches from one place to another, with no 'superior' officers looking over his shoulder. Call at this or that place, as he felt fit, and if he wished to tarry, if there was some lapse of time to explain, then a period of flat, calm weather could appear in the final drafts of the logs just as easy as you please, and no one the wiser. That way he could hunt Biddle-comb down, make inquiries, pass challenges, arrange meetings.

His thoughts moved along those lines as he stared aimlessly at the schooner, and it was a minute at least before he realized how odd her behavior was. He would have expected her to make for the *Roebuck* – that was the obvious destination for orders – but she had passed the big ship by and was still running upriver, still carrying everything aloft.

Possibly she was making for the fortifications, intending to drop the hook just below the *chevaux-de-frise* and send a boat ashore. Make a big show of hanging on to all her canvas until the last moment, a conspicuous display of alacrity for the admiral.

But if that was the case, then she was still pretty far out in the river, a half a mile away, in the center of the channel between Billingsport and Billings Island, and making right for the deadly submerged defenses. Was it possible that the master of the schooner was not aware of the danger? If he had just arrived with the fleet, then it was possible. It proved at least that he was no rebel, because a rebel would have known about the *chevaux-de-frise*.

209

Smeaton squinted, held his hand up to shield his eyes from the setting sun. The schooner showed no sign of slowing, no sign of altering course. 'What in the devil are you about?' he asked out loud, and then she struck.

It was the oddest sight, since the spike could not be seen above the surface – it looked as if there were nothing but unbroken water from shore to shore. The schooner was bowling along and then suddenly she just stopped, as if coming to the end of her leash, shuddering to a halt, the mainmast leaning forward with the momentum it still carried, ready to go by the board.

Almost instantly the schooner began to settle in the water, but she would not sink because she had speared herself on the *chevaux-de-frise*, and there she would remain, like the head of a traitor on a pike,

'And they give command to bloody idiots like that, and here I am a bloody second officer aboard a sloop!' Smeaton spoke out loud to himself again, thinking, I am starting to do that quite a bit. He scowled, shoved his glass in his pocket, walked fast back along the rampart. He was the only naval officer left at the fortification, left behind to supervise the crew of the *Merlin*'s longboat in pulling up the *chevaux-de-frise*, and as such it was up to him to go out and carry those idiots ashore. 'Forever pulling other's arses out of the fire,' he said.

He found the coxswain, Reid, and all of the boat's crew clustered on the inner ramparts, gawking at the schooner, the most diverting sight they had enjoyed in days, even more amusing than setting fire to the barracks.

'Reid, if you are quite done staring like an idiot, let

us get the boat under way and go and get those great chuckleheads off that heap of rubbish that was formerly a schooner.'

'Aye, sir. Come on, you lot,' Reid barked at the rest of the boat crew, then to Smeaton said, 'Pistols and cutlasses, sir?'

'What the devil for? Do you think our own people likely to attack us?'

'Well, beg pardon, sir, but watching that schooner, I weren't convinced she wasn't a Yankee-Doodle, not for certain.'

Smeaton was about to dismiss the man with a withering comment when he recalled a discussion along similar lines with the late Marine Lieutenant Page on a beach in New Jersey, so he said, 'Very well, pistols and cutlasses, if you think it so bloody important.'

Once the boat crew had gathered up their weapons, he led them out of the fort and down the worn path to the landing where the boat was tied. The sun was gone now, leaving only its glow behind, and the trail and the boat and the wrecked schooner in midriver were in deep shadows.

The crew tumbled into the longboat with practiced ease, taking their places on the thwarts, shipping oars, and giving way with only a few grunted orders from Smeaton.

It irked Smeaton to no end that this fool had run the schooner up on the *chevaux-de-frise*. That it would fall on him to get the wreckage clear was only a part of it. Now there was one less schooner for him to command, one less chance of his getting out from under Reeve's thumb. He was terribly far from a command of his own, he had no illusions on that score, still it irritated him that now there was one less dispatch boat in the service; that command had been given to someone clearly inept and he had made a hash of it.

Those dark thoughts occupied his mind as his men pulled with a steady, easy rhythm toward the wreck. The tide was flooding and Reid had to give her a bit of starboard helm to keep the longboat from also going on the *chevaux-de-frise*.

Night was coming on fast, the details of the wreck were indistinct, but Smeaton could see that her stern section had sunk, and only her forward end, about forty feet of it, from the midships to the bow, was still above water, hanging from the wicked spike. Her mainmast was gone but her foremast was still standing. Her people were clustered forward of that.

'Toss oars! In oars! Ready, lads!' Reid called out without consulting Smeaton, but Smeaton did not care. Let them play their games.

The oars came up, came inboard, and were laid along the thwarts as the tide and the way on the longboat carried it the last twenty feet to the wreckage. The forefoot of the boat hit the schooner's deck at the main-hatch coaming, where it emerged from the water, as if it were pulling itself to safety. The forwardmost men leapt out, the next two and the next two following, pistols unclipped from belts as soon as their feet found a grip on the slanting deck.

Smeaton could see no more than dark shadows and a huddle of people forward, but they seemed to be making no effort to get down to the boat, no effort to help, which was both odd and annoying.

'Here, stand out of my bloody way,' he growled, making his way forward, and the men who were

212

about to leap onto the schooner sat again and let him pass. He climbed over the gunwale, cursing as his shoe came down in a foot of water before it hit the sloping deck. He walked forward, uphill, toward the castaways near the knightheads.

'Here, now, who is the master of this vessel?' he called forward, trying to see through the dark. 'Doesn't anyone have a bloody lantern?' he asked the deck in general.

The answer that came from forward was not what he expected, not at all, for the accent was colonial, and the words, not addressed to him, were 'Front rank! Make ready!' followed by the sound of perhaps a dozen firelocks clicking into place. He felt suddenly hollow, a dried shell, as if the breeze might carry him away. It was the Jersey beach all over again.

'Jesus, Mary, and Joseph!' someone behind him cried, and then from forward another voice, another colonial accent, called, 'Do not move, do not any of you move or we shall fire into you!'

Smeaton rocked back as if he had been punched in the face. That voice, it was not possible! But that voice, how could he ever mistake it? He stepped forward, peered forward, the muskets aimed at him entirely forgotten.

'All of you there, drop your arms! Do it now!' A lantern snapped open, light spilled down the wet deck, onto the startled faces of the longboat crew. It danced across the small ripples on the river's surface.

'Biddlecomb?'

There was a pause, a silence, and no one moved. It seemed as if for that moment nothing in the whole world moved.

'Smeaton?'

The light came down the deck, was held higher, angled at him, and in the yellow glow around the edges Smeaton could see the man who was holding it, and that man was Isaac Biddlecomb. Smeaton's head swam, he felt his hands begin to sweat and shake. How could this be? How could this be?

'Smeaton. Dear God . . .' The words were soft, they carried all of the shock and surprise that he himself felt. And then Biddlecomb put the lantern down on the deck, balancing it on the hatch coaming so that the light shone up on them from below, making weird shadows on their faces. Biddlecomb stepped back, held a hand up to his people, said, 'Hold your fire! All of you, hold your fire!'

He pulled his sword and Smeaton pulled his as well, and a part of his mind noted how fine a weapon Biddlecomb's was, wondered how a Yankee-Doodle might have got his hands on such a blade. Smeaton understood that this meeting was something pre-destined, and with an insight that startled him he knew that Biddlecomb felt the same. This was more than the two of them, it was something much greater, much more profound than that.

'Put up your arms,' Smeaton called to his own men, his eyes never leaving Biddlecomb's. 'This is an affair of honor.'

He heard someone say, 'Isaac . . .' a low growl, wondered if it was the other one, Rumstick, but he paid no more attention to the vague warning than did Biddlecomb, and Biddlecomb paid no attention to it at all. The tips of their swords were wavering before them, steel seeking out steel, and they made little steps side to side, neither daring to make great moves on the wet and slanted deck.

214

Then Biddlecomb attacked, thrusting, catching Smeaton's blade, twisting, and Smeaton felt the grip of the sword starting to wrench from his hand. He twisted with Biddlecomb, not against him, freeing his sword before it was plucked away, stepped back, thrust, felt his sword knocked aside.

The first time it had been cutlasses, heavy, crude things that he was not accustomed to. But now he was fighting with his own blade, had always figured he would make short work of the Jonathan in that situation, but Biddlecomb had his own sword as well, and he used it to advantage. The bumpkin was not without some skill, but Smeaton would not have wanted it otherwise. How anticlimactic if he had killed him on the first pass!

Biddlecomb took a step up the deck and Smeaton took a step down, because Biddlecomb would not expect him to do that, and at the same time he lunged, attacking before Biddlecomb was settled in his stance.

He caught Biddlecomb unawares, and the rebel was just able to deflect the thrust, not hard enough to knock the blade away. Smeaton thrust again, felt his blade rasp against the target – bone or just a button, he could not tell – heard Biddlecomb gasp, saw him jump back.

'Bastard!' Smeaton cried, quite involuntarily, and prepared to lunge again. His foot came down in water, slipped on wet planking. He felt himself go down, twisting desperately so as to fall with his blade raised in some kind of defense.

He hit the deck on his right shoulder, looking up, sword in front. And there was Biddlecomb over him, lit from below by the lantern on the hatch, looking utterly insane.

He felt himself sliding down the deck and he kicked out to stop himself, but his shoes could find nothing but water. Biddlecomb's sword came down, and it stabbed into the deck with a heavy thud, exactly where Smeaton's throat had been half a second before.

Smeaton swung his sword in a great arc, felt it connect with Biddlecomb's, which was still planted in the deck. The momentum knocked it free, flung it back, twisted Biddlecomb around with the force. Smeaton saw the man's feet come up, felt the deck jar as Biddlecomb went down as well.

Smeaton rolled over on his stomach, his legs in water up to his knees, grabbed at the hatch coaming, pulled himself up the deck. On the edge of the lantern light he could see Biddlecomb thrashing to get to his feet. The first one up would be in a fine position to put a sword through the other.

Smeaton groaned, pulled his knees under him, put a foot flat on the deck. Then the dark was split by a great burst of flame, an explosion, the scream and rush of a ball passing close by. He staggered sideways, wondered if he had been shot. Thought, Is this what it is like to be shot? In that instant of flame and thunder he had seen the rebels huddled in the bow, lit from behind, had seen the shock on Biddlecomb's face as he too twisted around, stunned by the light and the noise.

A rebel gunboat. Smeaton realized at once what it was, one of the damned rebel gunboats that were forever dropping down to the *chevaux-de-frise* and firing on the fleet.

Damn the luck, damn it! he thought, even as he

216

and Biddlecomb found themselves again face-to-face, swords before them.

He heard a murmuring behind, his own men, fully aware of the danger they were now in, all but surrounded by rebels. He did not want to leave until Biddlecomb was bleeding his last – it seemed an affront to the Divine Being to do so, after the miracle of this meeting – but neither did he want to be a prisoner of the rebels, which was what he would be if he tarried a moment longer.

Smeaton took a stab at Biddlecomb, and Biddlecomb knocked the blade easily away, his eyes darting between Smeaton and the darkness from which the big gun had fired.

Biddlecomb did not know that the gun had been fired by a rebel, Smeaton realized. He did not know it was a friend coming down to him, and here was the chance to escape and to give the silky-tongued bastard a taste of his own.

The gunboat fired again, with the huge flame and noise of the single twenty-four-pounder carried in her bow, the ball screaming by in its trajectory for the anchored ships farther downriver.

Smeaton took a step back, moving with care lest he slip again, said, 'Here is our gunboat to collect you up. Do not think to fire on my men or it will go hard on you.' He took another step back. 'Reid, all of you, in the boat.' He heard his men clambering quickly into the longboat, but he kept his gaze locked on Biddlecomb's uncertain eyes.

'You son of a bitch!' Biddlecomb said, the words starting off as a growl, building, ending in a shout that seemed to propel him across the deck, sword slashing out, and Smeaton was just barely able

217

to fend it off. 'Running away, you coward? You bastard!' Biddlecomb said, gasping, putting all into the attack.

Coward. Bastard. Son of a bitch. The words were as insufferable as a blow, but Smeaton could hear the longboat pulling away. In a moment he would be left behind, and then even if he did kill Biddlecomb, he would be a prisoner of the rebels, and no doubt executed for killing their little hero.

Smeaton stepped back again, the water up to his knees, put a hand on the gunwale of the boat, held his sword in front of him, tip level with Biddlecomb's face. 'I shall seek you out, you bastard, and if you are not taken tonight' – which Smeaton knew he would not be – 'then meet me at dawn, the morning after next, on Billings Island right opposite of here.'

'As if I might trust you, you murdering bastard,' Biddlecomb growled.

Smeaton fixed him with his eyes, held his gaze, lowered his sword. 'An affair of honor.'

And Smeaton saw that the words had their intended effect, that Biddlecomb understood that on that point Smeaton could be trusted, trusted entirely. The rebel lowered his own sword an inch, said, 'An affair of honor.'

From the darkness beyond the bow of the wrecked schooner, Smeaton could hear the grind of oars, the rhythmic splash of long sweeps. The gunboat was coming down on them, but he could not take his eyes from Biddlecomb's.

And then he felt hands on his arms and shoulders, no gentle touch, but painful, crushing grips that lifted him bodily off the submerged deck and dragged him over the gunwale and dropped him in an ignominious heap on the longboat's floor-boards.

He lay there, looking up. The stars were blotted out by the great pall of smoke still rising from the barracks in Billingsport. The gunboat fired again, the flash lighting up the grim faces of the boat crew as they stroked like furies for the shore. He heard Biddlecomb's voice calling, 'Hold your fire! Hold your fire!' but he did not know if Biddlecomb was talking to the gunboat or his own people, or who might be firing at whom.

It was incredible, this meeting, but Smeaton felt himself overcome with a wonderful calm, as when hard liquor first begins to take hold. Here was proof of his destiny, proof of divine intervention.

Why had he said the day after next? Why had he not said tomorrow? Because he had been summoned back to the *Merlin* for a council in the morning, he recalled. And here was more proof of the divine hand, for even though he had forgotten the council he had been prevented from setting a date that he would not have been able to keep. He felt sick just thinking on it, just imagining how Biddlecomb would construe it as cowardice.

But it had worked out, and there would be no intimations of cowardice, for there was no cowardice in his heart.

And on the morrow, one day hence, his destiny would be fulfilled.

CHAPTER 15

Delaware *frigate of [f] Philad.*
Sr.
*its my Entintion to Prevent the Efusion of Blod as
mush as in My pour therfore I do Aquant you if
you Atimpt to throw Up Any Works So as to Anoay
Any Vessils from Passing or Repassing I shall Give
Orders for the City to be Demolished I am with
Mutch Respt.*
[&c.]

—CAPT. CHARLES ALEXANDER
TO THE COMMANDING OFFICER OF THE
BRITISH ARMY AT PHILADELPHIA

Freeman, McGinty, and the rest came back from
their foraging excursion well laden with food: a half
dozen gammons, a barrel of pork that had apparently
once been property of the British army, flour, corn
pone for ash cake, dried peas, and a fresh leg of
mutton; as well as small beer and, to Foote's great
relief, tobacco. The Gloucester County farmers had
been quite forthcoming when presented with a dozen
loaded muskets on the one hand and ready money on

the other, and they bade the men come back if they needed more.

McGinty selected two of the younger men as volunteer cooks and dispatched them to the galley. Freeman returned the money that remained in his purse. They all ate well that night, and the next morning, and by midafternoon it seemed to be generally understood, if not actually verbalized, that the men of the Fifth Pennsylvania would be on their way that evening.

They had just sprawled out on the quarterdeck, enjoying an after-dinner smoke or plug, each to his preference, when the cannonade began. McGinty was the first to hear it, sitting bolt upright from his nearly supine position, cocking an ear to the southward and saying, whispering really, 'Now, bloody hell, what's all that?'

The others sat up as well and listened. It started with one gun, then another and another, and soon the firing was continuous, off to the southwest and not so far. In the city, it would seem.

Foote stood, spit a stream over the side. 'Let's go have us a look,' he suggested.

The men took their now familiar places in the longboat, glad to be rowing without the six hundred tons of frigate towing behind, and made their way south, past Petty's Island, toward the main part of the Delaware River. The northern end of the city came into view, and the gunfire grew louder.

They came at last to the dogleg point on the Jersey shore, and before them, to the south, all of the city lay spread out, though indeed they could see little of it through the pall of smoke left by the steady discharge of the guns. A few of the taller buildings away from the river could be seen, as well as the various spires jutting up, but most of the waterfront was lost in the gray cloud. The breeze would pick the smoke up in great blankets and lift it away, allowing for a glimpse beyond before it was quickly replenished by the British batteries on the shore.

The object of the artillerymen's attention lay at anchor about five hundred yards from the waterfront: a frigate, the Stars and Stripes waving from her ensign staff, her own battery belching smoke and round shot at her enemies ashore. There was another ship as well, somewhat smaller, adding her firepower to the cannonade. Around them clustered a few small vessels, gunboats and such, also firing at the shore, but the frigate and the other ship were doling out and receiving the worst of it.

'*Delaware* and *Montgomery*,' Foote said.

'What was that, now, Mother Foote?'

'The big ship's the *Delaware*, the rotten tub, built by Coates. Continental frigate. The other's the *Montgomery*, Pennsylvania Navy. What they think they're about, I don't know, but it happens they're the two most powerful ships on the river, on the American side.'

'They'll not be for long,' McGinty observed. The men rested on their oars, the longboat's bow pointed upstream, and every moment or so McGinty gave the word for a pull or two of the sweeps, to keep them in place, as the current set them down toward the city and the murderous cannonading. They watched the *Delaware* take a brutal pounding, watched the *Montgomery*'s foremast go by the board, and then her main, which dragged the better part of her mizzen down with it.

'Well, that *Delaware*, the stupid bastard,' Freeman growled, 'he'd better pass a tow to *Montgomery* and get the hell out of there.'

Foote had been thinking much the same thing; if the British were to be held downriver, if his *Falmouth* was to remain safe, then those two ships would be desperately needed in the fight. But it was McGinty who spoke next.

'Too bloody late. They're done for, both of them.'

'Shut yer gob, Teague,' Foote growled. He did not want to hear that.

'I'd not lie to you, Ma Foote. Look at the bight in your *Delaware*'s anchor hawse. She's aground, and the tide falling still.'

Foote squinted, frowned, saw what McGinty was talking about. The anchor hawse was hanging slack, which meant that the ship was not pulling on the anchor, which could only mean she was aground. The ebb was not very old, it would be hours before she would float again, and there was not one chance she could live for hours through the beating she was taking.

The soldiers floated there for another half an hour, watching with horror and fascination. They saw smoke rising from the *Delaware*, smoke of a color and consistency altogether different from that of the gunsmoke, and they knew she was on fire. Ten minutes after that, the Stars and Stripes was hauled down. The men of the Fifth Pennsylvania took up their oars and pulled slowly back to the *Falmouth*. No one said a thing.

The deserters did not leave that day, nor the next, and it was soon understood that they were not going to leave at all, and so by unspoken consensus they

223

settled into a routine, daily rounds of shipkeeping, watchkeeping, and housekeeping.

September gave way to October, and the men aboard the *Falmouth* heard nothing more of fighting, save for occasional gunfire way off downriver. They kept a constant watch for British patrols, by land or water, but none appeared. It was as if they had towed the frigate to a different country, a land that had never seen warfare, for all the attention that was paid to them. And with Petty's Island blocking all view of Philadelphia it was difficult to believe that they were only three miles from their capital, the biggest city in America, now occupied by the most powerful army on earth.

The food ran out in the first week of October and the men gathered again, and again Foote gave Freeman what money he had and sent them off to purchase what they needed.

Foote waited until the soldiers were a mile away before gathering up his chisels, his bosun's chair, his several pots of paint. He slung the chair over the beakhead, settled in, let his eyes wander over her face, her hair and dress, let the wood tell him where it had to be shaved away. Just the finest of passes along her straight, thin nose, a sliver from her upraised arm for a suggestion of strength. Taut, lean muscle under perfect skin.

He did not even hear them approach, so utterly focused was he on her flowing perfection. McGinty's big voice made him jump, nearly drop his chisel. 'Ahoy there, Mother Foote, put it back in your breeches, now!'

Foote clamped his mouth shut, stared hatred at the big Irishman, felt his face flush red. Too angry even to tell him to shut his gob. He swung inboard, untied the bosun's chair, climbed up the ladder to the forecastle head. The soldiers were coming alongside in the longboat, but Foote ignored them, went below, and stowed his tools away.

He heard them coming up the side. Scowled, did not care to hear any of McGinty's shit. They had come to something of a truce between them, him and McGinty, hostilities limited to a few sharp words now and again. But Foote did not want to hear anything about . . . her. His strong feelings on the subject embarrassed him, and that made him angrier still.

He stamped up the ladder to the quarterdeck where the soldiers were depositing their newly acquired provisions. 'Ah, Mother Foote, I hope you satisfied yourself before we—'

'Stow it, Teague.'

McGinty nodded toward the bow. 'She would be Mistress Foul-Mouth, am I right?'

'Shut yer fucking gob, Teague, I mean it,' Foote growled, but McGinty was having fun now.

'Now, Ma, I meant no offense. But do ya know, I do believe I thrummed the little bunter that sat for you for the figurehead? Or sat on you, as it may be.'

'Son of a bitch!' Foote growled, felt his hand go for his sheath knife, felt the knife clear the leather as he leapt forward, grabbed a handful of McGinty's collar, jerked the Irishman toward him as if he were a child.

'Oh, will ya?' McGinty's hands were on Foote's collar, jerking him aside. The knife came around and then stopped in midswing, as if Foote's wrist had hit a thick tree limb. A blur of faded blue, and Freeman tore Foote's hand from McGinty's collar, grabbed McGinty himself, shoved him back five feet.

Foote struggled to free his wrist, but Freeman possessed a surprising strength; no other man aboard could have held Foote's wrist against his will. At last he twisted his arm free, but his rage was a flash in the pan and he put his knife back in its sheath.

Freeman turned to McGinty. 'Get the fuck out of here, Angus.' McGinty hesitated, long enough to let everyone know that he was going of his own volition, not by Freeman's orders or Foote's threats, and then he tramped off below.

Foote met Freeman's eyes, scowled, was met with an unwavering glare. Foote turned and stamped off aft.

The shipwright bit a mouthful off his plug, chewed it slowly, leaned on the taffrail, and stared down at the water. Anger and embarrassment at his excessive reaction, a longing to stick his knife in McGinty, churned in his head, along with fear of losing the *Falmouth* and a profound hatred of them all, British, Americans, all the warmongers. But Foote was not a man given to introspection; he just let it rage as he chewed and stared.

After some time – Foote had no notion of how long – Freeman came aft and leaned on the taffrail next to him. Foote braced for whatever idiot thing he might say, there was nothing he cared to hear, but Freeman just chewed his own plug and stared down as well.

Foote had almost forgotten the soldier's presence when Freeman finally spoke. 'McGinty's got a big mouth, but he ain't so bad, you know.'

Foote spit a stream overboard, looked up at Freeman. 'That's half-true, I'll warrant.'

226

Freeman spit as well. 'He saved our bacon. We'd all be dead or prisoners of the damned British if it weren't for him.'

'My arse.'

'It's a fact. At Brandywine.'

The two men looked down at the water again. After a space Foote said, 'Very well, Freeman, I can see you're with goddamned child to tell it, so tell it.'

Freeman stood up straight, rolled his quid in his cheek. In fact he didn't look that anxious to tell it, but it was hard to imagine Freeman looking anxious about much. Then, as if coming to a decision, he said, 'Right then, I will.'

CHAPTER 16

Describe the Battle. 'Twas not like those of Covent
Garden or Drury Lane. Thou hast seen Le Brun's
paintings and the tapestry perhaps at Blenheim . . .
There was a most incessant shouting, 'Incline to the
right! Incline to the left! Halt! Charge!' etc. The
balls plowing up the ground. The Trees crackling
over one's head. The branches riven by the artillery.
The leaves falling as in Autumn by the grapeshot.
> —A BRITISH OFFICER
> DESCRIBING THE BATTLE OF BRANDYWINE

The heat of August had lingered into September, and
on the morning of the eleventh it remained oppressive, muggy, the air still. The Fifth Pennsylvania was
spread out north of Chad's Ford, looking west.
Down a sloping, grassy field in front of them, across
a dry road and a marshy area of tall grass, the
Brandywine Creek ran blue and inviting.

Corp. Nathaniel Freeman, Second Platoon, Third
Company, sat beside the company's stacked arms,
Indian style, his regimental coat discarded for the
moment. The Fifth had been newly outfitted not

nine months before, and they displayed a uniformity not often seen on the Continental line. The uniform consisted of a dark blue coat faced with white, buckskin breeches, and blue stockings, and a surprising number of the men were dressed just that way. Still, Freeman knew the day would be hot, and he found himself envying those troops who had no regimentals, had naught but torn shirts and breeches to wear.

'Ah, Freeman, lad, there you are!'

Sgt Angus McGinty came lumbering up, his normally pink face flushed red with exertion and heat, beads of sweat standing out on his forehead. He had his musket over one shoulder, a dozen canteens over the other.

'McGinty. Why don't you sit down before you fall down?'

'I believe I will, lad, I believe I will.' He sat and pulled a twist of tobacco from his haversack, bit off a piece, and handed the twist to Freeman, who bit off a piece as well and handed it back. They sat silently, side by side, and stared past the creek at the great clouds of dust rising up in the southwest, dust kicked up by an enemy on the move: Howe, Cornwallis, the German butcher Knyphausen.

It was rolling country, low green hills covered with close-cropped grass and dotted with thick stands of wood, some of them acres across, some no bigger than a city lot. Dusty roads cut through here and there. The occasional farm or cluster of buildings, a tavern huddled up against the roads. The enemy troops themselves were hidden beyond the ridges of hills like the one on which the two Continental soldiers were sitting and watching.

'Now those lads, I should think, are right warm, marching about in their finery on such a morning,' McGinty said, pointing with his chin toward the dust. 'And we shall be all rested for them, when they come.'

'Reckon they're better fed than us,' Freeman said. The supply wagons had been pulled back two days before, and the troops had survived on whatever they could buy or beg from the local farmers.

'Oh, as to that, have no fear, boy-o. And hasn't Angus McGinty secured us potatoes and butter and a fine big gammon for our breakfast? Do you see yonder, that they are cooking it up now?'

Freeman twisted around to see where McGinty was pointing. A fire was burning, one hundred feet back, and over it a big black kettle hung from a tripod, carefully tended by one of the company's wives. Freeman felt his mouth water, a reflex he would not have thought boiled potatoes could inspire. He spit tobacco juice on the grass.

'Third Company'll have a full belly, sure, for today's amusements,' McGinty said, 'And that leaves but the problem of the platoon's water for the fighting . . .'

Freeman looked at the pile of canteens on the grass, and up at McGinty's pale blue, disingenuous eyes. He did not speak.

'You see, boy-o, we had a drawing of straws for the one who would fill the canteens, and you lost, as it happened.'

Freeman just stared at him and chewed.

'Oh,' McGinty explained, 'I drew for you, and you looking so contemplative here, I had not the heart to disturb you, but it was fair as ever could be.'

At last Freeman could not help but smile at the man's outrageous mendacity. He stood and collected up the canteens. 'You are a lying bastard of a feather merchant, McGinty. Next time just ask me to fill the damned canteens.'

'Oh, but, laddie, this is the United States of America! We are all great republicans here.'

Freeman slung the canteens over his shoulder. 'Lying about some drawing of straws ain't my idea of great republicanism,' he said, then headed off down the sloping field.

He came to the bottom of the hill and pushed himself through the tall grass that fringed the road, then crossed the road itself, his shoes crunching in the dirt and kicking up little clouds from the dry and dusty surface. He worked his way through the tall grass on the other side, through the soft earth, and down to the Brandywine Creek.

He laid the canteens down on the ground and stretched, breathed deep, turned his face toward the sky. It was a beautiful morning, with the sun making the earth warm and dry. He could hear the sounds of insects humming and buzzing, could smell the fragrance of the warm ground and of the green and brown bracken. And under it all was the Brandywine, calling with its soft, babbling voice.

He opened his eyes, looked down. A bird flittered up, black with bold orange patches on wing and tail, paused for a second in its relentless search for food, and then was gone.

Another deep breath, another luxurious stretch. Freeman was unwilling to let the moment go, one of those rare instances of privacy and peace for a soldier in the field. The irony of McGinty's silly charade was that Freeman would have volunteered in a minute to fill the canteens, for just this reason, as lowly as the job might be.

But he could not remain there all day, nor did he want to. That stretch of the creek was just north of Chad's Ford and the American center. Peaceful as it was, it would likely become a killing ground before the day was out. He grabbed up the canteens and waded out into the stream, relished the cool water flowing around his feet and soaking his stockings as he thrust the first empty container under the water.

He had just finished with the third canteen when the British artillery started in. There was no warning, no break in the otherwise tranquil morning, and then the flat thump of a fieldpiece, six-pounder by the sound of it, somewhere across the creek and to the south.

Freeman stood motionless in the stream, his ear turned to the fading report, and then the full battery let go. It was too far away to be an immediate threat, too far even for the noise to be bothersome, but it did mean the peace of the morning was over, that there would be no peace at all until nightfall, at the earliest.

He looked south. He could see the gray smoke rising above the ridge that stood between himself and the British artillery park, and on occasion the dark streak of a ball in flight. More artillery opened up, farther upstream from the first, more directly in line with where Freeman was standing. And then suddenly there was gunfire from behind him as well, the American gunners responding to the enemy's salute.

It was an odd place to be, between and below the

artillery barrage. On the hill on either side of the creek men were firing at one another, six-pound balls shot into dense groups of artillerymen with tremendous velocity, but below it, here in the creek, he was safe, even though he was probably closer to the enemy than any other American.

Freeman shook his head, chased the pointless speculation away. 'Standing here gawking like a motherless idiot,' he chastised himself, and turned back to the job at hand. One by one he dunked the canteens in the cold water, felt the buoyancy leave them as they filled, plugged them, took up the next.

He had eight of the twelve filled when he sensed something across the water. He paused, looked up. Freeman was not a city boy like some in the regiment, he had grown up on the frontier, had hunted since he was eight and had a sense for the woods that went beyond what he could see or hear.

In this case he could see nothing, but he remained motionless, poised and alert. A crow lifted off from the woods on the other side of the creek, squawking in protest, and flew away to the north. Freeman watched him, thought, That is not good.

He gathered up the canteens and backed away toward the shore, his eyes on the woods across the Brandywine. A flash, a puff of smoke, the crack of a gun, and he felt the canteens jerk in his hand. He looked down, saw one of them was shattered. He continued to step back, quicker now, his eyes on the far shore. He saw a head pop up, a black cocked hat, a green regimental coat that might have been lost among the foliage were it not for the red facings and cuffs.

'Jaegers,' Freeman spit, 'bloody, goddamned

233

Hessian jaegers.' Sent out ahead of the main body to probe for weaknesses in the Continental line. Not a group he cared to tangle with, not alone. But they were a long musket shot from him and could not cross the creek there, so far above the ford, so Freeman did not think himself in any great danger. He felt the shallow bank underfoot, turned his back to the Germans and disappeared into the tall grass.

He made his way back uphill, laboring against the climb and the weight of the full canteens. On the ridge to his right the American artillery was giving back almost as good as it was getting, the swarms of men around the mismatched fieldpieces attending to them like slaves to Egyptian kings of old. Each gun crew was loading and firing at will, and there was rarely a second during which one gun at least did not go off.

At last he came to the place where he had left his regimental coat. He deposited the company's canteens in a heap on the grass, looked around for McGinty.

He saw the Irishman over by where the potatoes had been cooking, and he looked as if he were possessed by demons. He was twirling around, arms flapping as if he were trying to fly. In those seconds between the guns going off, Freeman could hear McGinty's voice, loud with rage, though he could not make out what he was saying.

Freeman struggled into his coat, the time for informality being past, and ambled over to McGinty. A stray ball from the British artillery had gone wide of its target and by unhappy chance had struck the kettle dead center, tearing it and its contents apart, spreading bits of the pot and the tripod, potato, and ham over ten square yards. The woman who had been attending to the cooking sat on the grass, her eyes wide, the ladle still clutched in her hand. She seemed unhurt, save for the shock of the thing.

'Bloody piss-poor luck,' Freeman said when McGinty finally settled down, and he meant it. Since McGinty had first mentioned it, Freeman had been looking forward to a buttered potato with something akin to lust. He could not recall when he had been more disappointed.

McGinty glared at him, and then the irrepressible smile was back on his face and he said, 'Ah, the fortunes of war, boy-o. Though your hangdog face has done wonders to restoring me good humor!' He slapped Freeman on the back, called to the company to come and get their canteens.

Ten minutes later the order to form up came down the line, and the men of the Fifth Pennsylvania, along with the others standing on the ridge north of Chad's Ford, assembled in ranks. They were poised, ready to sweep down on the enemy's flank when their guns stopped and they made their drive across the shallows and into the American center, for such was surely their intent.

They waited for an hour. An hour and a half. Two hours. The anxiety of pending battle dissipated as the guns continued to pound and the British showed no sign of following up their artillery barrage with a frontal assault.

Noon came and the men were able to scrape up some little dinner, enough to keep the worst of the hunger at bay, and still the guns played on each other. Tension gave way to exhaustion, the men physically unable to maintain that degree of readiness, and one by one they sat and then reclined, and some even slept.

Second platoon, Third Company were all sitting, the dozen men occupying their little section of the Continental line. They were the northern end of the Fifth Pennsylvania, the right flank of Gen. Anthony Wayne's division. A little to their north was the left flank of Gen. John Sullivan's troops, to which they were linked.

Their captain, Caldwell, was off to the Lord knew where, searching for arse of a superior rank to kiss, as he generally was. Freeman and McGinty sat side by side, looking out over the Brandywine, over the hills at the flashes and the low-hanging smoke. Their ears were quite immune to the sounds of gunfire, they had been listening to it for hours and they no longer heard it.

It was strange, very strange indeed, sitting there, inactive, bored even, while the opening salvo of a great battle went on and on and on. Finally Freeman could stand no more. 'Here, McGinty, these are your people, why don't they attack us?'

McGinty grinned, did not rise to the provocation. 'Not my people, laddie. More your people than mine, for there are those who would still call a Yankee an Englishman, but an Irishman has never been thought of as such, and I pray to Jesus, Mary, and Joseph that he never will. But as to when they'll attack, I say, soon, boy-o, soon.'

And then the rumor, flashing along the line like electricity; they had been flanked. Cornwallis and Howe had stolen a march around their right, seven thousand British regulars forming up on Osborne's Hill, ready to drive into the American rear. It was

Long Island all over again, they said, and no hope of a rainstorm to stop them this time.

The exhaustion born of an excess of tension was gone, and Second Platoon, Third Company, the Fifth Pennsylvania, all of the Continental line formed up along the Brandywine, were alert again. The men were standing again, rechecking weapons, staring about, speculating. Officers rode up and down the line, rumor following in their swirling dust, but still the troops did not move. Another hour, and once more the edge began to dull.

'Ain't this always the goddamned way?' Freeman said at last. 'God, could they just let us fight instead of all the fucking waiting?'

But there was movement along the line, actual movement to their north. Stirling's division was on the march, and Stephen's turning away from the river and quick-stepping inland. The buzz of speculation grew in direct proportion to the number of troops realigning themselves.

And then Sullivan's division began to move, the division to which the Fifth Pennsylvania was hooked. Twenty minutes later they were gone, and Third Company became the right flank of the Contintental line.

'Captain, sir! Captain!' McGinty called out. Caldwell was riding by on his chestnut mare, the only captain in the regiment who kept a horse. He looked crisp, buttons, sword hilt, and boots shining in the sun, a model of soldierly decorum. Caldwell loved everything about soldiering, save for the doing of it.

He wheeled his horse to stop in front of his company. Freeman spit on the ground. He knew

Caldwell thought himself a grand fellow, condescending to talk to the regular troops. 'Yes, Sergeant?'

'Beg pardon, sir, but what's acting? We're hearing a power of rumors here.'

'Bloody Cornwallis has stolen the march on us again. You would think the great Incompetent-in-Chief would figure it out by the third time.' Caldwell spun his horse, pointed dramatically to the north. 'Do you see Osborne's Hill there? They are forming up now.'

The company's eyes turned north. A few low whistles, a few muttered curses. Four miles away they could see Cornwallis's troops, a long scarlet line along the ridge of the hill. It seemed to go on and on, a great red wave that would sweep forward over everything in its path. Bayonets flashed in the sun like fireflies, hundreds of them, thousands of them. The British had marched around the Americans' unprotected right flank and come up right behind their line.

'Stephen and Sullivan and Stirling and them are realigning themselves, forming up to meet Cornwallis,' Caldwell went on, happy to display his own grasp of the strategic situation. 'We are to remain put. Remember, men, we are now the right flank of the Continental line. If they hit us in the center, across Chad's Ford, as well they might, it is up to us to hold them to their side of the creek!'

McGinty saluted, and Caldwell saluted back and then rode off. 'Thinks he's a bloody general, thinks he's bloody Alexander the fucking Great,' McGinty said, still smiling at the departing captain.

'More he can make himself at home at headquarters, less chance he'll be where the lead is flying about,' Freeman said.

'Is it any wonder he hates Gen. George Washington, and the old man's always putting himself in harm's way? It can only set a bad example, and next it will be expected of all officers to risk being shot at.' McGinty pulled a watch from his pocket and flipped open the cover, then squinted up at the sun. 'Half-past three. If they don't bloody get on with it, there'll be no fight today.'

Freeman was about to sit, to let the exhaustion overwhelm him, when a new sound reached his ears, a thin, delicate sound, just audible in those seconds between gunfire. He frowned, cocked his ear. It was music, far off. He looked toward Osborne's Hill. The scarlet wave was rolling forward, as steady and straight as the countryside would allow, a long, impenetrable line. A lull in the gunfire and he caught enough of the music to recognize the tune. The British Grenadier.

They were all on their feet now, backs turned to the Brandywine, watching the British troops marching, marching toward a head-on collision with the American troops that had been shifted to face them. They could see parts of the Continental line where they were spread out along the crests of the hills, but it was broken, rolling, and partially wooded country, and that prevented anyone from seeing too far in any direction. Soon sections of the British line also disappeared from sight into the low areas between the high ground.

And then the British batteries ceased fire. The low, distant rumble was gone, the thunder cut by half, and soon the American guns fell silent as the gunners realized that no one was firing back.

It was quiet along the line, the strangest sensation,

after six hours of artillery barrage. 'Any moment now, lads . . .' McGinty said, and then, as if he had conjured it up with his words, the distant battle commenced. A great spattering of musket fire, a cloud of smoke rising above a hillside, drums, bugles, more muskets, field artillery going off here and there. The men of the Fifth Pennsylvania stood watching, four miles back, glad that it was not them in the path of the scarlet wave.

And then hoofbeats coming down the line and Freeman thought Caldwell was back, but it was not him, it was another officer, Maj. Edward Fitzgerald, from Washington's staff. Freeman had seen him before, knew that unlike Caldwell he was not a man given to dramatics. He wheeled his horse to a stop, looked around, scowled, demanded, 'Where is Captain Caldwell?'

'Beg pardon, sir.' Lieutenant Walton stepped forward, young and unsure and now nominally in command of Third Company. 'Beg pardon, but I thought he was off at headquarters.'

Fitzgerald continued to scowl. 'Well, never mind that. Lieutenant, I want you to form up closer on the left and incline your company down toward the creek, anchor the line there as best you can. We are expecting a thrust across Chad's Ford, and you might be in a position to turn their flank.'

'Yes, sir.' Walton saluted, clearly unsure of the orders. Fitzgerald looked at him, annoyed, then apparently decided he had no more time to waste with him so he returned the salute and rode off.

'Up, lads, up!' McGinty boomed, even before Walton had a chance to speak. 'You heard the major! It's all up to us, again, to save their bloody arses!

Come along, to the left, incline!' To Lieutenant Walton's evident relief the Irishman got the men into a semblance of a line and swept them forward and down the hill, until they were in a position angling away from the Brandywine Creek and more or less facing downstream toward Chad's Ford.

They had closed to a hundred yards north of Chad's Ford, were still dressing ranks, when the enemy hit the American center. British troops and German poured down the road and splashed into the creek, led by the Hessian fusiliers in their tall, shining caps.

They came at a charge, bayonets held low, screaming in their ugly guttural language. Halfway across the Brandywine, their momentum building, they ran right into a solid sheet of musket fire from the Americans clustered around the ford, the very point where Washington had expected the enemy to attack. The Hessians fell like ninepins, tossed aside, falling back on the men behind. Freeman could see men hit by a dozen balls at once, their feet lifting clean of the water as they were blown away.

But still the Hessians came, trampling their dead comrades in their effort to get across and use their bayonets against the Americans. More volleys from the shore, and now artillery as well, grape into the packed troops, and rank after rank fell.

'Come on, lads! Come on!' McGinty was shouting, standing ten feet in front of the company and waving them forward. Caldwell was nowhere to be seen, and Lieutenant Walton, white-faced, trembling, barely able to hold his sword, was not about to give orders, so McGinty took it upon himself. With a shout the Third Company rolled forward, some on

241

the dusty road that bordered the creek, some running along the sloping hill, and the Sixth Company, hooked to their left flank, rolled forward as well.

The Germans kept coming, kept coming, splashing into Chad's Ford and dying under the grape and musket fire. Freeman could see the bodies bobbing in the water, brown and red, a horrible mess of stirred earth and blood.

'Halt!' McGinty shouted, and the company stopped. 'Take care to fire by ranks! Front rank – make ready!' The company formed up, no thought involved, brought muskets up to shoulders. They were twenty-five yards from the ford, looking right at the Hessians' flank as the Germans pushed on, reaching farther and farther across the creek, as if the pressure of all those men behind were pushing them forward, despite the murderous fire from the Continental line.

'Fire!' and Freeman fired, felt the heavy jolt of the musket against his shoulder. Brought the musket down. His hand reached for another cartridge. He did not even think to look at what damage the volley might have done, could not have seen it anyway, for the smoke. His fingers found a cartridge, his teeth tore the end off, his thumb clamped down on the torn paper and poured a bit into the pan.

Over his shoulder the rear rank fired. Then he was pulling his rammer free, cocking the firelock, shouldering the weapon. Over the barrel he saw the situation; dead men, hundreds of them, it seemed, floating faceup, facedown in the river. Some crawling pathetically through the shallows. He saw a Hessian pause as his tall, silver cap was plucked from his head. He turned, looking for it, and then he was shot dead.

242

But the first of the Hessians were more than halfway across the ford. They would not be stopped. Slowed down, killed by the dozens, but not stopped.

All of those thoughts Freeman had in the half second before McGinty's big voice shouted, 'Front rank! Fire!' Freeman squeezed the trigger again, felt the jolt, and again began the rote mechanics of loading his musket. The smoke was thick, blotting out parts of the battlefield, the smell of it in his mouth and nose stirring up all sorts of memories, few of them good.

He brought his gun back to his shoulder, looked over the barrel at the enemy. They were a solid line, stretching from the west side of the Brandywine to the east. The Germans had made it across, were coming to grips with the Americans, hand to hand. He saw the blue coats of Hessian regulars, and redcoats as well as British units charged into the fight.

'Front rank! Fire!'

Blast, jolt, recovery.

'Fix bayonets!'

Freeman reached around his side and his hand closed over the round socket of his bayonet, and he pulled it out and locked it onto the end of his musket.

'March! March!' McGinty shouted, and Third Company stepped off, moving fast into the fight. Freeman could see little of what was going on: swirls of gray smoke, men moving in and out, muskets and pistols firing, Germans, British, and Americans locked in battle.

'Charge bayonets!' McGinty called, and Freeman slapped the butt of his musket under his right arm, wrapped his left hand around the barrel, and moved faster toward the fray. Lieutenant Walton was just to his left, his sword over his head, screaming, and Freeman was screaming too. Then Walton pitched forward and Freeman thought he had tripped until he saw the gushing wound in the lieutenant's neck where he had been hit by a musket ball. And then the officer was behind them, forgotten already as they plunged bayonets first into the fight.

It was a melee, desperate and confused, as the Americans tried to push the enemy back into the river and the enemy surged forward into their ranks, scattering them, breaking up the integrity of the companies and regiments, leaving them leaderless. Third Company was hitting them on the flank, and for a second the Germans did not see them coming and they paid the price for that.

Freeman hit the first man he came to, a Hessian, drove the long point of his bayonet into the man's side, just under his arm, heard the prolonged scream, saw the wide eyes, the blood flecking the thick mustache, the tall metal cap slewing sideways. He pulled the weapon free, turned to meet a bayonet coming at him, turned the blade aside, lunged and missed.

The Continentals fought with the passion of men defending their home, but the enemy fought with the coolness of trained and seasoned professionals, and inch by inch the Americans gave ground.

They were fully involved now, each man locked in his own private fight, with no thought for grand strategy, no thought for anything beyond the five-foot reach of his own bayonet-tipped musket. The world was lost in the smoke and the noise. No one

244

was giving orders. There was no plan. It was only fighting, desperate and awful, and Freeman had seen more of it than he cared to.

Then there came a shouting, a cheering, a yelling on the left. Freeman saw men running, a swirl of activity. Something had happened, something had turned the tide, one way or another. He knew the signs.

And then McGinty loomed up in front of him, hat gone, his face bright red, shouting in a voice that would carry over the din, 'Third Company! Third Company! Form on me! Fall back! Fall back!' He grabbed Freeman's arm, held it, shouted in Freeman's face, 'Bloody German butchers crossed at Pyle's Ford, downriver! The whole fucking left flank has collapsed! They took the artillery!'

'Third Company!' McGinty shouted again. It was as if he were calling dead men from the grave, but Third Company heard him and fell back and formed up, and he led them away from the fight, stepping backward, firing all the while.

The Germans and the British were pushing the Americans back in all directions, more and more troops splashing through the bloody water at Chad's Ford, and more coming up on the left. Artillery opened up, grape sweeping into the American lines, causing panic, scattering cohesive units and routing them. It was American artillery, captured and turned on its former owners.

Third Company continued to fall back, back to the place where they had spent all of that morning waiting, and back beyond that. They gave ground grudgingly, firing all the while, held together by the will and force of Angus McGinty's leadership. Another hundred yards back.

Freeman half turned to see what was behind them. A thick patch of forest, and on the high ground beyond that he could see the divisions, fully engaged, that had been realigned to meet Cornwallis. He could hear the sounds of that battle, even over the chaos of the fight in front of him. Smoke hung thick over the trees, lit up orange, and he realized that the sun was not so far from setting.

Hessians and British in their front and left, the Brandywine on their right, but at least there were Americans behind them. If they kept pushing back, then they might come right up against the other divisions, like two men standing back-to-back to fight off a mob.

There was more movement behind and to the left, something happening in the trees several hundred yards away. Freeman turned, expecting to see American troops from Sullivan's division who had been pushed back, but that was not it, not at all. They were British troops, scarlet regimentals, white shoulder belts, the tall hats of grenadiers. They came charging out of the woods and fell on the center of the American line, and that was the end of it.

Freeman looked with dismay as the Americans fled under this new assault. Where the British had come from he could not imagine, but there they were and they swept away any last chance of the Continental line holding together. The battle was lost, and there was just daylight enough left for the British to drive the Americans from the field.

And then, a more immediate concern; they were trapped. Third Company was cut off, with the creek to one side and the newly arrived British troops to the other. Visions of fighting to the death, of a ghastly prison camp, played in his mind. He had lived his life out of doors, did not think he could endure prison.

McGinty was there again, in front of the men, shouting, 'Come on, lads, into the woods! Into the fucking woods!' and then he was leading the way, racing for the cover of the trees and the deep late-day shadows of the forest two hundred yards away.

Freeman was not aware of the sprint, was not aware of anything until the moment he plunged through the bracken and let the cool, dark forest swallow him up and shield him from the horrors of battle. He stopped, threw his head back, gulped air. All those smells were there, the old smells: dry pine needles, rotting vegetation, the perfume of oak and fir, and under it all the smoke of battle.

He looked around. About half of Third Company had reached the woods, a dozen men. The rest dead, wounded, captured. The survivors were sprawled out on the ground, looking with wide eyes at him, at McGinty, and Freeman realized with some surprise that they were looking to him and the Irishman for leadership. They were the closest things to officers left, and ten years senior to the next oldest man.

McGinty, crashing like a moose through the undergrowth, and coming back from the edge of the woods where he had gone to see what was happening, spoke first.

'Well, laddies, the bloody British and their German puppies have won the day, and here we are, behind their lines and surrounded by the bastards.' He spoke softly, though there was no possibility of them being heard.

'So what're we to do, Sergeant?' one of the men asked, the most respectful tone Freeman had ever heard used to address McGinty.

'What you are doing right now, boy-o. Lie low, lie low, and once it is well dark, then Freeman and I will find the way to the promised land.'

It seemed a tall order to Freeman, and he did not know how he had come to be included in it, but he was far too tired to argue. Instead he lay down on the soft cover of pine needles, stretched out, and closed his eyes. He let the smells and the sensation of the forest wash over him, took comfort in their familiarity, memories of his home, memories that had nothing to do with Hessians and bayonets and bloody ground.

It seemed no more than a moment before a hand was shaking him, gentle but insistent. He forced his eyes open, but there was nothing to see, just blackness, as if everything he knew had been removed while he slept.

'Are you awake now, Freeman?' he heard McGinty's voice, a whisper, close by. He sat up on his elbow, and now he could make things out: the Irishman, dimly seen, stars through the gaps in the tall pines, a few shapes scattered around that he took to be the sleeping forms of the other men.

'Yeah, I'm awake.'

He pulled himself to his feet, picked up his musket. McGinty stood as well, looming over him. He could smell dried sweat and powder residue. He could still taste the gunsmoke in his mouth. He uncorked his canteen and took a big swallow. 'So what the hell do we do now?'

'I don't know, laddie, God's own truth,' McGinty

said softly, 'but pray don't let this lot know that, they'll die of despair. I reckon we best go scout about, see how things lie, and with the blessing something will present itself.'

Freeman nodded, loaded his musket. He could barely see the gun in his hand, but it did not matter, he did not need to see to do that. He tamped the charge down, returned the rammer, and turned to McGinty. 'Let's go, then.'

'You best lead the way, boy-o. I'm not much of a woodsman.'

Freeman nodded, cradled his musket in his arms, and moved off into the undergrowth. He was at home here, in the woods at night, a loaded gun in his hand. He felt more comfortable than he had in months. He heard McGinty behind him, noisy, cursing softly as branches whipped his face. He had not lied about his woodcraft.

They came at last to the edge of the trees, where the patch of woods yielded to open meadow, the ground across which they had earlier sprinted to safety. The moon was just making an appearance, giving some relief from the dark. The distant hills were covered with campfires, some burning bright, some just glowing embers. Six men generally shared a fire, and there were hundreds of fires, covering the ground as far as they could see. It was not an American encampment.

'We're well boxed in now, boy-o,' McGinty whispered, 'and our own troops on the far side of these cozy bastards.'

'We could go west, cross the Brandywine.'

'They'll have the fords covered, depend on it. Howe'll not make the same mistake that Washington

249

did. Perhaps there is some way around them, or through their lines.'

The two men moved out, skirting the edge of the trees, moving north, closer to the British encampment. In the distance they could hear an occasional cry, a loud laugh, a sentry's challenge to some unseen intruder, but they were invisible in the dark.

And then, a noise. Freeman stopped, held up his hand, and McGinty nearly collided with him. They stood utterly still and Freeman listened. It was a horse, moving at a walk, the hooves barely audible on the soft grass. He turned to McGinty, nodded toward the undergrowth, and the two men receded into the bracken.

The rider was coming closer; soon even McGinty could hear him. They crouched low and peered through the brush until he came into sight. A dark coat, blue most likely, but it looked black in the night, lighter cuffs and lapels. Moonlight glinted off tall, polished boots, a leather cap.

'Provost . . .' McGinty breathed the word. 'Watching the perimeter, seeing none of them bastards slips away.'

They watched the rider for a moment. He was moving slowly, alert, looking for any kind of movement. Freeman turned to McGinty, surprised to see the big man smiling. 'Oh, Freeman, and don't I have a grand idea?' he said, barely audible. 'Here's the bastard we want. Now I'll get him over here, and you club him good.'

Freeman pulled his long knife from the sheath. 'I'll do better than club him.'

'No, no, we don't want to mess up his pretty

250

clothes. The butt of your musket. There'll be time for the other later.'

Freeman turned his gun over, held it like a club, moved back into the undergrowth until he was entirely hidden.

McGinty fell with a crash, thrashed around, moaned, the noise jarring and frightening after the silence.

For a moment there was nothing, and then, 'Who's there?'

'Oh, dear God, will you help me?'

'Who is it? Who's there?'

'McGinty, Sergeant McGinty, Seventy-first Regiment . . . Oh, dear God!'

Freeman heard the rustle of the provost dismounting, the click of a pistol's lock pulled back. He heard soft steps on the grass and then the hesitant crunch as the provost stepped into the tall grass at the edge of the wood.

'What are you doing way the devil over here? Where are you, Sergeant?'

Freeman felt himself coil, every muscle taut, like a panther ready to spring. He heard the provost's footfall just a few feet in front of him, saw the tall black boot. Two more steps . . .

'Here, sir, here . . .' McGinty groaned. The provost took another step, another, and then Freeman was on his feet, swinging the musket in a great arc. The provost had time to look surprised, had time to half turn toward Freeman and begin to bring the pistol up, before the butt caught him in the back of the head, just above the neck, and pitched him forward. With no more than a grunt and a thud as he hit the ground, and to Freeman's relief the pistol flew from his hand and did not go off.

251

McGinty was up and on the man, unstrapping his helmet. 'Well done, lad, well done. Give us a hand with his coat, then.'

Freeman put his gun down, began unbuttoning the provost's coat, and only then thought to wonder what McGinty was intending. The Irishman was pulling off the man's boots and then his breeches, and then, to Freeman's surprise, began stripping off his own clothes.

Freeman sat back on his heels, looked up at McGinty, an inkling of the plan starting to come to him. 'Angus, what the fuck do you think you're about?'

'It's as simple as can be, me boy. I dress the part of the provost, "arrest" you damned Yankee prisoners, and march you right through the British lines and right away to a prison, as far as anyone will know.'

'You're mad. You'll hang if you're caught in that uniform.'

'Then let us hope I'm not caught. But the sad truth is, I'll hang in any event. I've a colored past, you see.'

Freeman could well imagine. It was a wild plan, and a hundred objections came to mind, but no alternatives, so he just shrugged and continued to strip the motionless provost.

Five minutes later an all but naked McGinty began to struggle into the provost's clothes. 'Now what makes you think you'll fit your fat arse into his uniform?' Freeman asked.

McGinty's big, pale body looked like a ghost in the moonlight. 'They don't pick the wee, frail, skinny lads like you for the provosts, Freeman.'

The uniform did fit, with some effort, though no

one would ever have believed it was tailor-made for the wearer.

'Let us be on our way then, shall we?' McGinty said, slinging the provost's shoulder belt over his neck.

'What about him?' Freeman nodded toward the figure on the ground.

'Oh, you done for him, lad, with that mighty swing. I reckon he's making his apologies to St Peter as we speak.'

'All right.' Freeman looked down at the provost's all but naked body. The last casualty of the Battle of Brandywine.

'You go back and join the lads, I'll ride along on the edge of the wood. When you see me, show yourselves. And would you be so kind as to take me proper uniform? I reckon I'll need it again.'

Freeman took the bundle of clothes and headed back through the dark forest. He heard McGinty soothe the horse, heard his breeches split as he mounted. At last Freeman came to the place where Third Company was camped out, sneaking up on them undetected. They were all asleep. If I were a jaeger, he thought, I could kill them all with cold steel, the woolgathering blockheads.

He woke them, told them the plan in a few words. None of them objected, they were too overwhelmed by their situation. He led them to the edge of the woods and they waited; ten minutes, twenty minutes, an hour. Freeman was beginning to suspect that McGinty had left them, gone off alone with his new disguise, when he finally appeared and dismounted with an ease that was surprising.

'Evening, lads,' he said, 'I've just had a look about. Seems to the north are units of the Forty-second, the

253

Seventy-first, and the Royal Highlanders, and them German bastards are on the hill yonder. We'll make our way through there; less chance them foreigners will wonder what's acting.'

'McGinty, you sure as hell seem to know a lot about the British army,' Freeman observed.

McGinty grinned. 'Ah, boy-o, the checkered past I mentioned. Now here we go, boys, and all in a line, if you please.' He had a rope in his hand.

'What do you reckon to do with that?'

'Why, I have to tie you together. If it don't look like you're my prisoners, then we're sunk, darlings.'

'Humph.' Grudgingly Freeman and the rest allowed their wrists to be bound, not so tight, just enough to look the part. When they were tied in a long line, McGinty swung back up into the saddle.

'Where are we going, Sergeant?' one of the boys asked.

'Where I told you, laddie. To the promised land.'

Foote spit into the dark river below, heard the tobacco juice hit the water. The sun had set half an hour before, and the Delaware was lost in deep shadow. He looked up at Freeman, who had paused to take a drink from his canteen.

'And that was it? The British and the Hessians believed you was prisoners and McGinty a provost?'

'I reckon so. We was only challenged once, and McGinty just tossed it off. He's a great one for making himself believed. No one else paid us any mind. We just marched right through the British lines, and once we was clear, McGinty changed uniforms and we was off, looking for the rest of the Fifth Pennsylvania.'

254

'You didn't find them.'

'No, but it weren't for lack of trying. Washington was marching and countermarching all over the sodding country. North, south, trying to keep between Howe and Philadelphia. We chased him for days, was nearly overrun by the British once. After a while we just give up. I reckon the others didn't care any longer about finding the regiment. Reckon I didn't either. So we just marched into the city. Didn't know Howe was right behind us.'

Foote nodded. Then footsteps on the quarterdeck ladder, a hulking shape in the dark, and McGinty was there. He nodded, said, 'Evening, gentlemen.'

Foote nodded back, said nothing. He imagined McGinty's presence, his greeting, was to be taken as some kind of apology. He considered whether he would accept it.

The three men stood in silence for some time, and slowly the tension eased away, like the slow disappearance of light on a summer evening. McGinty yawned, stretched, which made Foote and Freeman do the same.

'Do you know, Mother Foote, I have been thinking,' McGinty broke the silence.

'You surprise me, Teague.'

'Ah, ever the wit. No, truly, it is but a matter of time before the damned British make their way to this place, and then your dear *Foul-mouth* is lost.'

'So? What's to be done? We've towed her as far as we can. We can't sail her.'

'That is where you may be wrong, Mother, dear. I see below there's a power of rigging and such. Shroud gangs laid up, even a suit of sails it would seem.'

It annoyed Foote to think of the big Irishman poking around the *Falmouth*'s storerooms, taking inventory, and he was silent for a long moment.

'I may be just a stupid boatbuilder, Teague,' he said at last, 'but even I know you need spars to hang all that fine rigging and sails from. Masts?'

'Yes, it's true. I see there is no end to your knowledge. But as to masts and yards, if I am not mistaken, I saw a fine, full mast pond right down by the very ways from which this ship was launched.'

'Yes,' Foote said, gruff, noncommittal, but the thoughts were coming fast as he saw where McGinty was going. All of the *Falmouth*'s spars were already made. They were there, three miles away, bobbing happily in the mast pond.

'Very well, Teague,' Foote said, his hatred and anger entirely forgotten. 'For the next two minutes you get my undivided attention, so whatever you say, make it interesting.'

CHAPTER 17

Fort Mifflin October 7, 1777

*I wrote you a few Days ago informing of the Loss
of Billingsport . . . [As a result] a prodigious
Desertion has prevailed among the Galleys. A few
Nights ago Capt Montgomery lost Eleven Men,
last Night, after the Action, Capt Mitchel lost
Twelve: Three other Galleys are so reduced that all
their Men will not Man One Galley . . .*
—COL WILLIAM BRADFORD
TO THOMAS WHARTON JR, PRESIDENT OF
THE STATE OF PENNSYLVANIA

The men of the *Lady Biddlecomb*, and her namesake,
and her namesake's child, waited while the British
longboat pulled away and another, bigger vessel
pulled down on them. No one said a thing. They
were too stunned by the events of the past hour, the
schooner impaling herself on the *chevaux-de-frise*,
their captain suddenly locked in a mutually agreed-
upon duel with their would-be captor, the heavy
gunfire overhead.

Isaac Biddlecomb did not say a thing either. He just stood there, the point of his sword resting on the sloping, half-submerged deck, staring at the dark place into which Smeaton's longboat had disappeared. He knew he should be giving orders, saying something, doing something, even if it was wrong. The first thing he had ever learned about leadership was never to stand there, dumb and unsure, as he was doing now.

But he could not seem to make his mind or his mouth work. It was all too unreal. And now he was a prisoner of war. Again. And with Smeaton there to tell his British captors about his and Rumstick's history, it would be a speedy trial and a halter around their necks.

In any event, it was pointless to try to defend themselves against the British gunboat. They might fire one volley of small arms, and then the enemy would learn their lesson, would stand off and blast away with their big gun.

He might even have chosen that option were it not for Virginia and little Jack.

So stupid, so stupid, shipping them aboard a man-of-war. How greatly one's options were reduced with supernumeraries so precious aboard, a whole new area of concern that should not burden a fighting sailor. He finally understood his mistake when it was too late.

He turned just as the gunboat came looming up out of the dark. It was an odd-looking craft, really an oversize launch, perhaps forty feet in length mounting one big gun in the bow. A single mast was stepped just forward of amidships, but the two square sails were furled in favor of the sweeps and the greater maneuverability they provided.

'Put up your arms!' a voice called out from the galley.

'Yes, do as he says,' said Biddlecomb, weary.

'You are prisoners of the Continental Congress of these United States of America!' the voice said grandly.

It took a moment for the words to register, but when they did, it was like the sun breaking through thick clouds. Of course. Why else would Smeaton have run like a rabbit? He would not have missed Biddlecomb's capture for a peerage. Smeaton knew all along.

He tricked me, Biddlecomb thought, and he had to smile at that.

'We are Americans! We are Americans!' Biddlecomb shouted out, giving voice to his vast relief. He could see his men smiling, shaking their heads. The men at the galley's sweeps took another pull and tossed oars, and the galley slewed up alongside, turning and then bumping gently to a stop against the submerged *chevaux-de-frise*. A lantern was unshuttered, the light falling across the wreckage of the *Lady Biddlecomb*.

Isaac stepped up to the bow. 'I am Capt. Isaac Biddlecomb of the Continental navy. We were bound for Philadelphia. Didn't know there were obstructions this far downriver.'

In the lantern light he could see the galley's captain, holding the light, staring at the schooner. 'I reckon not,' he said. 'I'm Homer Warburton, captain of Pennsylvania galley *Liberty*. You fellows come on aboard, and . . . dear God, is that a woman? With a child? Here, ma'am, you first. Williams, Selman, stop staring like idiots and bear a hand.'

Little Jack was handed up and Virginia was helped

over the rail, though much of the help was in the form of unwanted pushing and pulling that only impeded her otherwise nimble climbing. Then the Lady Biddlecombs abandoned their vessel and climbed in as well, settling themselves amidships.

Another big gun went off, one hundred yards away, illuminating in its flash a galley much like the *Liberty*. And then another and another, all along the line of *chevaux-de-frise*.

'We drop down here every night,' Warburton explained, 'play our guns on the British, make it hot for them. If they get too close to the obstructions, we can drive them away before they get much done by way of removing them.'

'I see,' said Biddlecomb, sitting beside him.

'Ship oars!' Warburton called to his men. 'Give way now, to larboard, handsomely, handsomely, don't foul them sweeps in the fucking spikes . . . oh, beg pardon, ma'am.'

'Never think on it, Captain,' said Virginia. 'I have been much in company with sailors and I am used to their ways.'

The galley crew handled the sweeps well, pulling the heavy boat upriver, away from the gunfire and the muzzle flashes that lit up the night. Soon they were again enveloped in dark, and the fight downriver seemed very far away, as if it were not part of their world at all.

'Reckon I'll take you to the commodore,' Warburton said, answering the question a second before Biddlecomb asked it. He had just realized that the cluster of lights upriver were anchor lights. The vessels of the Continental and Pennsylvania navies arrayed against the navy of King George.

'He's shifted his flag to *Andrew Doria*,' Warburton continued, 'since the *Montgomery* was lost.'

Andrew Doria. Biddlecomb smiled when he heard that name. The *Andrew Doria* had been part of the first fleet, one of the first four vessels commissioned by Congress in late 1775. She and *Charlemagne* had both taken part in the raid on Nassau, the first United States fleet action, the first landing of the United States marines.

Warburton pushed the tiller over and turned the bow toward a specific anchor light, and a moment later the brig *Andrew Doria* loomed up out of the dark, looking much as she had when last Biddlecomb saw her.

Unlike some of the other ships in the fleet, *Doria* had not suffered great damage in their fight with the frigate *Glasgow* and had spent much of her time since cruising against the enemy. As the galley pulled up along her side, Biddlecomb had the sensation of meeting up with an old friend. It was a small comfort, but he welcomed any comfort at all.

'Holloa, *Andrew Doria*!' Warburton called out. 'We've survivors to see the commodore! Rig up a bosun's chair for the lady!'

'Oh, damn the hellish bosun's chair, I'm not helpless,' Virginia said.

'Ah, belay the bosun's chair,' said Warburton.

Virginia gathered up her skirts and tied them in a knot. She positioned Jack in her sling and scampered up the side of the brig as easy as any seaman, to the accompaniment of Warburton's cries of 'Eyes inboard, there!' Biddlecomb thanked Warburton for his kindness and followed his wife, and then Rumstick and the former Lady Biddlecombs after that.

261

A midshipman led Isaac and Virginia aft and down to the great cabin. A surly, harried-looking Commo. John Hazelwood sat behind his desk, sorting papers, moving them from one pile to the next, shaking his head. He left the Biddlecombs standing for several minutes, entirely ignoring them, and then finally looked up.

'Very well, who are you and what do you want of me?'

Biddlecomb felt himself bristle at the greeting. 'I am Capt. Isaac Biddlecomb of the Continental navy, sir, and I would expect a tad more civility in the presence of my wife.'

Hazelwood put down his pen, sat more straight in his chair. 'Biddlecomb? Captain Biddlecomb, the gunpowder fellow?'

Isaac, preparing for a harsh retort, was caught off guard by that. 'Yes, I suppose I am he . . .'

'Well, sir, I apologize. Let me shake your hand. Ma'am, an honor; pray, be seated. But of course, the uniform, Continental navy. I had thought at first you were one of these artillery officers, sent by that villain Smith to harass me. Adams, some wine in here, you lazy rascal.'

Once they were seated, with glasses of wine in their hands, Hazelwood said, 'Now, sir, I beg you, give me the particulars of how you happen to be here.'

This Biddlecomb did, telling him in perfunctory terms about the loss of the *Charlemagne* and the fight on the beach, the purchase of the *Lady Biddlecomb* (though calling her just 'the schooner'), and her subsequent loss on the *chevaux-de-frise*. He did not mention Smeaton, told himself it was not germane to the story.

'Well, a damned bad run of luck, I should say,' said Hazelwood after Isaac had finished. 'As to the *Falmouth*, she was ready to go down the ways when last I saw her. Don't know if she did or not. But even if she was launched, I can't imagine they kept her out of Howe's hands . . . hold a moment. Adams! Pass the word for Jeffries.'

As the call for Jeffries echoed down the *Doria*'s lower deck, Hazelwood said, 'Jeffries is from Philadelphia and he was a gunner on one of the gunboats that was there when that idiot Alexander surrendered the *Delaware*. Ah, here you are.'

Jeffries stepped into the great cabin and saluted. A young man, gangly, nondescript. 'Jeffries, when you were up by the city, firing on the batteries, were you anywhere near the yard of Wharton and Humphreys?'

'Yes, sir. No more'n half a mile north and five hundred feet offshore.'

'And did you see the *Falmouth*? You recall, the frigate that was building there? Just about ready to go in the water when Howe took the city?'

Jeffries frowned, looked away, picturing the waterfront as he had last seen it. 'I know the *Falmouth*, sir, never doubt it. I was there when her keel was laid. The master shipwright is a distant cousin of my mother's. But to tell the truth, sir, I can't recall seeing her. And I should think I would have noted it, if she was there.'

Jeffries's words gave Isaac hope, just the tiniest glimmer, but that was more than he had had in some time. If *Falmouth* was not in the city, then it was still possible she had been saved.

'Humph,' Hazelwood said. 'Very well, Jeffries,

263

thank you.' Once the young man had gone, Hazelwood said, 'I wouldn't be overly hopeful, Captain.
Even if they got her upriver, they ain't getting her
down again. Washington's been agitating for the
Naval Board to order them frigates burned, the *Effingham* and the *Washington* and I reckon the *Falmouth*
too. Can't say I disagree, even though I'm in the naval
line. Damned lot of trouble protecting them, and
more trouble by half if the British get them. They can
always find plenty of mischief for frigates to get into.'

'Yes, sir, I understand,' said Isaac, and he did, but
he knew that Hazelwood did not understand him.

The *Falmouth*.

She was more than just another ship now. She
had been more than that when he was first given
command of her, even when she was no more than a
name scratched into a blank space in a preprinted
commission.

She had been more than just another ship when he
had first unrolled the long drafts, had seen the lively,
weatherly craft represented by those dark lines on
paper. And now he had lost two ships trying to get to
her, two ships and the lives of half a dozen men.
David Weatherspoon had died trying to get to the
Falmouth. No, she was not just another ship. She was
the land of Canaan and he would lead his men there.

'So, Captain, what are your intentions? How do
you intend to proceed from here?'

'Well, sir,' Biddlecomb extemporized. He had not
really thought about it. Present considerations had
been too overwhelming to allow for thoughts of the
future. 'I suppose I shall apply to you for a vessel of
some sort. Anything to get me and my men upriver
where we can discover the fate of the *Falmouth*.'

'Men? Men, did you say?'

'Yes. I have with me the bulk of the *Charlemagne*'s crew, less those we have lost, though, to be sure, she was undermanned from the onset. Around forty men I should think, all able seamen. They were . . . are . . . to form the core of the *Fulmouth*'s company.'

'Oh, indeed,' Hazelwood said.

Biddlecomb could see that the commodore was turning over some plan. The unsubtle creature, he thought, if he thinks he is getting his hands on my men for his silly state navy, he is very much mistaken.

'Well, sir,' Hazelwood began, 'everything we have that will float is being used in defense of the river, not a punt nor a dory to be spared. However, I could give you a vessel of not inconsiderable size, if you and your crew would man it as part of our defenses here. Once the situation is brought to some conclusion, you would be free to proceed upriver and seek out your frigate, but until then you would have to put yourself under my command.'

'Humph,' was all Biddlecomb said as he turned the offer over in his mind.

'If you feel your orders would not permit this, then I could certainly put you ashore at Fort Mifflin, and you could proceed overland, though I fear for your crew if I do so. The army there has been quite unscrupulous in the matter of recruiting men.'

Hazelwood was leading with his trump card, and it had the desired effect. The core crew of able sailors was the most precious and irreplaceable thing that Biddlecomb had, and the only way to keep them together was to ship them as a crew on whatever vessel Hazelwood had in mind. Biddlecomb had no choice, and the commodore knew it.

'Very well, Commodore, I accept your generous offer,' said Biddlecomb. 'Pray, what ship is it that we are to man?'

'She is called the *Expedient*. She is new built and prodigiously armed and just the thing for greatly distressing the enemy. I am confident that you will find her very much to your liking.'

'What the hell is this?'

Rumstick stood by the gangway, mouth hanging open, staring around him, confused and distressed. Along the deck of the *Expedient* the other former Charlemagnes and Lady Biddlecombs also stared with wide eyes and gaping mouths at their new ship.

'It is called a xebec, a very sensible rig. The Arabs and the people of the Mediterrranean have employed it for centuries, and to great effect.'

'And bully for them heathens, I say, but didn't the commodore have anything that a Christian might sail?'

Rumstick did have a point, though Biddlecomb would not concede it. The *Expedient* was as odd-looking a craft as one was likely to find in the Western Hemisphere. She was about eighty feet on deck and had no bowsprit of any kind. In the place of the bowsprit a big twenty-four-pounder gun jutted out past the stem, and on her open deck were four nine-pounders. A raised quarterdeck enclosed the cabin aft, which might have been spacious for so small a vessel were it not for the eighteen-pounder that pointed aft and took up most of the room there.

But it was the rig that most bewildered the new crew. She sported two masts, just single poles, no topmasts at all, and on each mast was crossed a single long yard from which hung a triangular lateen sail. The rig would have looked more at home on the Nile than the Delaware, and Biddlecomb's men, as tradition-bound as sailors were wont to be, did not know what to make of it.

'Now, Mr Rumstick, think on the advantages. Precious little running gear to be manned or to carry away. She'll point like a schooner if she don't make too much leeway.'

'Aye, sir, and when we miss stays with some British frigate on our arse, we'll wish we had some of your heathen Arabs to show us how to work them damned lateen sails.'

'If I am not much mistaken, Lieutenant, one simply pulls on the sheets and the wind fills the sails and the boat goes, just like any other. Now let us have no more of this. The *Expedient* is the vessel we were given and we will fight her like we did the *Charlemagne*, and until we can reach the *Falmouth* we will be damned glad to have her. Mrs Biddlecomb and I will be turning in. Please see the men stood down to an anchor watch. Then in the morning we will figure out how to sail this stupid boat.'

With that he took Virginia's arm and led her aft under the low quarterdeck and into the privacy of the after cabin. There was a single hanging cot there, and some blankets left by the men who had deserted the vessel en masse after the fall of Billingsport. Isaac helped his wife into the cot and kissed his son and laid him in her arms and made them as comfortable as he could. Then he laid a blanket out on the deck, next to the eighteen-pounder, and lay on that, with another over him, and despite the utter lack of physical comfort, he slept.

CHAPTER 18

Gent^n.
The more I reflect upon the evil that may arise
from the Enemy's possessing themselves of our
unfinished Frigates up the Delaware, the more
convinced I am of the indispensable obligation we
are under to prevent it, effectually. – If no other
methods could be devised I should be for absolutely
burning them . . .

—GEORGE WASHINGTON
WRITING TO THE CONTINENTAL NAVY BOARD
OF THE MIDDLE DEPARTMENT

Once again they took to the river – Foote, the men of
the Fifth Pennsylvania – leaving the *Falmouth* astern.
Two hundred yards, and her looming shape was
lost in the dark, moonless night. They were as silent
as a rowed launch could be, with muffled tholes
and blades dipped easily in the river, no splashing,
no crabbing of oars. The former infantrymen were
developing a surprising proficiency in boat handling.
They did not speak, even though they were still
miles away from any place where they might be

overheard. Their faces and hands were covered with lampblack, and even from the stern sheets Foote could hardly make them out, just the dull lapels and cuffs of their regimental coats, moving in a steady rhythm.

Save for McGinty, sitting beside him in the stern sheets, steering the longboat with nudges of the tiller and the occasional whispered command. He had not applied lampblack, and his generally ruddy moon-face seemed to glow. He wore a civilian coat and hat, acquired from where, Foote did not know.

They hugged the north shore of Petty's Island, pulling for the main channel of the Delaware River. From behind the southern shoreline of New Jersey, more and more of the city revealed itself with each pull of the oars. Quite a number of lights were still burning, it being no later than ten o'clock. At another time Foote might have thought them pretty, glowing like a nearby constellation, but now there was something sinister and frightening about them, as if they were a threat to this secret mission.

McGinty steered the boat straight across the river, then turned it south and hugged the Pennsylvania side, keeping to the bank just north of the city.

'Here,' Foote grunted as they drew abeam of a small cut in the shore, the mouth of a creek that emptied into the Delaware and provided a dark and secret landing spot.

'Starboard, back water,' McGinty said, just a whisper, and the boat spun around like a leaf in a stream. 'Give way. Here, Mother Foote, put us ashore wherever you see fit.'

Foote took up the tiller and steered the boat toward the marshy shore, toward the point where he

269

knew the worn trail came down to the water. He had been rowing and sailing along the Philadelphia waterfront since he was a young boy, knew every twist and inlet. That made it all the more annoying that McGinty seemed to be taking the lead in this expedition.

The bow of the boat eased up into the mud, a barely perceptible cessation of movement. 'Toss oars,' Foote growled, and the oars came up. 'Here you are, Teague. Trail is right over there. Leads up to a road that'll take you into the city. I'm afraid you'll get your feet wet getting there.'

'You'll not carry me ashore, Ma?'

'No, but I'll be pleased to hold you by your ankles with your head underwater.' It was bad enough that they were following a plan of McGinty's devising, and made much worse because McGinty would tell none of them what it was. But Foote could not shake the story that Freeman had told about the escape after Brandywine. Foote would never have believed it coming from the Irishman, but he could not picture Freeman lying, or even embellishing the truth.

In the city to the south, not more than a mile away, a church bell rang out, immediately joined by another and another. 'There's ten o'clock,' said McGinty. 'You lot keep out of sight, and when it strikes midnight, meet me at the mast pond. I'll be waiting there.'

Foote wanted to ask again what McGinty intended, but he knew he would be put off with some flip remark and he did not need that aggravation, so instead he said, 'You be there, Teague, or we're off without you.'

'Good luck to you too, Mother,' McGinty said.

Foote could make out the glow of McGinty's smile through the dark, and then he was over the side, leaving the longboat rocking hard side to side as he jumped clean. A splash, a rustle of grass as he climbed ashore, an indistinct shape on the trail, and then he was gone.

The dark and the silence closed in on them again, an oppressive silence that was not relieved by the chirping of the frogs and the crickets, that was broken only by the occasional far-off sound from the city: a shout, a wagon rolling by, a sharp crack like a gunshot.

'Reckon we're as safe here as anywhere,' Foote said. 'Might as well lie on your oars till it's time to go.'

'If you don't object,' said Freeman, 'I'll post some pickets along the trail, in case anyone comes wandering along.'

'Fine with me.'

Freeman called out four names, and the men collected their gear and slipped over the side and up the bank, disappearing in the night just as McGinty had.

'Rest of you may as well relax,' Foote said because he felt he had to say something. He could just make out the forms of the men stretching out as best they could, finding the most comfortable positions on the hard thwarts and gunwales of the boat.

Soon the few whispered discussions ceased. No one moved, and Foote could hear rhythmic breathing. One man began to snore, but Freeman gave him a swift kick to silence him. Malachi was astounded at the men's ability to sleep anywhere, anytime. Worse than damned sailors, he thought.

He leaned back himself, stared up at the stars that filled the clear night sky, let his mind wander away. He let it wander downriver to the broad ocean, standing on the quarterdeck of the *Falmouth* with a full press of canvas overhead, heeled hard over, running her easting down, trim and fast. He saw the white water churned up by her stem, the figurehead in her beautiful, flowing gown, her arm stretched out before her, her knowing face turned into the wind.

These thoughts led naturally and unbidden to thoughts of the young woman on whom the carving was based, and Foote felt the familiar and unwelcome ache and stirring inside.

A woman would be a good thing right now, he thought. That woman in particular.

Foote had not always been so fortunate in matters of the heart. He knew full well why that was; it was the dandies, with their fine clothes and effete ways, who seemed to lure the women, not irascible and profane shipwrights such as himself.

But Susan, she was something different. He had seen her on the street, and the moment he ran his eyes over her perfect face and body, he knew that she was the one who must grace the bow of his perfect ship. And so he had asked her to sit for him, asked with not a hint of awkwardness, because this was not about the girl, it was about the *Falmouth*, and he was never backward for a second where the ship was concerned.

Only after half a dozen sittings did he become aware of her amorous regard for him. The very act of posing, sitting utterly still while he scrutinized every part of her, rendering her face, her arms, her breasts, her waist, in wood, seemed to arouse her.

That session started in the workshop but ended in the bedroom, as did each one after that.

But it had been a long time, and Foote was feeling the effects of abstinence. Perhaps these soldiers were used to going for stretches without a good thrumming, but he was not.

And then the bells rang out, midnight, to Foote's absolute amazement. He had been so absorbed in his thoughts that he had had no notion of the time passing, could not even recall the bells having struck eleven.

'Wake up, wake up, you lazy bastards,' Freeman was whispering, giving nudges and kicks all around. The four pickets appeared out of the dark and slipped back over the boat's side, and a moment later the infantrymen were all in their places, oars held vertically, ready for the command.

'Ship oars. Back water, all,' Foote growled, and the oars came down and the boat backed out of the creek and into the Delaware River. Malachi turned the bow south again, keeping a good five hundred feet from the waterfront and skirting along the city, marking each familiar building and dock as it passed abeam. He searched the dark for signs of a guardboat but could see none, reckoned the army would not think in terms of patrolling the water.

At last he recognized the contours of the Wharton and Humphreys shipyard: the lofting shed, the offices, the spar shop, the empty ways. He pushed the tiller over and pointed the boat toward the mouth of the mast pond, his eyes riveted on the shore, looking for movement, a British patrol.

The whole plan, the plan that had seemed so simple and rational aboard the *Falmouth*, suddenly seemed mad, suicidal. All this risk for a lower fore-mast and foreyard? If they could steal them, and if they could step the mast, it would still be just enough to give the ship steerage, and what good would that do? Keep the men occupied, setting it all up? What did he care if they were bored? But if he was made prisoner, then there was no one to watch over the frigate.

I'm frightened, that's the goddamned thing of it, Foote admitted to himself. He had been in more tavern fights than he could recall, had stood down many an angry shipwright or rigger, had on many occasions used force on strong but dumb yard workers who did not care for his management style. But this was something else altogether. This was not what he was accustomed to.

He swallowed, adjusted the boat's course, told himself that this was not the time to reevaluate the plan. He thought of McGinty, the arrogant bastard, skipping off into the city as if he were as free as General Howe. McGinty leading his men to safety as the British army pressed them back from the Brandy-wine. Was that son of a bitch braver than he? He felt anger replace the fear, felt himself tense up, his mind working faster, clearer. McGinty would not show him up, that would never happen.

The stone quay loomed up ahead, making a sharp edge against the lights of the city. Foote steered for the dark hole that he knew was the mouth of the mast pond, a man-made reservoir in the shipyard in which the spars floated to keep them from drying and checking before they could be put in service.

'Toss oars, boat oars,' he whispered, louder, more harshly than he had intended. The oars came up and were laid down on the thwarts, and the longboat's way carried it along. 'In the bow there, there's a chain across the mouth of the pond. Grab hold of it when you see it.'

'Chain's cast off,' came a voice from the dark, from outside the boat, and Malachi jerked in surprise, cursed softly.

'Teague, is that you?'

'Aye, Mother Foote, and right where I said I'd be.' The boat drifted up against the stone wall, just inside the mast pond, and they could see McGinty, crouched low, just above them. 'Throw us the painter, then,' he whispered, and the line was tossed ashore.

'Any patrols?' Freeman asked.

'None that I can see, but I've not been here above ten minutes.'

'Ten minutes?' Foote whispered. 'What the fuck have you been doing for two hours, while we've been sitting on our arses?'

'Ah, Mother Foote, I've been visiting this dear little bunter I know, down on Chestnut Street, and a fine time we had. You boatbuilders might go without, but a soldier needs a good thrumming now and again.'

Foote heard snickers. He felt his face flush with rage. Here he had been sitting in the damned boat dreaming about giving some doxy a flourish, and all the while McGinty had been off making the beast with two backs. If ever he could have stuck a knife in McGinty, it was at that moment, and he was glad that he was not within arm's reach of the man.

'All right, McGinty,' said Freeman, 'what did you do for the other hour and fifty-nine minutes?'

'Oh, you'll see, and any moment now. Mother Foote, would you care to select which of these fine spars we'll take?'

'Hold on, hold on, Teague, you stupid Irish bastard,' Foote said as he climbed out of the boat. He did not try to check the irritation in his voice. If McGinty made one more flip remark, he would beat him into paste and leave him on the dock, but happily McGinty seemed to realize as much and kept silent.

Foote stood at the edge of the mast pond, ignoring McGinty, looking around the familiar yard and the city beyond. He could hear people off in the distance, a horse's hooves on the cobblestones. More than one.

'What makes you think the British ain't going to send a patrol by here any second?' Foote asked at last.

'That,' said McGinty, pointing. Just beyond the confines of the Wharton and Humphreys yard stood the warehouse of Joseph Piercy, a prosperous merchant and well-known loyalist, a man who would have enthusiastically welcomed the British into Philadelphia.

Foote squinted, stared at the building, tried to understand what he was looking at. The few windows were lit up brilliantly, as if a formal ball were taking place inside. And just as he realized that the inside of the warehouse was on fire, someone raised the alarm. Somewhere in the city a bell began to ring; voices shouted, 'Fire! Fire!'

The big double doors of the warehouse swung open – Malachi could not tell if someone had pulled them open or if they had just burned through – and suddenly the flames came spilling up, leaping up the front of the building, looking for more material to consume but finding little on the brick face.

'Dear God, Teague, you'll burn the whole damned city down,' Foote said, but he could not help smiling at the sight of that infernal British tool Piercy's wealth going up in flames. Casualty of war. No insurance company would pay out a claim.

'Not a bit of it, my dear Foote. I'd not have set a wooden building aflame, but a brick building such as that will hold the flame inside, never doubt it.'

'This here's another area of your expertise?'

'It's been a handy thing at times, knowing how a fire will act. But see here, let us get the spars we need and be gone. The fire won't distract them forever.'

In the considerable light of the flames Foote could see men congregating, running about, shouting and waving their arms. They were no more than black figures against the orange and yellow light. Whether they were British or American, soldiers or civilians, he could not tell. McGinty was right; the fire would hold everyone's attention for a time, but it would not do so for long.

'That there's the foremast, and the foreyard's over there. Reckon we may as well take the bowsprit and fore topmast too.'

'Aye, and these two as well should do us.'

'What do you want with them two? We'll be lucky even to get the foremast in.'

'Sheers, Mother Foote, we need them for sheers for getting the mast in. Do you know nothing about rigging a ship? Have you never looked higher than the deck?'

'Shut your damned gob, Teague.' Of course they

277

needed sheers. 'You lot in the boat, pull up along here, we'll make up to the spars we need.'

The shouting around the warehouse was growing louder, as was the roar of the flames as they spread through the packed space. The light fell over the yard and lit up all the dark corners it could reach. Long shadows danced over the ground, but the men in the boat were shielded by the edge of the mast pond, working in the half-light of the shadow of the quay, invisible to anyone more than ten feet away.

Foote and McGinty jumped down into the boat, made their way to the bow. McGinty picked up one of the lengths of line they had brought with them, handed it to Foote. 'Clap a timber hitch around the—'

'Shut your goddamned gob, Teague, or I swear I'll cut your tongue out!' Foote could see the Irishman grinning, but again McGinty said nothing, just took up another coil and tossed a hitch around the foreyard.

It took twenty minutes to secure all of the spars, and in that time the pandemonium around the burning warehouse grew louder, but never closer, and the men in the longboat went entirely unnoticed.

'Give way,' McGinty said, his voice just a little softer than usual, and even that seemed unnecessary. The men leaned into their oars, pulled, leaned in and pulled again, and slowly the boat and its heavy drag began to move. The mouth of the mast pond slipped astern, and they came out into the river and the boat began immediately to slew around as the current caught the spars and tried to spin them away downstream. But that was no matter, because it pointed the boat in the direction they wished to go: north, back to the *Falmouth*.

The current and the spars made the rowing that much harder, but the men were used to it by now, and it was nothing compared with towing the frigate. Soon the rhythm was steady, the progress good, as they left the unsuspecting city astern.

Chestnut Street. That was what McGinty had said. The name gave Foote a spark of titillation, and he realized it was because *she* lived on Chestnut Street, she of the figurehead. He glanced over at McGinty. Foote did not know what he expected to see.

A lot of women live on Chestnut Street, he thought. A hell of a lot. There is not one chance in a thousand it could be her.

No, not one chance in a thousand. Still, he did not care for those odds.

Biddlecomb was surprised, pleasantly surprised, by the xebec's performance: her speed, her agility, her weatherliness, and the small amount of leeway she made when hard by the wind. All these things he noted in the journal, which he had found abandoned on the tiny desk in the tiny cabin aft. The last entry had been October 2nd and read:

Hazy weather, winds light from the south southeast. Fort at Billingsport overrun by British Troops this a.m. Much desertion among galleys. 2:00 p.m., First Officer and twenty Men took Long Boat to Shore, expressed Intention of not Returning. Much discontent among the people.

There was no entry for the 3rd so Biddlecomb

279

wrote simply, 'Moored, crew deserted,' then on the 4th noted his assuming command.

Now he struggled to describe in the spare prose of journel writing the sea trials they had conducted, the tacking, wearing, heaving to that he had put the men through so that they all might become familiar with the strange craft. He tried to recall all the events of the day worth noting, but he could feel her eyes on his back, knew that they were not done fighting, not by far, and he could not concentrate on the words.

He sighed, jammed the pen back in its stand, and swiveled around in the chair. She was glaring at him still. He held her eyes, glared back, and there they sat, each waiting for the other to speak.

The fight had started that morning. It had started soon after Isaac's suggestion that Virginia not remain aboard the xebec, but that was not the cause of it.

'I think perhaps it would be best if you continued overland,' he had said. 'We can put you ashore at Fort Mifflin, and I will have some men accompany you into Philadelphia.'

'I think that would be best,' Virginia agreed. 'I should never leave were it not for Jack, but now that we have him, I shall opt more for discretion in my valor.'

'Quite right. It would not be the thing for his mother to put herself in harm's way.'

'Nor, I assume, will his father go out of his way to seek danger.'

'No more than my duty demands. And rest assured I shall duck when the iron starts to fly.'

'I understand your duty, and I would not have you shirk it, for the sake of your honor. It is not that to which I refer. I refer to this thing with Smeaton, this childish duel. I assume you have no intention of meeting him? That telling him you would was a *ruse de guerre*?'

Isaac frowned. The words surprised him. Virginia, of course, knew everything about Smeaton and the *Icarus*, had heard every part of the tale. It had never occurred to him that she would think meeting Smeaton was any less part of his duty, any less part of preserving his sacred honor.

'I most certainly do intend to meet him. Do you think I could simply ignore an affair of honor? Be thought a coward?'

'Be thought . . . be thought a coward? By whom? Whose good opinion are you concerned with? Smeaton's? You are concerned that the man you most despise on earth will think ill of you?'

'Smeaton was not the only one to hear the challenge. Rumstick did, as did all my men, and I do cherish their opinion.'

'Don't give me that . . . that . . . spurious nonsense. There is not a man who knows you, Rumstick, any of them, who would think you a coward. With your record you need never prove yourself again.'

'Fine, but that is not the point. If only Smeaton and I knew of the meeting, I should not miss it, because, honestly, I am most concerned with my own opinion of myself. A man cannot disdain his honor simply because he thinks no one will find out. That is cheap honor indeed.'

'I do not believe this! Isaac, you are a father! You have a responsibility to your son, you cannot run off and fight in some idiotic duel like you are Sir

281

Lancelot. Think of Jack, think of your responsibility to him.'

'Do you think I am not?' They were nearly shouting now, talking as loud as they could without inviting the entire ship to listen. Isaac could picture the men on the quarterdeck above, straining to hear the voices coming up through the skylight as they stared off at the shore and pretended not to listen. It made him eager to be done with this.

'Jack is the most important thing in the world to me,' Isaac continued, 'and that is why I cannot allow the Biddlecomb name to be sullied by rumors of cowardice and dishonor.'

'Oh, you are a stupid man, just a stupid man! What do you think Jack needs more, a dishonored father or an honorable corpse?'

'You are so certain I will be killed? You have no faith that I might prevail?'

'That is not the point! If you had any consideration at all for your family, you would not put yourself in that position!'

This was absurd. How could he, the master of a man-of-war, absolute ruler of that floating state, be in such a position? Why should he, aboard his own ship, have to argue a point that any man would take for granted? Never, never again would she be allowed on one of his ships.

He stood, bent low under the overhead, snatched up his hat. 'That is enough. This discussion is finished. We will have no more of it.'

'Or what? You'll keelhaul me, Captain Biddlecomb? I am your wife, not one of your men. Your life or death mean far more to me than to them, and I have every right to argue for it.'

Biddlecomb had scowled, said nothing, retreated to the quarterdeck. Never again.

But that was that morning, and she was not off the ship yet, and while Isaac had enjoyed something of a reprieve that afternoon while he put the *Expedient* through her trials, had even managed to forget the argument enough to enjoy himself, had worked the men so hard that the knowing grins had been wiped from their faces, still he had to confront her, the one person on board over whom he could not exercise total control. That was why she would not remain on board much longer.

And so they sat in the great cabin, staring at one another, more angry than they had ever been in their year and three months of marriage.

'You are hardly dependent upon me for support,' Isaac said at last. 'Your father is worth more then I shall probably ever realize.'

With that, Virginia let out a sigh of disgust and looked away, her face set. 'How can you be so stupid? You think this has to do with money? You think the most important thing you are to Jack is a source of money?'

'No, I do not. I think the most important thing I am to Jack, and I pray I might be so, is an example of honor and decency. An example of manhood for him to take after. Tossing my honor away is not the example I wish to set.'

Virginia looked at him again. Anger and contempt. They were at loggerheads, neither could move. 'Will you be putting us ashore soon?'

Dear God, I hope so, you ungrateful bitch, Biddlecomb thought. 'Soon.'

'Good. There is nothing more we can say. You

283

seem intent on killing yourself, and your family be damned. I do not care to witness it.'

A number of responses swirled around in Isaac's head, bitter, angry words that would have stuck another knife in the wounded body of their marriage, but he remained silent, and thankfully, just when he felt he must say something, there was a knock on the cabin door.

'Come.'

Lieutenant Gerrish opened the door tentatively and peered in. 'Mr Rumstick's compliments, sir, and we shall be off Fort Mifflin inside fifteen minutes.'

'Very good. I'll be up directly.'

He stood and picked up his hat. Looked at Virginia and she looked back at him, but there was nothing more to say. He stepped through the door and left her there, her and Jack, alone.

CHAPTER 19

9th . . . Nine Rebel Galleys attacked our Battery of
2 medium 12 pounders but were beaten back. We
lost one Grenadier killed, three wounded and a
wagoner and two Horses killed.
      —JOURNAL OF CAPT. JOHN MONTRESOR

Biddlecomb came on deck to find a lovely and
tranquil setting, early evening on an autumn day on
the Delaware. The sun, brilliant in the clear blue sky,
was low in the west, casting its yellow light over the
banks of the river and the built-up ramparts of Fort
Mifflin, over the few ships and numerous boats of the
American fleet, leaving deep black shadows in their
wake.

The breeze was steady, if cold, and the xebec was
on her best point of sail, just a few points free, with
the fort and the anchored vesssels just forward of the
larboard beam. There was a relaxed attitude aboard,
the men's early apprehension about the strong rig
now all but ameliorated by the day's sail drills. They
moved slowly, conversed in low tones. Isaac heard
the occasional laugh from forward. It was all very

much at odds with his own mood, as if he and his men were marching in different rhythms.

While Isaac had been below, Rumstick had taken the *Expedient* nearly to the New Jersey shore, where he had skirted around the *chevaux-de-frise* that blocked the river, passing over the shallow banks of mud where the deep-draft British men-of-war could not. Now he stepped silently to the leeward side, giving the captain the weather side of the quarterdeck, and wisely did not try to engage him in conversation.

Biddlecomb looked out over the starboard quarter, to Red Bank on the Jersey shore. Fort Mercer seemed to glow in the evening light; the fresh-turned earth on her redoubts looked like gold. He turned and looked beyond the larboard bow at Fort Mifflin on Fort Island. The tops of the fort's walls still caught the sun, but the southeast-facing side was dark.

Forts Mercer and Mifflin, and seven ranks of *chevaux-de-frise*, were all that stood between the British navy and Philadelphia. And of course the *chevaux-de-frise* at Billingsport, but he did not imagine that they would remain for long, now that the fort was abandoned.

How long could the Americans hold them back, that irrisistible force? Two weeks? Three? God, but it all seemed so pointless, and for all his effort the British would still get the *Falmouth*, if they had not already. And he could die in a duel or destroy his marriage or forsake his honor. Those were his choices, he could choose any one of the three.

Well, we shall be into the fighting tonight, and perhaps a cannonball will make the decision for me, he thought, and then Virginia can mourn my death without blaming me for bringing it about.

With that happy thought he turned to considerations of seamanship, which were always a salve during times of distress.

'Mr Rumstick.' The first officer startled, then hurried over.

'Sir?'

'What have we for ground tackle?'

'Just the one bower, sir, and of no great size, but I reckon it'll hold well enough in anything short of a gale. All mud around here, good holding ground.'

'Indeed. And is it laid along?'

'Aye, sir, and Mr Sprout is up in the bows now . . . there he is is . . . ready to let go.'

'Very good. Let us come up to windward of that . . . what the devil is that?'

'Floating battery, as I understand it, sir. A sort of fort built atop a barge. They use sweeps to move them about.'

'Lord, I shouldn't like to try rowing that in any wind or current.'

'Nor I. But they're heavy armed. The one has twelve eighteen-pounders, the other ten. Get them in the right position and they could make it hot for any ship under their fire.'

'I can well imagine. In any event, let us luff up and come to an anchor just beyond them.'

'Hands, make ready to anchor!' Rumstick called, but the order resulted in more confusion than anything, as the new Expedients had never anchored the vessel, only weighed anchor the one time that morning. 'Here, sail trimmers, go to . . . where do you think you are going? If you are a sail trimmer, where might you expect to be, you sorry bastard? Mr Gerrish, bear a hand here!'

287

Gerrish plunged into the fray, directing men here and there, putting lines in their hands, pointing aloft and explaining what was going to happen, though his guess was no better than anyone else's.

The *Expedient* passed the floating battery and came into clear water beyond, and Biddlecomb said to the helmsman, 'Luff up!' The strange vessel turned up into the wind and the triangular lateen sails began to shiver, and Isaac called, 'Mr Gerrish, let go those sheets!'

The xebec turned slowly, slowly, until at last the wind was blowing directly down her deck. She paused and then began to move astern and Biddlecomb called, 'Let go!' and the anchor plunged down into the Delaware River. 'Mr Rumstick, please see to stowing the sails. I imagine the yards will have to be lowered to the deck. Mr Faircloth, a word?'

Rumstick hurried forward, bellowing orders in a voice calculated to mask any uncertainty he had in dealing with lateen sails.

Lieutenant Faircloth stepped aft and saluted.

'Lieutenant, as you know, I had hoped to reach Philadelphia with no trouble, which I see now was a stupid hope indeed. In any event, I would not have exposed my wife and son to this, had I known, and now I think it necessary that I get them ashore.'

'Aye, sir. And you need someone to see them safe into the city?'

Biddlecomb searched the man's eyes for a hint of ironic amusement, a glimmer of 'I reckon you'll be glad to be shed of that damned shrew,' but it was not there. Isaac felt ashamed of his paranoia. Faircloth was a gentleman, a real gentleman in every sense of the word, and he would never allow himself to find humor in such a situation.

'I am loath to ask you this, Elisha, and I would not if I thought we might see any action in the next few days that would be in your line, but I reckon it will be more of dropping downriver and cannonading the British. Not the stuff for your marines.'

'Of course, sir,' said Faircloth. 'I should remind you as well that I am a native of the city, know every road and ally. I submit, humbly, that there is no man aboard better suited to see Mrs Biddlecomb and your son into Philadelphia.'

'The city is occupied, as you well know. You'll have to go out of uniform, pretend to be a civilian. If you are taken and found out, the British might construe you as a spy.'

At that Faircloth waved a dismissive hand. 'Never think on that, sir. It will never be an issue, for I shall never be caught.'

Faircloth's assurance did much to ease Isaac's concern, and that concern, he understood, was made more acute by his current anger with Virginia. It was exactly because his less generous parts wished to see some harm befall her that he had to be certain it would not. He could well imagine the guilt he would suffer if she actually was hurt through his vengeful and petty negligence.

He longed to cross swords with Smeaton, or to plunge into the thick of battle, where the emotions – terror, hatred, rage – were so pure and uncomplicated.

Faircloth interrupted his thoughts. 'Just above the mouth of the Schuylkill River, on the north bank, there is a large farm, and the owner is a particular friend of mine. I am certain we can secure lodging there for tonight, more comfortable than this little boat or the fort, I should think, and then a carriage into the city on the morrow. If that is acceptable to you, sir.'

'Oh, very. I thank you, sir, thank you very much.' Faircloth was one of those men in whose abilities one had utter confidence. 'Mr Rumstick, the launch alongside, please, and a boat crew. Mr Gerrish, my compliments to Mrs Biddlecomb and the boat will be ready in five minutes to bear her ashore.'

That was cowardice, through and through, sending Gerrish below to fetch Virginia, but Isaac was willing to admit to himself that he was afraid of another confrontation, afraid of the bad feelings it would leave in its wake.

He did not know what he would say, or Virginia would say, when she came on deck, when it was time for her to leave.

He hoped desperately that she would apologize, that she would try to smooth things over. He did not want her to go with this anger between them, but neither was he willing to accept the blame and apologize first. He was not to blame.

Five minutes later she appeared, Jack held in the sling she had fashioned, Gerrish trailing behind, holding a bag with the few personal possessions she had left.

'Mr Gerrish, please take charge of the boat,' Isaac ordered. 'Mr Faircloth will direct you where you are to go.' Isaac turned to Virginia. 'Lieutenant Faircloth has agreed to see you into the city, Virginia,' he continued, formal and stiff. 'He knows of a place where you might spend the night and then get suitable conveyance tomorrow.'

'Very well.' She was not going to apologize, she was not going to yield an inch.

The boat crew climbed down over the side and took their places, and Isaac walked Virginia to the gangway. Gerrish handed her bag down and climbed down into the boat. Faircloth was already there, and the moment that Isaac had dreaded was on them.

He pulled the cloth away from Jack's little pink face, looked down at him with love, with longing and fear for the future, for all of their futures. 'Good-bye, little man,' he said softly, leaning over and giving his son a kiss. Jack cooed, grabbed a pudgy fistful of hair, and held tight with surprising strength. 'Such a strong little man you are,' Isaac said, smiling with genuine pleasure and carefully disengaging the little hand.

He straightened, looked at Virginia, but there was no warmth there. 'Good-bye, Virginia,' he said, fully aware that this really could be good-bye, the last good-bye. Between his fight with Smeaton and the defense of the Delaware River, it was perfectly reasonable to think that he might not live though the next few weeks, or that he might be captured and hanged or left to die of fever in some fetid prison.

He held her eyes. Now was the time for apologies, embraces, tearful kisses.

'Good-bye, Captain Biddlecomb. Fare you well.' She stepped through the gangway and down the *Expedient*'s side and into the boat.

Isaac watched her go, but she did not look up at him. He wanted to say something, but he could not. He could think of nothing to say, save for an apology, and he did not owe her that. He felt sick. Sick to his stomach, sick to his heart, sick through and through.

If Commo. John Hazelwood's sole intention had been to distract Biddlecomb from his marital woes, he could not have issued more effective orders than the ones he did. Even as the *Expedient*'s longboat was passing between Fort and Mud Islands, and Biddlecomb was taking pains not to watch its egress, a midshipman arrived from the commodore with orders for the xebec to join the rest of the combined fleet on their nightly attack on the British at Billingsport.

They weighed anchor immediately and worked their way clear of the anchorage with only a few nervous moments when Biddlecomb misjudged the speed with which the backed foresail would swing the *Expedient* off the wind and toward the galley anchored astern. They moved into open water and tacked back and forth and drilled with the guns while the rest of the hodgepodge fleet got under way.

It was just about full dark when they assesmbled and headed downriver, the oddest assortment of craft Biddlecomb had ever witnessed. There were two other xebecs, *Repulse* and *Champion*, the *Andrew Doria*, as well as the other veterans of the first fleet, *Hornet, Wasp*, and *Fly*. Along with those, the largest vessels, was a mosquito fleet of galleys, gunboats, armed boats, and fire ships and rafts. Over forty vessels were heading down the dark river to inflict their nightly damage on the British, a moving constellation of lights, like Henry Morgan's buccaneers off to the Isthmus of Panama, with the *Expedient* in their midst.

The dark fortifications at Billingsport were just abeam when the *Andrew Doria* opened up, her broadside throwing twenty-eight pounds of iron and enough light to illuminate the various British ships and boats working at removing the *chevaux-de-frise* or anchored just below it. One by one the gunboats and galleys moved into position and began their bombardment, loading and firing their bow guns at the barely seen enemy.

'Mr Rumstick, I reckon we can fire the bow gun or the stern gun or one of the broadsides,' Biddlecomb said to Ezra, standing beside him at the break of the quarterdeck, 'but we cannot employ them all.'

'No, sir. I reckon we can do the most damage with the twenty-four-pounder in the bow. Put the rest of the men on the sweeps so we can maneuver easy. Perhaps go to the stern gun when we head back up river.'

'Very good. Make it so.'

Five minutes later the sails were furled, the men now having some expertise in that evolution, and the sweeps run out and manned and the twenty-four-pounder banging away. It was the largest gun that Biddlecomb or any of the other Expedients had worked, and they were amazed at the noise and power of the big cannon. It was as unlike a four- or six-pounder as the *Expedient* was a seventy-four-gun ship of the line, an entirely new animal and the men liked it.

For an hour they blasted away, and the British returned fire, their larger ships rigged with springs to the anchor cables so they could bring their broadsides to bear. The night was lit up by the vicious cannonade, British and Americans pounding away at one another, the air filled with the shriek of passing shot and orders issued in hoarse voices and the occasional crash and scream as a shot hit home.

It was nearly ten o'clock when the first fire raft was employed. Biddlecomb did not even see them getting it in place, was not aware of it until it burst into flame just below the *chevaux-de-frise*. The fire leapt twenty feet in the air and swept over the pile of combustibles on the flat barge. It threw a great circle of light, illuminating everything within two dozen yards, including the boat that had towed it into place and cast it off and was now pulling back to the American fleet as if the devil himself were grabbing for their rudder.

The raft twirled in the current and drifted down on the anchored men-of-war. Issac could see a sloop now, caught in its light, a sloop not unlike the one that had driven the *Charlemagne* ashore. Smeaton's sloop. He thought for certain that the raft would fetch up alongside the ship, would catch it on fire and turn it into a great flaming torch. He was leaning forward, pounding the rail with anticipation, when two boats pulled into sight and easily grappled the raft and pulled it clear.

Another fire raft burst into flames, fifty yards away, and then another closer to the Jersey shore, and that, apparently, was enough for the British. By the light of the drifting fires Isaac could see boats cutting away the springs and the British men-of-war swinging in the current, bow-on to the Americans. Their guns fell silent as they would no longer bear, and the ships' companies began to win their anchors and loosen off topsails.

There was nothing hurried about it, no cutting and running from an overwhelming attack. The fire rafts seemed to pose no real danger; they were each in turn grappled and towed clear before they became anything like a threat to the men-of-war. It was as if the incendiaries and the cannonade had become more of a nuisance than was worth enduring, and so they were going to leave.

And tomorrow night they would be back, and the Americans too, and they would all do it again. And a few more of the *chevaux-de-frise* would be removed.

Slowly the American fire began to slacken as their targets disappeared downriver, until the final gun of the night went off and the Expedients could hear nothing but ringing through their dulled ears. The men at the sweeps had been backing water all night, a couple of strokes per minute, just to keep the xebec stationary in the current, keep her from being swept down and pinned against the submerged spikes.

On Biddlecomb's order they maintained that rhythm, holding the vessel where she was while one by one the other ships and boats headed back upriver to the secondary line of defense. At last the *Expedient* was alone.

'On the sweeps!' Biddlecomb shouted, much louder than normal, certain that the men's hearing was as dull as his own. 'Back water now! Stoke! And stroke! And stroke!'

The *Expedient* began to make sternway, began to head back upriver, stern first, as if she were disengaging from a fight, not wanting to turn her back on her opponent. When Isaac judged them far enough from the *chevaux-de-frise*, he called, 'Starboard, hold water! Larboard, give way!' and the xebec spun around in her own length.

'Give way, all!'

The *Expedient* headed upriver, the last of the American fleet. Biddlecomb did not wish to sail in company with the others. He was not going back up to Fort Mifflin, and he did not care to explain why. He was going to anchor in the shallows just above Billings Island.

Then, at dawn, he would see to his other business.

At an hour before dawn, Gerrish, who had been standing the morning anchor watch, stepped softly into the cabin and woke him. Isaac crawled stiffly out of his bunk, stretched painfully, and splashed some of the frigid water from his nightstand on his face. He dressed carefully, in his best uniform, the uniform he would be buried in, if it came to that. At that early hour, with his emotional bulwark knocked down, he could not help but think on that eventuality.

No matter the morning's outcome, he had as good as killed Smeaton already. Smeaton must have suffered some great shame at the loss of the *Icarus*, and the final insult of being set adrift on a grating, of being used as a means of his enemy's escape.

With his wealth and connections, Smeaton would not be a mere lieutenant on a sloop of war if he had not suffered some stigma for the *Icarus* affair.

Such humiliation would be a living death for a proud bastard like him. No, he had already done for Smeaton, and that was why it would be ironically just if Smeaton were now to kill him. That was how the Great Clockmaker seemed to arrange things.

With those somber thoughts Isaac slipped his shoulder belt over his shoulder, adjusted the way his sword hung at his side, pulled his coat on, and stepped up onto the quarterdeck. The air was cold and damp, the night absolutely black. No lights were out on the river, no nearby land loomed. The *Expedient* might have been floating in a cave.

Mr Gerrish moved out of his captain's way, wisely saying nothing. A moment later he turned the glass on the binnacle and rang out three bells on the small bell mounted above the rail at the break of the quarterdeck. Three bells. Five-thirty in the morning.

Steps on the quarterdeck ladder, and the gun-room steward appeared with a pot of something hot enough to emit steam and three mugs on a wooden tray.

'Coffee, sir? Piping hot, it is.'

'Coffee? I didn't . . .'

'Beg your pardon, sir,' said Gerrish from the other side of the deck. 'I took the liberty of ordering it up.'

Biddlecomb felt his mood brighten, as if the sun had suddenly popped up over the horizon to reveal a perfect mornng.

'Indeed, thank you,' Isaac said, and as the steward poured the blessedly hot liquid, he added, 'Please, Lieutenant, won't you join me. I wish my officers would take such liberties more often.'

Two minutes later Rumstick appeared on deck, dressed and ready to go. He took a mug of coffee, looked around, sniffed the air. 'Black as a damned coal mine, ain't it?' he said.

'Aye, sir,' Gerrish agreed. 'I've seen nothing move this entire watch. Like we were alone on the earth.'

'Humph,' said Rumstick. 'Throw in a few women and that might not be such a bad thing.'

'Indeed,' Gerrish agreed. 'We should repopulate the globe. Just imagine all of humanity descendant from the men aboard this ship.'

297

'Put that way, it is a more frightening prospect than what's already out there.'

'Very well, gentlemen,' Biddlecomb interrupted, in no mood for their silliness. 'If you are quite done rewriting the Book of Genesis, we have business to attend to.'

'Yes, sir,' said Gerrish. 'Are you certain you will not take an armed party? Beg your pardon, but I still think this might be a trap.'

'It is not a trap. This is Smeaton's last chance to regain some semblance of honor. He won't toss it away with such a deceit.'

With that, Biddlecomb and Rumstick climbed down into the jolly boat that was tied alongside and took their places, side by side on the center thwart, and picked up their oars.

'You still recall how to use them oars, Isaac?'

'I have had the chance to study others.' He pulled a small compass from his coat pocket and set it on the thwart between them. Gerrish untied the painter and tossed it down into the boat. Rumstick pushed off, and together they put their oars in the holes and pulled, falling into an easy rhythm.

'I recall the last time we were alone in a boat together,' Rumstick observed. 'Right after we took that one from that lieutenant who tried to arrest us in Newport. You recall?'

'I do. How long ago was that? Fifty years? Sixty?'

'Seems it. It was two, two and half years ago. A little more, in fact. Does seem more like sixty.'

They rowed for another fifteen minutes, making small corrections in their course to keep their heading just south of west. The sky began to lighten to a barely detectable degree, just the smallest relief in the blackness. Biddlecomb swiveled around, hoping to see the loom of Billings Island, which he imagined had to be close, but still there was nothing.

'Do you know what, Isaac?'

'What?'

'If I ain't mistaken, I think we are in a hell of a thick fog.'

Fog. Of course. It was hard to tell in the dark. But there should have been more light at that hour. They should have been able to make out the island. Just as he was about to concur with Rumstick's supposition, the bow of the boat ground to a halt, nearly toppling the two men into the bottom.

Rumstick tucked his oar on the thwart and climbed out. 'I reckon you found the Indies, Mr Columbus,' he said.

'Indeed.' Biddlecomb got out as well and they pulled the boat up the beach. 'I fear we will not find Smeaton quite as easily.'

They stood side by side and looked around. It was definitely lighter now; the air had a gray, diffused quality, and they could make out the beach at their feet and a good five yards in any direction. 'This way is as good as any, I should think,' Isaac said, pointing west.'

'Lead on,' said Rumstick, and the two men headed off with just enough light to keep from tripping over the rocks and driftwood scattered on the shore and the thick grass that in places ran down to the water.

Another fifteen minutes and it was full dawn, or so they guessed, judging from the light that filtered through the blue-gray mist in which they were enveloped. Visibility was a good fifteen feet, no more. They could hear water dripping from trees, the river lapping on the bank. The whole world seemed semiliquid, nothing solid save for the small patch of earth under their feet.

They stopped and listened.

'This is bloody futile, Isaac. How in hell are we supposed to find him in this?'

'Let me show you.' Isaac cupped his hands around his mouth. 'Smeaton! Smeaton!' His voice sounded odd, forlorn, as if the words were swallowed up by the fog.

And then, to their surprise, 'Biddlecomb? Are you there?' It seemed not so far off, though it was hard to tell in the fog.

'Smeaton? Where are you?'

'Here, follow this sound!' A tapping, like the flat of his sword on a rock, a noise for them to follow because it was beneath Smeaton to call to them.

'Same arrogant little son of a whore, ain't he?' Rumstick observed, and they headed off in the direction of the tapping.

The sound grew louder as they approached, but the direction from which it came was no more definite; it seemed first to their left, then their right, then right ahead once more. Biddlecomb could sense Rumstick's growing frustration as they stumbled after the annoying tap tap tap tap.

Ezra stopped. 'Smeaton, you little whoremongering—' he began to shout, then, like an apparition, a figure appeared from the fog just ahead of them, and then another. Dark, indistinct, shadowy forms.

'Ah, Rumstick, if I am not mistaken. Still showing off your Yankee-Doodle wit? Have you not yet been hanged?'

300

'It'll take more than you buggering British dance-masters to see me hung.'

'Thank you, gentlemen, that is quite enough,' Biddlecomb interrupted. 'Smeaton, you clearly recall Mr Rumstick, my second.'

'I shall never forget him. This is Lieutenant Calloway, my second.'

The other shadow stepped forward, a man somewhere in his thirties, dressed in the scarlet perfection of the marines. He held a long walnut box under his arm. He gave a quick bow, muttered, 'Honored.'

The two parties were five feet apart, and now they could make one another out, despite the mist that swirled between them. It was the third time in under two weeks that Isaac had faced Smeaton, but it was the first opportunity he had had to study him, the first time they had been face-to-face without weapons in their hands.

He did not look well. He seemed gaunt and drawn, and his clothes, which Isaac remembered as being finely tailored, seemed to hang off him. It may have been the fog, or the early hour, but the man he was facing seemed no more than the discarded shell of the former arrogant, wealthy, aristocratic prig that was John Smeaton. And Biddlecomb was glad. He hoped that Smeaton had suffered the torment of the damned.

'Well, Biddlecomb,' Smeaton began, and his voice at least carried the old attitudes, 'we have crossed swords thrice now. I thought perhaps pistols, for a change of pace? Though, now that I recall, you were frightened to meet me with pistols, was that not the case?'

Biddlecomb's eyes fell on the long box that the

301

marine was holding and his stomach dropped inside of him.

Pistols. He had not even considered fighting with pistols. He could still see Smeaton on the *Icarus*'s quarterdeck, shooting with ease bottles that bobbed in the water twenty feet away – a moving target from a moving platform. He was the best shot Biddlecomb had ever seen.

Isaac had avoided fighting with pistols the first time by claiming to be the challenged party. But no protocol would now allow him to refuse pistols, save to admit that he was afraid, and if he were to do that, he might as well just leave in disgrace, then and there.

'I have no objection to pistols. I see you were kind enough to bring your own.'

'Your second will choose and load your weapon for you?'

'Yes.'

The marine stepped up to Rumstick and opened the box, as if offering him a cigar.

Pistols. Biddlecomb swallowed hard, as discreetly as he could. Thought of Virginia. And Jack. God, why had he been so stupid? He would not live through this morning. He would be dead within ten minutes, and in his last moment with his beloved Virginia they had been in a mutual rage. He wanted to be an example of honor for little Jack, but how would the boy remember his father now? As a man who abandoned his family to satisfy some selfish revenge. A man who had entered into a duel he did not have the skill to win.

'Pretty damned wet out here,' Rumstick said, holding the beautiful weapon in his big hand. 'You reckon these pistols will fire?'

'They'll fire,' Smeaton said. 'You'll not get your master out of this with so weak an excuse as that. However, if you are afraid—'

'Shut your gob, Smeaton, you sniveling little prick,' Rumstick interrupted. 'Not everything anyone says is an excuse for cowardice, and if you need proof of that, I'll come over there and tear your arms off and beat you to death with them. Is that clear?'

Smeaton sniffed, said nothing, and Biddlecomb was surprised to see the marine, Calloway, fighting back a smile. That was the extent of personal loyalty that Smeaton was able to inspire.

At last the seconds were done. Biddlecomb and Smeaton removed coats and laid them on the ground, then took the pistols the two lieutenants offered.

'New pistols, Smeaton? I recall when you threw your others overboard, when you thought I was going to hang you. That was right before I put you and that little bastard Pendexter on the grating and set you adrift. Was that not humiliating, being found thus?' If he could make Smeaton angry, shake him a bit, there might be a chance.

'You would not understand. One needs honor to feel humiliation, and a rebel and traitor . . . a colonial . . . has none.' It was a good retort, but Smeaton bit the words off, and Isaac knew that some of his broadside had told. 'Ten paces, turn and shoot on Lieutenant Calloway's word?' Smeaton framed it as a question, but the tone was more along the lines of an order.

'I have no objections.'

The two men, the American and the Englishman, stood back-to-back, pistols raised in front of their

303

chests. Biddlecomb stared off into the distance as far as he could see, perhaps fifteen or twenty feet, before the world was lost in a gray purgatory. Here it was: the charge into the breach, the march to the gallows, the moment of going under for the third time. Imminent death.

He felt calm. Not frightened, just sad, infinitely sad. He recalled his anger with Virginia, but he could not understand it, could not summon the emotion or even the reasons for feeling it. He saw Jack, his eyes, his tiny hands.

'Gentlemen, on my count,' Calloway said. 'One, two, three . . .'

Isaac stepped off, marching to the hypnotic rhythm of Calloway's counting. He heard the sand crunching beneath his shoes, saw the mist recede before him. The butt of the pistol was warm under his hand. He could see a film of mist on the barrel. Perhaps it would not fire. But that would be like the hangman's rope breaking; they would just have to do it again.

'. . . seven, eight, nine, ten. Turn and fire.'

The moment, and now Biddlecomb was tensed, ready to fight, all thought gone save for survival and murder. He turned sharp, brought the pistol up as he turned, searched out the target. Smeaton was there, twenty paces away, but he was no more than a dark shade, a vague outline in the mist.

Biddlecomb peered over the sight of the gun, aimed for the bulk of the half-seen shadow, put pressure on the trigger, felt it yield under his finger.

And then from somewhere out in the mist someone yelled, 'Smeaton! Smeaton, where the devil—' and Biddlecomb fired and Smeaton fired, and the fog was lit up with the flash of their muzzles. The bullet

304

screamed by Biddlecomb's head, a half inch from his ear, the buzzing and the rush of air from the passing lead making him stagger sideways.

'Smeaton, where in the devil are you! Smeaton!'

A crunching on the sand, a shape looming in front of him, and there was Rumstick. 'Isaac, are you shot?'

'Nearly. Who is shouting? Is that Calloway?'

'No, Calloway was standing right next to me. I don't know who it is.'

'An armed party? Could this be a trap?'

'Perhaps. We best lose ourselves in the fog here.'

They stepped back, five feet, ten feet, until Smeaton and Calloway became almost indistinguishable in the mist and then were gone. Biddlecomb and Rumstick were standing in the open, perhaps twenty feet away, and they were as hidden as if they were buried in the sand. And from that vantage they listened to what was unfolding.

'Smeaton, where are you?'

'I am here.' Disgust, weariness in his voice.

'Smeaton . . . there you are. What are you about? They thought at Billingsport that you were here to fight a duel.'

'It is an affair of honor.'

'Yes, well, Captain Reeve is not much interested in your honor, such that it is, and he requires you return to the sloop immediately. He will not be pleased that it has taken me this long to find you. I have been looking the better part of an hour. We should have been back on board already. With whom were you having this . . . affair of honor?'

'It is none of your business, nor will I suffer you to speak to me with so insolent a tone. Remain here, I shall be but a moment.'

They could hear Smeaton's footsteps as he approached. Rumstick looked at Biddlecomb and smiled. 'Mother is calling him home, it appears.'

More footsteps, a pause, and then, 'Biddlecomb? Are you here, or have you run away?'

Biddlecomb pulled his sword. 'I am here, Smeaton.' He began to tap his sword on a rock. 'Just follow the sound.'

A moment later Smeaton appeared out of the mist and stopped five feet away. 'You will no doubt be most relieved to hear I have been recalled to duty.'

'Sounds like you're in for a spanking when you get home, little Johnny,' Rumstick supplied, but Smeaton ignored him.

'I shall not have the opportunity to kill you this morning,' Smeaton went on, 'but I have no doubt that you will be a prisoner shortly, unless you display your usual alacrity for running away. In either case—'

'Stow it, Smeaton,' Isaac said. 'I am in command of the *Expedient*. She is a xebec, lateen-rigged—'

'*Lateen* means them triangular sails, little Johnny,' said Rumstick.

'I know what a lateen sail is, you Yankee son of a bitch!'

'If you send word under flag of truce of where we may meet,' Isaac continued patiently, 'then I shall be there and we will settle this thing.'

'Very well, then.'

'Oh, Smeaton?' Rumstick said. 'There's one thing I've been meaning to ask you for some time now.'

Smeaton turned slowly, glared. 'Yes, what is it?'

Rumstick's left arm shot out, like a snake striking, faster than Smeaton could react. He grabbed the lieutenant by his shirt, jerked him forward, off-balance, and smashed his right hand into Smeaton's face, sending him sprawling to the ground, his nose crooked, blood sprayed across his chin and shirt even before he came to rest.

'Does that hurt?'

Smeaton touched his lip, looked at his finger, which was covered with blood. His expression was the most incredulous that Biddlecomb had ever seen. Smeaton had probably never suffered such an affront.

Smeaton looked up. 'A blow? You . . . you . . . Yankee bastard, you . . . filth . . . you dare strike me?'

'I reckon I did. I suppose I ain't so impressed with your pedigree.'

'How dare you?' Smeaton pulled himself to his feet.

'That was for Haliburton. Come over here and I'll give you one for Weatherspoon.'

'I will kill you for this!'

From out in the fog, the voice: 'Smeaton, hurry along!'

'Run along, little Smeaton,' Rumstick said.

'I will kill you!'

'So you said. But you still have Isaac to do first. After you kill him, then try me.'

Smeaton stepped back and stepped back again. Isaac could see his hands trembling, his face consumed with fury, looking even more horrible with the blood running down his nose. Isaac thought for a second that Smeaton might start to cry, so overwhelmed was he with rage. It was terrible, really, to see a human being, any human being, so swept up with hatred.

He turned and disappeared into the fog.

'We best get the hell out of here,' Rumstick said.

'They might have a whole landing party there, and little Smeaton might just lose all sense of his precious honor.'

'It won't do much for his position, returning to the sloop with a broken nose and nothing to show for it.'

'I know. Sweet, ain't it?' Rumstick was smiling again.

The two men turned and hurried back up the beach. The fog was already burning off; by the time they found the jolly boat they could see a hundred yards in any direction.

They took their seats on the thwarts and pulled for the *Expedient*. Below the *chevaux-de-frise* Biddle-comb could see the longboat bearing Smeaton and Calloway back to wherever they had been ordered. Isaac wondered what such a man was capable of, someone with so fine a sense of honor and position who had been so beaten down, so humiliated.

He imagined that it would not be long before he found out.

CHAPTER 20

Many of the Inhabitance of this City [Philadelphia], are very much Affected, by the present situation and appearance of things, while those on the other side of the question are flush'd, and in Spirits.

—DIARY OF ELIZABETH DRINKER

They sat across from one another in the carriage, rocking and bouncing in unison, sometimes talking, sometimes silent or looking out the window. Elisha Faircloth tried to be witty, tried to make their journey more enjoyable, but he could not entirely wipe away the sadness that Virginia was struggling to hide.

He stared out the window at the October-brown fields through which they passed. The clumps of trees that had survived the farmer's ax were starting to show their red and yellow plumage. The Pennsylvania countryside. The farms on the outskirts of Philadelphia. His home. He knew every foot of the land.

'You are not yourself a Quaker, sir?' Virginia asked, and Faircloth looked up, smiled.

'No, no. My family are Presbyterians, or some such. It makes it a bit awkward at times, you know, in the City of Brotherly Love, but we manage. The Quakers are not a bad lot, on the whole.'

'I have known a few of them, and I would agree. Religious tolerance, that is a big part of the Cause.'

'Your Rhode Island prejudice is showing. Or lack of prejudice. I think it more true that every group wants tolerance for themselves and the rest be damned. But in practice it would seem that there are so many groups wanting that, that the end result shall have to be universal tolerance.'

Virginia sighed, looked out the window, then back at him. 'This war has gone on for so long, Elisha. At first I had such grand visions. The army of Israel marching off to conquer the Philistines. Now I would welcome any means to achieving our ends. Stagger thoughtlessly into them, as you suggest. That would be fine.'

Faircloth smiled. 'Pray, do not disparage thought-less staggering. It has worked well for me for these thirty-seven years. Tonight we shall drink a toast to it.'

The bundle in Virginia's arms moved and cried out for feeding, so Elisha looked discreetly out the window. He and Virginia had dispensed with the 'Lieutenant Faircloth' and 'Mrs Biddleomb' formality while still in the boat pulling up the Schuylkill River. They had spent a comfortble night in the home of his friend there, a friend who had had no word of him for a year and a half, who was shocked to find him at the doorstep but welcomed him and Virginia effusively, eager to hear of his adventures.

That morning, after an expansive breakfast, they

were given free use of his friend's carriage and four, which was no mean dray but a beautiful piece of coachwork. Thus situated, as comfortable as they could be, they had rolled off across the countryside for the six-mile trip to Philadelphia.

Faircloth stole a quick glance at Virginia, then looked out the window again, craning his neck to see the spires of the city rising over the fields. Virginia was a stunning woman, he could not help but think it.

If she had been the wife of a man for whom he had less fear and respect and genuine affection, he might even have tried his luck with her. Had she been the wife of a Tory, he would have bedded her for certain, just on principle. But as she was Capt. Isaac Biddlecomb's wife, he would do no more than protect her in the manner he had promised.

At least I shall be in Philadelphia for a night or two, he mused. And while he would have to be very discreet – he was well-known in the city, even by some who would welcome the chance to report him to the British – still he had reason to hope for some amorous liaison. In Philadelphia he knew where to find love beyond the brotherly – or-sisterly – kind.

The spires grew more distinct, and around them rose the red-brick buildings that made up a goodly part of the former capital city of the United States. They rolled past the playhouse where Faircloth recalled with pleasure many evenings spent before the war. They were near the city now. He did not think they would go unmolested much longer.

From over their heads, the driver's gruff voice. 'Some kind of barricade up ahead, them damned lobster-backs.'

311

'Very well, just do as you are ordered,' Faircloth called back.

The carriage lurched to a stop. Elisha looked at Virginia and gave her a conspiratorial wink. 'Road-block. Can't allow any of this rebel vermin to crawl into the city.'

A man appeared at the window, wearing the cocked hat and red coat of British infantry. 'Right, then, who are you, where are you bound, and on what business?' Bored, condescending, antagonistic.

Faircloth sniffed, looked down his nose at the soldier, said in the haughtiest of tones, 'My name, Sergeant, is Makepeace, William Makepeace, and I do not care to be questioned about my comings and goings.'

'Well, I'm sorry Mr Makepeace, but I have orders to—'

'I am fully aware of your orders, Sergeant, as I am a particular friend of General Howe, and in fact am late for a dinner engagement with him at this moment. Please allow us to pass.'

'You got papers—'

'No, Sergeant, I do not. I live here, I am not in the habit of carrying papers in my own home. Now I insist you let us pass, or go and get your commanding officer. I have no time for this nonsense, being questioned by an enlisted man.'

The sergeant wavered, glanced off somewhere, probably in the direction of his commanding officer, and then stepped back and waved to the driver. 'Very well, you may go.'

The carriage lurched forward and they watched the fresh-turned earthworks, and the armed sentries pass from their view. 'That was very well done, Mr

312

Makepeace,' Virginia said when they were well clear of the soldiers.

'Thank you. British soldiers are like that, they are easily cowed by arrogance and presumptions of social superiority. Their officers see to it. It is in the nature of British society. If I were to try that with an American sentry, he would have dragged me out of the carriage and shot me, in the name of republicanism, even if George Washington himself were sitting beside me, and John Adams in your seat.'

'Your arrogance and presumption of superiority are most convincing.'

'That is because they are genuine.' He smiled to let her know he was making a joke. He was, of course, a gentleman of means, and he reckoned that she must know it. The manner with which he outfitted his marines would be proof enough.

She probably did not know that his father was the fifth-wealthiest man in Pennsylvania.

Of course, her own father had owned the *Charlemange* outright, and other ships as well, so he imagined that Virginia was no stranger to wealth herself.

Biddlecomb, as he understood it, had, by thirteen years of age, been a penniless orphan, a ship's boy. Now he had Virginia and the Stanton wealth. God, but he was a lucky man!

They passed into the city, and the hard-packed dirt roads gave way to the clatter and shaking of cobblestone. They rattled down Fifth Street, past clapboard houses and brick houses, their windows framed with dark shutters. They came to the intersection of Walnut. Virginia leaned forward and peered down the street.

'Reminiscing?'

313

'Hmm?'

'Reminiscing on your wedding day? Do not tell me you are not straining to see the church where you and Captain Biddlecomb were married.'

Virginia leaned back, smiled. 'You are right. I was.'

'Iaaac told me the particulars. He said it was bloody hot. They read the Declaration of Independence for the first time, like it was staged for you.'

'Yes.' Virginia was far away for a second, remembering.

Faircloth smiled. Independence for the United States, and something quite the opposite for Isaac that day. It was an irony Faircloth could appreciate. But Biddlecomb was the kind of man who was suited for marriage, generally.

'Elisha . . .'

'Yes?'

Virginia hesitated, and Faircloth knew what she was going to ask, and he knew he would answer, Yes, she was a fool to be angry and remain angry with her husband simply because he felt the need to defend his honor. What kind of a man would he be if he did not? They were fighting a war. There was every possibility that she would never see him again, alive or dead.

And then someone on the street laughed, loud, and Virginia startled and the moment was gone. They looked out the window again at the State House as they passed. The great brick edifice where the Continental Congress had met, where the Declaration of Independence had been signed. A British flag waved lazily at the flagpole, clusters of red-coated soldiers moved around the grounds.

Faircloth frowned. 'I am one of those who profess

314

that the loss of the capital is of no great consequence. Our nation is not dependent on fixed posts, and Howe's taking Philadelphia will gain him nothing. Indeed, it may be his downfall. But I confess that I am much distressed to see this.'

The coach moved past the State House and turned down Chestnut Street. 'At least the British occupation has relieved the crowding of vehicles in the streets. A year ago it would have taken us half an hour to move as far as we have in ten minutes. I suspect a good part of the population has fled, along with our esteemed Congress.'

Virginia looked out at the neat brick houses that stood shoulder to shoulder right on the edge of the sidewalk. 'We are almost there.'

'Pray, tell me again the name of the woman with whom you are staying?'

'Mrs Williams. She is a very old friend of the family, has been a widow these ten years or more. She lives here with her daughter, Susan, who is five years my senior. A sweet girl, if a bit of a . . .' Her voice trailed off.

'A bit of a what?'

'Well . . .' Virginia flushed, smiled. 'A bit of a tart.'

The carriage lurched to a halt and swayed as the driver climbed down. He opened the door and Faircloth stepped out and then offered his hand to Virginia, who stepped out as well, stretching and looking about. 'Nothing seems to have changed in the ten months since I was last here,' she observed.

The door to the nearest house flew open and a plump, ruddy-faced woman, gray hair tucked under a mobcap, came flying down the two granite steps and across the sidewalk, her skirts held clear of her feet.

'Oh! My precious Virginia! Oh, my, you are here at last, and we have been looking for you this past week and more! And my darling little Jack, let me look on you! Oh my, oh my, you are the very image of your father! Oh, oh . . .' She tickled the baby under the chin and then, noticing Faircloth for the first time, looked him over in a glance and said, 'Oh.'

'Mrs Williams, this is Elisha Faircloth, a dear friend of my husband's. Captain Biddlecomb is of course engaged, and Mr Faircloth kindly consented to escort me to your house.'

Mrs Williams gave an abbreviated curtsy. 'Charmed, Mr Faircloth,' she said, and went back to her hovering over Virginia and the baby.

Faircloth left Mrs Williams to her gushing. Standing framed in the door was a young woman whom he took to be Susan. She too wore a mobcap, a plain-looking garment, from under which tumbled the most extraordinary hair, blond in various shades, falling and spilling over her shoulders, framing a long neck, a lovely, sculptured face. Her breasts, which would have warranted Faircloth's attention in any event, were highlighted by her décolletage, with a line of teasing ruffle just along the edge, hiding her cleavage. The whole silk affair tapered down to a thin waist and then flared out again with the hoops of her skirt.

Faircloth paused, stared, with an uncharacteristic lack of calm disinterest. Susan cocked an eyebrow at him, an expression that might have meant anything, and then Virginia said, 'Oh, Susan, there you are. How very good to see you again.'

'And you, dear Virginia.'

They spoke in cool tones, just a touch of cattiness,

and Fairscloth had to smile. These two beautiful, headstrong young women. He could imagine that it would not take much for the fur to fly.

'May I introduce Elisha Faircloth?'

'Charmed,' said Susan, giving the same little curtsy as her mother, and then Mrs Williams was in charge of the party once more.

'You have arrived just in time for dinner and I reckon you are famished. Everything is in such short supply these days, what with the British taking the best of everything and our own army taking the rest, but I have managed to find a tolerable roast, and carrots and potatoes just in from my little garden, and we have scratched together . . .'

The litany of food, which belied its scarcity, continued as Mrs Williams ushered everyone into the house and directly into the dining room, seating them around the long table even as she directed the driver where to deposit the bags. Watching her, Faircloth could not help but think what a fine company-grade officer she would make. He could picture her standing amid the smoke and flying metal, calling out, 'Incline to the left! Take care to fire by divisions!' as she wiped her powderstained hands on her apron.

'Mr Faircloth,' a voice interrupted, and he found Susan looking at him from across the table. 'Might I inquire, are you of the Philadelphia Fairscloths?'

'I am. My father is Elisha Faircloth Sr.'

'I see,' she said, and Elisha could tell by her eyes that she did indeed see, that she was not insensible to the family's standing in the city. But there was still a coolness about her, as if he was somehow suspect.

317

Perhaps any acquaintance of Virginia's would be greeted thus.

'Now tell us, dear Virginia,' said Mrs Williams, seating herself at last, 'whatever has kept you so long?'

Virginia related the details of their trip from Boston, omitting Faircloth's name, giving no mention of his having even been on the ship, as they had agreed she would not. And though she played down the drama of the thing as much as was possible, she was met with a chorus of 'Oh, my's' and 'Oh, dear's' and 'You thing, how you have suffered! And you with a child!'

Nothing on the subject was said, but Faircloth had the impression from the various clucking noises she was making that Isaac was not faring well in Mrs Williams's esteem. She clearly disapproved of the danger in which he had inadvertently placed his wife and son, Virginia's own storm-into-the-breach attitude notwithstanding.

Susan played with her food, half listening and on occasion giving a sigh, as if some great thing were weighing on her mind. When Virginia was done with the tale, she looked up. 'And you, Mr Faircloth? You are not under arms? I should think you would be an officer in the Philadelphia Light Horse.'

'Oh, well . . .' Faircloth stumbled, and cursed himself for not having thought up a plausible explanation as to what he had been about.

'Mr Faircloth, I fear, is not in a position to discuss what he has been doing. We must be discreet while here in the city,' Virginia supplied. 'But you may rest assured that he has been most active in the Cause.'

'I see,' said Susan, and she looked at him with a new light in her eyes. He kept his expression grave and serious and nodded to her and she nodded back, but with a hint of a smile, coy and inviting.

There is nothing like a little intrigue, a touch of the mysterious, to excite a woman's fancy, he thought. Thank you, Virginia.

Perhaps he would not have to leave the house at all to satisfy his more base desires.

In the end he did leave the house, but only to go as far as the small and currently unoccupied servant's quarters at the far end of the little fenced-in lawn in the back.

By the time they had walked across the grass, Susan pulling him by the hand, and stepped into the plain, sparsely furnished room, Susan had become seemingly ravenous with desire. She spun around and kissed him as if she were drawing her very life from his lips, tangling her fingers in his hair, wrapping her arms around him, pulling at his clothing, while he, with a practiced ease, helped her out of her own.

She was more beautiful naked than clothed, which in Faircloth's experience was not always the case.

She looked her very best, he thought, the way he was seeing her at that moment, underneath him, her golden hair spread out in a great fan around her head, her long and delicate fingers clutching at the pillow or holding tight to the headboard, her lovely, smooth, tapered thighs pressed against his sides, her heels digging into the small of his back as she worked her body against his.

She gasped and bit her fist and then threw her head back and screamed with such enthusiasm that Elisha thought someone might kick in the door, certain that a murder was being committed. He covered her mouth with his, probed her with his tongue as she redoubled her motion, squeezing him with her legs, pulling his face down on her mouth, then down on her breasts.

She shrieked louder, tensed, and then her whole body went limp.

She panted for breath as Elisha continued to move inside her.

When all was done, they lay together, her head on his chest, which glistened with sweat despite the cool autumn evening. He ran his fingers gently through her hair, thought, This is far and away the best detached duty I have yet been ordered on.

'Oh, Elisha, this war is so dreadful,' she murmured after a few moments. 'And now will you have to go away from me?'

'I am afraid I will, my dear Susan.'

She sat up on her elbow, traced little circles on his chest with her finger. 'Will you come back to me?'

'Of course I will.' It was certainly the truth, insofar as he would one day return to Philadelphia and would look her up when he did. 'The war will not last forever.'

'I think you are a liar and no gentleman at all,' she said, but she was smiling and her voice was teasing. 'I think I shall not wait for you, not for a minute.'

'I should think you would not have to. There are men aplenty still, and none could be impervious to your charms.'

'There are men, to be sure. But none such as you, doing something so dangerous that you cannot even speak of it. Will you not tell me what it is you are about?'

'No. I cannot.' In fact, he probably could, but

he did not want to disappoint her or detract from the mystery. The reality of what he was – a mere lieutenant of marines, on a xebec of all things, would be dull indeed after the aura of intrigue he had created, at least in Susan's eyes. He did not want the truth to interfere with her rich fantasy.

'You are cruel to me. I have other men, you know, who are fighting for independence, and they tell me what they are about.'

'Indeed?'

'Oh, yes.' She put her chin down on his chest and smiled. 'I can be a very wicked girl.'

'I know.'

'I have a lover who is a shipwright, who has built some of the finest frigates in the Continental navy. For the last, he carved a figurehead in my likeness. What do you think of that?'

'I think there could be no more lovely image to adorn any vessel.'

'You are a flatterer. I have another lover who is a sergeant with the Fifth Pennsylvania, a great big fellow who would beat you soundly if he saw you here with me.'

'Let us hope he does not.'

'Do you think I am wicked?'

Elisha looked down at her lovely, teasing face. She was enjoying this, the tart, telling him about her other lovers. 'I do think you are wicked, but it suits you, you know?'

She slapped his chest with the flat of her hand. 'Beast. But here is the most wicked part of it. Neither of them know about the other, and they are both on the same ship, and not more than five miles from here.'

'They are part of the Pennsylvania Navy, then, keeping the British at bay?'

'No, they are on one of the new-built frigates that has been towed upriver. A mere shell, as I hear it.'

'The *Washington*, or the *Effingham*?'

'No, the *Falmouth*.'

Despite his attempt at disinterest – Faircloth did not entirely trust Susan or her professed Whig leanings – he could not hide his surprise at the name. She smiled, pleased to get such a reaction out of him. 'You are familiar with the ship? Don't lie.'

'I am familiar. I had heard a rumor that she was burned before launch,' he lied.

'Oh, no. She was launched and towed away and now is anchored just behind Petty's Island. It is but a matter of time before the British find her, I fear, and then my two dear men will be prisoners and I shall be more lonely than ever. But I shouldn't tell you this. I think you are a British spy.'

That was ironic, given his own distrust of her. Faircloth stroked her shoulder. He doubted that she was ever very lonely.

But this was extraordinary, what she was telling him. Here they had been going on faith and hope, not knowing if the *Falmouth* was complete or still intact or out of British hands, and she was telling him that the ship had indeed been saved and safely hidden, and not so far away. But not for long.

Biddlecomb had to be told this news. It was what they had suffered for this past month, what Weatherspoon and the others had died for, the thing for which the *Charlemagne* and the *Lady Biddlecomb* had been sacrificed. There was not a moment to lose.

Susan gave a low sigh, began to cover his stomach with little kisses, began to explore his body with her hands. He felt stirring in places where, ten minutes before, he had thought he might never feel anything again.

He thought, I cannot leave until first light in any event. Can't try to get through the roadblocks at night, I'd be taken as a spy for certain. He ran his own hand along the line of her thin shoulder and the small of her back and her firm, smooth buttocks, thought, First light, then, and not a moment later.

He was in his proper bed, the one that Mrs Williams had earlier directed him to, and in the deepest of sleep, when he felt a woman's hand on his shoulder, shaking him gently, a soft, feminine voice saying, 'Elisha? Elisha?'

He moaned slightly, thought, dear God, has she not had enough? He was not certain he could do it again, but as he came more awake, he guessed that probably he could.

He reached out and ran his hand along her leg – she was fully dressed, it seemed – and up along her stomach and around her waist, pulling her closer to him. He felt her hand on his, her firm grip as she removed his groping paw from her body.

He rolled back, opened his eyes, and in the light of the single candle she had brought he saw Virginia sitting on the edge of his bed.

'Oh, dear God!' he gasped, sitting bolt upright, pulling the blanket over his bare chest. 'Oh, dear God, forgive me . . .'

'No, never think on it. I am flattered. And I must say I am impressed with your stamina, Lieutenant.

After thrumming Susan all night I should think you would never have the energy for me.'

'Oh, Virginia, I thought . . . you never thought . . . ? What the devil are you doing here?' It occurred to him how very improper it was, that she should come into his bedchamber this way.

'We must go. It is an hour to dawn, we must be under way at first light.'

'What is it?' Faircloth was suddenly alarmed. 'Has something happened, some danger?'

'No, nothing like that.' Virginia was silent for a moment, staring at the guttering candle. She turned back to him. 'I must go back and see Isaac. I was a fool, was I not, to leave as I did? Angry at him, and just because he wanted to defend his honor, as any decent man would? I mean, what should I think of him if he was to shrink from such a challenge? I would loathe him if he were to hold his manhood so cheap, and yet I am so heartless when he will not?'

Elisha could see that she was on the verge of crying. He put his hand on her arm, a platonic, reassuring gesture, and she took it for that. 'Isaac is a proud man,' he said. 'We could not all love and admire him as we do if he were not.'

'You are right, and I was wrong, and worse I was a foolish and nasty witch. I must hurry back to him, I must apologize, beg his forgiveness. Oh, Elisha, I am frantic! He must have already met Smeaton by now, and even if he prevailed, he is still in the midst of fighting a war. What if he should have been killed already? Oh, God, however can I live with myself, knowing he went to the hereafter with my bitter words in his ears?'

'But you cannot take your baby back into the

fighting. He was damned lucky to come out of it unscathed. Isaac would not be pleased to see Jack in harm's way again.'

'Mrs Williams has sent for a wet nurse; Jack will be fine here until I return. I mean only to stay long enough to make my apologies and then go. I do not wish to be a burden any longer.'

'I can tell you, and I know this for a fact, you are no burden to Isaac. You are a comfort, despite the concern he has for your safety.'

'Thank you, Elisha.' She smiled at him. 'Perhaps he will ask that you escort me back again. Susan should be quite rested by then.'

'But I fear I shall not. I am no longer twenty years old, nor have I been for many years.'

Virginia smiled, squeezed his hand, and left him alone. He dragged himself from the bed, tired, aching, his nerves dull, and groped for his breeches.

He thought, This is perhaps the oddest night of my life.

But no, he thought on further reflection, he had certainly had odder still, if rarely so exhausting.

CHAPTER 21

Oct^r.

Wednesd^y 22^d

Billingsford E ¾ S ½ a Mile—

AM Warp'd thro' the Chiveaux de frize *in
company with the* Augusta *&* Liverpool. *At 10
Anch^d: with the S: B^r in 5 f^m muddy bottom . . .
At 1 p.m. His Majesty's Sloop* Merlin *& the*
Cornwallis *Galley warp'd thro the* Chiveaux de
frize *& Anch^d near us. At 5 Perceived a heavy fire
of Musketry at Red Bank and a Cannonading
from the Rebels' Vessels.*

—JOURNAL OF HMS *PEARL*
CAPT. JOHN LINZEE

On the twenty-second of October the British fleet
warped through the *chevaux-de-frise* at Billingsport.
It had taken them nearly three weeks to clear a
passage seventeen fathoms wide, to buoy it and move
their big ships through. Three weeks to accomplish
what might have been done in three days had the
Americans not tried to stop them.

They had done their work under a nearly constant

bombardment from the Continental fleet – gunboats and galleys, xebecs, schooners, and brigs. Their engineers had worked to drag the iron-tipped poles free from their cribs even as burning fire rafts and ships were floated down on them. Their men-of-war had sailed up to the *chevaux-de-frise* and anchored in support of the engineers, then dropped back downriver when the enemy's fire grew too hot. It was a difficult and dangerous task, but in the end it was done.

And to the Americans, who night and day tried to drive them from it, it was like trying to hold the tide at bay. There were minor victories – injuries doled out with the galleys' heavy bow guns, the pleasure of seeing Black Dick Howe's fleet driven off, the constant hope that one of the fire rafts would catch on one of the big ships – but those were mosquito bites to a bull.

Those sailors who did not desert the American fleet professed a near religious faith that Howe would be driven back, but few of them really believed it. They were fighting a delaying action. They could hold the tide back, for a while, but in the end it would overwhelm them.

And the most demoralizing aspect of the whole thing, the part that few thought about and none verbalized, was the utter pointlessness of it all.

Delaying actions had their place, to be sure. Washington had been fighting them almost from the beginning, forcing Howe to chase him and his tag and rag army all over the country, offering combat and then slipping away.

The last time was at a place called Germantown, two days after the British had taken the fortifications at Billingsport. A near-victory, a fight that actually put the illustrious Sir William Howe's army on the run, before British discipline conspired with fog and Continental blunders and misfortune to turn the battle around.

The Northern Army understood delaying actions as well. They had been fighting one against the British – first against Carleton and then Burgoyne – for over a year, leading them farther and farther into the woods of northern New York, weakening them like a pack of dogs on a bear, nipping, nipping, making the enemy exhaust himself with his own impotent rage.

Now there were rumors of a decisive battle, actually a series of battles, around the town of Saratoga, a fight in which Burgoyne had been trapped and his army taken. The Continentals had beaten the British army down, cut them off from supplies and reinforcement, and picked them apart.

That was what a delaying action could do.

It was not what would happen on the Delaware.

On the Delaware the British would eventually push the Americans back, sweep them aside, and join up with their army in Philadelphia. They would open and hold the supply route from the city to the sea, and then they could remain in Philadelphia for as long as they wished.

The clearing of the obstructions at Billingsport was the first crack in the dam, and once that crack had appeared, the flood was inevitable.

Those thoughts were certainly on the mind of Isaac Biddlecomb as he worked the *Expedient* down-river with the rest of the fleet, day and night, to drive the British off or to be driven off themselves. The inevitable failure of the Delaware River defenses occurred to him, depressed his spirit, along with that of all the other defenders.

And then on the morning of the twenty-second they watched the huge sixty-four-gun *Augusta* and the forty-four-gun *Roebuck* warp through the *chevaux-de-frise*.

But that was only a part of what worried Isaac Biddlecomb, and as it happened, the smallest part.

He worried first about Virginia, and though he told himself it was selfish, unprofessional, unpatriotic, to put his concern about his marriage before his ship and his men, such reasoning would not change a thing. He became physically sick when he thought about her anger, his foolishness, the fact that he might well die without even being able to set it right.

And then, like a dream, three days after she'd left, she had returned, with Lieutenant Faircloth beside her, apologizing that he could not prevent her returning.

They had embraced, there on the deck, there at the gangway, kissed deep, never saying a word, careless of their complete lack of decorum, of the grins and nudges and suggestive gestures that circulated among the men.

'I'm sorry, I'm sorry, I should never have risked abandoning you and Jack for something so childish as this affair with Smeaton.'

'No, my love, no, I would never have you compromise your honor for my foolish fears. I was selfish and petty. Pray, forgive me.'

Their conversation never went beyond that, never achieved any resolution beyond their both apologizing. They retired to the great cabin, where they were able to give one another a more physical display of their mutual relief and affection. With nothing but the single hanging cot in that small space, they made love on the deck, next to the stern gun, cushioned by the pile of their discarded clothes. It was the best they had ever had.

Four hours later Virginia was gone again, once more under the protection of Lieutenant Faircloth, whom Biddlecomb feared would resent being given that assignment a second time, but who in fact seemed positively eager to return to the city. Isaac recalled that Faircloth was from Philadelphia, reckoned he welcomed the opportunity to visit with family.

With the debilitating anxiety over his marriage put to rest, and his sexual appetite sated, Biddlecomb might have been content. But along with Virginia, Faircloth had brought a new consideration, one that awoke in Isaac a paternal concern that nearly rivaled that which he felt for his family.

The *Falmouth*. Word of his frigate. A rumor of her whereabouts.

Faircloth stresssed that he had no way of knowing the accuracy of the rumors, and he declined to indicate their source; he simply repeated what he had heard, but that was enough to fill Biddlecomb with anxiety and a desperate longing to be under way. Most rumors, in his experience, had at their core some germ of truth. Why would someone make up the story that Faircloth had related? It made no sense.

Confusion, uncertainty, lack of direction. It swirled around the American fleet and found a home in the great cabin of the *Expedient*.

They were at anchor, like most of the American

ships, just off the shore of Fort Island, two hundred yards from Fort Mifflin, the heart of the remaining Continental defense. Only three miles downriver they could see the British fleet working their way through the gap in the *chevaux-de-frise*. They could see it but they could do nothing to stop it.

'Well, damn it, we ain't officially attached to the navy here,' Rumstick offered. Biddlecomb had gathered his officers in the great cabin, solicited their opinions. 'We've done a hell of a lot for them, I reckon. Been under Hazelwood's command for over two weeks now, fighting almost every night, and with never an official order to do so. We were ordered to take command of the *Falmouth*, and I reckon we had best do it.'

Gerrish shifted uncomfortably. 'Mr Gerrish?' Biddlecomb prompted.

'Well, sir, Lieutenant Rumstick's right, to be sure, we're under no official obligation to continue with the fighting here, but orders are one thing and duty is another. I wonder if our duty is not to place ourselves where we might do the most good.'

'That is a valid point,' Biddlecomb said.

'It ain't up to us to decide where we would do the most good,' Rumstick countered. 'We have orders. Our duty is to follow orders. You can't have a navy with everyone deciding where his own duty lies.'

That was a valid point as well. 'Mr Faircloth?'

The marine let out a long sigh. 'Such a conundrum. I had thought that as a mere lieutenant I should not have to think on such things. But all philosophizing aside, it seems to me that if we do not stay and aid in the defense, then it is all the more likely that the route to the sea will be blocked, completely in British hands. Getting to the *Falmouth* will do us little good if we cannot then get her to sea.'

'Not necessarily,' Biddlecomb said. 'If the *Falmouth* is where your informant says she is, then she is in great danger indeed. We could tow her further up-river, up where the British would be less likely to get to her.'

Faircloth nodded. 'That is a good point.'

'Oh . . . damn it all to hell!' Rumstick said, his low threshold of tolerance for such nice discussion now met and surpassed.

'Gentlemen,' Biddlecomb said, 'I thank you for your counsel. This is my decision. Our orders were to proceed to Philadelphia and take command of the frigate *Falmouth*. These orders have not changed. We now have some word of her whereabouts, enough at least that we must act. More to the point, I shall go mad if we do not seek her out directly.

'I will go and see Hazelwood and ask permission to proceed upriver with the *Expedient* and try and locate her. As he is a commodore of the Pennsylvania Navy and we are under orders from Congress, he has no authority over us, only the xebec. All he can do is make us give back his boat, in which case we will find another. We've had famous luck in that regard, so far. Agreed?'

The officers nodded. 'Agreed,' they said in near unison, and then, as if God were offering his opinion, the rumble of cannon fire filled the cabin.

'What the hell?' asked Rumstick, and then they were all scrambling for the door, impatiently standing aside to allow Biddlecomb to exit first. They came out in the waist, which was lined with men peering over the bulwark, staring across the river at Fort

Mercer. They hurried up to the quarterdeck, lined the rail, and stared themselves.

A gray cloud of smoke was rising from the far side of the fort, rising from the line of trees four hundred yards beyond.

'Artillery,' Faircloth said.

'They're attacking Mercer,' said Gerrish.

For ten minutes the officers watched the flashes among the trees, the clouds of smoke billowing up from the woods. Red Bank, on which sat Fort Mercer, was only two miles away.

Then the artillery stopped and out of the woods came a great column of men, charging over the open ground, sweeping toward the fort in an arc from the south. Biddlecomb put his telescope to his eye, as did the other officers. He saw blue uniform coats, dark blue and light blue, and white as well.

'Hessians,' Faircloth said. 'Bloody Hessians.'

'Bloody German butchers,' Rumstick muttered.

Biddlecomb watched them advance across the open ground, waited for the blast of grape and small arms from the Americans in Fort Mercer, but the ramparts were silent. He was marveling at what a perfect view he had of the battle; he was looking right at the Hessian's flank. Then it occurred to him that perhaps he could do more than look.

He closed his telescope with a snap. 'Mr Rumstick, please buoy and slip the cable. Mr Gerrish, let us make sail. Mr Faircloth, I leave you in charge of the bow gun. We shall see if we can't make some sausage meat of these German bastards.'

In less than five minutes the *Expedient* was under way and she was not alone. Every vessel in the American fleet was either moving or getting ready to move, under sail or sweeps, making all possible speed for the south bank, desperate to bring their guns to bear on the Germans, who were just reaching the outer works of the fort.

Biddlecomb stood on his quarterdeck and watched the assault through his glass. He saw the Hessians hit the first ramparts and keep on going, saw them rush forward with unmistakable confidence, saw them throwing hats in the air. Over the mile and a half of river between him and the fort, he heard shouting, triumphant shouting, and he thought, I am too late.

And then the shouting was cut off by the sound of a volley, small arms and grape, and then another and another. Through his glass Biddlecomb saw the Germans stagger back, saw some turn and run, saw dozens fall under the fire coming from the defenders within.

There was confusion in the Germans' ranks. They were stopped by the sharp, overhanging poles of the abatis outside the redoubt, seemed not to have the means to get over that obstacle, and so they stood and endured the murderous fire from the fort. Here and there groups of men broke and fled, some making it to the trees, some being driven back into place by their officers.

Biddlecomb turned from the view in his glass to the view of his deck. The sails were set and trimmed to perfection. The *Expedient* would sail no faster than she was. In the bow the twenty-four-pounder was running out and Faircloth was positioning the hand-spike men in preparation for training the big gun around. Sprout and Rumstick were laying out an old sail to use as a drogue in lieu of their one anchor, which they had left on the bottom of the river in their desire for haste.

There were no orders he needed to give, nothing he could do to get into the fight faster. He could only hope that the Germans would not retire or prevail before he got there.

The Germans would not retire, that was soon clear. They were professionals, used to the battlefields of Europe, and the fort's first repulse would not be enough to drive them away.

They had fallen back, two hundred yards, and their officers were forming them again, getting them back into their disciplined columns, readying them for another headlong assault. Now that they knew the Continentals were waiting behind the redoubt, they would not stop until they came to grips with them.

They did not, however, understand the threat that was sweeping in from the water. They could not, Isaac imagined, or they would not be standing as they were, fully exposed to the small fleet racing across the river.

'Mr Gerrish, let us brail up the sails. Out sweeps.'

They were a quarter of a mile from the column, well within range of the twenty-four-pounder. The Germans were starting to move, advancing at a steady and mechanical pace. If any of them had noticed the new threat, they were doing nothing to avoid it.

'Mr Faircloth, you may fire at will.'

Faircloth called for the handspike men to train the gun around, but he was not the first of the Continental fleet to fire. Half a dozen boats, vessels faster than the clumsy *Expedient*, had pulled past them, and within half a minute of one another they let loose on the Hessian column.

Biddlecomb watched through his glass as the orderly line was blasted apart. One moment there was a solid column of men, then one of the fleet's guns blasted and a gap appeared, and in the gap, fallen men, dead and wounded.

And then the *Expedient*'s gun went off, a blast that shook the vessel as if she had run up on a rock, and Isaac's view of the battle was lost in the smoke.

He turned to Rumstick. 'I can't imagine the Germans will stand for much of this.'

'Let us hope not. They'll be getting their own help from the water, soon enough.' He pointed down-river, down toward Billingsport. The British ships that had come through the *chevaux-de-frise* were setting more and more sail, trying to cover the three miles to Red Bank in time to drive off the American fleet before the American fleet drove off the German infantry.

Augusta and *Roebuck*, the frigates *Liverpool* and *Pearl*, and the *Merlin*, Smeaton's *Merlin*, were all under way, all working their way upriver, trying to bring their overwhelming firepower to bear. The battle, which had at first involved only the four hundred Rhode Island troops holding Fort Mercer and the two thousand Hessians arrayed against them, had now become a naval battle on a theater-wide scale.

But the fight for Fort Mercer was over. By the time Biddlecomb pulled his eyes from the advancing men-of-war and looked back at Red Bank, the Hessians were in full flight.

There was no organization in their retreat, no orderly withdrawal. It was a rout, the soldiers running headlong for the protection of the woods, fleeing from the devastating fire from the fort and the American fleet. The field was covered with wounded and dead left behind, hundreds of men, carnage such as Isaac had never seen. He was happy to be seeing it from such a distance.

He could hear cheering from Fort Mercer, cheering from the other vessels. It spread to the *Expedient* and his own men cheered, and he let them, let them yell as long as and as loud as they liked. They had had precious little to cheer about as of late. And when the British fleet had them under their guns, they would have even less.

CHAPTER 22

Oct

Wednesd[y] 22[d] -

Billingsfort E ¾ S ½ a Mile—

Got under weigh'd with the Augusta, Roebuck,
Liverpool Merlin *&* Cornwallis *Galley & work'd
up the River in order to engage the Rebels' Vessels
and prevent their firing on our Troops who
appear'd to be much gall'd from the Enemie's
Shipping. ½ past the Rebels Galleys &c began
firing on us.*

—JOURNAL OF HMS *PEARL*
CAPT. JOHN LINZEE

James Smeaton stood on the heel of the *Merlin*'s
bowsprit, elbows resting on the top of the knight-
head, and peered upriver through his glass. He had
abandoned the quarterdeck twenty minutes before;
the view from there was too restricting with the
foresail set, and he found the company intolerable.
That feeling, he knew, was mutually held.

Smeaton knew what obsession was, understood it
intellectually, had even known a few men gripped by

one such passion or another. And now, he realized, he was himself a man obsessed. He still retained enough of his senses that he could step back and marvel at how all-consuming such an obsession was, but he could do nothing to break free of his desire, nor would he if he could.

Rather, he gave in to it, let it possess him, drive him, to the point where everything else – eating, shaving, standing his watch – became a mere annoyance, a distraction to his life's work. He lived them again and again, those scenes that had become the defining moments of his life: Biddlecomb forcing him onto that grating and setting him adrift, Rumstick's fist crashing into his face.

He was aware of the smirks, the stares, the amusement, the disgust, of his fellow officers, even the warrant officers and the men, as he came back aboard the sloop, his face imperfectly washed of blood, his nose crooked and swollen, his eyes turning purple. He had stood silent as Reeve lectured him, insulted him, abused him about not attending to duty, about fighting duels, about his poor performance as an officer. But Smeaton was numb to it. It made no difference. Duty and the Royal Navy were no longer what he was about.

He was staring upriver at the American fleet as back on the quarterdeck Reeve and the pilot, Matthew Croell, struggled to get the sloop up to Red Bank, to bring her broadside to bear on the little ships that were decimating the Germans attacking Fort Mercer, to keep from running her aboard the *Roebuck*, which was close by the larboard bow.

He had seen them immediately, the twin lateen sails of a xebec. They were nearly the first sails to be set when the rebel fleet got under way. How many xebecs could there be on the river? Even the idiot Yankee-Doodles, who probably thought they were re-creating the glory of ancient Egypt, so desperate were they to ape all things classical, could not have so many of them.

It was Biddlecomb. He knew it, felt it deep inside. Biddlecomb and Rumstick. The grating. The blow.

He stared with a concentrated hatred and his mind wandered and he saw himself as a giant, the Delaware River no more than ankle deep to him, as he stomped, stomped the little boats underfoot. He saw bits of broken planking, no more than toothpicks to him, floating up from the muddy bottom. He saw Biddlecomb and Rumstick in the palm of his hand, puny as insects, Reeve and Colcot and Croell flicked off the *Merlin*'s quarterdeck like crumbs from a table, their screams tiny and pathetic, the *Merlin* picked up and flung like a child's plaything.

'Mr Smeaton?'

He startled, flushed, as if the midshipman interrupting him could see his infantile daydream. 'Yes?'

'Captain's compliments, sir, and as you are forward already, would you mind laying into the foretop to watch for the fall of our shot? We're to engage at long range.'

Smeaton stared into the young man's eyes. He did not see the amused disdain of the others, but he knew it was there, just better hidden. He knew that his face, though now somewhat healed, was still purple and black, his nose swollen. Everyone found it disgusting or amusing or both. Once, such damage to his fine looks would have tortured him, but no more.

340

Without a word he hopped down from the bowsprit and climbed into the fore shrouds and aloft.

From his perch on the foretop Smeaton had an excellent view of the river and the American fleet above and the British ships below. Better than a mile separated the two sides, extreme range for cannon fire, but with the sun nearly down and the rebels' little ships inflicting such damage on the Hessians attacking Fort Mercer, they had no choice but to engage. They could not wait until they drew closer. By then it would be dark and the rebels would be gone.

The *Merlin* opened up just as Smeaton settled with his legs hanging over the edge of the top. He could see the shot falling like raindrops in the river, a mile away. He called down, 'Short!' Thought, Of course it's short, you damnable moron, firing from this range.

Astern of them the *Augusta* fired as well, a deeper and more menacing sound erupting from the two-decker's heavy battery. Her round shot reached to the Americans and beyond, sending spouts of water up among the many small ships and no doubt scoring a few hits, though Smeaton could not actually see any damage done. And there was *Liverpool* firing as well, and *Pearl* and *Roebuck*, as well as the fifty-gun *Experiment*, just arrived after having cleared the Hudson River of rebels.

And the rebels were firing back, even though all of their tonnage combined probably did not equal that of the *Augusta*, nor all of their guns her broadside. But they were maneuvering under sweeps, bringing their bows around to bear on the British fleet, and scoring not infrequent hits.

The thought crossed Smeaton's mind that the rebels were displaying an admirable amount of courage and fortitude in the face of an overwhelming enemy. And then he realized with horror what he was thinking – mentally praising the rebels – and he banished those thoughts from his head.

But for all there was to see from the top, his glass never strayed for long from the xebec, just over a mile away. He stared, sitting utterly still, but his thoughts raged. He felt like a cat, frantic to get at a bird through a window, like a dog snapping and barking at the end of its leash. He wanted desperately to engage at point-blank range, to blast holes through the xebec's frail scantlings. Had he been in command of the *Merlin*, he would have plunged right into the rebels' midst, firing away, fire ships and *chevaux-de-frise* be damned. But he was not in command, was not likely to be, and he could do nothing but watch.

The gun in the xebec's bow fired and fired, throwing out its pinprick of light every minute or so. With an entire ship's company manning a single weapon it was little wonder that their rate of fire was so high.

The muzzle flash grew brighter as evening closed in and the light of the day faded. The wind was light and did little to lift away the great quantities of smoke from the incessant gunfire. It hung like fog over the river, making it harder yet to see. Smeaton realized that he had entirely forgotten about reporting the fall of the shot, and no one of the quarterdeck had reminded him.

At last the flames from the guns were all that was to be seen of the rebel fleet. The word to cease fire passed among the British ships, and the guns were loaded one last time and then housed. All sail came in, save for topsails and jibs, as the ships felt their way upriver through the smoky twilight.

No word was sent to the foretop giving Smeaton permission to lay back to deck. He imagined that the vermin aft hoped he would stay up there all night, but he would not. He climbed down the futtock shrouds and down the fore shrouds and then ambled along the gangway to the quarterdeck. It was fully dark by the time he arrived.

Captain Reeve and the pilot, Croell, were by the weather rail, staring out toward the dark water. Croell was shaking his head, gesturing upriver. Smeaton thought, Pathetic son of a bitch, forever making his excuses.

'River used to be predictable as sunrise,' the pilot said, 'same shallows summer and winter. It's them damned obstructions the rebels have sunk, they've changed the current and that's changed the shoaling. That place where we touched, back there? Four fathoms. That was always four fathoms, never an inch more or less.'

'Yes, well, I had hoped to see the signal to come to anchor, but now I think it will not be forthcoming,' said Reeve. From the forechains, starboard and larboard, came the alternating plunk of the leads hitting the water, the calls of the leadsmen, 'Three fathom this line!' or 'Four and a half and shoaling!'

'The men in the forechains are only going to do us so much good, Captain. Them mud banks shoal fast. We'll be aground between casts. And I wouldn't think it amiss if the damned *Roebuck* would give us some sea room.'

343

'Right,' said Reeve, the sound of a man coming to a decision. 'Ah, Mr Smeaton, there you are!'

Smeaton crossed the quarterdeck with the enthusiasm of a man climbing the gallows steps. 'Sir?'

'Lieutenant, we are having the devil of a time with these mud banks and channels all shifting due to the damned rebels and their underwater obstructions. I need someone to go ahead of the ship and take soundings. The men in the chains won't answer, we could go aground between casts of the lead.

'I'm afraid this is simply too important for me to put it in the hands of a midshipman. You will take the gig and sound one hundred yards ahead of us. Pocock's the best leadsman aboard, take him. Carry a lantern and blink three times if we should come to an anchor, four to come about if the water shoals to two and a half fathoms. Is that clear?'

'Aye, sir.' Oh, it was clear. It was all clear – and had been for some time.

Ten minutes later Smeaton settled in the stern sheets of the gig and ordered the men at the oars to give way, and they drew ahead of the slow-moving *Merlin*. They passed under her figurehead, a man with a bare, muscled chest and long beard flowing aft that might be construed as the wizard of ancient lore, passed under her bowsprit that seemed so massive and majestic from the low angle of the boat, and then left the ship behind as they took their position half a cable length ahead.

'Very well, Pocock, you may begin casting the lead,' Smeaton growled. In the bow the leadsman stood and swung the conical lead back and forth, then tossed it forward, letting the marked line run through his fingers.

'Four fathom; four fathom, this cast.'

The leadsman's chant was as familiar a sound as the squeaking of the pumps or the slatting of canvas, and soon Smeaton no longer heard it. Rather he let his mind go back to those thoughts from which it never strayed for long.

They were both of them upriver, Biddlecomb and Rumstick, just upriver, within easy reach, but they may as well have been on the moon for all the good it did him. If he had just an hour of freedom, he could run them to ground, kill them both, but that was too much to ask for. He had no freedom, rather he was condemned to exile in the damned . . .

Boat. Smeaton sat upright, gripped the gunwale hard. He was in a boat, on the river, and all but lost from sight of the *Merlin* in the growing dark. Whatever had he been thinking? Here was the perfect oppportunity, further proof that it was the Almighty's will that he fulfill his destiny. There was no other explanation for the perfect symmetry of the whole thing.

'Here, pick up the pace, you bloody laggards, the sloop will run us down directly,' he growled at the men at the oars, and though a few eyebrows were raised and a few questioning looks shot along the thwarts, the men leaned into their oars and pulled with an increased tempo.

'Four fathom, four fathom . . .'

Smeaton looked astern. The *Merlin*'s topgallant masts and yards were still discernible in the setting sun, but her hull was no more than a dark shape against the river. He doubted if the gig was visible at all from her deck. They would be looking for the signal from the lantern.

Smeaton glanced at the compass on the thwart, nudged the tiller over a few inches. He had been steering north northwest, the heading that *Merlin* was on. But to find Biddlecomb he would need a course more like west northwest. He eased the tiller a little farther over.

'And four and a half, and four and a half. . . sir?'

'What is it?' He could see Pocock staring up at the smattering of stars overhead.

'Sir, are we on the right heading? Beg your pardon.'

'You just cast your lead and don't worry about our heading. Navigation is not your concern.'

'Aye, sir.'

'And you men on the oars, you are slacking again. Pick it up, pick it up, I say.'

A few coughs, a few sideways glances, but the beat of the oars increased, and the note of the water sliding under the boat went up in pitch and Smeaton nudged the tiller a little more.

'Three and a half, three and a half and shoaling . . .'

The *Merlin* was gone now, lost in the darkness as twilight settled into evening. And she was considerably more than one hundred yards astern; Smeaton guessed the gig was moving at three knots to the *Merlin*'s two. A quick sprint up to the rebel fleet, a white flag, a challenge or even a duel there on the xebec's deck, and back to their station before the sun was up.

'Three fathom, three fathom . . . Sir, are you quite sure of that compass? We must be steering close to north by west, a half west, and the sloop was making—'

'Silence! Yes, I am sure of the compass. Here, I shall signal for the sloop to put about.'

346

'But, sir, were we not to wait until two and a half fathoms . . .'

Smeaton swiveled around, held the lantern above the gig's transom, and flashed it into the dark, four times.

'Sir, don't you reckon—'

'Shut your impudent gob, you son of a bitch! You do not, do not, question my orders! Now, the lot of you, we have to get ahead of the sloop once more, now that she is on a new tack, so pull, double-time, pull!'

More coughs, and even a few murmurs, but once again the men followed orders, pulling hard, and Smeaton felt the light boat leap ahead. He put the tiller over more boldly this time – the men would expect a change of course if they were now trying to overtake the sloop – and settled the gig down on a heading that would take them right up to Red Bank, right up to the place where he had last seen the xebec.

They pulled for an hour, pulled past various lights on the shore, distant clusters of anchor lights, the dull glow of fireplaces burning in homes, many miles off. It grew cold, and the pace slackened, and the muttering came more and more frequently, but still the men followed orders and rowed.

Smeaton was aware of the ugly mood in the boat, but it did not concern him, and soon he put the men out of his mind as he searched the dark for some sign of the American fleet. He was aware of Pocock in the bow, glancing more and more frequently at the stars, saw him shake his head now and again. It was irritating, but he managed to ignore that as well as he considered what he might use as a flag of truce, what he might say to Biddlecomb when they met again, how Rumstick would look with a bullet through his face.

He could see no sign of the rebel shipping at Red Bank, but to the north was a cluster of lights that Smeaton guessed was the American fleet riding at anchor. They must have crossed back to Fort Mifflin. He put the tiller over again, swung the bow north.

'Toss oars!'

Smeaton looked up, startled. No one had the right to say that but him, and yet someone had. Pocock. And worse, the men obeyed, lifting their dripping blades from the water, staring aft at him with their suspicious and impudent expressions.

'What is the meaning of this? You ship your oars and give way now! Pocock does not give orders in this boat!'

'Sir, we've lost the *Merlin*. We're nowhere's near her now. What do you reckon you're doing?'

'What I am doing is of no concern of yours! You just follow orders, do you hear?'

'I hear, sir. But I think not.'

Smeaton was dumbfounded by this. It was mutiny, outright mutiny, completely ignoring his orders. But at the same time he understood that he had no authority over these men, because these men knew that their captain had no love for him or confidence in his abilities. Reeve and the others had stripped him of the moral authority he should have had over the men, by their failure to show him any respect. And without that, and with his being outnumbered in the boat, there was nothing he could do.

Well, there was one thing he could do. He brushed

his boat cloak aside and pulled his pistol from his belt, aimed it at Pocock, and pulled back the lock.

'You will obey my orders, do you hear?'

There was silence in the boat, only the lap of the little waves against the side. The men stared at him, not afraid, not angry, just impassive, as if they were waiting for him to finish so they could get on with their business.

'If you shoot one of us, it will be murder, sir, and you will hang.'

'Murder? This is mutiny! You shall all hang!'

'No, sir, I don't think so.'

God, he was right. The son of a bitch was right. Reeve would take Pocock's side, not his, officer though he was. And besides, what would he say to justify his actions? He had ignored his duty, gone off on his own. Pocock was trying to get him to go back and do as he had been ordered.

He felt as if all of the strength had been sucked from him. He lowered the gun – it was suddenly too heavy to hold – and rested it on the thwart. He threw his head back and gulped air, felt the tears welling up in his eyes. He fought them back. That would be the end, if he were to cry in front of these men. That would be the end.

How could it have come to this, when it had been God's will that he have his vengeance on Biddlecomb?

'Very well. I shall ignore this . . . insurrection. This time,' Smeaton said at last, finding deep inside himself a spark of that arrogance that had formerly passed for competence and authority. He eased the lock back to half cock.

'Ship oars. Give way.' With the same passive, silent disrespect, the men put their oars back in the tholes and pulled, and Smeaton put the tiller over, bringing the boat around to a heading just south of east, a direction in which they might realistically hope to find the *Merlin*. Pocock sat in the bow, watching him, watching the stars.

They pulled for another hour, slower this time, the men cold and tired. The same lights they had passed going upriver they passed going down, the same blackness, the same great void that was the Delaware River at night.

Smeaton pointed the bow toward a light that he was now fairly certain was an anchor light, perhaps *Merlin*'s.

As they made their way downriver, as the passion of his vengeance dulled and his return to the sloop became more imminent, Smeaton began to wonder what he would say. Had he pushed his luck too far this time? Reeve would certainly ask the boat crew what had happened. He would take that villain Pocock's word over his own.

The light grew brighter, closer, and then another one, another vessel, apparently, appeared behind the first. Smeaton began to be afraid.

They were still two hundred feet from the ship when he realized that she was not *Merlin*. She was much larger than the sloop, and the light behind was on a smaller vessel anchored nearby. *Roebuck*, perhaps, or *Augusta*, with their tenders. He held his course, which was bringing him past the big man-of-war. They drew within hailing distance and he realized that she was HMS *Experiment*, riding at a single anchor.

'Hoa, the boat ahoay!' The hail came from *Experiment*'s waist. 'From what ship?'

'*Merlin!*'

'Very well, come aboard!'

That was not the response that Smeaton had expected, but he did not care to argue the point, yelling up the side of the two-decker, so he steered for the boarding steps. Pocock grappled the main-chains with the boat hook as Smeaton climbed up the side and through the gangway.

Being acclimated as he was to the size of the *Merlin*, the *Experiment* seemed enormous, with great acres of deck space, a place altogether more befitting a gentleman. He looked around with satisfaction at the orderly bustle, the hundreds of men turned out and busying themselves about the deck, the blue-coated officers on their broad quarterdeck aft, set well apart from the mob.

It had just occurred to him to wonder what the men were so busy at, at that time of the night and with the ship at anchor, when the officer who had hailed him stepped up.

'Lt John Smeaton, second of the *Merlin*,' he introduced himself.

'Lieutenant Howard, I'm second here.' Smeaton saw the eyes flicker over his damaged face. 'The old man says we can give you the barge and the stream anchor, and crew for that, but that is all. We can spare no more. *Augusta* needs the longboat.'

Smeaton squinted, frowned. He had no idea what this Howard was talking about. 'Give us . . . the barge?'

'Yes, the barge, but that is all,' said Howard, making no effort to hide his impatience. 'They are lowering the stream anchor onto the davits now.'

'You have the advantage of me, sir. I confess I do not know what you are on about.'

351

'Are you not from *Merlin*?'

'I am. My party was sounding ahead, to see that the sloop does not take the ground.'

'Oh, indeed. Well, a bloody poor show you've made of it. *Merlin* is hard aground by the Jersey shore, has been these three hours and more. *Augusta* as well. Did you not know?'

'No . . . I . . . we . . . thought she was behind us. I was signalling . . . seemed to have lost her when she went about . . .'

'Perhaps you had best speak with the captain. Have your men come aboard.'

Smeaton watched Howard step aft and felt his stomach sink away, saw his bleak, bleak future laid out before him. Dismissed from the service, back to England in poverty, begging from his dear friend, the still wealthy but socially outcast James Pendexter, his fellow pariah. Back to the Colonies as a civilian, trying to hunt Biddlecomb down, turning quickly into a broken, sodden wretch.

He leaned out the gangway, shouted down to the boat. 'You lot, up on deck.'

In a moment Howard was back. 'Come along, please, the captain will see you.'

'Captain . . . Wallace, is it?'

'Yes. Sir James Wallace.'

Of course. It was Sir James now. Of all the damned luck. Wallace was well known as a cold and heartless disciplinarian, a man who would suffer no nonsense or breach of authority, beloved of the Admiralty, feared by his subordinates. Smeaton felt a cold dampness on his palms. He wiped them on his coat, followed behind Howard.

They made their way under the wide quarterdeck

and aft, to the bright-painted bulkhead that closed off the great cabin. The marine sentry stood aside, allowing Howard and Smeaton to pass.

The luxury of the great cabin was a comfort; it gave Smeaton a sense of his past life, of elegant balls and grand country estates, the season in London. The company of gentlemen, genteel society. He felt his tension ease. He straightened his posture, took in the fine surroundings, the mahogany furniture, the crystal glasses and decanter. A glass of port would be nice, would dovetail perfectly with this reawakening of his former self.

And then Lieutenant Howard called, 'Sir James? The lieutenant from *Merlin* is here, sir,' and from the day cabin within came a snort of disgusted impatience and Smeaton felt his confidence collapse like a topmast shot clean away.

'A minute, Mr Howard,' Wallace said. The minute stretched into two, then three, then four, the silence growing more awkward, Smeaton's palms sweating with abandon as he worked and reworked his story.

'Very well, come!'

Howard led the way into the great cabin. Sir James Wallace was sitting behind his desk, which was covered with logs and papers arranged in orderly stacks. Near the edge sat a silver writing set that looked as if it were on display in a shop window.

Wallace leaned back in his chair, regarded the lieutenants, pressed his fingertips together. His jaw was square and his face was lined in the way of men who had been all their lives at sea. His thin lips were pressed together and they were not smiling. His hair was dark on top and growing gray at the temples.

His uniform was perfect; the whites bright white, the blues deep and showing no sign of the damage brought on by sun or salt water. He would not have looked amiss in the Admiralty's waiting room even though he was in his own cabin, where he had the option of being as casual as he chose.

'Thank you, Mr Howard. You may attend to your duties.'

'Aye, aye, sir!' Howard saluted and was gone, a man not anxious to loiter under his captain's eyes.

Smeaton stood still, met Wallace's eyes, and then looked away, shifting slightly from one foot to the other. Wallace continued to stare, saying nothing, the pale blue eyes burning into Smeaton, until he thought he would scream. And just when Smeaton could bear no more, Wallace spoke.

'Tell me again, you are . . . ?'

'Lt John Smeaton, sir, second of the *Merlin*.' No offer of a chair, no glass of port.

'What happened to your face, Lieutenant?'

'I was hit, sir, by a splinter, at the action at Billingsport.'

'I see. And how do you happen to be here? Howard tells me that you were not sent by Captain Reeve.'

'Ah, no, sir . . . I . . . I should say we, myself and the boat crew . . . were sent ahead to sound the river, sir, to see that the sloop would not take the ground . . .'

Wallace leaned forward, elbows on the table. He fixed Smeaton with the stare, let him squirm a moment, then said, 'The *Merlin* took the ground some hours ago. How could you have gotten so far ahead of her that you would not know that? Howard

354

tells me you were coming from upriver when you came alongside.'

'Yes, sir . . . I . . .' Smeaton swallowed hard, as if he could choke down all the fear and misery that Wallace was inflicting on him, all the humiliation he had suffered at the hands of Reeve and Biddlecomb and Rumstick.

His mind raced through the labyrinth of lies he was laying out, stopped at the various dead ends, raced on, saw Pocock standing where he now stood, telling Wallace everything in that hearts-of-oak tone of the honest foretopman, the humble sailor man and all that horseshit that the public in England so adored.

And then he knew he was done with lies.

'It was an affair of honor, sir.' He looked Wallace straight in the eye, did not waver as he spoke. 'I willfully abandoned my post to seek out a man . . . a rebel . . . to call him out and kill him. I put my honor before my duty, sir, and I admit it.'

Satisfaction at last, watching Wallace's reaction, the eyebrows coming down, the frown that suggested confusion, as if he could not understand such blunt honesty, such a forthright admission of so heinous a dereliction. Smeaton imagined Wallace did not hear such things too often. The lieutenant almost smiled, thought, I should have tried this a long time ago.

But in an instant the former Wallace was back, the Wallace so beloved of his superiors. 'You know what you are saying? You abandoned your post, allowed the *Merlin* to take the ground? We shall have to burn her if we cannot get her off. You could hang for such a thing, are you aware of that?'

'Yes, sir. I would rather hang than allow my honor to be so sullied.'

Wallace leaned back again, shook his head in disbelief. 'This is an extraordinary thing, Smeaton, extraordinary. Who is this rebel, for whom you would throw away your life for the chance to kill?'

'Sir, I do not think it is a matter for—'

'Who?'

'His name is Isaac Biddlecomb, sir. He styles himself a captain in what they call their navy.'

The reaction was not what Smeaton had expected, not at all.

It was no surprise that Wallace had heard of Biddlecomb – he was already infamous in Royal Navy circles – but this was something else, something beyond mere recognition. Wallace's eyes went wide and he half stood, then sat down again as if he could not decide which to do. He leaned back and squinted at Smeaton, cocked his head, leaned forward.

'Isaac Biddlecomb? Of Rhode Island?'

'Ah . . . yes, sir, I believe that is he . . .' Wallace, Smeaton recalled, had been stationed in Newport, Rhode Island, when he was in command of the frigate *Rose*. Smeaton wondered if that was more than a coincidence.

'And you have a reason to believe he is here, on the Delaware River? You were attempting to make contact with him, to call him out?'

'Yes, sir. I know he is here. I have met him twice already, but the outcome was not satisfactory on either occasion.' He hoped that Sir James would not ask for particulars.

Wallace leaned back in his chair and again pressed the tips of his fingers together. The shock was contained now. He regarded Smeaton with his former disinterested stare, but Smeaton had gained enough confidence from the exchange that he did not flinch.

'You can find him again? Call him out? You must have thought you could, if you were willing to toss your very life away.'

'Yes, Sir James, I can.'

Wallace stood at last, stared out the window at the distant lights. It was a full minute before he spoke.

'I understand honor, Lieutenant. The need to preserve one's honor. And for that reason I will not only forgive your indiscretion and smooth it over with Reeve, but I will assist you on your quest. Did you see the cutter, anchored off our larboard quarter?'

'Yes, sir.'

'She is the *Sparrowhawk*. Tender to *Experiment*. I will put her at your disposal, let you use her as you see fit. Take her upriver, find this Biddlecomb, and call him out. You may finish this affair. I'll not ask after the particulars.

'Lieutenant Howard will have to take nominal command of the tender, of course, I could not ruffle his feathers so by giving her to an officer from another ship, but he'll follow your directions. I'll explain to Reeve that I need you for this, I'm certain he can spare you for a time.'

Wallace turned at last, held Smeaton's eyes. 'Is that acceptable?'

It was a dream now, too extraordinary to be real. From a halter around his neck to a cutter at his disposal in less time than it would take to issue a death sentence. A command of his own, in essence, to have until such time as he had killed Biddlecomb and Rumstick, and perhaps even called Reeve out, if he could manage it. He and Reeve were, after all, equals in rank now, lieutenants called captain by courtesy.

At least he imagined that he would be called captain, once he was aboard the *Sparrowhawk*. It was only proper.

'Yes, Sir James, that is quite acceptable.'

CHAPTER 23

October, 1777
Thursday 23
Billings Port Fort SE 1 Mile Roebuck *SEbE 1 – dº.*
& the Rebel Fleet EbN 3 Miles—
at 2 a.m. Weighd & Came to Sail up the River. at
7 dº the Augusta Roebuck Pearl Liverpool *&*
Coll Wallis Gallie. Engaged the Rebel Fleet &
Forts. The Merlin *Aground on the Jersey Shore.*
> —JOURNAL OF HMS *CAMILLA*
> CAPT. CHARLES PHIPPS

It gave Malachi Foote some small sense of relief to see the bustle of activity on the foredeck, the sound of mauls pounding shoring under the beams that would take the weight of the shears and the foremast, the gangs of men manhandling the heavy spars that would act like cranes to set the new foremast in place.

The air carried the smell of tar and the crackling of rope pulled taut as others of the *Falmouth*'s crew turned mere cordage into runner pendants, fore shrouds, forestay, spring stay, deadeye lanyards. His beloved *Falmouth* was alive. She was not lying beaten in a corner, waiting for the executioner to come, but rather fighting back, tunneling out of her prison.

It was a relief to witness this. But the feeling was a far cry from optimism, because beneath it all was the gunfire – muted, distant, but incessant.

They had become used to the gunfire from down-river, reckoned it was the fleet and the garrisons in the forts holding the British fleet at bay, making it hard for them to remove the obstructions in the river. There had been gunfire almost every night, and often during the day as well.

But this time it was different. This time it had started at sunup and had not let up at all, a constant rumble, an uninterrupted blanket of sound. Over the trees they could see the cloud of gray smoke lifting over the river, ten miles away, something they had never seen before. It put the men on edge, infused the day with an amorphous anxiety. This was a determined battle, a full-scale fight. Something was happening, and whatever it was, Foote could not imagine that it was good.

And on top of all that was his irritation with McGinty, the annoying fact that the Irishman was running things as far as getting the foremast in, the gnawing truth that it had all been his idea. Foote knew spar making, knew how to build tops and caps and trestle-trees, but the rigging and stepping of masts was not his purview at all. He had no choice but to allow McGinty to do it.

McGinty stood at the forward edge of the fore-deck, hands clasped behind his back, looking aft, running his eyes over the sheers, making sure that all was in readiness.

The sheers were made up of the fore and main

topmasts, lashed together at their heads with their bases resting on either edge of the foredeck. They formed a huge *V*, lying flat on the deck, with the apex pointing aft.

The upper block of a big four-part block and tackle hung from the point where the two masts were lashed together, and the lower block was led forward and made fast to the gammoning knee at the ship's bow. Various guys, tail tackles, and girtlines ran off in all directions. It looked like a great tangled mess to Foote, but McGinty seemed satisfied.

'Very well, boy-os, listen to yer dear McGinty, and listen good!' the Irishman shouted, and the deck went silent. 'On the after tail tackles . . . yes, that's you lot there . . . take up the strain. That's well, now hold it. Mother Foote, have you the capstan rigged, at all?'

The sound of his name jerked Foote from his reverie. 'It's been ready this half hour and more, Teague. Waiting on you, as ever.'

'Very well, then. On the capstan, heave away, heave and pall!'

The men stationed at the capstan, aft on the quarterdeck, began to march around, the long capstan bars held against their chests, and the pawls clicked faster and faster as they picked up speed.

''Vast heaving, you bloody, motherless lubbers!' McGinty shouted, and the men froze. 'It's not a bloody footrace! Slow and steady! Now, heave away!'

Once more the men stamped the capstan around, slower this time, their pace constant. The pawls lifted and fell with a clocklike rhythm and the strain came on the four-part tackle. Foote watched it all, wanted to jump in, wanted to be in charge or at least be an indispensable part of the operation, but he did not know enough about it to offer anything more than brute strength. He climbed up onto the foredeck, put his shoulder under one of the sheers, stood ready to lift.

The tail tackle attached to the heels of the sheers groaned as the strain came on them, and the fall of the four-part purchase was pulled bar tight, and McGinty shouted, 'All right, you lot, heave away! Mother Foote, that means you! Heave now, laddies, heave!'

McGinty bounded aft and put his shoulder under the sheer opposite of Foote, and with an audible grunt he pushed. The point of the great V began to rise off the deck as the sheers were pulled from where they rested horizontally up to the vertical. Higher and higher they rose until the men pushing could do no more good and the ones hauling the tackle with the capstan were taking all the strain.

McGinty stepped forward again, stood directly under the sheers and looked up. They looked like the two legs of a giant straddling the deck. 'Hold the capstan!' McGinty shouted, and the men stopped their circular march. 'Take up them guys! On the tail tackles, heave and belay! There she is, lads!'

The men looked up, the veteran infantrymen turned apprentice riggers, and saw the sheers towering over the deck. And though the apex of the V was no more than thirty feet over their heads, still it was an impressive sight on a vessel with no rig at all, and the men cheered, smiling and slapping one another on the back.

'They're good boys, you know.'

Freeman stood beside Foote, nodded toward the

jubilant men on the quarterdeck. 'Reckon we are deserters, no getting around that. But these boys ain't the lazy, shirking type, not like some. Does them good to have something to do, something to feel proud of.'

Foote spit over the rail. 'That's nice.'

'Sure, I know you don't give a rat's arse about how they feel. Wouldn't expect you to. But it might do your boat here some good too.'

Foote looked at Freeman and gave him something that resembled a smile. He liked the corporal, saw in him a mean, uncouth, yet kindred spirit. 'It's a ship, it ain't a boat. And any good we can do for her, well, I do give a rat's arse about that.'

'All right, lads, all right!' McGinty shouted. 'That's cheering enough, it's just the *Foul-Mouth*, you didn't raise the great bloody pyramid of Egypt! Now, someone nip down into the beakhead and cast off the block from the gammoning knee. Let's get that mast alongside here, I'd like the bloody thing in before the war ends.'

The soldiers-cum-riggers turned to with a will, racing to obey McGinty's every order. Foote marveled to watch it, reckoned a part of it was the novelty, the activity after so many weeks of boredom. But part of it as well was McGinty's natural ability to inspire. Foote was a candid enough individual that he could admit as much, at least to himself. If the yard workers at Wharton and Humphreys had shown half the enthusiasm of McGinty's men, there would be frigates for every captain on the navy list.

The thought of the navy list made Foote think once more about Biddlecomb. Bloody shirking, cowardly, backwards Biddlecomb. A month late and never a word. Where the hell was he? Sipping coffee in some coffeehouse in Boston, no doubt, as far from the enemy as he could get, feet up, enthralling his fellow captains with tales of his daring exploits. And the actual preservation of the ship he left to whoever was willing to do it, and if that was no one, then let the British have her.

Goddamned navy officers.

It took the young and well-motivated crew of the *Falmouth* another two hours to get the foremast rigged for hoisting and stepping. This part, at least, crossed into Foote's domain, and he spent the intervening time preparing the step and the partners to accept the mast and laying out the wedges that would hold it in place.

The heel of the mast was designed to rest in a mortise cut in a block of wood called a step and bolted to the keelson at the very bottom of the ship. To get there, it had to pass through holes, or partners, in each deck.

At last all was ready, and with a word from McGinty the men stamped the capstan around once again. The mast lifted slowly off the deck, hanging by the block and tackle from the apex of the sheers. The huge pole seemed to float up and up, toward the top of the *V*. The sheers and beams groaned under the load, the cordage creaked with strain, but everything held, everything worked, and soon Foote, who was guiding the heel of the foremast, said, 'That'll do, Teague,' and McGinty called, 'Hold the capstan!'

Foote swung the heel of the mast over the hole in the deck down which it would go, and McGinty called, 'On the back rope . . . yes, you lot . . . haul away!'

The back rope, attached to the head of the mast, pulled the long pole more toward the vertical until soon it was hanging all but straight up and down over the partners.

'You can lower away, Teague!'

'Surge the capstan, surge way!'

'Surge, ho!' shouted the man tending the line around the capstan as he slacked it away. Foote guided the heel of the mast down toward the partners and wondered where these fellows had picked up such sailorly phrases.

At a steady rate the mast was lowered until the heel passed through the hole in the deck. Foote, despite himself, thought of the girl on Chestnut Street. The figurehead. Susan.

There are hundreds of girls on Chestnut Street, he thought again.

Susan was more than just a girl now; she was the beloved figurehead, the fantasy in his lonely cabin. She was the *Falmouth*. That was why he could not stand the thought of McGinty thrumming her.

There are hundreds of girls on Chestnut Street.

'Hold the capstan! Mother Foote, are you going to stand there and stare like you've never seen the like before, or are you going to go below and see the mast through the next deck?'

Foote looked up, once more surprised from his reverie. He wondered about the state of his mind, that he should so often drift away. 'Shut yer fucking gob, Teague,' he said, and hurried below.

He climbed down into the waist and then went forward, under the foredeck, where the mast was hanging through the partner above, twisting slightly and swinging in a tight circle. It was a strange sight, that heavy spar seeming to levitate over the deck. Foote took hold of it, steadied it, positioned it over the partner in the main deck.

'Lower away!'

From the deck above, McGinty's voice: 'Surge the capstan! Surge away, easy, easy!' The mast came down again, passing through the main deck on its way to the hold, and once he guessed it was halfway there, Foote called, 'That's well!'

In the same manner the mast was eased down through the berthing deck, and Foote took up a lantern and went down into the hold, where he would guide the mast the last few feet, fitting the tenon cut in the heel of the mast into the mortise in the step.

He positioned the mast over the step as best as he could. 'Ease away, half a fathom!' he shouted, as loud as he could, to make himself heard two decks up.

He waited. Nothing happened. 'I said, ease away, half a fathom, Teague, you lazy, deaf—'

'I heard you, Mother Foote, damn me, how could I not?' McGinty's voice was close, and Foote turned to see him on the ladder, coming down into the dark hold.

'Now, what the hell are you doing down here, Teague? This ain't the time to sneak away for a nap.'

The Irishman stepped down on the slanting bilge and came forward. They were alone in the hold. The only light came from the lantern and the hatches that communicated with the waist, giving the place a weird, twilight quality.

McGinty stepped up beside Foote and looked up at the heel of the mast and then down at the step.

Foote opened his mouth to make some comment but stopped. There was an odd quality about McGinty at that moment, a seriousness that Foote had not seen before, and it gave him pause.

Then McGinty stuck his hand in his pocket, fished around. 'I'd been saving this, Malachi, for a time when I might find myself in some real trouble. But I think we can put it to best use here.'

He pulled his hand from his pocket and held it open, palm out. Resting there was an imperfectly round yellow disk. Foote looked closer, squinted, and his mouth opened in surprise. It was a gold doubloon, like that of pirate lore, not a new-minted one but an ancient coin with its markings worn nearly smooth. A valuable bit of specie in the cash-strapped United States.

'What do you reckon to do with that?'

'Put it under the heel of the mast.'

'Coin goes under the mainmast.'

McGinty smiled at that. 'Boy-o, we'll be lucky to have even the one, I shouldn't go holding out for a mainmast now.'

Foote nodded and McGinty silently laid the coin in the mast step, then turned toward the hatch and shouted, 'Surge the capstan, easy now!'

From two decks up they heard the sound of the line creaking around the barrel of the capstan. The mast began its descent once more, and Foote and McGinty together grabbed hold of it and positioned it over the step as it came down. The tenon eased into the mortise. With a groan and a settling motion it came down on top of the gold coin and the foremast was in place.

Foote met McGinty's eyes and they shared a half

smile. 'Well done, Malachi, well done,' the Irishman said.

Foote pulled his plug of tobacco from his coat pocket, tore a piece off with his teeth, handed it to McGinty. 'You know, McGinty, you ain't so bad for a fucking lazy Irishman.' Then, embarrassed by this display of raw and unchecked emotion, Foote spit into the bilge and hurried back on deck.

There was a festive atmosphere there, the men congratulating themselves on their accomplishment, and the congratulations were warranted. It was not the great pyramid of Egypt, but still it was a difficult task and one they had accomplished well, with spars they had stolen on their late-night raid.

What good it might do them, Foote did not know.

And then from downriver, a rumble, an explosion, not gunfire but something deeper, more prolonged, more profound than that. The men fell instantly silent and looked away, over the tops of the trees. A great column of black smoke was rising from some distant fire, sharply defined against the amorphous gray of the ongoing artillery barrage.

They felt the deck under their feet tremble, saw the guys supporting the sheers quiver like harp strings.

'What the hell was that?' someone asked, but no one could give him an answer.

Foote looked at the column of smoke, shook his head. No one cared more than he about getting the *Falmouth* to safety, no one hoped more than he that getting some kind of sail on her might help accomplish that, but he was not certain how. And now it seemed he would have to come up with an answer to that question, and quickly.

It made him angry that that should be his concern.

He was only the shipwright. The *Falmouth* had a captain, and it was his responsibility to take care of her now.

He thought again of Biddlecomb, grew angry again as he did. They had expected him to arrive before the British overran Philadelphia. Now Howe and those sons of bitches had been comfortably ensconced in the city for almost a month, and the Lord alone knew what was happening downriver. And there was still no word, no sign of Biddlecomb.

Nor did Foote expect to see him soon. No doubt he had abandoned all thought of reaching his command – which he was damned lucky to have – once he heard that the British were close by. That was just like all those bastards in the navy. Avoid the enemy at all costs.

It was just as well that Biddlecomb had given up so easily. The *Falmouth* should not go to one so undeserving.

Isaac Biddlecomb, captain of the xebec *Expedient*, nominal captain of the *Falmouth*, was, at that moment, just nine miles downriver of where the *Falmouth* lay. It had taken him over a month to get that far, had cost him two ships, the lives of half a dozen of his men, including young David Weatherspoon, whom he had loved. It had nearly cost him his marriage, had nearly cost him the lives of his wife and child and his own life as well.

But now he had reason to believe that the *Falmouth* was safe, for the moment, and he had a good idea of where she was, and that knowledge was making him frantic to get upriver.

After the glorious defense of Fort Mercer, after the

garrison in the fort and the fleet on the river had driven the Hessian attackers away, after he and his men had helped save the American defenses on the river, it had seemed a good time to go. He had determined that in the morning they would make their way upriver and find the *Falmouth*, and when they did, he would send the *Expedient* back down to Hazelwood.

He had decided not to ask the commodore's permission after all. It was a cowardly decision, and he knew that, but there was just too great a likelihood that Hazelwood would say no.

Now the morning brought a scene that was entirely unexpected: two British men-of-war, a sixty-four-gun ship and a sloop of war, Smeaton's sloop of war as best as he could tell, hard aground on the mud. Their sails were neatly furled and they were heeled over slightly, as if they were sailing with the wind on their beams, but they had the dull, motionless, dead quality of vessels that had taken the ground.

The ships were the focal point of the British navy's activity, with boats hauling kedge anchors astern to heave the ships off, gangs swaying casks and spare guns and stores out of their holds to lighten them, more boats plying between them and the other big men-of-war that lay at anchor nearby.

The British had all the men and equipment, all the resources they might need, to get the two ships free. But in the night the wind had shifted into the north, and Biddlecomb knew that that would keep the tide from rising as high as it had been when they went aground. He did not think that all the British forces in North America could pull them off the mud.

And to further impede the Royal Navy's effort, the rebels had opened up at first light.

The firing had been brisk at first, as the gunboats and the artillerymen at Forts Mifflin and Mercer tried to make it too hot for the fleet to remain. Not until 7 a.m. did the Americans realize that the two ships were aground, stranded under their guns.

In ten minutes the brisk shelling became a constant and murderous barrage as every gun that would bear was turned on the British fleet, and every gun crew served their weapon fast and with an enthusiasm they had not felt in weeks.

Under sail and sweep the mosquito fleet moved downriver, pushing through the great banks of smoke that they were creating, circling in like wolves sensing wounded prey. Bow guns and broadsides poured shot of all size and description into the stranded vessels and into the ships that were attempting to render aid.

The British, for their part, were not simply enduring the insult. They were fighting back with all they had, and their cumulative power was terrific, more than the entire Continental navy and all the state navies together could boast.

The sixty-four that was aground – Rumstick believed it to be the *Augusta* – was fighting for her life, blazing away with her broadside at Fort Mifflin and any ships foolish enough to get within her arc of fire, even as her crew and those sent to assist struggled to get her free of the mud. Defending and aiding the *Augusta* was a ship of fifty guns, another of forty-four, and various frigates and sloops and galleys. It was, all together, an awesome display of force, gun for gun far more than the Americans could hope to muster.

Biddlecomb had never seen the like and hoped never to see it again. The entire river was covered with ships, ships of every description, all firing at once, pounding away at each other. The British trying to free their stranded vessels, the Americans firing into their midst, the big men-of-war blasting away with broadside after broadside.

'It is our maneuverability, do you see, that will win us the day!' Rumstick nearly shouted in Biddle-comb's ear. They were all but inured to the gunfire, hardly took note of it after three hours of the noise. It was only when one or the other tried to speak that they became aware of how overwhelming it was, how numb their hearing had become.

'Yes?'

'Yes, sir! This river work, too confining for those big bastards! Our little ships can hit and run, no worries of going aground!'

Biddlecomb nodded. It was easier than speaking. He thought of making some flip comment, to the effect that it was a relief that the Americans had no cumbersome ships of the line, or mentioning the advantage of the forts firing from their stable platforms, but shouting over the gunfire took too much effort. Instead he thumped Rumstick on the shoulder, pointed upriver.

Down through the crowd of gunboats and floating batteries came a small brig, all plain sail set, running right for the stranded *Augusta*. Isaac could see no one on her decks, no guns manned along her sides. She sailed placidly downriver, like a yacht that had inadvertently stumbled upon the battle.

Then two cables from the *Augusta*, flames licked up from the brig's hold, spreading along her decks.

'Fire ship!' Gerrish ran aft and pointed, then saw that Biddlecomb and Rumstick were already watching her progress. Dark smoke poured out of her belly and rolled down over the British sixty-four, her intended victim. Flames reached her mainmast and caught on her mainsail, and soon that was burning well, the fire spreading through the rig.

A figure appeared on her quarterdeck. He climbed over the taffrail and slid down the painter to the boat that was being towed astern, then two more men followed him. They cast off the line and took up the oars and pulled for all they were worth back to the American fleet.

'Brave sons of bitches!' Biddlecomb observed. They had stayed with the brig until the last moment, but even that bold move was not enough. A British longboat, double-banked and moving fast, pulled up under the brig's bow. A grappling hook flew over the bulwark and caught, and a moment later the burning vessel was towed clear and let go, drifting harmlessly away from the British fleet.

'Can't say we've had much luck with them fire ships,' Rumstick observed.

'No, but see here!' Biddlecomb pointed toward the *Augusta*. Wisps of dark smoke were rising out of her, ill-defined veils that were quickly whisked away, then quickly replaced.

'On fire, sir?' Gerrish asked.

'I think so.'

'The fire ship never caused that.'

'No, I think not. It must have been burning already. But it doesn't look so bad. I should think they will be able to get it out. More the shame.'

The battle continued unabated for the next hour,

the noise rising and falling like the crash of surf, the constant frenzied gunfire seemingly from all quarters and in all directions.

Isaac thought of the noble portraits he had seen of sea fights, the great men-of-war in their lines of battle, fleet sailing past fleet and each ship firing one into another. This action was not like that. This was chaos, fortifications and ships of every size and description, firing wherever they found an advantage, often lost in their own choking smoke.

Biddlecomb thumped Gerrish on the shoulder, pointed toward the *Augusta*. 'Never been so pleased to say I was wrong!' he shouted. 'They didn't get the fire out, and they won't now!'

The smoke rising from the *Augusta* no longer came in tenuous wisps but in great columns, roiling out of the upper gunports and through the hatches, obscuring the masts nearly to the tops and blowing away downwind. It was thick and black, not like the gray-white smoke of the guns, and it blotted out the Americans' view of everything downwind.

Rumstick ordered a fresh crew on the *Expedient*'s single bow gun, directed their fire toward the fifty-gun ship, then came aft, grinning. '*Augusta*'s done for! And look there! Ain't that Smeaton's sloop?'

He pointed south toward the Jersey shore. Half a mile away, the stranded sloop lay heeled over in the mud. A column of black smoke was rising from her as well, and an orderly procession of boats was pulling alongside and then sheering off.

'They must have fired her! Set it themselves!' Biddlecomb shouted. 'They are abandoning her in too organized a fashion for anything else!'

'Fine by me!' Rumstick shouted. 'I don't care if

the devil himself set her afire, as long as she burns!'

The British were giving up, conceding the day. The boats that swarmed around the *Augusta* and the sloop were no longer concerned with getting them free. They were getting the people off and leaving whatever was left for the flames.

And the others, the fifty-gun ship, the forty-four, the frigates, all of them were dropping back downriver, letting the current drift them back toward the lower *chevaux-de-frise*, out of the fight.

It was just past noon, and the Americans had held the river.

Isaac realized that he and Rumstick and Gerrish, and Faircloth as well, who had joined them aft, were all grinning like idiots. This was the second time in twenty-four hours that they had had the sensation of victory, pleasant and unfamiliar as it was, and they deserved to enjoy it.

Then, a sound from *Augusta*, a muffled thud or explosion. They looked up together, and as they did, the ship exploded, her decks bursting up and out, flinging all the contents of her hold up, up into the air in a great burst of flame and smoke and shattered wreckage.

Her masts blew aside like cornstalks and tumbled into the water, and more flame shot out from her gunports as if she were vomiting fire. The entire hull was lit from within, bright even in the noon sun; the air was filled with the sound and with the wreckage, flying up and out in a great circle of destruction.

Biddlecomb stared, his mouth and eyes wide. The debris looked as if it would never come down, and just as he realized that it had reached the top of its ascent, he realized as well that a good portion of it would come down on them.

'Stand from under!' he shouted, but there was nowhere to run. They could not get below before the debris came back to earth.

He crouched and flung his arms over his head and saw the others do the same, and then it was like a hailstorm, with bits of flaming wood and metal and cordage falling all around them.

He heard Rumstick grunt and curse as something hit him, felt something bounce off his own back, saw a quarter block with part of a topsail sheet still rove through hit the deck at his feet and bounce, leaving a great dent in its wake. It seemed forever that they stood in their absurd positions, tensed, ready to be struck down by something, the heel of a mast, the fragments of a gun carriage.

And then it stopped, and a dreamlike quality settled over the river. For the first time since dawn the guns had ceased firing. Isaac looked around the *Expedient*. Bits of flaming wreckage were strewn around the deck, but already the men were stamping them out, and dumping buckets of water over the bigger ones.

The *Augusta* was no more than a shell, a shattered wooden bowl filled with burning material. Her upperworks were splintered and she was settled lower in the water. The flames rose above her to the height of her former maintop. Biddlecomb just watched and shook his head. As much as he hated the British navy and all that served her, he found himself hoping that no one had been left aboard.

Half a mile beyond, the sloop was engulfed in flames, belching out black smoke just as the *Augusta* had done. Soon it would be her turn to blow. But the British ships were already beyond long cannon shot, coming to anchor down by Billingsport. The battle was over, for that day at least, and the Americans had won.

Biddlecomb looked up at the sun. 'Five hours of daylight left. I reckon that's enough time to get up past the city and around Petty's Island.'

'Reckon you're right, sir,' Rumstick agreed.

'Think I should ask the commodore's permission, Lieutenant?'

Rumstick squinted at the many vessels on the river, the patches of gunsmoke that hung tenaciously on the water. 'Reckon the commodore has enough on his mind. Be doing him a favor, sir, not forcing him to make one more decision.'

'I quite agree. Very well, then, let us go.'

Ten minutes later the bow gun was housed, the sweeps stored down, and the twin lateen sails set and drawing in the northerly breeze, and the xebec *Expedient*, and the last of the Charlemagnes, made their way upriver. To the *Falmouth*.

Capt. James Wallace stood alone on the weather side of the quarterdeck of His Majesty's ship *Experiment* of fifty guns, staring vaguely forward. He seemed as if he were looking at nothing at all, but his men knew that he was in fact watching everything, seeing everything, and he knew that they knew that.

That was why the current evolution – coming to an anchor with the best bower – was going smoothly, silently, uneventfully. The Experiments knew better than to make a hash of anything under Sir James's eye, especially something so simple and routine as setting a three-ton anchor made fast to three hundred feet of cable twenty-four inches in circumference.

They knew that nothing less than perfection would be tolerated, and so that was the level they had attained.

It had been a bad day, and Wallace was furious, though, like his watchfulness, it was not evident. They had been bested by the rebels. Beaten. There was no reason to soften the truth of their defeat with euphemisms. They had been driven off, two ships destroyed, one of them a sixty-four, as big as the flagship *Eagle*.

And there was Smeaton. He had been like a pebble in Wallace's shoe; not the day's biggest problem, but an irritant, making everything that much worse. The lieutenant had been prancing around the quarterdeck all morning, always on the verge of approaching, clearly eager to get his hands on the *Sparrowhawk*, as he had been promised, and be gone.

What Wallace really wanted to do was crush him, professionally if not physically. He reckoned that Smeaton was as responsible as anyone for the loss of the *Merlin*. But Smeaton might get him Biddlecomb, and that was what he wanted above all else.

That thought gave him some glimmer of hope, some suggestion of happiness through his black mood, like the first flicker of a lighthouse on a dark coast.

Biddlecomb.

Early in 1775, Wallace, then in command of the frigate *Rose*, had been sent to Narragansett Bay to put an end to the Rhode Islanders' flagrant smuggling. He had done so, effectively, efficiently. But Biddlecomb was the worst of them, and he had slipped away. Had wrecked his ship on Popasquash

Point and escaped on foot. Had escaped from Wallace's then third lieutenant, Norton, and a shore party of marines, had stolen the *Rose*'s longboat and disappeared.

The next time they met, Biddlecomb had led a mutiny aboard His Majesty's brig *Icarus*, and though the *Rose* had beaten the *Icarus* to kindling, Biddlecomb had once again escaped. And Norton had died trying to stop him.

Biddlecomb. Wallace had set the frigate *Glasgow* as a trap for him in Bermuda, had actually captured the bastard, and Biddlecomb had managed not only to escape but to retake his own ship and capture a storeship full of gunpowder, which had revitalized Washington's supply-starved troops around Boston. Biddlecomb, who had carried that villain Franklin to France and had had the effrontery to attack British shipping in British waters.

Wallace told himself that it would be of great benefit to the British war effort to capture that son of a bitch and make an example of him, and in that he was not wrong. But he also knew that that was not his entire motivation. Sir James Wallace could not bear to be bested, and in his darker moments he had to admit that that was exactly what Biddlecomb had done.

He wanted that bastard dead more than he wanted anything else in life.

He could not send the *Sparrowhawk* away during the morning's fight because she would have been taken immediately by the rebels, white flag or no. Smeaton was too excited or too stupid or deluded to realize that. But now the rebel fleet was dispersing, heading back toward Fort Mifflin and the protection of its heavy guns. Now Smeaton might have a chance to approach under flag of truce, to find Biddlecomb and perhaps even to kill him.

'Lieutenant Smeaton,' he called, and Smeaton darted across the deck, stopped, and saluted. 'You may take the gig and go aboard *Sparrowhawk*. I shall send Lieutenant Howard over directly, and then you can get under way and see about delivering your challenge.'

'Aye, aye, sir. And, sir, to make certain you recall, this is an affair of honor, a fight between gentlemen, and as such, I must reiterate, I am bound by the protocol governing such things.'

Wallace fixed him with his expressionless stare, held him again like a bug on a pin, watched while he began to squirm. 'Do not presume to tell me the nature of your task, Lieutenant,' he said at last.

'Oh, no, sir, no, never, I just . . .' Smeaton backed away as he spoke. 'I shall be off, then, sir. And thank you.'

Wallace gave him a wave of his hand by way of dismissing him, and Smeaton practically fled to the waist and then down into the gig alongside. Once Wallace saw the boat appear beyond the *Experiment*'s bulging tumblehome, pulling for the *Sparrowhawk* anchored nearby, he said, 'Lieutenant Howard, would you step over here, please?'

Lieutenant Howard stepped briskly across the deck, having learned that Wallace expected a crisp and quick response, close to, but just short of, undignified fawning servility.

'Sir?'

'Lieutenant, I will need you to take temporary command of the *Sparrowhawk*.' Wallace paused,

380

sighed, said, 'It is . . . complicated. Lieutenant Smeaton has certain intelligence of a rebel captain named Biddlecomb, thinks he can get near him. It would be very much to the good if we could capture him and make an example of him. He has caused too much trouble already, too much by half.

'Smeaton thinks this is an affair of honor, thinks he's calling Biddlecomb out. I want you to humor him as much as needs be . . . it will not be a pleasant task, I understand . . . and help him find Biddlecomb. When he does, you are to take Biddlecomb yourself, alive if you can, and bring him back. You'll have to take him by force, I should think, so see that all the men aboard the tender are issued side arms and take another half dozen steady men from this company. Take the gig and the jolly boat as well, they may be of some use. Is that clear?'

'Yes, sir, perfectly clear. But this Smeaton, sir, his affair of honor . . . ?'

'Once you have arrested Biddlecomb, then Smeaton is of no concern. His "honor" is not such that it is worth a gentleman's time to consider.'

'Aye, sir!' Howard saluted, then walked forward along the gangway. The gig was already pulling back for the *Experiment*.

Wallace stared aimlessly upriver. How very odd these past twenty-four hours have been, he thought. He had experienced the most extraordinary range of emotions, he, a man who prided himself on being as steady as a ship in a millpond.

The rebels and their fortifications and their little ships, slaughtering the Hessians at Fort Mercer, had sent him into a rage. The Yankees' reason for fighting, their justification for this civil war, was so

381

clearly wrong, so obviously without legal or moral or logical justification. And yet so many men had to die because of it.

When he thought on it, it made him crazy, so he generally did not think on it.

And then Smeaton. He had been ready to destroy the man for his negligence, his letting the *Merlin* get aground, even after the lieutenant's refreshingly candid admission of wrongdoing. But when he had spoke the name *Biddlecomb*, Wallace felt as if he had been punched in the stomach.

Biddlecomb.

He had almost forgotten about Biddlecomb, and now here he was, and possibly within his grasp. The old wound was opened fresh. He was once more desperate to get his hands on the man.

An affair of honor. Such a joke. Laughable if it were not so pathetic.

He did not know who Smeaton was at first, did not know why the name was familiar, where he had heard it, or in what context. After their interview it had come back to him.

Smeaton had been first officer aboard the *Icarus* when Biddlecomb had taken her. Honor, for him, would have been to die trying to put down the mutiny, or failing that, to put a pistol to his head. But he had done neither. He had instead crawled through the court-martial, ignored all the ugly talk, accepted the disreputable demotion to second officer aboard a sloop of war. The man could not fight an affair of honor. He had no honor left to defend.

So Smeaton could serve as a tool, a stalking-horse for him, Sir James, to find Biddlecomb. Smeaton was good for nothing else.

CHAPTER 24

Red Bank, October 23ᵈ 1777
May it please Your Excellency
This will acquaint Your Excellency that early this
morning we carried all our Galleys to Action, &
after a long & heavy firing we drove the enemy's
Ships down the River except a 64 Gun Ship & a
small Frigate, which we obliged them to quit
as they got on Shore & by accident the 64 Gun
Ship blew up & the Frigate they set on fire them-
selves.

—COMMO. JOHN HAZELWOOD
TO GEORGE WASHINGTON

With the wind out of the north and the tide against them it was slow going for the *Expedient*.

They made their way close-hauled around the northern shore of Red Bank Island, a move that excited no comment, as most of the American fleet was at anchor there. Once past the island they were able to haul their wind for a reach to the southeast, a considerably faster point of sail for the xebec.

And Biddlecomb was grateful for that, for once

383

they passed through the American fleet, it was clear to any observer that they were heading off on their own, upriver. But with the wind to their advantage they soon left the other vessels behind, clearing the tip of League Island before any embarrassing questions were asked, or any orders issued that might interfere with their design.

At Gloucester the river turned sharply to the north and their progress slowed down considerably, as they were forced to make short boards from one bank of the river to the other, fighting wind and current. It took them the better part of three hours to make the two and a half miles up to Philadelphia, but by then the tide had begun to flood and the surge of water helped push them upstream against the northerly breeze.

It was a fortuitous thing, the change of the tide. Along the city's waterfront they could see the hastily constructed batteries, the muzzles of the long guns sweeping out over the river. The Delaware was just under a mile wide at that point, and the *Expedient* was forced to hug the Jersey shore, shrinking from the heavy guns, and making just the shortest of tacks to keep at the extreme range of the artillery. Were it not for the flood, they would have made no progress at all.

In the flag locker Gerrish found a British ensign, and so they flew it, by way of deception, though they did not reckon on deceiving anyone, being as they were clearly avoiding the batteries in the occupied city. Nor was the British navy likely to employ so outlandish a rig as that which the *Expedient* sported. But Isaac thought it might at least give them pause, make some subaltern in charge of a battery send for his superior officer before taking the responsibility of opening fire.

And it would seem that it worked to that effect, for they had cleared half the city before the first gun took the first ranging shot at them. Biddlecomb could see the puff of smoke, coming from nearby the yard of Wharton and Humphreys, a place he knew well. The ball fell well short, as did the next, and most of the other dozen or so shots that were fired.

That, apparently, was enough for the shore batteries, and after that futile cannonade the *Expedient* beat unmolested past the city.

A few hours before dark they came abeam of the channel that passed south of Petty's Island. They tacked one last time and fell off, felt their speed increase dramatically as the wind came over the larboard quarter.

Isaac stood at the break of the little quarterdeck, searching the shoreline with his glass. His feet were tingling, his palms sweating, and he found himself clenching his teeth until his jaw ached.

He told himself to stop it, made a conscious effort to stop tensing up, but he was filled with a sense of anticipation such as he had not felt since he was a boy.

The *Falmouth*. For three months he had thought about her, studied her plans, tacked her, wore her, fought her to glory and riches in his mind. She had been the motive, the leitmotiv, behind every action. Smeaton had been a distraction, the fight on the Delaware River an unavoidable delay. The *Falmouth*, that was what he was about.

And now he was almost aboard her. He looked longingly at the xebec's bow, wanted to run up there so that he could see the *Falmouth* those few seconds before she came into view from the quarterdeck, but for the sake of his dignity he resisted.

'On deck!' Gerrish called from the top of the foremast. 'There's a ship tucked in there all right, right up by the Jersey shore!'

Biddlecomb swallowed hard, paused until he could trust his voice, and called, 'Very well! You may come down, Mr Gerrish.'

After an agonizing five minutes she was visible from the quarterdeck. The southeast tip of Petty's Island seemed to draw aside, revealing the ship made fast to the low, distant shore, three-quarters of a mile away. Telescopes snapped to eyes as Biddlecomb, Rumstick, and Faircloth took their first look, and forward the men lined the rail, as appreciative as the officers of the effort that had gone into reaching that particular place.

'Seems to have a lower foremast stepped,' Rumstick observed. 'And a foreyard crossed, it appears . . .'

'I suppose that is as far as they got in rigging her, before the city fell,' Faircloth offered.

'I suppose . . .' Rumstick equivocated. 'Generally, though, you'd put the mizzenmast in first, if you was getting them in by sheers. You'd expect that, before the foremast, and certainly before the foreyard, in the natural order of things.'

Biddlecomb did not join in their discussion, could not verbalize the sensations washing over him. He was like a bridegroom at an arranged marriage, seeing his bride for the first time and finding her more lovely than he could ever have imagined.

She was high in the water, so high that he had to guess she had no ballast in her, which made it even more odd that there should be a mast in place, even

386

if only a lower. But that afforded him a nice view of the run of her bottom, the graceful way her hull swept up from the round turn of the bilge amidships to the narrow part at the rudderpost and up under the stern.

Her bow was sharp, an unusually narrow entry, just as he had seen in the drafts, and he could well imagine the speed and weatherliness that would result. Her sheer was not so great that she looked bowed, or so little that she looked stiff and slab-sided, but rather an elegant, understated sweep from bow to stern. He could see the quarter galleries aft, real quarter galleries, not the little badges carried on brigs and sloops. Her sides were oiled, with just a few tastefully painted strakes.

Isaac smiled, thought, So this is love at first sight. God help me if Virginia knew that I was thinking such things.

They stood on and were able to see more and more details of the *Falmouth* as they approached, and nothing they saw altered Isaac's first impression of naval perfection. Quite the opposite, in fact, and the praise grew more and more grand as Rumstick and Faircloth and Gerrish pointed out this or that aspect of her construction. And all the while Biddlecomb just watched, smiled, remained silent.

They were just over a cable length away when Isaac finally spoke. 'Mr Faircloth, tell me again how she happens to be here?'

'Well, sir, my, ah, informant was not entirely certain of the details, but it would appear that the shipwright and some other fellow towed her here just before the British took the city. I am not certain how.'

'But why here? The other frigates are much farther upriver. I would think the *Falmouth* is terribly vulnerable here.'

'Indeed, sir. I can only guess, but I would think that this was as far as they were able to tow her. As I said, my informant did not know all the particulars of the matter.'

'I see.' Isaac knew Elisha Faircloth well enough to guess that his 'informant' was probably too busy screaming and digging her fingernails into his back to be of any great help, but she had been right about the frigate's location, and for that he would be forever grateful.

They closed to twenty yards from the frigate, rounded up, and dropped anchor in the stream. The ship loomed over them now, powerful and threatening in appearance, even with the empty gunports along her side. There was no sign of activity, no sign of any living soul aboard her.

After a few moments of waiting for a hail or some indication of who might be aboard, Biddlecomb said, 'Let us have the longboat alongside. Mr Faircloth, an armed party of marines, I think, since we have no notion of what we might encounter. You can fit ten in the boat, I should think. Mr Rumstick, pistols and cutlasses for the boat crew.'

They pushed off from the xebec's side, pulling slowly for the frigate. Biddlecomb sat in the stern sheets, wedged between Faircloth and Rumstick, while Mr Gerrish, under protest, was left behind to see after the *Expedient*.

Faircloth peered at the figurehead with his glass until it was lost around the turn of the bow.

'Extraordinary,' he said.

They were all the way up to the boarding steps before someone appeared on the frigate's deck: two men, one dark and in want of a shave, a battered three-cornered hat on his head, the other big, hulking, with red hair bursting out from under a military-style hat. The big one wore some kind of uniform. Both were pointing muskets down at the boat.

'Who the fuck are you?' the smaller man asked. 'What do you want?'

It was not the welome Biddlecomb had dreamed of, a far cry from being piped aboard with all the ceremony due the first captain of a newly commissioned ship. It was the welcome of besieged men in desperate times.

Rumstick answered before Biddlecomb could. 'This is Capt. Isaac Biddlecomb, captain of United States frigate *Falmouth*.'

That at least invoked a response, a startled look from the civilian, quickly suppressed, and followed by a wad of tobacco expertly spit into the river. 'Biddlecomb? A little late, ain't you?'

Rumstick was getting mad, and that was never a good thing. 'Who the hell are you, you little chuckleheaded son of a whore? You don't talk to the captain of this ship that way, you—'

'We have been delayed,' Biddlecomb broke in. 'We have fought every inch of the way here, and we do not care to be greeted thus. Who, sir, may I ask, are you?'

But this time it was the big redheaded man who spoke, a jolly, welcoming voice, in an accent that was thick and Irish. 'Have no mind of this one, Captain, we're damned glad to see you, damned glad. I am Sgt Angus McGinty, of the Fifth Pennsylvania, on a temporary detached duty to protect the dear *Foul-Mouth*, do you see, and this unpleasant son of a bitch is one Malachi Foote, master shipwright.'

'Master shipwright?' Biddlecomb asked, despite his annoyance. 'Master shipwright of the *Falmouth*? And you had a hand in her design too, did you not?' He could picture that name on the draft, next to Humphreys's.

'I am. And I did.'

'Well, sir, I commend you. I have had only the most cursory look, but I can see from that that this ship is unparalleled. The sharpness of her entry alone, I should think, will give her the heels of any other ship her size, and I am with child to see how her stiffness is affected by the deadrise you have given her.'

It was an absurd way to carry on a conversation, yelling up and down the tall side of the ship, like talking to a guard in a tower, but Biddlecomb saw that his words had an unintentional effect on Foote, could see the man's expression soften, the downturn of his mouth ease just a bit.

'Very well, come on aboard,' he said, putting his gun up, forgetting, apparently, that Biddlecomb was the one man in the world who needed no one's permission to board the *Falmouth*.

Isaac stood and grabbed onto the boarding step and stepped up, a tricky move with the vessel so high in the water. He climbed, noted the tumblehome as he went, and stepped through the gangway.

He had assumed that the two men, Foote and McGinty, were the only ones aboard, and so he was

390

startled to find a dozen armed men in the waist, all dressed out in the same uniform as McGinty.

'Surprised we are so well manned, are you, Captain?' McGinty asked with a big grin and a slap on the back that made Biddlecomb immediately wary. 'These are my lads, the detachment from the Fifth. This here is Corporal Freeman, I'd be lost without him. But it's Mother Foote, here, runs the show, or did, until you arrived to relieve us of his tyranny.'

'Shut your bloody gob, Teague,' Foote said, and to Biddlecomb's surprise the big man smiled. Isaac had seen fists fly more than once over the use of that moniker.

'Come along, come along, then,' McGinty said as the men from the longboat came one after another up the side. Rumstick stepped through the gangway, nodded, shook hands with McGinty as the two sized one another up, as big men will when meeting another of their size.

Faircloth came next, looked around the deck, smiled appreciatively. After going from the *Charlemagne* to the *Lady Biddlecomb* to the *Expedient* – vessels in descending order of luxury – the *Falmouth* seemed utterly palatial.

'Pray, sir, tell me,' Faircloth said to the shipwright, Foote, 'the figurehead, do you know who carved it?'

'I carved her,' said Foote. He had seemed to Biddlecomb to be relaxing a bit, but the question put him back on the defensive.

'Extraordinary!' Faircloth said with enthusiasm. 'Mind you, I am no expert on such matters, but I have seen what sculpture London has to offer and

I can assure you, I have never seen its equal. Might it be Susan Williams who sat for you?'

Foote glanced over at McGinty, who was following the conversation, then growled, not pleasantly, 'She did. You know Miss Williams?'

'Indeed, sir,' said Faircloth, 'she and her mother are particular friends of Captain Biddlecomb and his wife. Mrs Biddlecomb is at this moment staying with her in the city.'

'Oh,' said Foote. 'Well then, I reckon that makes the head even more appropriate.'

'Indeed, and I share Lieutenant Faircloth's enthusiasm,' said Biddlecomb.

Of course Faircloth had met Susan, Isaac thought. He would have, escorting Virginia to the Williamses' house.

Isaac also knew Susan, knew her well, in fact. And Susan knew this fellow Foote, had sat for the figurehead – if nothing else – and so it all fell into place. The informant, Faircloth's enthusiasm to see Virginia back again.

Thankfully, Faircloth was the soul of discretion. Isaac could see that a bit of male grunt-and-thrust humor at that moment might have led to gunplay on the deck.

Then McGinty spoke and the fragile tension broke like thin ice. 'Be ever so careful what you say around himself about the whittling, Captain, for he is damned touchy about it,' and even before Foote could order him to shut his gob he added, 'Now, will you not come forward, sir, and allow me to show you what little we've managed to accomplish, while waiting on your honor?'

Biddlecomb allowed himself to be steered forward.

392

He ran his eyes over the long run of the deck, the fresh paint, the unmarred planking, as he half listened to talk about sheers and lower masts and runner pennants and shrouds. He let the sight and the smells, the subtle motion of the vessel underfoot, overwhelm him, let himself become lost in the sensuousness of the thing. For the first time in his life he felt as if he had come home.

CHAPTER 25

*The Court in pursuance of an order from The
Viscount Howe Admiral of the White and
Commander in Chief of His Majesty's Ships and
Vessels in North America directed . . . to enquire
and examine into the Cause of the Loss of His
Majesty's Sloop* Merlin *. . . are Unanimously of the
opinion that the Sloop took Ground in endeavoring
to get into Action with the Rebel Armed Vessels,
by the Shoal having Shifted out farther than the
Pilot was acquainted with that every proper
means were Used to get her off . . . We do therefore
acquit Captain Samuel Reeve, His Officers and
Ships from having in any respect failed in their
duty.*

—OPINION OF THE COURT-MARTIAL
ENQUIRING INTO THE LOSS
OF THE SLOOP *MERLIN*

Things had gone well aboard the *Sparrowhawk*,
Smeaton thought, despite Lieutenant Howard's
failure to understand the proper chain of command,
his failure to yield complete control of the cutter to

him, his disregard of Wallace's stated intention that he do so.

The problem had become apparent almost immediately. Smeaton had come aboard first, had sent the gig back for Howard in what he reckoned was a considerate gesture. Still, it took Howard half an hour to come aboard – a maddening delay – and when he did arrive, he brought with him a boatload of armed men and more in the jolly boat. With never a word to Smeaton he ordered both boats tied up astern even as he stepped through the gangway.

Smeaton said nothing, not wishing to upset Howard by countermanding his orders. As long as Howard's silliness did not interfere with the mission, then he would not embarrass him by pointing out mistakes, such as the excessive number of men he had brought, or the plethora of boats. After all, Howard and the Sparrowhawks were there only to convey Smeaton on his search for Biddlecomb, whereupon he would kill the rebel and be done with it.

By the same token, Smeaton did not give commands for winning the anchor or loosening off sail, waiting instead for Howard to come aft. He felt it only right that he grant Howard the courtesy of consulting with him first before issuing the orders. He understood the humiliation of forced subservience, and with a generosity brought on by his change of fortune he did not wish to inflict it on another.

And so he was fairly taken aback when Howard, without so much as looking at him, shouted, 'Bosun, bring us to short peak. Topmen, away aloft! Loosen all plain sail!'

The crew scattered to their tasks, and it seemed as

if everyone aboard was occupied with something, save for Smeaton, and that was not the thing, not the thing at all.

'Lieutenant?' Howard turned, as if noticing Smeaton for the first time. 'Yes?'

'I think perhaps I shall give the orders for making sail and such, from here on out.'

Howard stared at him, in what Smeaton realized was a copy of Wallace's stare. 'I think not,' Howard said, and said nothing more.

Smeaton made no reply because he could think of no reply to make, so he stood silent while Howard got the cutter underway, set all plain sail and put her close-hauled for the American fleet.

The *Sparrowhawk* was a lovely vessel, about sixty feet along her flush deck and armed with ten four-pounders. Her rig appeared too tall for her size, her bowsprit too long, but those oversize spars gave her a great turn of speed. She carried a flying jib, jib and fore staysail, along with a huge gaff-headed mainsail, and for square sails, a course, topsail, and t'ga'n's'l. Close-hauled as she was, under fore and aft canvas, she could move very fast and point very high indeed.

It would have taken her no time at all to close with the rebel fleet, and so it was an unpleasant surprise to Smeaton when Howard ordered them to tack and keep below the upper *chevaux-de-frise*, just out of long cannon range of the American ships.

'Lieutenant' – Smeaton bit off the word – 'we are to close with the rebels and gain intelligence as to Biddlecomb's whereabouts, so that I may dispatch him.'

Howard turned and looked at him, his expression that of a frustrated parent addressing a habitually naughty child. 'We are not going to sail straight into the rebel fleet, white flag or no. An officer of the British navy may respect a flag of truce, but there is no telling what that type will do. We shall wait until it is dark, or close to.'

There was no denying the logic of that, or that Howard seemed to have everything so well in hand that there was little Smeaton felt the need to do, so he kept to himself and played out in his mind various scenarios by which he would kill Biddlecomb.

Soon it was approaching dark and Howard came over to the taffrail where Smeaton was standing. His tone was somewhat contrite. Smeaton imagined he had finally come to his senses regarding Wallace's orders.

'Lieutenant,' Howard said, 'pray tell me what you know of this Biddlecomb's whereabouts, how we might locate him?'

'He arrived on the river in a schooner, some weeks ago, and promptly wrecked it on the rebel's own *chevaux-de-frise*. Through various means, it is not important how, I have discovered that he is in command of one of the rebels, which one I do not know. I have seen several. He was involved in that horrid business, firing on the Germans at Fort Mercer. As to his precise location at the moment, I should think he is up with the other rebels.'

'We shall skirt around the *chevaux-de-frise* and see if we can't snatch up one of these rebels and glean what information we can from them,' Howard said, his tone like an order, and then, as if once again recalling that he was supposed to consult with Smeaton, he added, 'If that is satisfactory?'

'Quite.'

The shallow-draft vessel easily cleared the mud banks along the Jersey shore and stood upriver in the fading light, unnoticed or ignored by the anchored rebel fleet.

It was their good fortune to stumble across a small gunboat, pulling from Fort Mercer over to Mifflin. They overtook her, luffed up alongside, pointing two dozen muskets at the startled crew, and captured her without a fight, without even a voice raised in protest.

Lieutenants Howard and Smeaton both stepped across to the decked-over section of the captured boat, half a dozen armed Experiments behind them. 'Who is in command here?' Howard asked. 'Or is this barge run by one of these committees you rebels so love?'

'I am the captain.' A man stepped forward, late twenties, with the air of a seaman about him. 'We are your prisoners.'

'Indeed you are,' said Smeaton. 'We are looking for an Isaac Biddlecomb, captain of one of the xebecs. Do you know of his whereabouts?'

'There're some xebecs anchored up by Fort Mifflin. But I don't know any Biddlecomb.'

There was a long pause, and then Smeaton said, 'That is as much as you know?'

'Yes.'

Smeaton pulled his pistol from his belt, cocked the lock, pressed it against the man's head so hard he forced the American to take a step back. 'I ask again, that is as much as you know?'

'Yes!'

'Here is a choice for you to consider.' Howard stepped closer to the man. 'If that is indeed all you know, then we shall take the lot of you prisoner, and you will be shipped off to the prison hulks in New York City. You are no doubt familiar with them? However, if you happen to recall something more, then we shall let you go. We have prisoners enough without you pathetic lot.'

The captain of the gunboat, who had not flinched when a cocked pistol was pressed to his head, was clearly impressed by the threat of a slow, horrible death by starvation and disease in the fetid hell of the prison hulks. Their reputation was well-known, and their filthy, vermin-ridden decks were to be avoided at any price.

'I seen one xebec heading upriver right after the fighting,' the man said reluctantly. 'I didn't think her to be *Repulse* or *Champion*, so she might be the other, the one your friend is commanding.'

'Heading upriver? Up past the city?'

'No, she was making for the Schuylkill. Don't know where she was bound.'

'Mind you,' said Howard matter-of-factly, 'we shall be taking you along, and if it becomes clear you have lied, then it is off to the hulks for you. Now, the Schuylkill, you say?'

The man frowned, looked between Howard and Smeaton, seemed to gauge how serious they were, then said, 'Maybe not. Maybe she was heading up toward the city.'

'Ah, very good,' said Smeaton, lowering the gun and easing the cock back. 'Now please, come aboard, and we shall be off.'

The captain of the gunboat stepped reluctantly aboard the *Sparrowhawk*, and with a few sharp words from Howard the cutter was underway again, leaving the surprised and grateful crew of the rebel vessel behind in the early-evening darkness.

Up past the city. Smeaton could not imagine what Biddlecomb was about, leaving the rebel fleet behind, running past the guns of occupied Philadelphia.

'The man is a coward, just a bloody coward, running from the fight,' he said to himself, but he did not really believe it. He had seen Biddlecomb in a number of circumstances now, knew him to be a villain, a traitor to his king, a criminal and a mutineer. But with genuine and private candor he had to admit that Biddlecomb was also a man who respected honor, and no coward.

The *Sparrowhawk*, fast and weatherly, made a quick run past the rebel fleet, sandwiched as they were by the British navy below them and the occupied city above. The tide had begun to flood some hours before, which made their passage upstream that much quicker. It was only two hours past sunset when they rounded up in front of one of the riverside batteries in the British-held city of Philadelphia and dropped the anchor in four fathoms of water.

Howard ordered the jolly boat pulled around and two men to man the oars. He and Smeaton crowded into the stern sheets and were taken to shore at the foot of the battery, where they were greeted by a captain of artillery backed by two dozen armed men.

'Forgive the troops, gentlemen,' the artillery officer said, gesturing at the soldiers behind him as he helped the lieutenants up the steps of the landing. 'Lot of these damned rebels running up and down the river. Can't trust any flag. Had one go by a few hours ago, flying the Union Jack, but never a proper British navy vessel.'

'Really,' said Smeaton. 'That may well be the one we are after. Was it a xebec?'

'Could have been. What in hell is a "xebec"?'

'Two masts,' Howard explained, 'no bowsprit, lateen sails.'

'It had sails shaped like triangles, if that is what is meant by *lateen*. As to the bowsprit, I'll own I didn't notice. They stayed pretty much to the Jersey side, which is why we reckoned they was rebels, that and the singular look of the thing. Kept well out of long cannon shot, more the shame.'

'And they continued on upriver?' Smeaton asked. He could feel the anticipation growing.

'Can't say for certain. About two miles north of here there's an island that splits the river—'

'Petty's Island, yes, I know it,' Howard interrupted.

'Petty's Island, exactly. This . . . xebec . . . took the southern channel. Disappeared around the point there and that was the last we seen of her. Don't know if she went any further than that.'

'Southern channel, you say . . .' Howard mused. 'That is most helpful, sir, most helpful indeed. I thank you. Now we must be under way once more.'

And ten minutes later they were, sailing close-hauled for a long board across the river, then a tack back to the Pennsylvania shore, and another toward Jersey, which, with the aid of the flood, brought them to the mouth of the southern channel around Petty's Island.

'Do you know the river at all, Smeaton, this far up?' Howard asked, condescending, uninterested.

'No, I do not.'

'Well, Biddlecomb does, I should imagine. Vessels

401

sailing with the flood generally take the northern channel, when sailing upriver. If this Biddlecomb took the southern, I should think it is because he had some specific destination in mind. I intend to anchor here and send the boat out to see what that destination might be.'

Smeaton was growing angry, had been all day. Through a combination of aristocratic stoicism and the thrill of hunting Biddlecomb down like a dog, he had managed to hold it in check until then, but he found he could no longer.

'His destination is of no matter. There is no need to reconnoiter. You are here to get me to him so that I might fight him and kill him. No more.'

'I disagree.'

'You are not in a position to disagree!'

'Oh? Am I not?'

Smeaton clenched his teeth. It was Pocock and the boat all over again. The men aboard the *Sparrowhawk* would not listen to him, a stranger from another ship. He had no authority aboard the cutter. All he could do was let Howaard do as he wished and hope he did not make a hash of the whole thing, then see that Wallace meted out fit punishment when all was done.

'Very well, Howard, do as you wish. We shall see what Captain Wallace has to say about this when we return.'

'Indeed we will,' Howard said, and then to the helmsman said, 'Let us round up here,' his discussion with Smeaton at an end.

The little jolly boat was sent out, with two men again at the oars, the tholes well muffled, and a midshipman in the stern sheets. An hour later it returned, the men pulling hard, the midshipman looking as if he might explode from excitement before he could even give his report.

'Xebec's down there, at anchor, and there is a frigate as well, sir, tied right up to the bank! Foremast is in and the foreyard crossed, but it don't look like they even have the ballast in, and never a gun that I could see.'

'Is that so . . .' said Howard, and then turning to Smeaton, who had wanted to remain aloof but could not, said, 'Might that be where Biddlecomb was bound? Perhaps he was going to meet up with the frigate, take command of her?'

'Perhaps. But the point is this: we now know where he is, so let us get under way under flag of truce and let me call him out. That is what this is all about. I insist, insist, sir, that you follow Captain Wallace's instructions! I shall see you court-martialed if you disobey his orders.'

Howard sighed, seemed to come to a decision, and Smeaton imagined that his words had finally struck home.

'That is it, Smeaton, I have had quite enough. My orders from Captain Wallace are these: I am to capture this Biddlecomb and bring him back. I am to use you in whatever way I can to bring that about. That is your sole function in this operation, sir, and now that we have found him, I have no more need of you. And now it would seem we have a frigate to capture as well, a prize that I shall be delighted to bring in. So, pray, shut your goddamned mouth and let me see to things from here on in?'

Smeaton staggered back, as shocked as he had been after Rumstick's blow. This was too much, too much by half.

'This is an affair of honor—' he managed to stammer.

'This is a military affair, Lieutenant, no more. The Royal Navy is not concerned with the last vestiges of your honor.'

'This is too much, sir! I must demand satisfaction!'

Howard actually smiled at that. 'Please do not interfere or I shall have to see you detained below, under guard. If you behave, then I shall allow you to participate in the cutting-out expedition we will be undertaking tonight. Is that understood?'

Smeaton just stared at him, in shock, in disbelief, in wide-eyed horror.

Wallace had used him to get to Biddlecomb, had toyed with his sense of honor, played him for a fool.

It was the final, the ultimate, betrayal.

CHAPTER 26

*If . . . they [the British] should by Surprise, or force,
obtain the Frigates above Bordentown, and bring
the whole in aid of their Ships in a general attack
upon our little Fleet (thus surrounded) we may,
but too easily without the spirit of divination
foretell the consequences – their destruction will be
certain & inevitable.*

— GEORGE WASHINGTON
TO THE CONTINENTAL NAVY BOARD
OF THE MIDDLE DEPARTMENT

Smeaton could do nothing, nothing, but watch in
sick disbelief as preparations were made. His stomach
churned, his mind raced through a thousand considerations, decisions, suspicions, as Howard laid out
the plans for the attack and the cutting out of the
frigate, the capture of Isaac Biddlecomb.

Smeaton stared in mute horror as small arms were
issued, men assigned to this boat or that, officers told
which part of the ship they would be boarding.

And then it was quiet, the men stood down to rest
before the expedition, which was to take place at

three, that dark, dead time of night when surprise would be most complete. Soon only Smeaton and the lookouts and the midshipman who was officer of the deck were awake, and only the lookouts and the midshipman were aware of their surroundings.

Smeaton's mind was somewhere else, in a place where he could try to make sense of what had happened to him. He had been so certain of his destiny, he had seen all the signs of divine intervention in his quest to reclaim his honor and his rightful place.

And now this.

It was not possible that his honor and reputation was some heavenly joke, as it was apparently an earthly one. It was not possible. And yet here he was, brought to the edge of regaining his good name and then pushed aside.

And Biddlecomb would think that he, Smeaton, had forsaken their duel, daring only to confront his enemy with overwhelming force. Biddlecomb would think that Smeaton had been afraid, that he had arranged for the cutting out to avoid an honorable affair.

And that, Smeaton realized, was the most intolerable notion of all. That Biddlecomb should think him afraid, that Biddlecomb should go to his death believing that he, John Smeaton, Esquire, had brought his army to avoid fighting Biddlecomb man to man.

The very thought made him panicky, terrified. He told himself that Biddlecomb's opinion should be the last thing that mattered to him, but it was not, not at all. It was ironic, to be sure, but Biddlecomb's opinion was what mattered most.

And then, like warm sleep settling on him, came the understanding that he had to face Biddlecomb, that he could not let Howard or Wallace or anyone, human or otherwise, stand between him and his fate. And if it was God who was tormenting him thus, then God Himself could be damned.

He ambled forward slowly, his movement attracting no attention. It was a dark night, with no moon, and he could barely see those few men on deck, and in turn he imagined that they could barely see him, if at all.

At the gangway he paused and glanced down, over the side. The launch was directly below and the jolly boat was tied up to the mainchains, astern of the launch. It would be an easy step from one to the other.

He could feel the beat of his heart, and his breathing sounded loud to him in the still night. He half turned and looked along the deck. The midshipman was standing aft on the quarterdeck, bored, staring distractedly toward the shore. The lookouts, no more than dark shapes, appeared to be staring off into their assigned quadrants. No one was paying him any attention.

He took a step toward the gangway, then another. Put a foot on the first step and stepped down, and down again. No alarm, no voices raised. He took the next few steps quickly and lowered himself as softly as he could into the longboat, then climbed aft and over the transom into the jolly boat.

Now he could hear movement on the *Sparrowhawk*'s deck, steps coming toward the side, attracted by the noise, soft though it was. With shaking hands he untied the painter and pushed the boat off the cutter's side. The space between ship and boat widened and he stumbled aft, balancing awkwardly, and sat on the thwart and took up the unfamiliar sweeps.

'What the hell . . .' he heard from the quarterdeck above, and then another voice, softly, 'It's that lieutenant. Sir? Sir? What the devil is he about?'

Smeaton managed to get the oars outboard and bring the blades down into the water and pull, a clumsy and inefficient motion, but enough to shoot the light boat along. He could see the figures watching him, heard one say, 'What should . . .' and another, 'Here, go fetch Mr Howard.'

He pulled again and the *Sparrowhawk* fell farther astern. Lean forward, oars down, pull; he began to fall into a rhythm as the mechanics of rowing, something he had not done in years, began to return. He could feel the speed and momentum of the jolly boat building.

The hard wood under his palms, the pressure of the blades in the water, the motion of the boat, felt good and pure and honorable, and his heart felt lighter with every yard he put between himself and that treacherous cutter. He could see figures running around the deck now, but he could hear nothing because the men on the *Sparrowhawk* were still trying to keep quiet.

He didn't know what Howard would do. He didn't know what he himself would do either, for he had not thought this out at all, had just acted, for once, and it felt right. He would find Biddlecomb and call him out. That was the plan in its entirety. He would regain his honor, or by Biddlecomb's hand or by Howard's hand he would die in the attempt.

* * *

'Damn it, damn it, damn it, damn it!' Howard repeated like a mantra, pounding his fist softly on the quarterdeck rail and staring at the patch of darkness into which Smeaton had just disappeared. 'Damn it.'

That stupid, stupid bastard.

It was the kind of situation that ambitious lieutenants such as Howard fantasized about, the sort of thing that occupied their thoughts above all else, even more than dreams of country estates or lovely and willing young women. Here was Isaac Biddlecomb, one of the great villains of the war, the man that Capt. Sir James Wallace, for some reason, was desperate to capture, along with a new-built frigate, all within his grasp.

At the very moment that the lookout had knocked on his cabin door, he had been thinking about where in the Colonies he might buy his epaulet, after being promoted to commander.

It had all been laid before him, like a banquet, and now Smeaton was going to knock the table over, scatter the whole thing on the ground.

'Sir . . .' said the midshipman, hesitating. He was still reeling from the tongue-lashing Howard had given him. Howard could hear the fear in his voice. 'Sir, I could go after him. The longboat could catch him, easy enough.'

'No.'

The longboat could overtake the jolly boat, that was true, but catching him meant finding him on the dark river, and that might involve all kinds of noise, perhaps even gunshots.

No, Smeaton wanted only to fight Biddlecomb, and Howard was certain that that was what he was going to do, and he did not think Smeaton would purposely betray the *Sparrowhawk*'s presence. But when Smeaton appeared alone on the frigate, Biddlecomb would guess that more men were nearby – the jolly boat had to have come from some vessel – and he would bolt.

Howard turned to the midshipman. 'Turn the men out with their weapons. Under no circumstances are any guns to be loaded. Redistribute the men that were assigned to the jolly boat. We will cut the frigate out now. I want every boat under way in ten minutes.'

It had been a long and exhausting day, coming at the end of a long series of long and exhausting days, and most of the men aboard the *Falmouth*, those late of the *Charlemagne* and those late of the Fifth Pennsylvania, were asleep. Only a handful of them remained awake: her captain and first officer, lieutenant of marines, her shipwright, Angus McGinty, a few sailors and soldiers on the fo'c's'le head, the lookouts fore and aft, who stared all but pointlessly into the dark night.

The officers and Foote sat on the quarterdeck, engaging in little bursts of conversation, then falling quiet again, enjoying the night and their ship. All the stories had been told: the *Charlemagne*, the *Lady Biddlecomb*, the provosts, the towing of the frigate, the fight at Fort Mercer, the raid on the spar pond. Each group had proved to the other their bona fides, their claim to a part of the great ship that had nothing to do with warrants and orders from Congress.

Now the talk, when it came, was general: the state

of the defenses downriver, the situation in occupied Philadelphia, the battle at Germantown that had almost been won by the Continental Army. Conversation of no great depth or consequence, just a reason to remain on deck. They were loath to give up the moment, to close their eyes and sleep and stop looking at their ship.

Finally McGinty stood, stretched, and yawned, like a bear ready to hibernate. 'That's it for me, lads. I'm off to sleep that fine slumber of the innocent.' The others nodded their goodnights and McGinty climbed down the scuttle and was gone.

A minute later Biddlecomb stood as well, and the others followed, deciding by silent and mutual agreement that it was time at last for bed. 'Great cabin's waiting on you, Biddlecomb,' said Foote, who could not seem to get his tongue around the word *captain*. 'Ain't much there, beyond the deck.'

'I have had ample experience sleeping on decks as of late. I shall be famously comfortable.'

Foote turned to Rumstick. 'I been sleeping in the first officer's cabin, didn't get the chance to shift my gear. Ain't much . . .'

Rumstick held up his hands. 'Never think on it. I'll find some place to bunk. It's a big ship.'

And then from the lookout forward, words stammered, startled and afraid: 'Damn me! Who . . . what . . . you there, who are you?' The lookout ran across the fo'c's'le head and aft along the gangway, unslinging his musket as he ran, and the men on the quarterdeck ran forward, Biddlecomb in the lead.

The lookout stopped at the top of the boarding steps and pointed the musket down, and Biddlecomb stopped and looked where the gun was pointing.

Floating alongside the *Falmouth* was a small boat, just visible in the dark. A single figure was seated on the thwart, more the suggestion of a man than anything definable on that black night.

And then from the water below came that clipped and aristocratic tone that Isaac had first heard almost two years before, in the black hold of the *William B. Adams*, as he shrank behind a stack of casks from the British press gang. 'I am Lt John Smeaton. I am looking for Isaac Biddlecomb.'

Incredible. Smeaton, here, alone in this little boat. Had he rowed up from Billingsport? The voice was lacking its former authority, the arrogance that ran like a musical theme through his every word, but still there was no mistaking it.

'I'm here, Smeaton. Are you alone?'

'I am.'

Foote appeared with a lantern. He opened the shutter and the weak light spilled down the side of the frigate and just barely illuminated the figure of John Smeaton, sitting alone on the thwart. He looked small, like a child rowing a boat built for an adult. Isaac hesitated, uncertain how he should react to this surprise, then said, 'Very well, come aboard.'

The men on the gangway stood aside to allow the British naval officer to pass. It was an odd sight, an awkward moment, and then Rumstick helped make it worse by saying, 'Your nose is healing up nicely there, little Smeaton.'

Smeaton looked at Rumstick with the purest hatred and then turned to Biddlecomb. 'You know why I am here. We have an affair of honor that is not yet settled.'

Smeaton did not look well. His face was quite pale

compared to those of the men around him. It seemed to float above his dark coat like a ghost. His cheeks looked hollow and his nose was crooked and dark patches were under his eyes, vestiges of the black eyes that came with a broken nose. Without thinking Biddlecomb said, 'God, Smeaton, you are a fright.'

Smeaton appeared to be a man at the end, the kind who volunteered to be first into the breach or to take the lead in a futile charge. Coming alone aboard an enemy frigate was not so very different from those things. It wasn't bravery, it was the absence of everything else.

Smeaton took a step back, pulled his sword from its scabbard. The lookout leveled the gun at his head, pulled back the lock. Smeaton did not even blink.

Biddlecomb shook his head. 'No. The situation is much altered now. There'll be no fight. You may go.'

Smeaton scowled, but in his eyes he looked afraid. 'I have gone to great lengths to see this through. If you have any honor at all, I suggest you defend it.'

'No.'

'Defend yourself, you son of a bitch,' Smeaton said louder, with a bit of the old arrogance creeping in, 'or admit to all these men that you dare not fight. Then what of your reputation? The great rebel captain?'

Biddlecomb shook his head again. 'That won't work here. This is not the *Icarus*, Smeaton, and these men are not a crew of mutineers and outlaws. They are sailors and soldiers in the armed forces of these United States. My authority over them is a legal one, it comes from the Congress, and even if you don't recognize it, they do. Most of these men have sailed with me for some time. I think they will not question my authority.'

Smeaton glanced around, as if looking for some signs of insubordination, some indication that the dozen men gathered there would turn on their captain if he declined the challenge. But Biddlecomb knew Smeaton would not see it because it was not there. These men had been tempered by the journey to that place, had fought beside him in the long-running battle to claim the *Falmouth*, and they would not be turned against him by the words of a disgraced British naval officer.

'So that is it? Cowardice? After all of this we see your true colors, your true nature, your cowardly heart?'

'You'll not lure me in with that bait. I have no need to prove my courage. Your precious navy has given me test enough and I have not been found wanting, I dare say.'

Biddlecomb was surprised by what he was feeling, or more to the point, what he was not. No rage, no need to run a sword through Smeaton. Vengeance, which had only a few weeks before seemed so desperately important, now seemed a little thing, not worth pursuing. He wondered if that was what Smeaton seemed so afraid of: that he, Biddlecomb, would consider him too insignificant to be worth raising a sword against.

'Listen here, Smeaton. I have a wife, I have a young son. My life is worth something. I'll risk it for my country, I'll risk it for my honor. I've done so and I'll do so again. But it was never for honor that I fought you. You have never tarnished my honor in any way, though I have yours. It was for vengeance, and that is a luxury I cannot indulge. I'll not risk my neck just so you can regain your own lost honor.'

Smeaton paused and lowered his sword until the point rested on the deck. He looked as if he might cry, looked more miserable than any other man Biddlecomb had ever seen, and despite himself, Isaac felt sorry for him.

'You'll not fight me?'

'I will not.'

Smeaton looked up at the stars, took a deep breath, swallowed hard. He looked down again, met Biddlecomb's eye. 'I have lost everything, Biddle-comb, everything. My fortune, my dignity, my position in the navy. I have been betrayed by my own people. Because of you. And so now I must beg you . . . I have never begged in my life . . . but now I must beg you, don't do this thing to me. Fight. Please.'

Biddlecomb felt pity, actual pity, rising up out of the murk. Smeaton was pathetic, a wretch in every sense of the word. Was it possible that pity could motivate him, Capt. Isaac Biddlecomb, to fight this man?

'Please . . . Captain . . .' said Smeaton. 'It is all I have left. My ability to do this, it is the only thing left.'

Yes, it would. Isaac shook his head in disgust, disgust with Smeaton, disgust with himself. I do not believe this, he thought, even as he gestured for Smeaton to follow him down into the waist. I do not believe this.

Smeaton nodded, a small gesture, but one that conveyed every nuance of his gratitude. Isaac heard his steps behind as they went down the ladder to the waist and the long stretch of empty deck where the guns would go. The other men still on deck followed as well, solemn, as if at a funeral.

Isaac turned, faced Smeaton. He pulled his sword from its sheath, felt the lovely balanced weapon floating at the end of his arm.

Smeaton stepped back, brought his sword up to a defensive position, took a small step to one side. With that simple motion he went from Smeaton the broken, pathetic fool to Smeaton the deadly swordsman, Smeaton the man of dignity.

Once more the failed lieutenant had led Isaac Biddlecomb into a fight against all his will and better judgment.

Isaac stepped with care, circling away from Smeaton. Fine, you little bastard, he thought, I am no ham-fisted bumpkin with a sword, and with that he made an exploratory lunge, felt the weight of Smeaton's blade, the quickness of his arm, and then drew back.

The points of the swords danced around one another, like snakes looking for the chance to strike, and then both blades came together, clashed, clashed again, drew apart. Smeaton thrust straight at Isaac's chest, a fully extended lunge, and Isaac leapt back, arched his back, knocked the point aside even as it pierced the front of his coat.

Smeaton had looked so pathetic, so weak, pleading for the chance to redeem himself. Isaac realized with further disgust that he had been led into this in part because Smeaton did not look to be a formidable adversary. But the loss of his dignity had not slowed his reflexes.

The dozen or so men on deck were fully engrossed

in the fight, standing amidships or under the gangways like spectators under a roof, watching the swordplay in the waist. The former Charlemagnes, the former infantrymen, those who had been posted fore and aft as lookouts, all were staring intently at the duelists, entirely ignorant of anything beyond that confined space.

Nor was Biddlecomb thinking about anything further than the sweep of Smeaton's sword. There was an all-consuming intensity about the moment, a body-and-soul involvement that allowed for no outside distractions. Isaac understood on every level that distraction meant death.

They had circled one hundred and eighty degrees, coming together in clashes of steel and then drawing apart. They were well matched as swordsmen, both very good, both out of practice with this sort of civilized swordplay.

Smeaton attacked, taking a step and then another, thrusting straight. He feigned to the right, and Isaac took the bait, and even as he moved his sword to defend against the trick, Smeaton swung his own blade around and thrust.

Isaac leapt back, quick enough to avoid a fatal wound, but not fast enough to avoid taking an inch of steel just below his left shoulder. He gasped, stepped back, his sword still up, still ready to defend.

The wound burned and ached with a dull pain. Isaac touched it with his left hand, looked at the dark blood on his fingers. He had been cut enough times to recognize the sequence of sensations. His eyes met Smeaton's and the two men just stared for a second. Such a wound would have meant victory in a fight to first blood, but this was way beyond that.

'Son of a bitch!' Biddlecomb said, and the last word propelled him across the deck, and this time it was Smeaton who stepped back under the onslaught, his sword flailing to keep Isaac's off. The banging of steel against steel filled the waist, filled Biddlecomb's ears as he slashed and slashed, waiting for that opening, that mistake on Smeaton's part that would allow him to get past the man's guard and end the nonsense for good.

And then, a thump alongside, a heavy thump, not the jolly boat swinging into the frigate but something much bigger.

Isaac stepped back, eyes on Smeaton, sword ready, but his ears and his concentration were elsewhere. He warned himself not to lose his focus, but then there was another noise and suddenly a clash of weapons, muskets being handled, feet on the boarding steps, more boats against the hull. A grappling hook flew up over the bow and grabbed on to the short rail there.

Isaac turned to Smeaton, who was also looking around in shock and surprise. 'Smeaton, you lying son of a bitch! You said you were alone, you bastard! Is this what you mean by "honor"?'

A British naval officer appeared on the gangway above, raced aft, and behind him came a dozen armed seamen, pistols in hand, cutlasses banging against their sides. More were clambering over the bow, larboard and starboard.

Malachi Foote came racing past, fleeing for the cover of the quarterdeck, and disappeared below.

None of them had seen the attack coming because none of them had been watching, and no one had heard it over the sounds of the fight.

Smeaton found his voice at last. 'Biddlecomb, this was none of my doing! I came here on my honor—'

'Stow it, Smeaton, you son of a whore! I know what your honor means now, you bastard.'

Smeaton's mouth hung open and he shook his head from side to side. At the sound of footsteps on the ladder, the two men looked up. The gangway was lined with seamen, British seamen, aiming their short-barreled muskets down into the waist, as if at animals caught in a pit. The officer who led the expedition stepped into the waist.

'Ah, Smeaton, thought I would find you here. And this, I take it, is the rebel Biddlecomb? Glad you didn't kill him, Lieutenant.'

Smeaton frowned and Isaac could see that his hands were trembling as if he had palsy. 'You bastard,' Smeaton said, his voice like a rasp on wood. 'You bastard. This was none of my doing, Howard. You tell him this was none of my doing!'

'Nonsense,' said Howard, 'don't deny yourself the credit, Smeaton. You led us right to him. We should never have caught him, and taken the frigate as well, were it not for you.'

'You bastard!' Smeaton screamed, the purest of sounds, unadulterated by any tinge of emotion beyond rage. He took two steps forward, brought his sword up over his head. Howard crouched, clawed at the brace of pistols clipped to his belt. The sword came down in an arc, like a Viking battle-ax, as Howard freed the pistols, brought them up, thumbed the hammers back, and discharged both barrels into Smeaton's chest.

Smeaton was blown back to Biddlecomb's feet, crumpling to the deck, the sword falling with a clatter

419

beside him. Glassy eyes stared up at the stars. A trickle of blood ran out of the corner of his mouth. More spread out from under him, making a dark spot on the new wood, soaking into the pine-planked deck.

Isaac looked down at his face. Smeaton's lips moved, just a little bit, and in a harsh whisper, choked with blood, he said, 'Biddlecomb . . .'

Isaac knelt down on the deck, leaned over him. He could not tell if Smeaton knew he was there. The dying lieutenant just gazed up at the stars. Then he said it again.

'Biddlecomb . . .'

And then he was dead.

Isaac stood up, looked at the corpse at his feet. Smeaton had not lied to him. It had been an affair of honor, or so he had believed, and he had died by his countryman's hand rather than let his bitterest enemy think otherwise.

'This was the noblest Roman of them all . . .' Biddlecomb heard himself mutter the words.

It was the most pathetic thing he had ever witnessed.

'It's better for him this way, truly,' said Howard without the least bit of sympathy. 'Might even write it up that he died in the cutting out. Not so far from the truth, really. And now, Biddlecomb, we must talk.'

Isaac pulled his eyes from the dead officer and looked up at the living one. Living, and in possession of the *Falmouth*.

Biddlecomb and the Charlemagnes had come all that way, had had possession of the frigate for six hours. And now she, and they, were in British hands.

CHAPTER 27

These Frigates have been only officer'd & no Attempt ever made to man them . . . The Men we have are, for the most part, Militia . . . taken on Board merely to assist in getting the ships up to this Place.

—CONTINENTAL NAVAL BOARD
WRITING TO GEORGE WASHINGTON
OCTOBER 26, 1777

Clad only in breeches, wool stockings, and woolen undershirt, Angus McGinty stretched out his full length on the cot, feet well over the edge. He felt the muscles in his body relax, like the strain coming off a halyard as the yard settles in its lifts, and he sighed.

And then from overhead, the clash of steel, sword on sword, and he was instantly up, feet on the deck, perched on the edge of the cot and listening. He heard footsteps overhead, two men, and then the swords again. There was no shouting, no stampede of feet. It was not an attack, just a duel of some sort.

'Now what the bloody hell is this?' he muttered. Perhaps Foote had pushed someone beyond his limits, made some rude remark to someone who, unlike McGinty, was not so willing to smile and shrug it off.

Was it over that little bunter, Susan Williams, that Foote seemed so obsessed with? The marine officer had known her, and in Angus's experience, to know her was to . . .

'Ah, Jesus, Mary, and Joseph,' he muttered next, grabbed up his boots, and pulled them on.

He stood, bent low, just able to see in the feeble light of the lantern hanging in the tween decks. There was another burst of swordplay and he wondered if he should bring his musket. And then a heavy thump on the side of the ship, and then another, and feet on the boarding steps, and he knew that something was very wrong.

He snatched up his musket and the shoulder belt with his cartridge box and bayonet and flung the door open. Freeman was there, dressed and armed much as McGinty.

'Freeman,' he said in a harsh whisper, 'something's acting. Go turn them others out, tell them to load weapons and fix bayonets. And them sailors as well, with anything they got. And tell them to be quiet and keep their bloody gobs shut!'

Freeman nodded, hurried forward, and McGinty was alone. And then he heard more running feet, one person, making for the scuttle, and he wondered what craven bastard that was, fleeing from the attack. He took a step aft and Malachi Foote came racing down the ladder.

McGinty grabbed him by the arm, brought him up all standing. 'Mother Foote, what's acting?'

Foote jerked his arm but could not break the big

man's grip. 'Get your fucking hand off me, Teague! It's the British, they're cutting the frigate out!'

'And what are you doing?'

'I'm trying to get my musket, you cowardly bastard, so I can kill at least one of them!' Foote hissed.

'Well, hold up, and maybe we can kill more than that.' McGinty released Foote's arm.

'Don't you tell me what to do, Teague, you son of a whore! Those bastards will not take this ship without I do something to defend her.'

'You're a brave man, Malachi, but you can be a stupid one as well.'

They heard the shuffle of feet behind them, and out of the gloom came Freeman leading the dozen armed men of the Fifth Pennsylvania and twenty-five or so former Charlemagnes, some carrying muskets, some pistols, some cutlasses or sheath knives.

'There's a smarter way to do this, Foote,' said McGinty, in his most mollifying tone.' Now what are we facing, topside?'

'Boarding party, armed with muskets and cutlasses, maybe forty men. They come over the bow and amidships, complete surprise. Took the deck with never a fight.'

'What was—' McGinty began, and was cut off by two pistol shots, fired together, the thump of a body on the deck.

'They'll come down here next,' growled Freeman, 'better if we meet them first.'

'So much for me fancy plans,' said McGinty. 'You lot, there, with Freeman.' He pointed to a group of soldiers and sailors, directed them to the after scuttle. 'You, there, with Mother Foote; the rest with me!

Once I shout, then you all storm the deck and yell like the devil has your arse in his teeth! Go!'

The men rushed forward and aft, and McGinty led his division to the ladder leading to the waist. He paused at the bottom and looked up. Framed against the stars were half a dozen men, but he could not tell if they were on his side.

Then one of the figures turned and McGinty could just make out a face looking down at him and he heard, 'Damn! Lieutenant, there's—' and McGinty brought his musket up to his shoulder and fired. In the flash he saw that the man had been an English sailor and now was dead.

McGinty took the steps two at a time, felt a scream building in his gut, the passion of a thousand years of Irish warlords driving him up into this enemy aboard his ship.

He burst from the scuttle screaming, bellowing, driving his bayonet before him. A gun went off in front of him and he reckoned he must have been hit, but he did not feel it, just thrust the bayonet into the shooter, twisted, pulled it free. He saw Freeman aft, leading the charge forward from the aftermost scuttle, pinning those in the waist between the two divisions.

McGinty screamed again, twisted around, swinging his musket like a club, and caught a man on the side of his head a second before McGinty would have taken a cutlass in the back. Through the fray he could see Foote leading his own men up and out the forwardmost scuttle, driving the British forward, and beyond him the Yankees, Biddlecomb and Rumstick and the others, falling on the startled men who had been guarding them.

Guns were going off all around as his men and his enemies used the one shot they would get before plunging into the fighting with cold steel, hand to hand. Reloading in such a melee was not an option.

A cutlass flashed in front of him, and he moved his musket barrel too late to stop it. He felt the blade bite his arm, felt the burn of the cut, and he slammed the butt of his musket into the attacker, knocked him aside, and with a fluid, practiced motion – only possible for a man of his size and strength – he flipped the gun over and drove the bayonet home.

Bayonets. That was the thing, he realized, as he searched out another victim. The boarding party did not have bayonets. They wouldn't if they were sailors. The damage his dozen men might do, armed with those weapons, was greater than the enemy might hope to do with three times the number of cutlasses and swords.

'Bastards!' McGinty screamed, low, building, venting fury like a bear baited by dogs.

He plunged forward, saw a lieutenant in front of him, drove his bayonet forward as the officer tried in vain to knock the weapon away with his light sword. The momentum of the heavy musket carried the blade past the attempt to deflect it. McGinty thrust it into the man's side. The officer gasped, dropped his sword, collapsed to the deck, and McGinty reared back, swung around, screamed, 'Who's next, ya bastards, who's next!'

The answer was no one. The fight was over, the British sailors flinging their weapons to the deck, putting their arms over their heads, allowing pistols and cutlasses and boarding axes to be pulled from their hands.

The waist was covered with heaps of fallen men, men leaning on whatever they could find, gasping for air, clapping hands over wounds, falling to their knees in exhaustion, in shock, from loss of blood. The surprise, the ferocity of the attack coming up from below had overwhelmed them, and the bayonets had done the rest.

McGinty stood still for a moment, breathing, letting the tension drain. He could feel the cut on his arm now; it hurt like a son of a bitch, and he could feel the gunshot wound now as well. It had torn up his shoulder and he could not tell if the bullet was still lodged in him or had passed through.

A big man loomed up beside him, as big as himself, and for a second he stupidly thought it was his brother, Patrick, but it was in fact Rumstick.

'Reckon you saved our bacon, Sergeant,' Rumstick said in what McGinty guessed the man considered to be a song of praise. Just like Foote, another one of these damned taciturn Yankees.

'I thank you, Rumstick, but it was our lads, you know . . .' McGinty's voice trailed off. Where was Mother Foote? He looked across the deck for his familiar outline but could not see him. 'Forgive me a moment, Lieutenant.'

He made his way forward, looking over those leaning against the rails and seated on the hatch coamings or lying on the deck, but Foote was not among them.

He saw a British lieutenant lying on his back, dead in a big patch of blood, with what appeared to be two bullet wounds in him. He paused, recalled the pistol shots he had heard. But there was no time to puzzle over the man's death. He moved forward.

The line of Malachi Foote's advance toward the bow was marked by the litter of wounded men. It terminated just near the break of the foredeck, which was as far forward as they had pushed before the surrender of the cutting-out expedition.

Concern turned to fear and then certainty as McGinty walked forward and did not find the shipwright among the living or the dead.

By the time he passed the forward hatch he had no doubt that the figure lying crumpled by the break of the foredeck, the man who had pushed the farthest through the enemy, was Malachi Foote. And when he hurried up to the man, knelt beside him, rolled him over, there was no satisfaction in being right.

'Oh, Mother Foote, what have you done, man?' he said in a low and soothing voice. He lifted Foote's head and shoulders, cradled them in his lap. There was a bullet wound in Foote's chest, just below the heart. He was still alive, but would not be for long.

'Teague . . . ?'

'It's me, Malachi. We beat them, we did. They did not take the ship, the bastards.'

'Good . . .' Foote's voice was weak, sounded as if he were speaking from a long way off. 'So thirsty . . .'

McGinty turned his head. 'Get me some water up here! Get me some fucking water!' He intended to hide the desperation in his voice, but it came out unbidden.

'You can tell me now, McGinty . . .'

'Tell you what?'

'The gal . . . on Chestnut Street . . . the figurehead. Susan Williams . . . she the one . . . you been thrumming?'

'Williams? Do ya not mean Lizzy Batchalor, lives

427

on Chestnut Street, at the corner of Second? Is she not the one who sat for the figurehead?'

Foote shook his head, a feeble motion.

'Oh, then I'm all turned about. I don't know any Susan Williams, on me mother's grave.'

'They found her, Angus. The British found . . . *Falmouth*. You have to get her out of here . . . they'll come again.'

'Of course, Malachi, of course, if I have to pull her me own damned self, I'll see her out of here.'

Foote's body shivered, as if caught by a sudden chill, and his lips turned up in a vague suggestion of a smile. 'Not so bad . . . for a lazy Teague . . .'

McGinty heard footsteps behind him but did not look up. He closed his eyes, felt the tears squeeze out between his lids and run down his cheeks.

'Here's some water, Sergeant . . . like you asked for . . . ?'

'He don't need it now, lad. He got no fucking use for it now.'

Biddlecomb was thankful for the dark and for the corporal, Freeman, who was rounding up prisoners and organizing the men. It gave him time, if only a few moments, to think, to try to understand what had happened, what might happen next.

As a sailor, Isaac was used to fast-changing circumstances, emergencies appearing with no warning, and the instant reactions and decisions needed to cope with them. But now he found himself reeling from the events of the past half hour, all but overwhelmed by shock piled on shock.

He had the luxury of two and a half minutes of uninterrupted consideration, and then Freeman

428

appeared in front of him, saying, 'Captain? I got the prisoners all seated on the deck there, with a guard over them. Have some of my boys looking after the wounded, but there ain't so much they can do.'

'Good. Very good, Corporal.' Isaac felt himself returning to the reality of the moment.

'This one here' – Freeman indicated with a jerk of his thumb a man standing behind him and off to one side – 'says he's an American, pressed into the service.' Freeman's tone made it clear how un-impressed he was with that story.

Biddlecomb turned to the man. 'Yes?'

The figure stepped forward, clutching his hat in his hand. He had the look of a seaman, experienced, if a bit past his prime. When he spoke, his accent was hard to place. West Indies, perhaps.

'I was aboard a privateer, sir, out of Portsmouth, in Virginia, sir, and we was taken by a British cruiser just off the Capes. They said I was a deserter from the British navy, sir, and they pressed me into service. I swear to God it's the truth.'

'Humph,' said Biddlecomb. The part about being taken from a privateer was no doubt true, but Isaac doubted that the impressment story was. The man had probably volunteered for the British navy to avoid the prison hulks where most captured sailors were sent. Biddlecomb could not entirely blame him for that decision.

'I can't tell you what a relief it is, sir,' the man continued, 'being freed like this, and I hope I can have the chance to serve you and fight these bastards again.' He had a knack for the sincere turn of a phrase.

'You were rated able-bodied?'

'Aye, sir. Foretopman, and you know how picky them privateers is.'

Biddlecomb did indeed. And he could certainly use a foretopman, but the man no doubt had intelligence of the enemy, which was of much greater value at the moment than his ability to hand, reef, and steer. The *Falmouth* did not in any event sport much that needed handing or reefing.

'Where did this cutting-out party come from? What ship?'

'The cutter *Sparrowhawk*, tender to *Experiment*, which is still down by Billingsport. The cutter's anchored a mile or so up that way.' The man pointed into the dark, toward the southern shore of Petty's Island.

'Cutter? Were there many men left behind?'

'No, sir, just an anchor watch. A midshipman and four or five men, no more.'

Biddlecomb nodded, considered this information. They would have to take the cutter before she escaped with news of their presence, that much was certain. But what they would do beyond that he did not know.

He rubbed his head, tried to think, but nothing would come. 'Freeman, please find the officers and ask them to step over here.'

A minute later Rumstick and Faircloth appeared, and then the Irish sergeant, McGinty.

'Where is Mr Foote?' Biddlecomb asked. 'He's not an officer, but I reckon he should be here.'

'Dead, Captain,' said McGinty, 'died in the defense of his ship.'

'Oh.' Isaac did not know what more to say. He had hardly known the man. Rude, argumentative,

430

but brilliant in his craft, and passionate. That had been Biddlecomb's impression. It was all the impression he would ever get.

He turned to the emancipated Virginian privateer. 'I'll thank you to tell these gentlemen what you told me about the cutting-out party.'

The man related the story again and the officers listened in silence. When he was done, Biddlecomb said, 'We must take the cutter before she can carry news of us to the fleet. But I'll own I'm at a loss as to what to do beyond that, and I would welcome suggestions.'

'We can't remain here,' offered McGinty. 'If they found us once, they'll find us again. The frigate has got to be moved.'

'We towed her this far,' Freeman said. 'We got a power more men and boats now, we could tow her further upriver.'

'Beg your pardon, but sod that, I say,' said Rumstick. 'We can tow her to the headwaters and the damned British will still get her. Might be a year from now, but they will. And she don't do anyone any good up there. We have to try and get her to sea, get her someplace we can fit her out. I vote we try, and if we don't make it, we burn her. If we're just going to tow her upriver, we may as well burn her now and be done with it.'

Heads nodded at that sentiment.

'Quite right, Rumstick,' said Faircloth, 'but that leaves the thorny question of how to get a ship with only one usable sail past the batteries in Philadelphia and the entire British fleet in the river below. Can't say I relish the thought of sailing right through the enemy's lines like that.'

431

Those words were followed by silence, for Faircloth had raised the greatest, and most insurmountable, objection. Between them and the sea lay all the ships of Black Dick Howe's fleet.

And then Freeman gave a little cough, the prelude to the speech of a man who does not wish to speak, and everyone turned to him.

'Well, ah . . .' he began, and then summoning his nerve, said, 'I was thinking, see, McGinty had this notion, back after Brandywine, when we was trapped, sort of like we is now, except without a ship, do ya see? He got us through the lines by . . . ah, hell, McGinty, you tell the damned story.'

And then all eyes were on McGinty, who looked confused at first, then smiled as it dawned on him what Freeman was getting at. 'Well, sure, boy-o, I see what you mean. We marched right through the British lines, acting like we was prisoners already! And it worked like a charm, so it did.'

In broad strokes McGinty related the tale of their escape from behind the British lines, and as he did, it became clear how the story related to their own circumstances, and suggestion was piled on suggestion until something like a plan appeared. It was a wild plan, improbable, unlikely to succeed, but it was a plan, and that was more than they had had five minutes before.

'Oh, damn me, but that's a fine one,' said the Virginia privateer, who had remained with the officers, unbidden and unwelcome. 'And won't Sir James just shit fire when he hears what we done!'

'Sir James?' Biddlecomb asked.

'Captain of *Experiment*, ship that the *Sparrowhawk* is tender to. Sir James Wallace.'

Wallace. James Wallace. Sir James. Captain of the *Experiment*, former captain of the frigate *Rose*. Biddlecomb felt his stomach twist.

Wallace knew him, knew what Biddlecomb had done with the *Icarus*, with the *Glasgow*, his exploits off the coast of England. He had no delusions about how much Wallace wished to see him publicly executed.

If Wallace was downriver, it meant two things. First, it meant that there was at least one captain who would not easily be played for a fool. Suddenly the wild plan, about which Isaac had actually felt a glimmer of optimism, seemed more suicidal than anything.

The second thing that it meant was that he, Isaac Biddlecomb, could not, under any circumstances, allow himself to be taken alive.

CHAPTER 28

November, 1777
Moderate Breezes p.m. anchor'd with the B^{t}B^r in 6
fms abrest Red Hook and moored with the Stream
Anchor, we see under Red bank 2 floating
Batteries and Some Rebel Ships.
                    —JOURNAL OF HMS *EXPERIMENT*
                        CAPT. SIR JAMES WALLACE

First, they needed to take the *Sparrowhawk*, and that
was accomplished with little effort and no bloodshed.

By way of disguise, Biddlecomb borrowed an
official British-navy coat and hat from Lieutenant
Howard. Howard was in too much pain from the
wound McGinty had delivered and was too sullen to
object, beyond pointing out that Biddlecomb would
be hung as a spy if caught in the enemy's uniform.
But since Biddlecomb had no doubts about his being
hung in any event if caught, the argument carried
little weight.

Once the prisoners were secured below in that part
of the *Falmouth*'s hold designed for just that purpose,
Biddlecomb and Rumstick and the handpicked men

took to the boats that Lieutenant Howard had left grappled to the side. They rowed easily downriver, guided by the Virginian privateer, who, having an experienced seaman's sense of direction, took them right to the anchored cutter.

A voice from the cutter called, 'What boat is that?' and the Virginian replied, '*Sparrowhawk*!' and there were no questions raised as they came alongside. Not until a dozen armed Americans were spread out on the deck did the midshipman realize his mistake, and by then it was far and away too late for action.

Isaac had been to dinner parties that had required more thought and planning – and had involved more physical danger – than the taking of the *Sparrowhawk*.

They sailed the cutter back and anchored her near the *Falmouth*. A crew of five volunteers manned the *Expedient* and she was sent off, running past the city with the blessed wind over her quarter and her presence hidden by the dark. And then, after posting lookouts fore and aft, the Falmouths slept.

Exhausted as they were, sleep was not the thing they wanted most. More than anything, Biddlecomb, Rumstick, the officers, the men of the Fifth who had fought to preserve the frigate, and the Charlemagnes who had fought to get to her wanted to bring the ship to safety, wanted to get on with the job of saving her.

But the plan that they had devised required perfect timing, just the right number of daylight hours and no more. Such timing was problematic enough for ships that relied on the vagaries of wind and tide; they would not help themselves by trying to hurry it along. Nor would it help if all hands were ready to drop from fatigue.

And so they slept. And every few hours, those who

were privy to the plan made their way to the deck to see that the wind still held out of the north, because if it veered, then they were sunk, figuratively, and perhaps literally. But all night it held, and all through the next morning, and acute anxiety settled into dull worry, for even though the wind was steady out of the north and seemed as if it would remain that way, every man knew that it could change at any moment, including in the middle of executing their planned escape.

The early hours were taken up with preparations, with scrutinizing charts, and with funerals. Half the prisoners were released under guard to help bury their own in a proper manner, as proper as could be done under the circumstances, and the Americans did the same.

McGinty found Malachi Foote's saw and cut a section from the bulwark and lettered the words to the shipwright's headstone on it. The men clustered around the fresh grave as he put it in place.

'Forgive me, Mother Foote, for the damage I done your fine ship,' he said, nodding toward the make-shift grave marker, 'but now you'll have a piece of her with ye, even after we see her safe away.'

By noon they were ready to go. Biddlecomb stood on the quarterdeck of his new command and looked aloft, but there was not much there to see, so he looked along the deck instead. On the foredeck Rumstick was keeping an eye on the towrope that ran from the bitts, out the hawse pipe, and down to the *Sparrowhawk*'s fife rail.

'All ready, Mr Rumstick?' Biddlecomb called, and Rumstick gave an affirming wave of his hand. 'Cast off, fore and aft!' Biddlecomb called, and head- and stern-fasts, doubled around trees ashore, were cast off and the frigate eased away from the bank.

Over the bow he could hear the squeal of a halyard sheave as Angus McGinty, in temporary command of the *Falmouth*'s first prize, His Majesty's armed cutter *Sparrowhawk*, ordered the mainsail set.

'Foretopmen, away aloft! Ungasket and let fall!' Biddlecomb called next. It seemed a bit silly, giving that order, when there was only the lower foremast in place and only the foresail bent, but he knew of no other way to phrase it.

In any event, it carried the meaning he intended and the shrouds were instantly filled with men racing up the battens that had been lashed across them in lieu of ratlines and lying out along the single yard. The gaskets were cast off and the clean, new sail tumbled down and hung in its buntlines and clew garnets.

Over the bow Isaac could see the *Sparrowhawk*'s mainsail fill with the breeze as the gaff was swayed into place. A second later the British ensign appeared at the peak. It was a huge flag, one intended to be flown from an ensign staff, and it made a grand show there, high in the rigging. That was good. They wanted to be certain that it was seen.

Under his feet, Isaac felt the tiniest of jerks as the strain came on the towrope and the little cutter began to pull the frigate along. He looked over the side, saw the shore just starting to slip past as the ponderous hull gathered way.

'Set the foresail!' he called, and waiting hands let go of buntlines and leechlines, eased clew garnets, and hauled the two sheets aft. The sail snapped in the breeze, filling for the first time, collapsed, and then filled again as the yard was braced around.

Rumstick called aft, 'Towrope's slack!' He was grinning. The *Falmouth* was alive, moving under her own power, pushed toward the sea by the pressure of the wind on her own sail.

Just past the weather leech Isaac could see men lying out on the *Sparrowhawk*'s yards, casting off her square sails, and a moment later they too were set and drawing. The cutter pulled ahead, moving faster than the frigate. The strain came back on the towrope and once more the *Falmouth* was aided in her effort to get downriver.

'Shall I set those flags, sir?' Gerrish asked.

'Yes, Mr Gerrish, please set them now.'

Gerrish held the piles of bunting as Ferguson hauled away on the ensign staff's halyard, peeling the cloth from the lieutenant's arms and spreading it in the wind.

First came the British white ensign, with its bold cross of St George and the Union Jack in the canton, which they had found aboard the *Sparrowhawk*. And below that, the flag of the United States, thirteen red and white stripes, a circle of white stars in the blue canton. A flag that some unknown hand had lovingly sewed for the frigate. Now it flew below the British ensign, the international sign of a vessel that has been taken as a prize.

'Mr Faircloth, you'll see your marines do not wear their regimentals?'

'Aye, sir, though they shall be sorely disappointed. Again.'

Thus tethered together, like a small boy leading a huge, docile cow, the *Sparrowhawk* and the *Falmouth* made their way downriver. They hugged the southern shore of Petty's Island close, since the north

438

wind was on the beam there and the *Falmouth*, high in the water, was sagging off to leeward in a dreadful manner. Only the tugging of the *Sparrowhawk* kept her from being blown down to the Jersey shore.

They struggled like that for an hour, until they cleared the narrow channel around the island and turned due south, with the wind right astern. At that point the *Falmouth* was on the one point of sail that she could maintain with ease, with the breeze running down the length of her deck and filling the big foresail.

The tide was on the last of the ebb, which helped them as well. It also meant that they would be bucking the flood, and their speed slowed considerably, just as they tried to pass through the British fleet. But Isaac wanted to be through the *chevaux-de-frise* at Billingsport just as the sun was going down, and it was too much to hope that the tide would be with them as well.

'Sir?' Gerrish stepped up and saluted. 'Beg pardon, sir, but the *Sparrowhawk* seems to be making for the center of the river. Shall I call to that McGinty fellow to favor the Jersey shore, shy away from the British guns?'

'No, no, never. Why would a lieutenant in the British navy, with so fine a prize to show off, shy away from the city? Were I such a fellow, I would want to flaunt it.'

Gerrish considered that. 'True enough, sir.'

'I don't wish to come it the war-weary veteran, Mr Gerrish, but I can tell you – and this is from my experience as a merchant captain as well – one must avoid trying to do this sort of thing by half measures. Such a *ruse de guerre* as this must be complete, no pretending to be British and then shying away from the British guns.'

'Indeed, sir.'

Despite the pleasure of thus tricking the British batteries along the waterfront, no one aboard the two ships was insensible to the danger they were in, plodding along within easy cannon range of the enemy. The tension along the *Falmouth*'s decks was palpable; men talked in clipped sentences when they talked at all, and they took every chance they had, short of seeming too obvious, to glance over at the city passing down the starboard side.

They were halfway past the former capital when they had their first indication that they had even been noticed. Isaac heard a sound, something, coming over the water and was suddenly afraid an alarm was being passed. He felt his stomach, which had been easing, twist up again, felt his feet tingling. He swept the waterfront with his glass, settled it on the battery just abeam of them.

And then he recognized the sound: cheering. He twisted the tube of his glass and brought the battery into focus. He could see red-coated men standing on the ramparts, waving hats, could hear the muted sound of their 'Huzzah!' floating the half mile over the water. He laughed out loud.

From the foredeck, Rumstick called, 'I do believe they are giving us a cheer!'

'I believe you are right, Mr Rumstick! Be damned rude if we didn't return it. Everyone, up on the gangway, let's give them three hearty ones back!'

Like children on a great lark the men of the *Falmouth* crowded the gangway from the foredeck to the taffrail and on Rumstick's command returned the cheer from the shore with gusto, yelling with the enthusiasm of men who had been to the brink of ruin and saved.

'Huzzah! Huzzah! You stupid, motherless bastards!' Ferguson at the helm waved his hat and shouted with abandon. From over the bow Biddlecomb could hear the Sparrowhawks cheering as well.

And then they were past the city, past Windmill Island, past the point where the British guns could train far enough around to reach them if those manning them suddenly realized that they had been fooled. The first obstacle between the *Falmouth* and the sea was behind them.

The town of Gloucester passed along their larboard side and they turned almost due west, bringing the wind once more on their beams. The *Sparrowhawk* tugged the frigate along, as close as they dared to League Island, once more giving the nearly unmanageable *Falmouth* all the room to leeward that they could give.

Fort Mifflin came into view, two and a half miles away. They could hear the occasional smattering of gunfire on the river beyond, no more than routine exchanges of artillery. And that was a good thing. Biddlecomb reckoned they had concerns enough without having to tow the frigate through a full-scale battle.

It was three o'clock in the afternoon, with another three hours left before full dark, when Red Bank Island came broad on the larboard bow, revealing the American fleet anchored behind. McGinty turned the *Sparrowhawk* more southerly and Ferguson put the wheel a few spokes over to keep the *Falmouth* in her wake.

Rumstick made his way to the quarterdeck. 'Now we'll see if them fellows on *Expedient* did like they was told,' he said.

Biddlecomb put his glass to his eye, swept the line of small ships anchored downriver from them. He settled on a xebec, but after scrutinizing it realized it was *Repulse*. He shifted the glass and found *Expedient* three ships away. He could see her moving through the water as the crew won her anchor. The brig next to her was doing the same.

'Things seem to be in order.' He paused, watched for a moment, then lowered his glass. He was starting to have misgivings. Perhaps he should have let Hazelwood in on his plan.

But if he had, there was every chance that the commodore would have refused to allow it, arguing the unlikelihood of its succeeding and the need for all ships to aid in the defense of the river. And then Biddlecomb would have had to argue that a commodore of a state navy had no authority over a captain in the Continental navy. Then Hazelwood would have informed him that his being in charge of the Delaware River defenses gave him authority over every American vessel on the river, and it would have gone on from there.

No, Biddlecomb thought, better to apologize later than to ask permission, as was so often the case.

Ferguson continued to ease the big wheel to larboard, following the *Sparrowhawk* around as the cutter fell farther and farther off the wind, making her head for the shallow water around the southern end of the *chevaux-de-frise* extending out from Fort Island. If the *Falmouth* had had her ballast in, if she had been down to even a few feet of her waterline, she would not have been able to skirt around the obstacles. As it was, it would be close.

'*Expedient*'s under way, sir,' Gerrish reported, 'and the brig and a couple of the gunboats as well.'

'Good, good,' said Biddlecomb. He scanned the fleet up by Fort Mifflin. *Andrew Doria* was there, that familiar brig, and Biddlecomb imagined that Hazelwood was aboard her. But she was too far away to present much of a problem.

And then, from off the starboard beam, the rumble of gunfire, first one big gun and then several going off at once. The *Expedient* had fired, as had the others, even as they were setting more sail. The blanket of smoke was rolling off to the south and the little ships were pushing it aside as they gathered way.

The *Falmouth* came around the western end of Red Bank Island and settled on a heading for the passage through the chevaux-de-frise as the ships fired again, a rumble like thunder from their big bow guns.

'Strange, ain't it, sir?' said Faircloth. 'You get so used to the sound of the shot flying by, or hitting the ship. It doesn't seem right.'

'No, it does not. But I won't complain.' Nor had Biddlecomb any reason to. The rebel ships were doing a fine job, firing away like things possessed, trying to prevent a British cutter and her prize from running through the gauntlet of their fleet to the protection of the British ships beyond.

It was nice, for once, to be fired upon with unshotted guns.

Captain Wallace looked up from the chart spread across his table, frowned, cocked his ear to the open window aft. With the wind out of the north and the tide just past slack water, the *Experiment*'s stern windows were facing downriver, giving him a view of Billingsport and a few of the ships anchored down by Chester, but allowing him no view of what the enemy was doing.

For most of the day it had been nothing much: a few exchanges between the frigates and the rebel fleet, some long shots from the fort, the usual waste of time and powder. A swarm of boats had been sent to salvage what they could from the charred and still smoldering remains of *Augusta* and *Merlin*, and the rebels had been firing on them, hampering their efforts to deprive the Yankees of the ships' great guns.

But now his ear caught something else, a concentrated fire, volleys of big guns going off. It was not the coordinated sound of a British broadside, but the haphazard sound of the rebel fleet, with their mismatched guns, firing in earnest on something.

He looked down at the chart, where he had been sketching his plans for the reduction of the rebel fortifications, and continued to listen as the distant fire continued and even built in intensity. He considered going on deck, wondered if this development warranted time away from his work.

Then he heard hurried footsteps outside, the muted exchange with the marine sentry, the knock on the door.

'Come.'

A midshipman stepped through the door held open by the marine. He was panting, his face flushed with excitement. Wallace frowned. It was not at all the kind of display he wished to see from his officers.

The boy had a long way to go before he would don a lieutenant's uniform on that ship.

'Mr Jones's compliments, sir,' the young man panted, 'but *Sparrowhawk*'s in sight, coming through the rebel fleet, and she looks to have a prize, a big bastard, sir, and they're all firing on her!'

Wallace fixed the midshipman in his stare, remained silent, held the boy like that until he was certain that his displeasure with such enthusiasm had registered. Then he said in an even tone, 'My compliments to Mr Jones, and please inform him I shall be on deck directly.'

'Aye, sir,' the now humbled midshipman said, then saluted and disappeared. Wallace rolled his chart up again and replaced it in its pigeonhole, put his pencils and parallel rule back in the desk drawer, scooped the pencil shavings up in his hand and dropped them out the stern window, then took up his hat and telescope and made his way on deck.

It was a fine afternoon, with a steady eight knots of wind out of the north northwest and blue sky dotted with clouds. Sir James climbed up the ladder to the quarterdeck, and the officers moved en masse to the leeward side, leaving the great stretch of deck on the weather side free for him.

He was anxious to see what Jones had reported, but it was his custom to first inspect the ship and her surroundings whenever he came on deck. He had done it so long he was no longer even aware of it, though his officers most certainly were. He looked first at the sky, then ran his eyes down the *Experiment*'s rig, then along her deck, and at last outboard, noting that the tide had just begun to flood.

At last he looked upriver and called, 'Mr Jones, pray step over here. What of *Sparrowhawk*?'

Jones, the *Experiment*'s second officer, acting first officer in Howard's absence, stepped with acceptable alacrity across the deck. 'There, sir, fine on the starboard bow. She came around Red Bank Island just a few moments ago and looks to be making for the open water below the *chevaux-de-frise*. The rebels have just now seen her and opened fire.'

A dozen questions sprang fully formed in Wallace's mind. What ship might that be that the *Sparrowhawk* was towing? How did Howard think he could get a deep-draft vessel over those shallow mud banks? Surely the rebels would blow them out of the water before they even reached the passage.

He climbed into the mizzen shrouds halfway to the mizzen top and put his telescope to his eye. He found the *Sparrowhawk* in the lens and brought the image into focus.

It appeared to be a frigate, new-built rebel frigate, pierced for twenty-eight guns or so. Lower foremast stepped, foreyard crossed, foresail set. An odd bit of rigging but still a fine-looking ship. She was very high in the water, which made her look even more un-wieldy, but that at least answered the question of how Howard thought he would get her over the shallows.

As to the rebels, they were getting under way as fast as ever they could, and firing as fast as they could with their assorted guns mounted on their ill-begotten vessels. They were making a great show of it, but they seemed to be doing little damage, and the *Sparrowhawk* was returning fire on the few vessels within the arc of her guns.

He turned his glass toward Fort Mifflin. The guns there were silent. It was a long shot for them, and the chance of hitting one of their own vessels was as good as their chance of hitting the cutter.

Sir James turned his glass to Fort Mercer and saw that it was silent as well. He had heard from a number of deserters about the internecine fighting among the rebels, the army in the forts and the navy on the river refusing to cooperate in any endeavor.

Perhaps that was a part of what he was seeing now. Such an attitude would certainly help Lord Howe and the fleet in their task of clearing the river of impediments to British navigation.

Wallace lowered the glass, blinked his weary eyes a few times, then took in the whole before him. A little smile crept over his lips.

Well done, Howard, well done, he thought.

Biddlecomb had to be a prisoner aboard the *Sparrowhawk*. Howard knew better than to return so soon without him. And he had a prize as well, a magnificent prize, as good a ship as one could hope to capture from these tag-and-rag Yankees. He climbed back down to the quarterdeck.

Lieutenant Jones was still where he had left him, staring upriver through his glass. 'Sir,' he said, even before Wallace's feet had touched the deck, 'those Yankees are firing with more effect now, it appears. Oh, there goes a section of the prize's taffrail! And I see a few holes in *Sparrowhawk*'s mainsail, I believe.'

Wallace looked upriver through his glass once again. Some of the rebel ships from up by Fort Mifflin had dropped down, and they seemed to be firing with great accuracy. He could see actual damage being inflicted on the cutter and the frigate. 'Here goes *Roebuck*,' he observed.

Capt. Sir Andrew Snape Hamond of the forty-four-gun *Roebuck*, anchored much closer than *Experiment* to the upper *chevaux-de-frise*, was taking up on the spring line he had rigged to his cable, swinging the ship's broadside around until it would bear on the rebel fleet. A moment later she opened up, sent a hail of iron into the smaller ships, making it too hot for them to close on *Sparrowhawk* and her prize.

The cutter, in turn, was almost up to the sunken obstacles, almost to the point where they would pass over the mudflats and be safely back in the protective arms of the British fleet. And Lieutenant Howard would get his epaulet. Sir James would see to that.

A twenty-four-pound ball slammed into the *Falmouth*'s side, just below the quarterdeck rail, and sent a shower of small splinters over the deck, stinging the men there like a swarm of bees.

'Damn,' Biddlecomb said. 'We're on your bloody side!'

'I don't think they're in on the joke, sir,' said Gerrish, plucking a three-inch splinter from his hand. A trail of blood ran out from the point where the splinter had pierced his skin.

'I think not.' There was no time to inform the whole fleet of what they were intending, nor had Biddlecomb wanted to, because he wanted to keep it from Hazelwood. He had hoped to pass through the American fleet before those not privy to the situation could close with them, but it was not working out that way. The ships anchored up around Fort Mifflin had dropped down and opened fire with surprising dispatch. They were still a good ways off, but their big guns were finding their target.

It would not last for long, however. The *Sparrow-hawk* was almost up with the southern end of the *chevaux-de-frise*, and once the two ships rounded that point, the Americans would not dare to follow. The submerged obstacles were the invisible border between the real estate owned by the British, and that still in American hands.

A ball screamed over the deck and would have severely wounded the mainmast, had there been a mainmast there to wound.

At least they are making the show more real, Isaac thought, looking for something good in their situation. He hoped very much that none of his men would be killed by American fire. That was a guilt he did not care to live with.

And then more fire, not from the American fleet but from farther downriver, a great wall of sound, the broadside of a big ship. Biddlecomb looked up in surprise. One of the forty-fours, *Roebuck*, if he was not mistaken, had taken up on a spring line and brought her broadside to bear, firing into the American gunboats. And one by one the Americans were hauling their wind, or spinning around under sweeps and heading back toward Fort Mifflin, out of range of the British guns.

Biddlecomb met Rumstick's eyes and the two men smiled and shook their heads. The irony of the British navy thus delivering them from harm was so obvious that it was not worth commenting on.

Ten minutes later they were past the *chevaux-de-frise*, over the mud bank, and back into deep water. A little catch underfoot as the *Falmouth*'s keel touched bottom, no more than that, and before Isaac even had time to worry they were over with never a pause in their progress.

'Look'ee here,' said Rumstick, still grinning. He nodded toward the wrecks broad on either bow, the *Merlin* to larboard and the *Augusta* to starboard and only a few hundred yards apart. They were little more than charred skeletons rising out of the water. A few wisps of smoke still rose from their remains.

'They make fine-looking channel markers, don't they?' Rumstick said. 'Wish these bastards'd put more of 'em out the same way.'

'Indeed,' said Biddlecomb, but he had too much on his mind to enjoy sight-seeing.

They were past Philadelphia and through the American fleet, with only the one minor foul-up of being fired upon by their own side. He looked up at the sun. Two hours of daylight left, perhaps a little less. Two hours to get three miles downriver and through the buoyed channel cut through the *chevaux-de-frise* at Billingsport. With only eight knots of wind and the tide starting to flood and the slow progress of the frigate under tow, that would be about right.

Then they would be down with the British fleet anchored off Chester just as the sun was setting. The fleet, if they believed the *Sparrowhawk* and *Falmouth* were captor and prize, would expect them to anchor nearby, but of course they would not. Under cover of dark they would continue along until they reached the Atlantic and the nearest safe harbor.

It might work. So far everything had gone as well as could be expected. It made Isaac profoundly nervous.

They skirted along the edge of the lighter-colored water, which marked where the mud bank reached out from the shore, ready to grab the keel of any unwary vessel. McGinty, for all his annoying false bonhomie, was proving to be a fine seaman, and he kept the *Sparrowhawk* right where she should be and the *Falmouth* right behind her.

They swapped cheers with the *Roebuck*, just as they had done with the British batteries in the city, and then Biddlecomb turned his glass toward the British ships clustered up around Billings Island. He could see the frigates *Liverpool* and *Pearl* and the big *Somerset*, which he recognized from her days in Boston Harbor.

And there was another, a fourth-rate, her yards perfectly square, her sails neatly stowed, everything about her perfect, and he knew that she was the *Experiment*, and on her deck, perhaps looking back at him, was James Wallace.

He let his glass fall to his side, stared at the big ship a little over a mile away. James Wallace. That name was so associated with all of the horror and the tragedy that had first brought him into the fight against England, was so connected to the terror and the uncertainty of those early days, that just thinking it brought the old fear back.

He felt sick, felt his palms sweat, had the absurd desire to run below, to duck behind the bulwark so he could not be seen. He told himself he was being irrational; Wallace was only a naval captain, albeit a good one, but Biddlecomb had faced good captains before and lived.

Such logic did nothing to assuage his fear. Rational or not, he knew that Wallace was not just another captain to him and never would be.

The *Sparrowhawk* and then the *Falmouth* turned more southerly, away from the anchored ships at Billings Island, making for the marked channel leading through the *chevaux-de-frise*. Another hour at the most and they would be through and Wallace would be behind them. Biddlecomb felt he could face anything once he knew those obstacles stood between him and Sir James.

'Don't seem to be any concern among them,' Rumstick observed, looking at the ships through a glass of his own. 'No one making sail or slipping a cable. Nothing at all, I can see.'

'Good. Let us hope that it remains that way for the next hour or so, and then it will be dark and we will be on our way.'

And then the foresail snapped, the beautiful, gentle curve of the canvas collapsed as the air faltered. It filled again, then collapsed once more.

'Oh, no,' Isaac said. 'Oh, no, no, no . . .'

And then the wind was gone, and the current began to carry them back upriver again.

CHAPTER 29

It must not be imagined that any force will be sufficient entirely to execute the purpose of blocking up all the rebels' ports and putting a total stop to their privateering; for along so extensive a coast, full of harbors and inlets, many ships will in spite of our efforts get in and out by taking advantage of their knowledge of the coast, of dark and long nights, and events of wind and weather favorable to their purpose.

—EARL OF SANDWICH
FIRST LORD OF THE ADMIRALTY
TO LORD NORTH

Sir James watched with pride as his first officer brought the cutter and the captured frigate through the hail of rebel gunfire, through the tricky shallows at the southern end of the *chevaux-de-frise*, and up to the clear, deep water that stretched between the tender and the *Experiment*. Howard had always had the stuff of a fine officer. This action would garner him that most sought-after of steps – his own command.

But the pride began to fade, and confusion followed behind, as the *Sparrowhawk* did not close with *Experiment* at all, but rather continued on a more southerly course, as if making for the channel through the *chevaux-de-frise* at Billingsport.

And then the confusion gave way to anger as it dawned on Sir James what Howard was up to. He was not going to bring the prize to Wallace at all, he was going to tow it down to Chester, where he could present it to the admiral in person.

That stupid, stupid grasping little villain, Wallace thought as he watched the cutter and the prize draw abeam of the *Experiment*, a little over half a mile away. Stupid. He would not get an epaulet now. No command for him. He, Sir James, would see to that.

Despite the uncharacteristic play of emotions inside, Wallace remained stoic, unmoved in any external way, and as was often the case, one of his inferior officers verbalized what Wallace was thinking. This time it was Jones, still standing beside him by tacit consent, and staring at the *Sparrowhawk* through his glass.

'Now what the devil is he about?' Jones said out loud, and Wallace snapped, 'I have no notion,' biting off the words in such a way that Jones took his eye from the glass and looked at him, which made Wallace angrier still.

And then Sir Jamees felt a fault in the wind, a dying breath that played over his face, a sensation that could not go unnoticed after the better part of a lifetime at sea. He looked to windward, saw the *Roebuck*'s ensign hanging limp.

He looked due south. The sails on the *Sparrowhawk* and the prize were slatting and then they were still. The towrope between them sagged and disappeared in the river. The cutter and her prize sloughed around as the flood tide began to carry them back upriver.

It was as if God Himself had ordained that Howard desist in his traitorous, self-serving actions.

A flash of white water appeared under the *Sparrowhawk*'s bow – the cutter's anchor, set to prevent their being carried back on to the mudflats. A moment later the current pushed the tide-rode vessels back into line. The towrope lifted out of the river and the tender's best bower held them both in place.

'Mr Jones, get the gig alongside. I want you to go over to the tender and ask Mr Howard, for me, just what it is he thinks he is doing.'

'Aye, aye, sir,' said Jones, hurrying off.

Howard would be standing there on the cutter's deck, watching the gig approach, knowing he would have to explain himself even before he was basking in the warmth of Lord Howe's praise. Sir James considered how foolish the man would feel, how profoundly he would realize his mistake. Sir James felt the smile creeping back over his lips, but he kept his mouth set firm.

'Aw, bloody, bloody hell,' McGinty muttered.

There was some satisfaction in knowing he had been prepared for this situation, had cockbilled the anchor and ranged the cable along for running. It was a relief that the hook had a good purchase in the soft bottom and would hold both ships against the tide, at least until the height of the flood. But overall it was infuriating. They were almost there.

'Damn the wind! Damn, damn bloody wind,' he muttered again. He had seen it so many times, that conscious malevolence that the wind seemed to display.

'So now what?' Freeman asked the question, though everyone aboard was listening for the answer.

'Ah, it's nothing, boy-o. Have no fear of this. It's a wee quirk in the wind that you often get near sunset hereabouts. The breeze'll fill in again soon, never you doubt it.'

McGinty sounded convincing enough, and he saw the relief in the men's faces, though in truth he had no idea if such a thing would happen. He had never sailed on the Delaware River before. And while such a lull in the breeze at sunset was not unknown in other places, he had no idea if it was generally the case here. For all he knew the wind would not come back for days.

'Sergeant!' The lookout up at the *Sparrowhawk*'s crosstrees called down, never taking the glass from his eye. 'Looks like a boat's coming, from over where them other ships are.'

'Very well, lad, well spotted,' McGinty called, and then thought, Oh, grand. And this will be the bloody admiral, come to see what we're about.

At least they would come to the *Sparrowhawk* to inquire, McGinty realized, and that was good. A situation like this needed someone with a quick wit and a nimble tongue. He was not at all convinced that the Yanke Biddlecomb could talk his way out of a tricky situation.

Nor would talk alone, even his clever talk, buy them much time. Something else was called for as well.

'Keep an eye on this boat,' he said to Freeman. 'I've got to fetch something for them.'

By the time McGinty came back on deck, struggling with a heavy seabag over his shoulder, the boat was nearly alongside. It was a lightly built gig, of the type used to ferry captains around. He could see a lieutenant in the stern sheets, a boat crew single-banked at the oars. The men were not armed, and for that he was thankful.

The officer gave an order and the oars came up and the gig eased alongside.

McGinty leaned over the rail and looked down at the lieutenant, who was no more than four feet below him, the cutter's sides being as low as they were. 'Lieutenant, how are you, sir?' McGinty asked with a smile.

'Who the devil are you?'

'McGinty, sir. Bosun's mate.'

'McGinty?' The lieutenant scowled and McGinty realized that this officer was most likely from the *Experiment* and would expect to know all the tender's crew. 'Where is Lieutenant Howard?'

'The lieutenant's down below, sir.'

'Well, please inform him that Lieutenant Jones is here. I am sent by Sir James to inquire as to his intentions.'

'Of course, sir.' McGinty turned and addressed an empty space of deck. 'You there, go and fetch the lieutenant.'

'Might I come aboard?' Jones asked in a tone that implied this was not really a request.

'Of course, sir. But here, Lieutenant Howard sent up this parcel of dispatches and orders and such he took off the frigate, and might I drop it down to you?'

'Yes, yes,' said Jones peevishly.

457

'Stand clear.' McGinty grabbed on to the seabag with both hands, took a breath, and heaved it up. He felt his muscles tearing with the effort and realized he had put far more round shot in the bag than was entirely necessary. With a grunt he hefted it over the side and let it fall.

Lieutenant Jones leapt aside as the bag smashed into the bottom of the gig and kept on going, tearing out a big section of the garboard and a part of the keel before plunging to the bottom of the river. There was half a foot of water in the gig before Jones could stammer, 'What the bloody hell . . . !'

'Oh, Lord, I am sorry, sir, them orders wrapped in lead, I never thought it would go through the bottom,' McGinty said. 'Quickly, quickly, come aboard! Here, clap on to this line! That's right, right up the steps! Bloody boat must have been rotten right through!'

The startled boat crew came aboard, soaked from the waist down. They and the sputtering, furious Jones were led below, where Corporal Freeman and a dozen armed men were waiting to greet them.

Ten minutes after arriving at the *Sparrowhawk*'s side they were prisoners of the rebels. They sat quietly on the lower deck and stared at their captors, too confused by this quick turn of events even to mutter a protest.

The lookout at the *Experiment*'s foremast head sang out, 'On deck!' and Wallace himself replied, 'Deck, aye!' He was eager to hear what was happening. In half an hour it would be too dark for a man aloft to see anything smaller than a man-of-war. In an hour it would be entirely black.

'It looks . . . it looks like the gig has sunk, sir! Boat crew's on the cutter's deck!'

Wallace felt his eyes narrow and the corners of his mouth turn down. The gig sunk? What in the devil was going on? The whole thing was growing more and more outlandish.

Howard's career was over, that much was certain. He was the second of Wallace's lieutenants whose career had been ruined by Biddlecomb.

His third officer aboard the *Rose*, Lieutenant Norton, a promising young man, had disgraced himself by letting Biddlecomb take the ship's longboat from him and escape. But Norton had had the good fortune to die while trying to capture the rebel again. Wallace did not think Howard would be so lucky.

And then Sir James had an awful thought, one that made him take a step back, made his mouth hang open despite himself. What if Biddlecomb had not been taken? What if it was Howard who was a prisoner and Biddlecomb was now in command of the *Sparrowhawk*?

No, it was not possible. Such a thing could not happen. How would Biddlecomb defeat Howard and a party of armed, handpicked men?

And yet . . . and yet . . . Despite his loathing the man, Wallace had no delusions about Biddlecomb's skill, and his luck. He had slipped away before, slipped through the best nets that he, James Wallace, and the British navy had spread.

Sir James shut his mouth, tight, and composed himself, despite the sick dread spreading through him like a disease. He looked to windward. There was not a breath of air, but he knew that this lull often

459

occurred just before sunset, that the breeze would fill in again soon.

He stepped up to the break of the quarterdeck. 'Loosen off all plain sail. Stand by to slip the anchor cable.'

No one on board could have anticipated that order, but to the Experiments' credit they leapt to it as if they had been standing by for an hour, waiting for those exact words. In less than five minutes the sails were hanging in their gear and the cable was ready to run.

And now, Wallace thought, we need only a breeze.

So damned close, Biddlecomb thought. That was what made it so utterly maddening. If he pulled his eyes from the *Experiment* and looked past the *Falmouth*'s bow, he could see the line of buoys leading through the *chevaux-de-frise* to the open water beyond. Nothing but the wide Delaware Bay between the two ships and the Atlantic Ocean.

But it was not to be, because of a fluke in the wind. He had retained some measure of hope when McGinty had shown the good sense to anchor. He had even felt one last remaining spark of possible salvation when the Irishman had dropped something right through the bottom of the *Experiment*'s gig and taken the boat crew prisoner.

But in the fading light he had seen the *Experiment*'s sails loosened off, and that meant that Wallace had smoked them, that he was coming himself to investigate, and bringing his fifty-gun ship with him. There would be no escaping that.

Even if they did get a breeze, even if they made it through the buoyed channel, the *Experiment* would follow right behind. They could never outsail her, and even if they avoided her all night, then she would be there at first light.

Isaac had not forgotten Lieutenant Howard's words: 'And this, I take it, is the rebel Biddlecomb?' If Howard knew of his presence on the river, then Wallace did as well, and Wallace would not care to see Biddlecomb escape again.

He was just gathering the courage to order the *Falmouth* put to the torch when he heard the foresail snap, felt the returning breeze on his face. He waited for it to die away, but it did not. Rather, it came in a more spirited gust and the foresail began to fill and the *Falmouth* and the *Sparrowhawk* began once again to stem the tide.

In the fading light he could see smiles along the deck, men clapping each other on the back. It had apparently not occurred to them, as it had to him, that it was too late, that they had been discovered and that capture was now imminent.

The *Experiment*'s sails were tumbling off the yards as unseen men on her deck sheeted home and ran away with halyards. Her headsails were backed and her bow began to swing off the wind. The topsails were mastheaded, halyards belayed, yards braced around. The fifty-gun ship was under way, and she was heading toward them. Her jibboom, thrust out ahead of her, looked to Isaac like an accusatory finger, pointed right at him.

But from over the bow came the unmistakable creak of rigging taking up the strain of wind in sails, and on the dark evening water Biddlecomb could just see the first of the channel markers slipping by as the two ships gathered way once more.

Well, Biddlecomb thought, if these poor bastards haven't figured out that we can't escape now, then I most certainly will not tell them.

And then the next of the channel markers caught his eye, and in his stomach he felt that familiar pressure: not fear, but an idea being born. He felt the soles of his feet tingle. It was a welcome sensation, and he smiled as he called Rumstick aft.

It would be dark by the time *Experiment* reached the channel through the *chevaux-de-frise*, but that did not matter to Wallace. They were on a river, and the beauty of rivers was that they left an enemy with little room to run. By dawn at the latest, Biddlecomb would be his prisoner.

He knew that Biddlecomb was at the bottom of all this, knew as certainly as he could without actually seeing the man, which, oddly enough, he had never done.

There was no other explanation for why the *Sparrowhawk* and the prize were once more running away downriver. Lieutenant Howard might be foolish enough to continue on toward the flagship, but Jones would not join him. Jones was too invested in seeing Howard disgraced, and thus becoming the *Experiment*'s first lieutenant himself, to disobey any of his captain's orders.

The pilot on the leeward side of the *Experiment*'s quarterdeck was prancing around as if he might explode, fiddling nervously with his telescope. Wallace ignored him until he could stand it no more, then said, 'Pilot, is there something on your mind?'

'Aye, Sir James, aye,' the pilot said, nearly running across the deck. 'Beg pardon, sir, but this is a tricky business, a tricky business, indeed, running around on the river thus, and the sun all but gone.'

'I should imagine. It is fortunate that we have a pilot on board.'

The irony was lost on the pilot, who continued as if Wallace had not spoken. 'With these submerged obstacles, sir, the bars have all shifted around. Pray recall what became of *Augusta*, sir.'

'*Augusta* was not sailing through a buoyed channel, sir, and we are. Beyond that it is deep water all the way to the sea, nearly.'

The pilot collapsed his telescope and then pulled it open again in a nervous fidget. 'Aye, sir, but we've lost sight of the buoys already, sir.'

Wallace looked forward, saw that the pilot was right. Even in those few moments that they had been talking the darkness had closed in so that the buoys and the channel were lost to sight, and the dark outline of the rebel frigate was just visible as it passed through the passage cut through the *chevaux-de-frise*.

'Never fear about that, pilot.' Wallace turned to the midshipman behind him. 'Get a boat crew in the . . .' What boats were there left? Boats and lieutenants, he seemed to lose quite a few of both to Biddlecomb. But that would end.

'In the yawl boat. Take a lantern and show it astern and row along the northern line of buoys. Keep the ship in sight. We will follow behind. Will that serve, pilot?'

'Yes, sir,' said the pilot, who did not seem pleased at all but at least understood that he had argued with Wallace as much as Wallace was willing to tolerate. 'And leadsmen in the chains, perhaps, sir?'

463

'Yes, very well.'

They were forced to heave to to get the yawl boat in the water and away, and by the time they braced the foreyards around again, it was full night, with a blaze of stars overhead, brilliant in the moonless sky. The *Experiment* plowed slowly downriver, the helmsman following the instructions of the quartermaster, who was watching the bobbing lantern ahead. From forward came the cry of the leadsmen, a sound they had become quite accustomed to, having been so long on the river.

'Six fathoms! Six fathom, this line!'

'Beat to quarters. Clear for action.'

Wallace said the words softly, and they were relayed forward, more and more voices picking them up, bosun's calls piping down the hatches, the noise building with the sound of stamping feet, bulkheads coming down, guns hauled back along the deck. In less than a minute the silent ship was filled with noise and a riot of coordinated activity. Close to three hundred men were aboard *Experiment*, and every one of them was set into motion by the half dozen words that Wallace had uttered.

Eight minutes after he spoke the words, the first of the big guns was hauled up to the gunports. Wallace watched with satisfaction the men at the quarterdeck twelve-pounder heaving at the train tackles, felt the deck shiver below his feet as the big guns on the gundeck below were run out.

The first of the channel markers slipped down the starboard side just as the rumbling subsided. Sir James could not imagine that he would have the chance to use the guns; even Biddlecomb could not be foolish enough to go up against a fifty-gun ship

464

with a cutter. But they were going into action, and he would be derelict to do so without preparing for any eventuality.

What was more, he enjoyed the awesome potential strength of the ship ready to fight – like the sensation of holding a loaded and cocked pistol, only many, many times greater.

Sir James had never known fury like that he had known that night. The closest had been the last time Biddlecomb had slipped through his fingers. But now they were under way, now they were cleared for action and closing fast with the *Sparrowhawk* and the frigate – and Biddlecomb, he was certain – and the fury settled into the comfortable sensation of plunging into action, with a reasonable certainty of success.

He looked over the quarterdeck rail as the next buoy slipped by. Foolish pilot, they are like old women, the lot of them, he thought.

The *Sparrowhawk* and the prize were lost in the darkness, but he knew that they could not be above a mile downriver, and they were moving at half his speed. He reckoned on catching up with them within the hour, an hour and a half at the most.

'Two spokes to larboard,' the quartermaster said with just a hint of urgency in his voice. 'Two spokes, steady there . . .'

Wallace looked up from the buoy and looked around the horizon at the dozen or so lights that were visible. He could see a few fires burning at Billingsport Fort, the only indication of the men still stationed there. They were almost directly ahead of the *Experiment*.

He frowned, had an uneasy feeling that something

was not right. He looked over the taffrail. The anchor lights of the other ships in the squadron were right astern. He looked upriver, felt his dread growing.

'Pilot,' he said, and then from forward the panicked call of the leadsman: 'Two fathom! Two—'

And then the *Experiment* lurched to a stop, her bow running silently into the mud, sending a few unwary souls stumbling and falling to the deck.

Wallace regained his balance and glared around the quarterdeck. Every man was frozen in place. None dared move or speak. No one met his eye.

He felt the rage building up inside him like a pot left to boil. His hands were trembling, his teeth gnashed together, his vaunted self-control was slipping away. He snatched the telescope from the pilot's hands, raised it over his own head, and smashed it down on the deck. 'God damn it! God damn all your bloody eyes to hell!' he screamed.

Never before in his life had Sir James Wallace so completely lost control.

Isaac Biddlecomb could feel the mud, thick on his hands. He wiped his hands on his coat, but his coat was soaked through and covered with mud as well and was useless as a towel.

The small anchors holding the buoys that marked the channel had sunk deep in the soft mud of the river bottom. It had been a struggle to dislodge them, a messy task hauling them aboard and re-setting them, making the path lead not through the *chevaux-de-frise* but right up to the shallow banks along the Jersey shore.

He could see nothing of the *Experiment* as he worked, but he could not miss the sound of her clearing for action. The stamp of hundreds of men, the rumble of big guns running out, carried easily over the water and spurred him and the twenty others in the longboat to work that much faster.

Even when they managed to finish before the *Experiment* overhauled them, he was not certain it would work. Any number of things could go wrong, in any number of ways Wallace might discover what Biddlecomb had done. They might have to burn the *Falmouth* still and sail away in *Sparrowhawk* until she too was run down, at which point they would run her ashore and try to escape overland.

'That's the last of them, sir,' said Woodberry in the bow of the boat.

'Very well. Ship oars. Giveway, larboard. Give way, all. Put your backs into it, men, we must catch the ship up now.'

The men bent into the oars, pulling hard, and the longboat raced through the water, running down-river after the *Falmouth*, which had continued on without them.

Biddlecomb held the tiller steady as he swiveled around and looked back upriver. He could see a light, low on the water, a lantern in a boat perhaps.

'Hold a minute,' he said, and the oars came out of the water and paused and the way came off the boat.

Behind the faint light Isaac was certain he could see the loom of the man-of-war, her high canvas blotting out the stars as she passed. It was only the dimmest of outlines, but he had seen enough ships in the night to know what they looked like.

It was silent, save for the drip of water from the blades of the oars. There was no way to tell what was happening upriver.

And then from out of the dark, and not so far away, the sound of something hitting a deck, glass shattering, the sound of a man's voice, shouting, barely in control. And that was followed a second later by bosun's pipes, the stamp of feet, the squeal of blocks swaying boats over the side.

Isaac turned back to his men. He was grinning and he could see that they were too. 'I do believe that they have gone aground,' he said, and from forward Woodberry replied, 'I reckon you're right, sir. And the tide just ebbing now, and the wind foul for them. Reckon they'll be on the mud for a while.'

Someone in the middle of the longboat began to raise a cheer but Isaac cut him off. 'No, no! They still have boats, you know. They can still come after us in boats. Let us get back to the *Falmouth*, quickly now.'

The men bent to the oars again, and soon the longboat was skipping along. Ten minutes later the *Falmouth* rose up over them, like a ghost ship in the dark, and ten minutes after that they were all back aboard, with the longboat towing astern.

Fine on the starboard bow and six miles distant the lights of the fleet anchored off Chester made a little constellation on the river. But the *Sparrowhawk* and the *Falmouth* would be invisible to them, and Isaac was not concerned in the least about any threat from that quarter.

His only consideration was for what lay beyond their bow, and that, he knew, was only sheltering darkness and deep and open water.

It took them three blessedly uneventful days to sail out of the Delaware Bay and up the New Jersey coast to Great Egg Harbor.

The morning after their run through the British fleet had found them alone on the lower reaches of the Bay with never a sail in sight, and not one was seen from Cape May to Great Egg Harbor Inlet.

At noon on the third day Isaac Biddlecomb stood on the deck of his new command and watched the familiar headlands of Absecon Beach and Peck Beach pass down either side and Great Egg Harbor open up before him. He felt the motion of the ship change as she moved from ocean swells to protected water, felt himself relax for the first time in quite some time.

He wanted to sleep, he intended to sleep, he and all his men, for several days. Then, when they were rested, they would consider where to find spars and rigging, food and ballast and guns and powder for their frigate.

He took his speaking trumpet and walked forward along the gangway and then to the foredeck. He leaned over the rail at the break of the beakhead bulkhead and called down to the *Sparrowhawk* through the trumpet.

'The cutter, hoay!'

McGinty waved, called back, 'Holloa!'

Biddlecomb's respect for McGinty had grown considerably over the past few days. Biddlecomb had not liked him, not trusted him, at first, had not been comfortable giving him command of the *Sparrowhawk*. He thought McGinty might make a hash of it or even cut and run at the first sign of trouble. But none of the former Charlemagnes had wanted to leave the *Falmouth* after taking possession of her, and after all they had been through Isaac did not have the

469

heart to order it, so he had given the Irishman the job.

As it happened, McGinty had performed marvelously, far better than Biddlecomb would have expected. It was no mean task towing a big, unballasted vessel, particularly in a river, but the man's seamanship had been up to the task. Biddlecomb hoped to convince the man to stay with the *Falmouth*, perhaps even get him a commission, or at least appoint him master's mate.

'Just up the harbor are a set of warping posts!' Biddlecomb called down. 'I reckon you can lay us against them and we'll make fast, then warp into the dock!'

'Aye, Captain!'

It took the better part of an hour to get across the harbor and close with the waterfront from which they had sailed with the *Lady Biddlecomb* a month before. McGinty brought the *Sparrowhawk* in line with the warping posts, pulling the *Falmouth* up with those heavy pilings sunk in the harbor bottom.

With faultless timing he cast off the towrope, and for the first time in her life the *Falmouth* sailed unencumbered, making a good knot and a half and covering all of two hundred feet before her foresail was clewed up and the warps passed over the posts and checked and the ship came to a stop.

The *Sparrowhawk* made a wide arc around the harbor, tacking and tacking again, and then came up under the *Falmouth*'s counter. McGinty turned the bow into the wind and let the square topsail come aback, neatly heaving the little man-of-war to in the frigate's lee.

'Well done, Sergeant!' Biddlecomb called down.

'Thank you, sir! And well done yerself!'

Biddlecomb smiled, waved his thanks. 'You can take the cutter right up to the dock you see yonder, wind's fair for it!'

'Aye, sir!' McGinty shouted, then paused and said, 'Now, sir, the lads and I had a mind to do some privateering!'

Of course, Isaac thought. They all want to ship on privateers. Scourge of the navy. He would be sorry to lose McGinty's expertise, but there was nothing for it.

'I understand! Let's talk on this later, but first we must . . .'

Why was McGinty telling him this now?

'Oh, now hold just a moment!' Biddlecomb shouted, but McGinty just smiled and waved. He called an order forward and the topsail was braced around and the cutter gathered way again.

'Godspeed to you, Captain!' McGinty shouted from the taffrail as the wake began to stretch out behind the *Sparrowhawk*.

'Come back here, you son of a bitch! Bring that goddamned cutter back here! Damn it! Damn your eyes! That is a prize of the United States Navy, you rutting, thieving Irish bastard!' Isaac shouted, feeling his throat burn with the effort, but McGinty just kept smiling that big dumb smile, just kept waving as the *Sparrowhawk* headed for the inlet and the sea beyond.

Finally Biddlecomb stopped screaming. He spun around once in impotent rage, then sighed and watched as the *Falmouth*'s first prize grew smaller and smaller, sailing away.

Seventeen seventy-seven. The year of the hangman, and it was not over yet.

Isaac hoped that the halter would find its way around McGinty's neck.

But it was not for him to know, he understood, not for anyone to know, on whom the hangman next would call.

THE END

HISTORICAL NOTE

The arrival of Lord Richard Howe ('Black Dick' for his dark complexion and less than sunny nature) as admiral of His Majesty's naval forces in North America in 1776 signaled the first cooperative offensive effort by the British army and navy since the start of hostilities over a year earlier. It would be expected that the two services might finally work together; after all, the commander of the land forces, Gen. William Howe, was the admiral's younger brother.

In 1777, Gen. William Howe decided on a number of different actions, but one of the few he undertook was to capture Philadelphia, the capital of the newly formed United States.

In some ways Howe's actions were similar to those of Gen. George McClellan, the American Civil War general who was obsessed with capturing Richmond. As with McClellan's drive for Richmond, many felt that Howe's capturing Philadelphia would have little effect on the enemy.

But unlike McClellan, who could not be made to understand (or who did not care to understand) that the enemy's army, not their capital, was the objective, Howe had already tried many times to bring Washington to a decisive battle. If George Washington was not always a success at winning engagements, he was brilliant at not losing them in any conclusive manner, and in keeping his army intact. Ultimately, that was what would win the war.

And so, tired of chasing Washington and his band around New York and New Jersey, General Howe had his brother transport the army to the head of the Chesapeake, where they marched overland and took the capital, after once more beating but not destroying Washington, at Brandywine. Predictably, there was consternation at Philadelphia's capture. Even if losing the capital did not hurt the cause strategically (the Congress and other government functions had slipped away a week before), it did not do much for morale.

Washington and a few others, however, hoped that Howe's taking the city would not only fail to help him but might be his downfall. Benjamin Franklin, upon being told that Howe had captured Philadelphia, replied, 'No, Philadelphia has captured Howe!'

Such optimism was based on the belief that Howe might become trapped in the city and cut off from supplies coming overland, much as the British army in Boston had been half-starved while besieged there. The Americans held the Delaware Bay and the River, effectively cutting off that route, and Washington and Howe both knew that the rebels could cut off any overland supply lines into the city as well. The British absolutely had to open the water routes to Philadelphia.

The Americans had long understood the importance of the water approaches to the city, and well before the fall of Philadelphia had set up formidable

474

defenses. These consisted of lines of underwater obstacles, called *chevaux-de-frise*, which were heavy timber cribs, supporting long poles tipped with iron points, sunk in the river, waiting for an approaching ship to impale itself. The lines of *chevaux-de-frise* were supported onshore by fortifications, which would drive away any attempts to remove the lines. In this way they functioned like the perimeter barbed wire of later wars, which would hang an enemy up while the guns fired on them.

The first line of obstacles was at Billingsport, but the fort defending them was lightly manned and easily overrun by troops from an advance squadron sent around by Admiral Howe to begin clearing the river.

The fort, however, was not the only resistance the British encountered. The rebels had above the *chevaux-de-frise* a fleet of assorted vessels under John Hazelwood, commodore of the Pennsylvania State Navy. Between harassing fire and fire ships and fire rafts, it took the British at Billingsport twenty days just to remove enough of the obstacles to make a channel wide enough for their ships to pass. And once they did, they were faced with considerably more *chevaux-de-frise* upriver, supported by the more formidable Forts Mercer and Mifflin. It took the powerful British fleet almost another month to push through the homegrown defenses there.

The loss of the *Augusta* and the *Merlin* was one of the biggest hits taken by the navy. Indeed, the *Augusta* was the largest ship that the British lost fighting Americans in both the Revolution and the War of 1812, though her loss was more a fluke than the result of any American actions.

To this day it is not known how the *Augusta* caught fire. At the court-martial held aboard *Somerset* (and attended by Sir James Wallace, among others) every officer answered that the fire began in the cabin aft and its origin was not known. Capt. Francis Reynolds testified that the fire was well under way by the time he discovered it.

Midshipman John Reid was the only one to offer an opinion of how she caught fire. When asked 'Do you know by what means she took fire?' he answered, 'I suppose by her wads,' meaning that flaming bits of wadding from her guns must have blown back aboard and set her on fire. Each of the officers testifying was asked if the guns firing were windward or leeward guns, and each answered windward, so clearly the men sitting on the court had the same thought about the wadding. It remains the most plausible explanation.

The *Merlin* was set on fire by order of Lord Howe, who knew the sloop of war would be largely destroyed anyway when the *Augusta* blew up, which would happen once the fire reached her magazine. The explosion, when it did come, was felt as far away as Philadelphia and was the cause of much rejoicing among the beleaguered American defenders.

In the end the British navy did push through the Americans and open the water route to Philadelphia. It was inevitable given their vast superiority in ships, men, supplies, and weapons. They were aided too by the typical lack of cooperation between American army and naval forces, between Continental and state organizations.

But that said, the American resistance was bravely done, the fighting as determined and spirited as any during the entire war. The defense of Fort Mifflin, which finally fell on November 15, almost two months after the capture of Philadelphia, was possibly the boldest defense of any post during the Revolution.

The loss of the Forts Mifflin and Mercer meant the end of the rebels' hold on the river. Some of Hazelwood's ships managed to slip past the city and escape upriver, but most were burned, including the xebecs *Repulse* and *Champion*, the Pennsylvania Navy ship *Montgomery*, which managed to survive her beating off the Philadelphia waterfront, and the *Andrew Doria* and *Fly*, veterans of that first U.S. naval raid on Nassau.

In the end, after all of the effort and bloodshed, the British had complete control of Philadelphia and the surrounding countryside and water approaches.

In May of the following year, Gen. William Howe was replaced by Gen. Henry Clinton, and by the middle of June Clinton began to evacuate the city. The taking of Philadelphia, the capital of the United States, had done the British not one bit of good.

GLOSSARY

Note: See diagram of brig (pages viii and ix) for names and illustrations of all sails and spars.

aback: said of a sail when the wind is striking it on the wrong side and, in the case of a square sail, pressing it back against the mast.

abaft: nearer the back of the ship, farther aft, behind.

abeam: at a right angle to the ship's centerline.

aft: toward the stern of the ship, as opposed to FORE.

afterguard: men stationed AFT to work the aftermost sails.

apron: a curved timber situated above the joint between the keel, which forms the bottom of a ship, and the STEM, which forms the BOW.

backstay: long ropes leading from the topmast and topgallant mastheads down to the CHANNELS. Backstays work with SHROUDS to support the masts from behind.

badges: small ornamental windows on either side of the great cabin, much like small QUARTER GALLERIES.

banked: a boat is *double-banked* when men seated on the same THWART pull oars on either side of the boat. *Single-banked* means men, one man per thwart with

479

oars alternating PORT and STARBOARD along the length of the boat. Thus a boat rowed double-banked has twice the number of oars pulling as one rowed single-banked.

beakhead: a small deck forward of the FORECASTLE that overhangs the bow. The crew's latrine was located there, hence in current usage the term *head* for a marine toilet.

beam reach: sailing with the wind ABEAM.

belay: to make a rope fast to a BELAYING PIN, CLEAT, or other such device. Also used as a general command to stop or cancel, e.g., 'Belay that last order!'

belaying pin: a wooden pin, later made of metal, generally about twenty inches in length to which lines were made fast, or 'belayed.' They were arranged in pinrails along the inside of the BULWARK and in FIFE RAILS around the masts.

bells: method by which time was marked on shipboard. Each day was generally divided into five four-hour 'watches' and two two-hour 'dog watches.' After the first half hour of a watch, one bell was rung, then another for each additional half hour until eight bells and the change of watch, when the process was begun again.

bight: a bend in any part of a rope. Any part of a rope might be a bight, save for the ends.

binnacle: a large wooden box, just forward of the helm, housing the compass, half-hour glass for timing the watches, and candles to light the compass at night.

bitts: heavy timber frame near the bow to which the end of the anchor cable is made fast, hence the term *bitter end*.

block: nautical term for a pulley.

boatswain (bosun): warrant officer in charge of boats,

sails, and rigging. Also responsible for relaying orders and seeing them carried out, not unlike a sergeant in the military.

boatswain's call: a small, unusually shaped whistle with a high, piercing sound with which the boatswain relayed orders by playing any of a number of recognizable tunes. Also played as a salute.

boatswain's chair: a wooden seat with a rope sling attached. Used for hoisting men aloft or over the side for work.

boom: the spar to which the lower edge of a FORE-AND-AFT sail is attached. Special studdingsail booms are used for those sails.

boomkin: a short SPAR projecting out at an angle from the BOW at the end of which is attached a BLOCK through which the fore TACK is led.

booms: spare SPARS, generally stowed amidships on raised gallows upon which the boats were often stored.

bow: the rounded, forwardmost part of a ship or boat.

bow chaser: a cannon situated near the BOW to fire as directly forward as possible.

bower: one of two primary anchors stored near the BOW, designated best bower and small bower.

bowline: line attached to a bridle that is in turn attached to the perpendicular edge of a square sail. The bowline is hauled taut when sailing close-hauled to keep the edge of the sail tight and prevent shivering. Also, a common knot used to put a loop in the end of a rope.

brace: line attached to the end of a YARD, which, when hauled upon, turns the yard horizontally to present the sail at the most favorable angle to the wind. Also, to perform the action of bracing the yards.

brake: the handle of a ship's pump.

break: the edge of a raised deck closest to the center of the ship.

breast hook: thick timbers mounted perpendicular to the STEM to reinforce the BOW.

breast line: a dock line running from the BOW or STERN to the dock at a right angle to the centerline of the vessel.

breeching: rope used to secure a cannon to the side of a ship and prevent it from recoiling too far.

brig: a two-masted vessel, square-rigged on fore and main with a large FORE-AND-AFT mainsail supported by a BOOM and gaff and made fast to the after side of the mainmast.

brow: a substantial gangway used to board a ship when tied to a dock.

bulwark: wall-like structure, generally of waist height or higher, built around the outer edge of the weather decks.

bumboat: privately owned boat used to carry out to anchored vessels vegetables, liquor, and other items for sale.

buntlines: lines running from the lower edge of a square sail to the YARD above and used to haul the bunt, or body of the sail, up to the yard, generally in preparation for furling.

cable: a large, strong rope. As a unit of measure, 120 fathoms or 240 yards, generally the length of a cable.

cable tier: a section of the lowest deck in a ship in which the CABLES are stored.

cant frame: frames at the BOW and STERN of a vessel that are not set at right angles to the keel.

cap: a heavy wooden BLOCK through which an upper mast passes, designed to hold the upper mast in place against the mast below it. Forms the upper part of the DOUBLING.

caprail: wooden rail that is fastened to the top edge of the bulwark.

capstan: a heavy wooden cylinder, pierced with holes to accept wooden bars. The capstan is turned by means of pushing on the bars and is thus used to raise the anchor or move other heavy objects.

cascabel: the knob at the end of a cannon opposite the muzzle to which the BREECHING is fastened.

case shot: a type of shot used in cannons consisting of a quantity of musket balls in a tin cylinder called a canister. When fired, the canister blows apart creating a shotgun effect.

cathead: short, strong wooden beam that projects out over the BOW, one on either side of the ship, used to suspend the anchor clear of the ship when hauling it up or letting it go.

cat-o'-nine-tails (cat): a whip with a rope handle around an inch in diameter and two feet in length to which was attached nine tails, also around two feet in length. 'Flogging' with the cat was the most common punishment meted out in the navy.

ceiling: the inside planking or 'inner wall' of a ship.

chains: strong links or iron plates used to fasten the DEADEYES to the hull. The lower part of the chains is bolted to the hull, the upper end is fastened to the chainwale, or CHANNEL. They are generally referred to as forechains, mainchains, and mizzenchains for those respective masts.

channel: corruption of *chainwale*. Broad, thick planks extending from both sides of the ship at the base of each mast to which the SHROUDS are attached.

chevaux-de-frise: underwater obstructions, generally

consisting of iron-tipped poles, firmly secured and designed to tear the bottom out of a passing ship.

clear for action: to prepare a ship for an engagement. Also the order that is given to prepare the ship.

cleats: steps nailed onto a ship's side from the waterline to the GANGWAY for the purpose of climbing aboard.

clew: either of the two lower corners of a square sail or the lower AFT corner of a FORE-AND-AFT sail. To clew up is to haul the corners of the sail up to the YARD by means of the CLEWLINES.

clewline: pronounced *clew-lin*. A line running from the clew of a square sail to the YARD above and used to haul the clew up, generally in preparation for furling. On lower, or course, sails the clewlines are called CLEW garnets.

close-hauled: said of a vessel that is sailing as nearly into the wind as she is able, her sails hauled as close to her centerline as they can go.

cockbill: said of a yard that is adjusted so as not to be horizontal. Said of an anchor when it is hanging from the CATHEAD by the RINGSTOPPER only.

conn: to direct the helmsman in the steering of the ship.

course: the largest sails; in the case of square sails, those hung from the lowest, or course, YARDS and loose footed. The foresail and mainsail are courses.

crosstrees: horizontal wooden bars, situated at right angles to the ship's centerline and located at the juntion of lower and upper masts. Between the lower and the topmasts they support the TOP; between the topmast and the topgallant mast they stand alone to spread the SHROUDS and provide a perch for the lookout.

cutter: a small vessel rigged as a SLOOP and much

favored by smugglers. Also a small boat used aboard men-of-war.

deadeye: a round, flattish wooden BLOCK pierced with three holes through which a LANYARD is rove. DEADEYES and LANYARDS are used to secure and adjust standing RIGGING, most commonly the SHROUDS.

dead reckoning: from *deduced reckoning*. Calculating a vessel's position through an estimate of speed and drift.

dirk: a small sword, more like a large dagger, worn by junior officers.

dogwatch: two-hour watches from 4 to 6 p.m. (first dogwatch) and 6 to 8 p.m. (second dogwatch).

doubling: the section where two masts overlap, such as the lower mast and the topmast just above the TOP.

driver: a temporary sail, much like a studdingsail, hoisted to the gaff on the aftermost FORE-AND-AFT sail.

elm tree pump: an older-style pump, generally used as a bilge pump, consisting of a piston in a wooden cylinder that reached from the deck to the bilge.

fall: the loose end of a system of blocks and tackle, the part upon which one pulls.

fast: a rope by which a vessel is tied to a dock, what is today called a dock line. Thus a *head-fast* secures the head of a vessel, the *stern-fast* the stern, etc.

fathom: six feet.

fife rails: wooden rails, found generally at the base of the masts, and pierced with holes to accept BELAYING PINS.

first rate: the largest class of naval ship, carrying one hundred or more guns. Ships were rated from first to sixth rates depending on the number of guns. Sloops, brigs, schooners, and other small vesssels were not rated.

fish: long sections of wood bound around a weak or broken SPAR to reinforce it, much like a splint on a broken limb. Also, the process of affixing fishes to the spar.

flemish: to coil a rope neatly down in concentric circles with the end being in the middle of the coil.

fore and aft: parallel to the centerline of the ship. In reference to sails, those that are set parallel to the centerline and are not attached to yards. Also used to mean the entire deck encompassed, e.g., 'Silence, fore and aft!'

forecastle: pronounced *fo'c'sle*. The forward part of the upper deck, forward of the foremast, in some vessels raised above the upper deck. Also, the space enclosed by this deck. In the merchant service the forecastle was the living quarters for the seamen.

forestay: standing rigging primarily responsible for preventing the foremast from falling back when the foresails are ABACK. Runs from under the foretop to the bowsprit.

forward: pronounced *for'ed*. Toward the BOW, or the front of the ship. To send an officer forward implied disrating, sending him from the officers' quarters AFT to the sailors' quarters forward.

fother: to attempt to stop a leak in a vessel by means of placing a sail or other material on the outside of the ship over the leaking area. The sail is held in place by the pressure of the incoming water.

frigate: vessels of the fifth or sixth rate, generally fast and well armed for their size, carrying between twenty and thirty-six guns.

furl: to bundle a sail tightly against the YARD, STAY, or mast to which it is attached and lash it in place with GASKETS.

futtock shrouds: short, heavy pieces of STANDING RIGGING connected on one end to the topmast SHROUDS at the outer edge of the TOP and on the other to the lower shrouds, designed to bear the pressure on the topmast shrouds. When fitted with RATLINES they allow men going aloft to climb around the outside of the TOP, though doing so requires them to hang backward at as much as a forty-five-degree angle.

gammoning: heavy lines used to lash the bowsprit down and counteract the pull of the STAYS.

gammoning hole: hole in the STEM through which the GAMMONING is passed.

gangway: light deck planking laid over the WAIST between the QUARTERDECK and the FORECASTLE on either side of a ship, over the guns, to allow movement from one end to the other without having to descend into the waist. Also, the part of the ship's side from which people come aboard or leave, provided with an opening in the BULWARK and steps on the vessel's side.

gantline: pronounced *gant-lin*. A line run from the deck to a BLOCK aloft and back to the deck, used for hauling articles such as RIGGING aloft. Thus, when the rig is 'sent down to a gantline,' it has been entirely disassembled save for the gantline, which will be used to haul it up again.

garboard: the first set of planks, next to the keel, on a ship's or boat's bottom.

gasket: a short, braided piece of rope attached to the YARD and used to secure the furled sail.

gig: small boat generally rowed with six or fewer oars.

glim: a small candle.

grapeshot: a cluster of round, iron shot, generally nine in all, wrapped in canvas. Upon firing, the grapeshot would spread out for a shotgun effect. Used against men and light hulls.

grating: hatch covers composed of perpendicular interlocking wood pieces, much like a heavy wood screen. They allowed light and air below while still providing cover for the hatch. Gratings were covered with tarpaulins in rough or wet weather.

gripe: to securely lash a boat in the place in which it is stowed by the use of heavy ropes called gripes.

gudgeon: one-half of the hinge mechanism for a rudder. The gudgeon is fixed to the sternpost and has a rounded opening that accepts the PINTLE on the rudder.

gunwale: pronounced *gun-el*. The upper edge of a ship's side.

halyard: any line used to raise a sail or a YARD or a gaff to which a sail is attached.

headsails: those sails set FORWARD of the foremast.

heave to: to adjust the sails in such a way that some are full and some ABACK with the result that the vessel is stopped in the water.

heaver: a device like a wooden mallet used as a lever for tightening small lines.

hoay, holloa: the hail to gain someone's attention and the answer acknowledging that hail.

hogshead: a large cask, twice the size of a standard barrel. Capacity varied but was generally around one hundred gallons.

holystone: a flat stone used for cleaning a ship's decks.

hood-end: the ends of the planking on a ship's hull that fit into the rabbet, or notch, in the STEM or sternpost.

hoy: a small vessel, chiefly used near the coast, to transport passengers or supplies to another vessel.

hull down: said of a ship when her hull is still hidden below the horizon and only her masts or super-structure is visible.

jolly boat: a small workboat.

keelson: a piece of timber laid FORE AND AFT over the floor timbers of a vessel, an interior counterpart to the keel.

lanyard: line run through the holes in the DEADEYES to secure and adjust the SHROUDS. Also any short line used to secure or adjust an item on shipboard.

larboard: until the nineteenth century the term designating the left side of a vessel when facing forward. The term *port* is now used.

leech: the side edges of a square sail or the after edge of a FORE-AND-AFT sail.

leeward: pronounced *loo-ard*. Downwind.

letters of marque: a commission given to private citizens in times of war to take and make prizes of enemy vessels. Also, any vessel that holds such a commission.

lifelines: ropes running the length of the deck, or along BOOMS or YARDS, for the seamen to hold onto in rough weather.

lifts: ropes running from the ends of the YARDS to the mast, used to support the yard when lowered or when men are employed thereon.

limber holes: holes cut through the lower timbers in a ship's hull allowing otherwise trapped water to run through to the pumps.

line: term used for a rope that has been put to a specific use.

log: device used to measure a vessel's speed.

longboat: the largest boat carried on shipboard.

lug sail: a small square sail used on a boat.

mainstay: STANDING RIGGING primarily responsible for preventing the mainmast from falling back when the main sails are ABACK. Runs from under the maintop to the BOW.

make and mend: time allotted to the seamen to make new clothing or mend their existing ones.

marlinespike: an iron spike used in knotting and splicing rope.

mizzen: large FORE-AND-AFT sail, hung from a gaff ABAFT the MIZZENMAST.

mizzenmast: the aftermost mast on a three-masted ship.

painter: a rope in the BOW of a boat used to tie the boat in place. Also, one who paints, a never-ending task on shipboard.

parceling: strips of canvas wrapped around STANDING RIGGING prior to serving.

partners: heavy wooden frames surrounding the holes in the deck through which the masts and CAPSTAN pass.

pawls: wooden or iron bars that prevent a windlass or CAPSTAN fron rotating backward.

pintles: pins attached to the rudder that fit in the GUDGEON and form the hinge on which the rudder pivots.

plain sail: all regular working sails, excluding upper staysails, studdingsails, RINGTAILS, etc.

port: the left side of the ship when facing forward. In the eighteenth century the word was used in helm directions only until it later supplanted LARBOARD in general use.

post: in the Royal Navy, to be given official rank of captain, often called a post captain, and thereby qualified to command a ship of twenty guns or larger.

privateer: vessel built or fitted out expressly to operate under a LETTERS OF MARQUE.

quadrant: instrument used to take the altitude of the sun or other celestial bodies in order to determine the latitude of a place. Forerunner to the modern sextant.

quarter: the area of the ship, LARBOARD or STARBOARD, that runs from the main SHROUDS AFT. Also, the section of a YARD between the SLINGS and the YARDARM.

quarterdeck: a raised deck running from the stern of the vessel as far forward, approximately, as the main-mast. The primary duty station of the ship's officers, comparable to the bridge on a modern ship.

quarter gallery: small, enclosed balcony with windows located on either side of the great cabin AFT and projecting out slightly from the side of the ship. Traditionally contained the head, or toilet, for use by those occupying the great cabin.

quoin: wedge under the breech of a cannon used when aiming to elevate or depress the muzzle.

ratline: pronounced *ratlin*. Small lines tied between the SHROUDS, horizontal to the deck, forming a sort of rope ladder on which the men can climb aloft.

reef: to reduce the area of sail by pulling a section of the sail up to the YARD and tying it in place.

reef point: small lines threaded through eyes in the sail for the purpose of tying the REEF in the sail.

rigging: any of the many lines used aboard the ship. *Standing rigging* is employed to hold the masts in place and is only occasionally adjusted. *Running rigging* is used to manipulate the sails and is frequently adjusted, as needed.

ringbolt: an iron bolt through which is fitted an iron ring.

ringstopper: short line on the CATHEAD used to hold the anchor prior to letting it go.

ringtail: a type of studdingsail rigged from the mainsail gaff and down along the after edge of the mainsail.

round seizing: a type of lashing used to bind two larger lines together.

run: to sail with the wind coming over the stern, or nearly over the stern, of the vessel.

running rigging: see RIGGING.

sailing master: warrant officer responsible for charts and navigation, among other duties.

scantlings: the dimensions of any piece of timber used in ship-building with regard to its breadth and thickness.

schooner: (eighteenth-century usage) a small, two-masted vessel with FORE-AND-AFT sails on foremast and mainmast and occasionally one or more square sails on the foremast.

scuppers: small holes pierced through the BULWARK at the level of the deck to allow water to run overboard.

scuttle: any small, generally covered hatchway through a ship's deck.

service: a tight wrapping of SPUNYARN put around STANDING RIGGING to protect it from the elements.

serving mallet: a tool shaped like a long-handled mallet used to apply service to RIGGING.

sheer: the lengthwise curve of a ship's side from BOW to stern, as viewed from the side.

sheet: line attached to a CLEW of a square sail to pull the sail down and hold it in place when the sail is set. On a FORE-AND-AFT sail the sheet is attached to the BOOM on the sail itself and is used to rim the sail closer or farther away from the ship's centerline to achieve the best angle to the wind.

ship: a vessel of three masts, square-rigged on all masts. *To ship* is to put something in place, thus shipping CAPSTAN bars means to put them in their slots in the capstan.

short peak: indicates that the vessel is above the anchor and the anchor is ready to be pulled from the bottom.

shrouds: heavy ropes leading from a masthead AFT and down to support the masts when the wind is from ABEAM or AFT.

slack water: period at the turn of the tide when there is no tidal current.

slings: the middle section of a YARD.

sloop: a small vessel with one mast.

sloop of war: small man-of-war, generally ship-rigged and commanded by a lieutenant.

slop chest: purser's stores, containing clothing, tobacco, and other items that the purser sold to the crew and deducted the price from their wages.

snatch block: a BLOCK with a hinged side that can be opened to admit a rope.

snow: a two-masted vessel, square-rigged on foremast and mainmast, like a BRIG, but generally larger than a brig and setting a square sail on the mainyard. Snows have a short mast just behind the mainmast, stepped on the deck and terminating under the maintop, on which is set a big gaff-headed FORE-AND-AFT sail called a trysail.

soundings: water shallow enough to measure with a depth gauge, traditionally a lead line. Being 'in soundings' generally means a vessel is close to shore.

spar: general term for all masts, YARDS, BOOMS, gaffs, etc.

spring: a line passed from the stern of a vessel and made fast to the anchor cable. When the spring is hauled upon, the vessel turns.

spring stay: a smaller STAY used as a backup to a larger one.

spritsail topsail: a light sail set outboard of the spritsail.

spunyarn: small line used primarily for SERVICE or seizings.

standing rigging: see RIGGING.

starboard: the right side of the vessel when facing FORWARD.

start: to open, in reference to a cask.

stay: STANDING RIGGING used to support the mast on the FORWARD part and prevent it from falling back, especially when the sails are ABACK. Also, to *stay a vessel* means to TACK, thus *missing stays* means failing to get the BOW through the wind.

stay tackle: system of BLOCKS generally rigged from the MAINSTAY and used for hoisting boats or items stored in the hold.

stem: the heavy timber in the BOW of the ship into which the planking at the bow terminates.

step: to put a mast in place. Also, a block of wood fixed to the bottom of a ship to accept the base or heel of the mast.

stern chasers: cannons directed AFT to fire on a pursuing vessel.

stern sheets: the area of a boat between the stern and the aftermost of the rowers' seats, generally fitted with benches to accommodate passengers.

sternway: the motion of a ship going backward through the water, the opposite of *headway*.

stow: as relates to sails, the same as FURL.

swifter: a rope tied to the ends of the CAPSTAN bars to hold them in place when shipped.

tack: to turn a vessel on to a new course in such a way that her BOW passes through the wind. Also used to indicate relation of ship to wind, i.e., a ship on a 'starboard tack' has the wind coming over the STARBOARD side.

taffrail: the upper part of a ship's stern.

tarpaulin hat: wide, flat-brimmed canvas hat, coated in tar for waterproofing, favored by sailors.

tender: small vessel that operates in conjunction with a larger man-of-war.

tholes: pins driven into the upper edge of a boat's side to hold the oars in place when rowing.

thwart: seat or bench in a boat on which the rowers sit.

tiller: the bar attached to the rudder and used to turn the rudder in steering.

tompion: a plug put in the end of a cannon to prevent water from getting into the barrel.

top: a platform at the junction of the lower mast and the topmast.

top-hamper: general term for all of the SPARS, RIGGING, and sails; all the equipment above the level of the deck.

train tackle: arrangement of BLOCKS and tackle attached to the back end of a gun carriage and used to haul the gun inboard.

truck: a round button of wood that serves as a cap on the highest point of a mast.

trunnions: short, round arms that project from either side of a cannon and upon which the cannon rests and tilts.

truss: heavy rope used to hold a YARD against a mast or bowsprit.

tween decks: corruption of *between decks*. The deck between the uppermost and the lowermost decks.

waist: the area of the ship between the QUARTERDECK and the FORECASTLE.

waister: men stationed in the WAIST of the vessel for sail evolutions. Generally inexperienced, old, or just plain dumb seamen were designated as waisters.

warp: a small rope used to move a vessel by hauling it through the water. Also, to move a vessel by means of warps.

water sail: a light-air sail set under a BOOM.

waterways: long pieces of timber, running FORE AND AFT along the point where the deck meets the upper edge of the hull. The SCUPPERS are cut through the waterways.

wear: to turn the vessel from one TACK to another by turning the stern through the wind. Slower but safer than tacking.

weather: the same as *windward*, thus 'a ship to weather' is the same as 'a whip to windward.' Also describes the side of the ship over which the wind is blowing.

weather deck: upper deck, one that is exposed to the weather.

weatherly: said of a ship that sails well to windward while making little leeway.

weft: used to mean a flag, generally the ensign, tied in a long roll and hoisted for the purpose of signaling.

whip: a tackle formed by a rope run through a single fixed block.

wooding: laying in stores of wood for cooking fuel.

woolding: a tight winding of rope around a mast or YARD.

worming: small pieces of rope laid between the strands of a larger rope to strengthen it and allow it to better withstand chaffing. Also, to put worming in place.

yard: long, horizontal SPARS suspended from the masts and from which the sails are spread.

yardarm: the extreme ends of a YARD.